THE
DEVIL'S
SHEPHERD

Also by Steven Hartov

The Heat of Ramadan
The Nylon Hand of God

THE
DEVIL'S
SHEPHERD

• • •

Steven Hartov

WILLIAM MORROW
An Imprint of HarperCollins*Publishers*

HarperCollins books may be purchased for educational, business, or sales pro-
motional use. For information please write: Special Markets Department,
HarperCollins Publishers Inc., 10 East 53rd Street, New York, NY 10022.

FIRST EDITION

Designed by Nicola Ferguson

Printed on acid-free paper

Library of Congress Cataloging-in-Publication Data

Hartov, Steven.
    The Devil's shepherd / Steven Hartov.
        p.   cm.
    ISBN 0-688-14121-8
        1. Intelligence officers—Israel—Fiction. I. Title.
    PS3558.A7146 D48 2000
    813'.54—dc21   99–052627

00   01   02   03   04 /BP 10   9   8   7   6   5   4   3   2   1

May the road rise to meet you,

May the wind be always at your backs,

May the sun shine warm upon your faces,

The rains fall soft upon your fields and,

Until we meet again,

May the Lord hold you in the palm of His Hand.

ACKNOWLEDGMENTS

. . .

The writing of a novel is a long and arduous journey. This one would not have seen completion but for the unconditional love and support of my sister and brother-in-law, Susan and Paul Berman. Along the way, many others also helped carry the load, offered their wisdom, surrendered secret knowledge, endured me with patience, and even risked their own safety. I am grateful to you all: Lt. Col. (L.O.F.) Michael D. Epstein, Albert Zuckerman, my mother and father, Claire Wachtel, Lt. Col. (res.) Shaul Dori, Samuel M. Katz, Arye Rubel, Milton Schonberger, Richard S. "Buddha" Meyers, David Bale, Fred Pierce, Mike Marcus, Lt. Col. Charles J. F. McHugh, Shlomo Baum, Yaakov "K," Alon and Yael Shafran, Evelyn Musher, Klaudia Berkow, James Dator, Maja Nicolic, Dr. Hermann Heller, Otto Haan, Nicholas Burns, Bernard E. Gross II, Special Agent Gary F. Truchot, Rami Hatan, Nigus Fisseha, Mulualem Anemut, Muluget Yegezaw, Tinneke Dirckx, Avi Nesher, Mizuki Ogawa, Rick Washburn, Roger Berger, Christina Denzinger, Lee Malecki, Sgt. 1st Class Jerry Ginder, Bernie Hasenbein, Andrew Norman, Howard Goldberg, Joseph Vernon, Donald Maas, Ryder Washburn, Lia Yang, and David Hansberry.

This manuscript has been reviewed by the IDF Military Censor, which is a requirement with which I must comply, given my background.

Help I'm steppin' into the Twilight Zone.
This place is a madhouse, feels like being cloned.
My beacon's been moved under moon and star,
Where am I to go now that I've gone too far?
Soon you will come to know . . .
When the bullet hits the bone.

—Golden Earring,
"Twilight Zone"

THE
DEVIL'S
SHEPHERD

PROLOGUE

• • •

Eritrea
April 26, 1993

MAJOR EYTAN ECKSTEIN prayed that the bullets would kill him before he heard the gunfire.

Such was the way of ballistics, especially across open water, and he wrestled the urge to look back from the prow of his black Zodiac assault boat at the fading strip of midnight beach. Even at this range of half a kilometer, the heavy 7.62 mm round of a Dragunov sniper rifle could leap out faster than the speed of sound and sever his dreams, long before its sonic report reached his dying ears. If he was lucky, he would feel virtually nothing at all.

"*Zeh beseder.* It's all right," he silently persuaded himself in Hebrew. "*Ahf echad lo echieh l'tamid.* Nobody lives forever."

He paddled on, first the right side, then the left, watching his aluminum oar blade slice a flat sea shimmering with the pearls of an evil moon. The blazing orb should not have been up there at all; it was supposed to be obscured by clouds, and he cursed the army meteorologists and tried to think. Of nothing. Not of home, not of his wife, not of his son. *There is no future. There is only now.* Like the moments before a parachute jump, thoughts were your nemeses, instincts your only allies. Fantasy brought fear, fear broke concentration, and a flagging brain would react a split second too late, and then . . .

Just row, he ordered that other Eckstein, the cold professional one, while the hair at the nape of his neck stood straight up and stiff as the arms at a neo-Nazi rally.

The major had not always cringed at the possibility of being shot. As a young paratrooper, then an officer, and finally a senior operator with the Special Operations division of AMAN—Israel's military intelligence branch—he had swaggered into gunfire with the idiocy of ignorance, as do most young men whose flesh has not yet been scarred by spinning slugs of lead and brass. But later on, he had been wounded. Badly. His knee still ached from it, his memory held a vintage taste of that vicious flashback. He knew what it would feel like and he tried not to show that he trembled with the knowledge.

Just row.

Ahead, the gray unlit hulk of an Israeli Navy *Aliyah* class missile boat bobbed clumsily in the undulating swells, engines silent, its form growing larger, but slowly, so slowly. Eckstein fought another urge, to go prone now and paddle like a madman. But his wards were huddled just behind him in the rubber Zodiac, watching their shepherd very carefully. He could feel their eyes on his back, and so he knelt, spine erect.

First the right side, then the left. Just slice the Red Sea, part the waters, think about Moses . . . He grimaced slightly, chastising himself for his biblical comparisons as his muscles strained with the oar. *I suspect we might be having some delusions of grandeur here, Major.*

There were eleven *falashas* in Eckstein's "stretch" Zodiac Hurricane and eight more boats behind him, carrying a few remnants of the Ethiopian Jews who had been airlifted to Israel during *Operation Solomon* back in '91. *Solomon* had been a public relations triumph for Jerusalem, over 14,000 black Jews spirited to the Promised Land in less than forty-eight hours. Ethiopia's then-dictator, Mengistu Haile-Mariam, had happily snatched a thirty-five-million-dollar bribe from the Israeli government in exchange for turning a blind eye to the rescue, and promptly fled his war-torn country for Zaire.

But tonight, with the first general Ethiopian elections set for dawn and the province of Eritrea on the verge of independence, various and sundry rebel bands were pillaging the countryside, getting in their last licks. There was no one left in power to pay off, so Eckstein's mission,

Operation Jeremiah, was barely *Solomon*'s pauper cousin and strictly a covert operation.

The falashas gripped the gunwales of the rubber boat; silent, polite, mostly women and children, a couple of "old men" of fifty. A grandfather wearing an incongruous Sinatra fedora slipped a silver-plated Old Testament from his worn tweed coat and began to bob over the pages. The refugees were surely frightened, and possibly ashamed, for Eckstein had had to strip the women of their bright white *shama* shawls and their tin jewelry, and the handsome mothers in their burlap smocks clutched their children to their breasts, shy eyes lowered, waiting, watching.

Yet they trusted Eytan Eckstein, whom they knew only as "Anthony Hearthstone." They had listened to him when he came to their secret villages in Gondar, along with that burly bear of a man called "Schmidt," who was in fact Lieutenant Colonel Benjamin Baum, Eckstein's superior and SpecOps Chief of Operations. The two strangers had to say no more than, "It is your turn. Come with us to Israel," and the joyous tribal leftovers of *Beta Israel* abandoned their meager belongings to join a month-long trek by foot, wagon, truck, and finally here, to the sea.

The danger, besides the sun, starvation, and disease, was from Amin Mobote and his Oromo Liberation Front. The Oromo rebel leader was furiously jealous of the Eritrean independence bid and determined to upset the elections by any means possible. Ambushing and killing over one hundred falashas and their Israeli rescuers would do nicely. And so, as the ragtag convoy grew, following their Israeli pied pipers from Asmara to Akordat to Keren, through the searing wadis and the frosted mountains to Nakfa and Karora, and finally to the beaches of Ras Kasar, the OLF had probed. Like hyenas after wildebeest they had fallen on the weak, the slow, and the sickly who strayed.

Eckstein, Baum, and three support men from Queens Commando— the AMAN cover name of their SpecOps unit—had strict orders not to engage. But the rebels were growing dangerously bold, so on the last night before the final dash to the sea the Israelis had laid their own ambush. Igniting a seemingly frivolous campfire, they had drawn in the OLF probe, fired a brace of deadly Claymore mines, then herded their flock into poultry trucks and sprinted the last twenty-eight kilometers to the beachhead . . .

Eckstein broke his own rules of engagement now and began to think, making hollow promises to himself.

No more after this. No more. It's your last field mission, Eytan. Onward and upward to a desk in Jerusalem. It's enough. You've proved you're not your father. He ran from the Nazis, you ran straight at the enemy. Over and over and over. You can stop now . . .

He was aging, hurtling toward forty. It was not physically apparent, for his blondish ponytail was misleading, his physique boyish, and the sun of these continents had tightened and camouflaged the tired flesh around his pale blue eyes. But inside, his memories overflowed. Inside, he was sixty-five.

First the right side, then the left.

A pool of phosphorescent algae glowed green around the blade of his oar, and the missile boat beckoned. He could see a naval crewman gripping the handles of a fifty-caliber machine gun on the beachside gunwale. He could see the amber combat bulbs glowing from inside the bridge.

He glanced down between his knees at an olive canvas parachute bag. "Anthony Hearthstone" was zipped up in there: his frayed jeans and chambray shirt, his forged British passport, his "pocket litter," his press credentials from *Stern*, his cameras. Now Major Eytan Eckstein had emerged once more, clad in black fatigue pants and canvas Palladium commando shoes soaked through from the wading. He was shirtless except for a cordura assault vest, magazines of nine-millimeter ammunition, a Browning Hi-Power pistol, a smoke grenade, and a field dressing. On the beach a naval commando had handed him a small packet from General Itzik Ben-Zion, commander of AMAN SpecOps. It contained Eckstein's genuine dog tags, military ID, and prisoner of war card. He was a soldier again, in theory no longer summarily executable as a spy, but to Mobote's rebels it would make no difference. A warm African breeze full of brine prickled the hair on his arms. He was cold.

He suppressed the thoughts of gunfire and glanced over his left shoulder. Just behind him, Bayush Addisu sat cross-legged on the hard rubber flooring. Like all the refugees, she wore a water skier's life vest painted black, and she stroked her four-year-old son as he slumbered in her arms with the womb-like rocking. She opened her mouth and the accursed moonlight flashed from her smile. Eckstein felt the muscles twitch his lips as he grimaced in return. At the rear of the Zodiac two naval commandos from Flotilla 13 crouched at the flanks of the silent Evinrude 40 engine, rowing steadily outboard with their young muscles. They wore no diving gear, only black wetsuit tops and fatigue trousers, their mini-Uzis clipped to the new high-tech chest harnesses that Eckstein had never seen before.

The rest of the Zodiacs curved behind to the south in a long arc, much too visible under the betraying night of star clusters and the earth's bald-faced satellite. Benni Baum was back there somewhere, bringing up the rear in the last boat, and Eckstein wished they had reversed their positions. He felt like a lazy farm boy allowing his aging father to plow the fields on a blazing August afternoon. Baum was supposed to be out of it already. Baum was supposed to be retired, at home in Abu Tor, cursing his boredom and tending his garden. But he was a stubborn old bull and he had stayed on to help with *Jeremiah*, and in the field he was still the boss, by experience and by rank.

"You'll take the first boat," Baum had said when they broke through the brush and came upon the beach and the naval commandos suddenly rose from the water like someone's aquatic nightmare.

"Up your ass, Benni," said Eckstein.

"That's an *order*," Baum growled.

"I see your point."

While the two officers and their three SpecOps men separated the falashas into small groups, the naval commandos secured the beachhead, then called in the Zodiacs from the missile boat. The rowing-in seemed to take forever, but the outboards could not be fired up, for if Mobote's men were still tracking the flock the roar of marine engines would bring them on like a wolf pack.

Still, it had gone fairly smoothly, even though the falashas had backed away like frightened sheep at the sight of the strange rubber alligators, having never seen anything like them. And now they were all away, nearly to the missile boat, perhaps twenty minutes from making full throttle for the distant Gulf of Aqaba. Eckstein willed his neck muscles to soften as he watched the dot of Benni's distant boat bumping over the shallow shore swells and the beachhead team of commandos backing up with staggered discipline into the water, sweeping the beach with their gun barrels. They carried light weapons of choice, Colt Commandos or mini-Uzis, their flippers linked to their combat webbing. They were going to *swim* to the missile boat, a feat of which Eckstein found himself jealously annoyed.

He turned back toward the gray mass of the sleek hull out ahead. It was larger now, like a bobbing fifth of whiskey, and he could see rope ladders dangling from the gunwales. Just a few more paddle strokes, maybe a hundred, he reckoned. *First the right side, then the left,* and he remembered Baum's whisper in the dark, just before Eckstein pushed his laden Zodiac from the beach into the curling surf.

"This is all so unnecessary." The colonel had gestured at the tensed commandos crouching on one knee, weapons poised, hissing into commo gear. Eckstein looked at Benni, while the beefy bald man shrugged and pointed. "We could have just stood on that dune with a white flag and a suitcase full of cash. Mobote would've probably joined us for a bonfire and a *kumsitz,* sent us all off with a kiss."

Eckstein had just grunted, then pushed off for the sea. But now he smiled.

Simple bribery. Not a bad idea, come to think of it. Benni Baum was many things, including a genius tactician and practical cynic, and in the field even his jokes were often the fruits of operational lifesavers. *Well, next time,* Eckstein decided, then remembered that he had just sworn off field operations forever.

His ears pricked up like a dog's as something plucked at the water not two meters from the Zodiac's prow, and just as the flash from the beach registered on his retina and the choked report of the rifle reached him, the truth thundered in his head.

This is *the next time!*

The rest of it happened all at once. From the hillocks of brushy dune just above the slim beach a line of star-shaped flashes burst the night open, throwing *Jeremiah's* boats into horrific silhouette, their occupants frozen like teenagers caught skinny-dipping as the cannonade of Kalashnikovs rolled across the water. From somewhere behind, one of Eckstein's men yelled *"Ta'tan'kak!"* in Amharic, and the heads of the falashas bowed to the floors of their Zodiacs like Moslems at midnight prayer as quick lines of green tracers crisscrossed overhead and hissed into the swells.

Eckstein's heart muscle froze for a millisecond, then he caught a breath and turned to yell orders at his boat crew. But the commandos were instinctive and well-trained animals and all the Zodiac pairs reacted simultaneously. The men facing the beach unclipped their mini-Uzis, came to their knees, and opened up with controlled bursts of spaced red tracers back at the hillocks, ineffective as their nine-millimeters were at such a range. The starboard men kicked the Evinrude blades into the water and hauled on the starters, and in the shallows of the beach itself the withdrawal team quickly abandoned their retreat, went prone in the surf, and hammered back at the hillocks on full auto.

The prow of Eckstein's Zodiac suddenly lurched forward and rose precariously into the air, and he lost his paddle as he dove onto the rubber nose cone, scrabbling for the rope handholds and throwing his weight down. Feeble yelps reached him from behind, then were snuffed out as the engine screws bit and the big palm of a wave smacked his head, filled his ears, and stung his eyes He shook it off, sputtering and straining to see and hear again.

Up ahead, the roar of the missile boat engines coming to life seemed to split the sea beneath the crackling reports of small-arms fire. He could hear guttural shouts, quick boots slamming the ship deck, and then the fifty-caliber opened up, echoing over the water like a madman's gavel on a steel drum as the explosions stuttered and the shell casings rang off the railings.

The missile boat's fast attack hull turned quickly, listing hard to port as it came around, heading right *for* him. But the commando crew at Eckstein's stern were just as quick and they charged straight for the sharp bow, then suddenly veered the Zodiac hard to starboard as the missile boat driver cut his engines to coast again. And just before Eckstein passed behind the shelter of the mother ship, he turned back to see his pathetic little convoy, still in formation, Uzis buzzing like angry wasps. He squinted, then opened his mouth in horror, for the last Zodiac, *Benni Baum's* Zodiac, had gone flat and deflated in the waves, its engine fuel ignited by tracers, spitting pools of fire into the sea.

Eckstein's rubber craft bounced off the high steel hull of the missile boat, then came back in again, and someone reached down from the boarding ladder and grabbed his vest, but he caught the crewman's hand and switched it instead to the Zodiac's rope grip. And all at once the mission changed, *Jeremiah* became *Baum*, only *Baum*, and Eckstein spun on his refugees and began to snatch at them; arms, clothes, bodies of thin skin and unfed bones. He hauled them over his head one after another like sacks of potatoes, smearing each one against the rope ladder until other hands took them away, and he heard himself yelling at the naval crewmen.

"Kadima! Kadima! Kadima!"

He wanted all of them gone, he wanted his boat back, empty and fast. The last falasha's worn sneakers slipped on the rubber prow, half her legs splashed into the sea, then someone had her by her armpits and Eckstein was spinning again to his crew. But they already knew what he wanted and he crashed onto his back to the hard nippled deck as they roared away from the missile boat, arcing wide to swing around the stern and head back for Baum. Another naval commando team had davited a fiberglass *Snunit* assault craft over the rails there, and they freed it and it crashed keel-flat into the water with a tremendous splash. Someone fired a parachute flare into the night, and as it popped Eckstein glimpsed flippered forms leaping from the stern deck after their craft.

He crawled back onto his stomach, hugging the prow again as the Zodiac came around and picked up speed, passing the missile boat on the side exposed to the beach. From the shore, the rebel AK-47 bursts had been joined by the jackhammer of a PK light machine gun and a trio of Russian-made rounds cracked the air overhead and punched into the thin FAC hull just above his hair. He winced hard as he passed beneath the navy's fifty-caliber, the young gunner pivoting the heavy weapon and playing murderous timpani on the butterfly trigger. Then something *thonked* from the forward deck, the ship's bow was momentarily thrown into hard silhouette by the tube flash of an Israeli fifty-two-millimeter mortar, and moments later the shell exploded in the dunes too far behind the beach hillocks and a naval officer berated the mortarman in a torrent of Hebraic curses.

Eckstein instinctively reached for his pistol, then left the Hi-Power in its holster. What the hell could he do with it at this range, anyway? Throw it? Instead, he fumbled for the small pickup beacon pinned to his vest and twisted the phallus head until it glowed green, determined at least to not be killed by *friendly* fire.

Just out front, the surviving Zodiacs were coming on hard, the lead craft already passing him to reach the missile boat and disgorge their cargo. But Eckstein and his crew broke through the rescue flotilla, racing back toward the dwindling smudge of oily fire that had been Baum's pathetic craft, and he could feel his heart hammering against the sea-slickened rubber as a pattern of green tracers suddenly appeared out front only a meter above the waves. He smeared himself flat as the Zodiac slipped beneath the quilt of zipping neon projectiles and something clanged off the Evinrude and one of the commandos grunted, but they kept on.

Behind them now even more covering fire began to spit from the missile boat, a chorus of echoing rattles and pinging shell casings as the crews' M-16s and Galils bucked in long bursts, and on the beach the rebel guns at last slacked off into stutters. Eckstein lifted his head, searching the undulating sea. An acrid film of rifle and camouflage smoke drifted over the water like mist above a loch. Somewhere a heavy Israeli tracer struck rock on the beach and went careening off into the night like a red Roman candle. One of the beachhead commandos fired off a Mecar, and the rifle grenade exploded in a plumed flash that flickered over the sea like a disco globe.

He spotted the mahogany heads of Baum's surviving falashas bobbing in the small waves, the water glistening in their woolly scalps. Another empty Zodiac raced by on his left flank, then slowed as naval commandos rolled into the sea and began passing the refugees back into the craft.

But Eckstein only had eyes for Baum, and he flicked them madly over the water, seeing nothing, the gunfire no longer registering in his ears as he panicked.

Where is he? He cringed as his search foundered and he felt himself choking, helpless, like a child who'd left his dog in a burning building. *Where are you?!* He wanted to scream, but screaming made you a target, and then his fingers dug into the heavy balloon of boat rubber and he foolishly came to his knees and arched his body out over the water and he *did* scream.

"*Benni!*"

Nothing. Absolutely nothing.

"*Benni!!*"

"Stop shouting."

Eckstein spun his head to the sound of Baum's voice. There he was, just off the starboard pontoon, his bald head bobbing in the moonlight like an upended buoy. Incredibly, the colonel was smiling.

The *Snunit* assault craft zoomed by close, its gunner firing a MAG light machine gun at the beach from the bow, and the wake flowed quickly toward Benni and washed over his head. He came up again, spitting, and he raised his voice.

"Get me in before the idiots drown me."

Eckstein stretched out his hand, and already his crew were turning the craft around as Benni gripped the sinews of Eytan's arm. Eckstein leaned out, grabbed Baum's trouser belt, and the Zodiac almost flipped as the major hauled his whale of a colonel aboard . . .

They were the last men to board the missile boat. Baum was breathing like an asthmatic and Eckstein was not much better off as they climbed the rope ladder, with Eckstein's shoulder butting up into Baum's rump. They barely negotiated the rail and fell to the deck, where they slumped, soaked and trembling, amidst the crowd of grateful falashas sitting cross-legged and thanking God. A pair of navy medics were counting heads and checking for injuries, while more of the crew still crouched at the rails, popping off rounds at the beach. The fifty-caliber still spat angrily, making the falashas squeeze their quivering hands over their ears.

The *Snunit* assault craft roared by trailing taut nylon ropes in the water, having picked up the naval commando team from the beachhead, their elbows locked into loops in the ropes as they slid along the wavetops like limp acrobats. The *Snunit* driver raised a thumbs-up as he passed—he would rendezvous with the mother ship "upstream."

Eckstein watched as the muscular captain of the missile boat turned from the stern and came wading forward through the refugees, a strange expression of amusement at his lips. He was hatless, carrying a Motorola, and his kibbutznik red curls glistened beneath the parachute flares. He yelled to his riflemen at the rails.

"Sink the Zodiacs."

There wasn't time to haul the empty rescue craft on board. Even though the rebel gunfire had been suppressed to the occasional snipe now, Mobote's reinforcements might arrive at any moment. The young riflemen moved to the opposite rails and fired down into the rubber boats.

The boat commander made his way to the bridge, stopping for a moment to grin down at Baum, who wagged a finger at him.

"The comptroller will have your ass for that, Ami," Baum warned.

"He can bill me." The commander sneered and made to move on when there was a sharp bang from the beach and, a split second later, the finned rocket from an RPG screamed by just aft of the stern, then arced lazily down into the water.

The boat commander frowned angrily, spat some orders into his walkie-talkie, and all at once from a turret forward of the bridge the terrible roar of a multi-barreled Vulcan Air Defense System buzzed like a gigantic hair clipper. Its streams of twenty-millimeter tracers stretched to the shoreline and chewed along the hillocks, obliterating sand, brush, flesh, steel, and bone alike.

Everyone on deck, including Eckstein and Baum, jerked spasmodically with the unearthly howl. Then it stopped, the echo keening back over the water. Silence. Not a peep or retort from the beach.

"*Zonot.* Whores," the boat commander muttered, as if to justify the slaughter. Then he holstered the Motorola and walked away, shouting orders.

The big twin engines began to rumble, and very quickly the pitching hull of the missile boat settled as it picked up speed.

Eckstein leaned back on a rail spar and stretched his legs out, trying to will his calf muscles to stop twitching. He realized that in those fierce moments of the firefight, when he'd been sure more than once that each breath was his last, few images had flickered in his brain. No memories. No longings. No last wishes. For a brief instant, only the face of his son.

He looked at Baum, who was rubbing sea salt from his thick eyebrows, smearing it back over his bald pate. Baum craned his thick neck, catching a glimpse of the receding wrecks of the Zodiacs and the thin smoke and brushfires on the distant beach. Then he turned to Eckstein and shrugged.

"I told you. A white flag and a suitcase of cash. I don't need this much excitement."

Eckstein tried to smile, but his face would not function. This was it. No more. He didn't need it, either.

He felt the breeze from the forward speed lifting his wet hair as they began the run north for the Gulf of Aqaba and Eilat. He watched as Benni patted the breast pockets of his soaked khaki shirt, came up with a box of Marlboros, then opened it and frowned at the squashed, drowned cigarettes. Baum tossed the crumpled box over the side.

"Well," said Eckstein, "you should quit anyway."

PART ONE

VOLUNTEERS

• • •

There are no good-tempered generals.

—Michael Shaara,
The Killer Angels

I

*   *   *

THE GIRLS AT the main gate of the Israel Defense Forces Command General Headquarters appeared as delicate as swimsuit models. They were tall and slim, with fine features, modest lipstick, and no more than a touch of eyeliner, and they wore their young strong hair pulled back beneath old-style "overseas" caps. Their olive-drab blouses and trousers failed to camouflage athletic bodies tanned nut-brown from working under a Tel Aviv sun, and as they gracefully slalomed between the lines of waiting vehicles, checking drivers' identification cards and examining passengers with cool smiles, it was easy to imagine them as harmless as the perfume girls at Bloomingdale's. But they were some of the best gunwomen in the IDF order of battle.

The *Kiria*, as General HQ is called, is a massive plot of unmatched architectures just off of Kaplan Street. Girded by kilometers of high pylon and razor-wire fences, patrolled by elite infantry in open armored cars and full battle dress, it houses the command centers of every military and intelligence branch. And each independent structure of glass and steel, stucco or stone is equipped with a means of descent to the much larger balance of the Kiria's bowels, where neither the impact of nuclear nor biological warheads shall impede the conduct of a war.

At Victor Gate, the main entrance to the complex, perhaps the

Steven Hartov • • •

female gatekeepers' relaxed air was buttressed by their faith in the hydraulic steel teeth that could instantly thrust from the roadbed, stopping anything short of a main battle tank. Yet the hints that these young women were also deadly shots lay in the types of sidearms nestled in their waist holsters. The pistols were not standard issue, which meant that each not-quite-twenty-year-old girl had earned the right to be selective, having proved her killing prowess on the close-quarter range at Mitkan Adam.

They were not debutantes.

Eytan Eckstein's royal blue Ford Fiesta was only sixth in line now, but something was holding up progress, most likely the movement within the Kiria of the minister of defense en route to a sitdown with the chief of staff. The five sedans before him were all white Subaru staff cars with black IDF plates, and as the early Mediterranean sun began to turn the vehicles into microwave ovens, their windows rolled down and their drivers' bronzed arms dangled outside, impatiently flicking ashes.

The constant clutching and shifting was hard on Eckstein's once-wounded knee, and Benni Baum, squeezed into the small passenger seat, watched his major's rippling jaw muscle and clucked his tongue.

"You could declare yourself disabled with that leg, you know," said Benni. In the Israel Defense Forces, being wounded and disabled in action afforded a soldier compensatory privileges unequaled by any other army. "You could be driving a Mercury."

"Itzik would love that," Eytan snorted. "He'd chain me to a desk forever, and with the surgeon's blessing."

"Now *that* would be a travesty," Baum huffed sarcastically. He had been trying to lure Eckstein out of the field for some time, though he was unsure of his own motives. Baum was slated to retire altogether from the army and had only extended his tour to help Eckstein with *Jeremiah*. In turn, he believed that Eckstein should follow the natural progression, stop "playing spy" and run a unit from "inside." Yet he suspected himself of a selfish wish, that Eckstein should hold down an office in Jerusalem so that he, the retiree, would retain an ally in SpecOps. Someone to visit, someone to keep him in the game should gardening and clicking his heels to Maya's redecoration commands prove to be loathsome.

"*Tiyeh retzini.* Be serious," said Eckstein. "Can you picture me working in Itzik's little circus?"

"It's not such a bad idea."

"You've forgotten why we've stayed in the field, Benni. So he doesn't have to actually *look* at us."

Eckstein and Baum were admittedly the best of General Itzik Ben-Zion's officers, but the commander resented their operational coups, while forced to employ them if he wanted to continue to bask in their glories.

"Well, everyone has to come in from the heat eventually," said Benni, twisting the title of the novel that launched John le Carré's fame. He lit up a fresh Marlboro. The ashtray was already overflowing.

"Thank you for the advice. Crude, yet borderline poetic," Eckstein replied. "But it would be like jumping from a volcano onto an iceberg."

Baum laughed. Eckstein was right, of course. Even though Baum held the title of Chief of Operations, he made sure to hold most of his meetings, briefings, and rendezvous outside of Jerusalem headquarters. Not that he actually suspected Itzik of wiring his office, which would have been difficult since it was electronically swept once a week by the internal security detachment known as "Peaches." Baum had simply been weaned by the Mossad back in the 1960s, when street corners, cafés, and empty orange groves *were* the office and such habits were ingrained for the sake of security. But most importantly, these personal quirks kept him out of Itzik's line of sight, as the lumbering colonel knew that he was always a ripe target for inconsequential assignments concocted by his general.

"I want to change," Eckstein suddenly said, but he used the verb *l'hachlif*, which also means "switch."

"Departments?" Baum's tone was incredulous. He could not really envision Eckstein going back to Training again, or taking a straight AMAN desk where you analyzed Syrian troop concentrations by having your field agents monitor prostitute flow.

"Clothes." Eckstein shifted in his seat, snatched up one of Baum's cigarettes, and stabbed the car lighter. He was tempted to honk the horn, but the gatekeepers would probably respond by pulling him out of line and searching his trunk. Neither he nor Baum had slept in over thirty-six hours, and his eyes stung as if invaded by sand, his mouth mealy and his stomach sour.

The missile boat had zigzagged north through the Red Sea, then run the demarcation line straight up the Gulf of Aqaba, where just south of the resort city of Eilat they offloaded the refugees onto a "civilian" snorkel boat. An air force C-130 picked them up at the local airport, and the already culture-shocked Ethiopians were subjected to further technical thunder and wonder, opting to pray and sing Amharic folk tunes rather than peek out the portholes at the Negev Desert sweeping below.

Officials of the Jewish Agency and the Joint Distribution Committee took charge at Jerusalem's Atarot Airport, but Eckstein's dawn fantasy of limping off home to catch his young son before the school day began was dissolved by a messenger driving the major's own Ford and waving a note from Ben-Zion. As always, Itzik's missive was polite, flowery, and *so* apologetic: "0800 hours. Meeting at the Kiria. B.Z."

Eytan and Benni had managed to borrow some sandals and T-shirts from a kibbutznik acquaintance en route to Tel Aviv, but they were both still wearing their miserably damp fatigue pants.

"My ass is chafing," Eckstein complained.

"It's *not* the trousers, my son," Baum observed.

"First you're a literary sage, now you're Sigmund Freud. I can't keep up."

One of the gatekeepers approached Eckstein's window. She was a sergeant, tall like a volleyball player, her coal-black hair pulled into a slick ponytail. Her thumbs were hooked into a white Sam Brown belt and one set of short scarlet fingernails tapped on the butt of a Jericho nine-millimeter pistol.

"*Boker tov,*" Eckstein greeted her as he handed over his AMAN ID card, and her mouth made a perfunctory smile as her eyes flicked from his photo to his face. She returned the card and bent her head to look in at Baum, who was sitting there holding his own card next to one of his jug ears. His thick-necked, bald head in person and the laminated image were easy to compare, and this time the sergeant smiled a real smile, showing a sharply chipped front tooth that made Eckstein wince for her boyfriend. She waved them through.

General Headquarters is, for all its military traffic, one of the most attractive plots of governmental real estate in Israel. It is something of a military Disneyland, a maze of clashing architectures: Here a row of Quonset huts washed in snow-white "seed," there a towering glass structure topped by a honeycombed "widow's walk," which in turn sprouts another tower of clustered dish antennae.

The feature that beautifies the camp is its abundance of carefully manicured plants. Tropical palms, Lebanese cedars, and Jerusalem pines are garlanded near their roots by blood-red poppies, purple bougainvillea, wild daisies, and tiger's-eyes.

The building to which Eckstein and Baum were headed, the Office of the Prime Minister, is a classic leftover from the British mandate whose stone walls are barely visible now for their thick quilt of climbing vines. On the pristine walkways before the porticoed entrance, young privates are constantly hosing flowers, and Colonel Margaliot, who has master-butlered the building since he was a sergeant major, screams at them. "Not so hard! You'll kill the plants! A light spray! A *light* spray!"

He is a big man with a black goatee in pressed fatigues, field insignia, and shirt sleeves that have been widened so he can neatly roll them to the shoulders over massive biceps. When you are an invited, visiting officer, Margaliot will gladly make you coffee in the prime minister's kitchen, then sit with you and sip some of the black mud himself. But if you have no business being there, his face of a friendly "sharif" will turn to storm, and he'll likely toss you into a hedgerow by the seat of your pants.

In accordance with Israeli military and socialist traditions, the prime minister's office is not the private enclave of a head of state, but a suite of modest boardrooms and secure meeting spaces utilized by the various intelligence and Ministry of Defense branches for "special projects" and emergency sessions. However, when the PM himself does appear to make use of his quarters on the restricted upper floors, everyone else has to scramble for alternate facilities, because Margaliot is out there, extending his threatening palm like an angry traffic cop.

Eckstein and Baum pulled into the large parking lot just across the street. Apparently there was some sort of emergency session in progress, because the lot was jammed with well-scrubbed white staff cars and big brown Chevrolet Suburbans, all sprouting multiple antennae like a flock of science fiction insects. Field radios crackled from open windows, and drivers in pressed uniforms lounged around the vehicles, handsome young men who looked more a propos to magazine ads for blue jeans. They sipped coffee from paper cups, smoked, or polished their fuselages with soft rags, and when Eckstein and Baum emerged from the blue Fiesta, leaving no staff driver behind, the chauffeurs assessed them as low-ranking officers of no import. Either that or intelligence agents, who often shun drivers in order to reduce the pairs of ears privy to their conspiracies.

The two men crossed the street to the prime minister's office, where Margaliot was fussing over some tulips, the sun already beading his large forehead. He came erect when he saw Baum.

"Geppetto and Pinocchio!" Margaliot bellowed, then squinted at the officers, their scruffy sandals and damp trousers, and their T-shirts emblazoned with the Israel National Softball League emblem. "Bet I know where *you've* been. Surprised there aren't catfish flopping in your pockets."

Baum grunted under his grin. "What the hell's happened to security in this country?"

"The press already broke it, pictures in this morning's *Yediot.* Falashas and their rescuers, your faces blacked out, of course. Didn't you see the photographer?"

"I can only see my bed," said Eckstein.

Margaliot laughed. "Well, I'd top you up with coffee, but your king awaits." General Ben-Zion's substantial ego had its own reputation in these circles. Margaliot waved them through. "Better move. He's in one of the clean offices, Number Twenty-One at the back."

The "clean office" was one of those nondescript debriefing rooms entirely devoid of decor. No plants, no desktop family photographs, no patriotic posters or calendars from the Society for the Preservation of Nature to warm the gray plaster walls. There were two steel desks, one white telephone, four metal chairs, and an unplugged standing fan next to the single wide window. The only odor was from a thin film of disinfectant on the speckled tile floor, which evoked sense memories of surgery theaters or public restrooms, depending on one's experience.

Eckstein had been to hundreds of meets in such sanitized cubicles, and they always chilled him inexplicably. You could murder a man in such a lifeless space and easily dispatch the evidence with a roll of paper towels and a bottle of window cleaner.

Yudit Greenberg, General Itzik Ben-Zion's secretary, sat cross-legged next to the desk on the left, tapping a pen on a hard-backed record book. She was a first lieutenant now and at Itzik's behest one of the few SpecOps personnel who almost always wore a uniform, the olive drab tunic and slacks tailored to her young, elastic figure. Yudit's long black curls, green eyes, and mischievous smile sometimes ambushed Eckstein with brief erotic fantasies, which he forgave himself because she was so physically similar to his wife, Simona.

In stark contrast to Yudit's uplifting image, Raphael Chernikovsky sat at the desk itself, bent over a black laptop and enveloped in his perpetual mist of gloom. Despite his departmental sobriquet, "Horse," Chernikovsky was anything but a physical thoroughbred, and his prematurely bald pate, steel-rimmed spectacles, and question-mark posture were indicative of the burdens he hefted as Benni Baum's operational troubleshooter.

The Russian immigrant held the rank of captain in AMAN, yet no one could recall ever seeing him in uniform, even at the private post-mission celebrations where such attire was permissible. It seemed that Horse lived in eternal mourning over his role as the bearer of bad tidings, a stammering, brilliant analyst whose lot was to defuse the fantasies of overoptimistic plotters. Today, he wore a tan, short-sleeved shirt with unfashionably large white buttons, and he hardly looked up as Eckstein and Baum entered—a sign that he was already privy to the future, and it was bleak.

Eckstein was surprised to see Uri Badash perched on the desk to the right, his black T-shirt and roll-cuffed blue jeans ending with white Nikes crossed on a chair seat. Badash was a career officer in the General Security Services, known colloquially as *Shabak*, the third major intelligence arm after AMAN and Mossad. Shabak's domain was essentially domestic counterintelligence, its powers akin to Germany's BfV or the American FBI. However, in a country whose border and citizens were under constant threat from terrorists and enemy spies, the GSS also held enormous responsibilities for protecting air and sea ports, El Al Airlines, and heads of state.

Badash had risen to the post of GSS chief of counterintelligence, but his film-star image of slick black hair and smooth-peanut-butter skin belied the mental pressures of spy-hunting and traitor-trapping. General Ben-Zion respected the GSS man, but he never invited him to a SpecOps event unless there was a specific Shabak "need to know."

This should be interesting, Eckstein thought without pleasure as he smiled at Badash and rotated his hand, palm up, the silent Israeli gesture asking, "What's going on?"

Badash returned another gesture indicating, "Just wait," and behind Eckstein, Baum closed the door with his foot.

Itzik Ben-Zion turned from the window where he had been standing with his hands clasped behind his back, apparently looking through the glass at Margaliot's garden, but most probably admiring his own reflection. He was an imposing figure, one of the tallest general officers in the IDF. He was dressed in full Class Aleph uniform, perfectly pressed, the rust-red jump boots of his early airborne days spit-shined American-style. Israeli officers did not usually display "fruit salad"—rows of ribbons and medals—as these were only granted for major campaigns, courses of command, or absurd acts of bravery. But Itzik wore every trinket to which he was legally entitled. The coarse hair poking from his open shirt collar was going bristly and gray, but his head was still blessed with a heavy crop of it and his dark eyes, astride a sharp, prominent nose, were clear and calculating, the corners unmarred by smile lines. A pair of pilot's Ray-Bans was perched in his hair, and his fingers tapped the butt of a SIG Sauer P226 on his belt, the gift of a Swiss intelligence counterpart.

Eckstein glanced at the pistol, thinking that the general would love to finally dispatch with him and Baum in a fashion that no doubt tempted him regularly.

"You're late," Ben-Zion growled.

"We're early," Baum immediately retorted. "Africa's on daylight savings time."

Ben-Zion nearly snapped a reply, then executed a quick time zone calculation and realized Baum was baiting him. Baum's favorite pastime was playing mental tennis with his general, and Ben-Zion rarely even managed to return a serve, only winning at all by taking his ball home in a huff.

Eckstein, who was even less tactful than Baum when it came to their commanding officer, nevertheless tried to alter the impending rancorous atmosphere. He turned to Badash, with whom he'd done business for many years.

"*Ma enyanim, Uri?* What's up?"

"*Ha'chaim manyenim.* Life's interesting." The Shabaknik smiled.

"Badash's presence here is not social," said Ben-Zion as he folded his arms.

Eckstein raised an eyebrow and looked at Raphael Chernikovsky, who appeared to be melding with his laptop and the latest version of Windows.

"Horse?" Eckstein said with feigned confusion. "Can you pull up the military code of conduct and see if there's a reg against greeting 'enemy' officers?"

Uri Badash chuckled and Yudit smiled and opened her record book, while Horse wondered if the major was serious and Baum lit up a cigarette. Now that the usual hostilities were comfortably commenced, everyone was ready to play their traditional roles. The general began with some light sniping.

"I've already been briefed by the navy," he said, as if revealing a schoolyard tattletale. "You got yourselves into quite a firefight."

Baum looked at Eckstein. "Ami is such a fucking gossip," he said, referring to the missile boat commander.

"*Jeremiah* was supposed to be *covert*, gentlemen," Itzik admonished. "A subtle footnote on this whole falasha thing."

Eckstein put a palm to his own chest and jutted his chin. "*We* didn't start the shooting, Itzik." The IDF tradition of addressing everyone by first name often dissolved all pretense of formality and respect.

"And if you remember, Itzik," Baum chimed in, "the Africa desk warned us that Mobote would try to scuttle it."

Baum backed up, resting his heavy shoulders against a blank wall and blowing out smoke rings of impatience. Eckstein joined him there, and in their strange attire and unshaven faces they looked like the impending victims of a Central American firing squad.

"Still," Itzik pressed. "The naval commandos said they could hear you coming all the way from Karora."

"Traitors," Eckstein muttered.

Baum looked at his major. "Maybe we should have dispensed with the marching band."

"I think it was the cheerleaders." Eckstein picked up his cue. "All that dancing and squealing."

Yudit was working hard to suppress a snicker, while Ben-Zion waved his arms in disgust.

"All right, all right." The general squelched the banter. "But still, this was *not* supposed to be a small war."

Eckstein's fatigue was besting his tolerance, but he stuck his hands into his damp trouser pockets to avoid actually jabbing a finger at his commander. "I don't remember *you* out there ducking bullets, Itzik." The general stiffened, raising his head, and Eckstein could feel Baum mentally trying to rein him in, but he went on. "They threw a shitload of small arms at us, and we nearly lost a Zodiac load, *including* Baum. But we still got them all out and we're here, high and wet, so what the hell do you want?"

"Eytan," Baum whispered, touching the major's forearm, and Eckstein exhaled a sigh and slumped against the wall. After so many years of suffering Ben-Zion's congratulations disguised as criticism, Benni had become immune. Eytan, however, would always be offended by it.

"We're tired," Eckstein mumbled as something of an apology.

The general nodded once, frowning at the floor. "Yudit, get them some coffee."

The lieutenant looked up at her boss with a remonstrative glance.

"*Ani mevakesh.* If you *please*," Itzik added, and Yudit smiled and rose from her seat. They had an interesting father-daughter thing going, without any of the sexual banter so common to high rankers and their comely adjutants. The men made an effort not to watch her sway from the room.

Ben-Zion took the sunglasses from his hair, folded them, and hung them from a pocket. Then he faced the window, perhaps examining his own character.

"I don't like being chained to the office, Eckstein," he confessed. "No more than you *really* like being in the field at this stage."

Eckstein was always surprised when Ben-Zion revealed a human quandary, or perceived such in another man. He took it as a reciprocal apology. "So? Let's switch," he suggested.

"I couldn't," said the general. "Nor could you. We are here to do what we do best."

Eckstein looked at Baum, whose expression said that Itzik's temporary humanity was unsettling him as well.

"You both did well," the general conceded. No one in the room breathed, including Uri Badash. It was a historical moment. And it passed quickly. "However, *Operation Jeremiah* has to be extended. On an emergency basis."

"Did we miss something?" Baum asked. "We picked up everyone on the list."

Ben-Zion turned from the window again.

"No, you did not miss anyone. And I know you are supposed to be cashing in, Baum. But I'd like you to extend again."

Eckstein and Baum just stared at their commander, their limp postures and expressions slightly comical, reminding Uri Badash of Laurel and Hardy. Itzik looked at his fingernails. They were short, filed, and very clean.

"There's a group of about fifty more refugees, somewhere outside of Addis Ababa."

"So, let them walk on in to the embassy compound," said Baum. "They've certainly done that before."

"It's not that simple," said Itzik.

"Why?" Eckstein asked.

"They are all children."

Eckstein took in a breath, feeling a cord tightening around his chest, fighting it, hating Itzik for knowing him and Baum so well. He searched quickly for an exit.

"Why not use Rick Singer?" he suggested, referring to an American-born officer who was rapidly rising in SpecOps. "He *loves* kids."

"And *you* hate them?" Itzik snorted. He had seen Eytan rushing home to his son too often. "Besides, you already know the territory."

"But we're blown."

"Not in the south, Mr. Hearthstone. Unless you have been terribly unprofessional."

Yudit strode in with a tray of white demitasses and a *finjon* of Turkish coffee, no doubt a gift of Margaliot, and she walked the tray around. Badash gladly accepted the muddy brew, as did Ben-Zion, since he had ordered it. Baum sipped some as a delaying tactic, while Eckstein declined and the lieutenant resumed her stenography seat.

"Make up your minds, gentlemen," said the general. "It's a two-weeker. Tops. And after that, thirty days' leave."

Baum nearly spit out a stream of coffee. "Excuse me?" You had to be half dead for Itzik to grant you leave. Unprecedented. There was a catch. He was hiding the bulk of the iceberg. Eckstein was thinking the same thing.

"What's the rest of it?"

"You know the drill." Itzik shrugged. "First, you sign on."

SpecOps regulations held that you never fully briefed field officers until they were manifested for a mission. Itzik almost always used this compartmentalization policy as bait, knowing that intelligence officers are, for the most part, secrecy junkies.

"Well? Do you volunteer?"

"You could just issue an order," Baum reminded him.

"Yes, I could."

Ben-Zion waited while Baum and Eckstein exchanged full looks, reading each other's thoughts.

"She'll murder me," Eckstein muttered, and Benni knew that Eytan meant Simona, who was already at the end of her rope regarding Eckstein's career and endless absences. He always managed to stay around the Jerusalem office for an acceptable period between missions. But this would mean going right back out again.

"It's only two weeks." Baum lifted his shoulders.

"Marriages can be killed in a weekend," said Eckstein.

"True. But look at mine. I've been trying to kill it for thirty years."

Eckstein smiled. Well, he was going to quit out of field operations anyway. Two weeks wouldn't make a difference. He nodded at Baum, who turned back to their general.

"For the sake of family harmony," Baum said, "Eckstein and I would prefer not to volunteer for this mission."

"I see." If anyone understood the concept of plausible deniability, it was Itzik. "In that case, I order you to execute the assignment, or suffer courts-martial."

Benni raised his hands, palms skyward. "Who could refuse such delicate persuasion?"

"Good." Ben-Zion clapped his own hands together, but he suppressed the urge to actually say, "Gotcha." There would be no formalities, nothing to sign, no waivers of any kind. Baum and Eckstein were military officers, not civilian employees. Itzik barked at Chernikovsky, "Horse, pull up a mission code."

Chernikovsky winced like an abused puppy, but he began tapping his keyboard until a program appeared that randomly selected operational titles. Although the two officers would be returning to the same area of operations, for reasons of security it would be considered a virgin assignment.

"*Mechashef. Sorcerer*," said Horse in his heavy Slavic accent.

"Good enough," said Itzik. Not that he could have chosen an alternate code even if he wanted to. He put his hands in his snug trouser pockets and began to pace. "So, the crux of *Operation Sorcerer* . . ."

Eckstein pulled up an empty chair and straddled it, while Baum stayed against the wall, found that he had smoked all his Marlboros, and came up with a pack of Time. At this point, Yudit began recording the proceedings in earnest. Later, if there was an operational disaster, someone would want to trace its flaws.

"Last week, while you were still running *Jeremiah*," said Itzik, "there was a walk-in to our embassy in Addis Ababa."

"Walk-in" was intelligence slang for an uninvited guest, usually appearing at an official government facility and offering valuable information of one sort or another. These volunteers showed up regularly at Israeli embassies and consulates around the world. They were listened to politely by low-ranking foreign ministry staffers and rarely had anything concrete to offer. There were, however, rare exceptions.

"One Jan Krumlov," Itzik continued. "Ring a bell?"

Eckstein shook his head. Baum, however, never forgot the names or ranks of foreign intel officers, regardless of when he had learned them. He touched his bulbous nose as if it was the button to his memory bank.

"Czech intelligence. A captain in the StB, I think."

"Czech *counter*intelligence," Itzik corrected. "He is a lieutenant colonel now, or was. And he ran that section." Itzik waved at Chernikovsky again in dismissive, regal fashion. "Give them a sketch."

Horse tapped some more keys. His laptop was not linked to the AMAN mainframe, but he had downloaded the relevant files. He cleared his throat.

"Krumlov, Jan. Born in Prague, 1956. Catholic school, psychology degree University of Prague. Father, Czech national. Mother, Polish refugee from . . ."

"Skip to the employments, Horse."

"Uhh . . . military, two years armored corps. Recruited by the *Státní Tajna Bezpecnost* 1977. Language school at Patrice Lumumba, counterintel courses Moscow. Has English, French, German, and Arabic. Afghanistan, 1980 to '81. Lebanon, 1982 to '84. Three African posts: Uganda, Kenya, and Somalia. Back to Prague in '87, ACO counterintel. Appointed chief of section 1989."

"Any previous involvement with us?" Ben-Zion wanted to know if Krumlov had been the target of or opposition to any Israeli operations.

"*Shlili.* Negative, not counting standard field support of Soviet trackers playing cat and mouse with us in Beirut," said Horse. "And I already checked with the civilians." He meant the Mossad, whose greater license to operate on foreign soil included Czechoslovakia. "They have pretty much the same file."

"Because they got it from us," Eckstein said proprietarily.

"Or *we* from *them.*" Baum corrected him in a fatherly, instructional tone. Having begun his career as a young Mossad officer and then transferred to AMAN, he harbored none of the interservice jealousies common to many other officers.

"So? What's he offering?" Eckstein pulled the black elastic band from his ponytail and regathered the sea-dampened hair. Ben-Zion watched him, frowning. The hairstyle was suited to Anthony Hearthstone, but the general still disapproved of such untidiness. "If it's more bullshit about Syrian T-72s, we don't need it," Eckstein scoffed. The Czechs were still the major suppliers of Syria's armored corps.

Ben-Zion wagged his finger at his major. "It is nothing like that."

He looked at Uri Badash, and the GSS man thought it was his turn to jump in, but the general went on. "First of all, he is offering us the children."

"What the hell does that mean?" Baum growled.

"Six months ago, Krumlov went permanently absent without leave from Prague. The Russians put out a wet order on him, missed him twice. Than he shows up in Africa with a bodyguard of mercenaries, running protection for U.N. relief convoys. He is biding his time, waiting for an opportunity to hook into *us*."

Baum and Eckstein were silent now, realizing that this was not going to be the tale of a simple walk-in.

"He finds that opportunity in a village north of the Ethiopian capital, where a French nurse is running a sort of orphanage for abandoned children. She's having her stores raided by rebel groups, so Krumlov takes over."

"And now he's Bing Crosby." Eckstein frowned.

"Right. A real Father Kindness. So he comes into the embassy, offering us the falasha kids." Ben-Zion paused for a moment, enjoying the drama. "And something else." Now he turned to Uri Badash and pointed a finger like an orchestra conductor cueing the string section. Badash uttered a single word.

"*Chafarperet.*"

Baum and Eckstein exchanged confused expressions, then looked back at Badash.

"A *mole*?" Baum asked. "Where?"

"Here," the GSS man said.

Eckstein, momentarily speechless, jutted his chin into his chest and pointed at the floor. Did Badash mean *here*, as in the Kiria, or perhaps the prime minister's office itself?

Badash smiled at Eckstein's shock, but shook his head as Ben-Zion took over again.

"He claims to know the identity of a man inside Dimona. A man who would make Vanunu look like a vengeful schoolgirl."

"*Yo.*" Eckstein whispered the Israeli equivalent of "wow." Dimona was the not-so-secret site of Israel's nuclear reactor in the Negev Desert. Underground, in six sublevels of hardened production and research facilities, were the manufacturing cores of the state's nuclear weapons arsenal. In 1985, a disgruntled Dimona employee named Mordechai Vanunu had secretly photographed top-secret sections of the plant, left the country, and spilled the story of Israel's nuclear weapons stockpile to a London newspaper. He had subsequently been lured by an Israeli Mata Hari from London to Rome in a "honey trap" sprung by the Mossad, captured and returned to Israel for a trial *in camera*, and convicted and sentenced to eighteen years in prison.

Vanunu had been reviled by the Israeli populace as the worst kind of traitor. Yet, in point of fact, once his clumsy attempt at spying had been discovered, the government had decided to let him run with it. His story and photographs served as a public warning to the Arab confrontation states. Despite Israel's repeated denials, she had the bomb, and she would use it. There was no longer any way to defeat her on the conventional battlefield.

"Right," said Badash, responding to Eckstein's invective. "This isn't about some pissed-off kid from Be'er Sheva out to save the world. This traitor's passing the information on."

"To whom?" Baum demanded.

"Krumlov won't tell," Itzik said.

"Of course not," Eckstein muttered. "That would make it easier for us to run the rodent down, and then our Czech hero would have nothing to sell."

Baum pushed himself away from the wall and began marching around in small circles, his hammy fists on his wide waist. "So, who says he's not bluffing?"

"Krumlov?" Badash asked.

"Yes, Krumlov!" Eckstein growled.

Badash was not offended by Eckstein's vehemence. The idea of an Israeli turncoat, which was a rare and terrible anomaly, caused bloods to boil all around.

"He offered a key word," said the GSS man. *"Keshet."*

"Oh, shit." Eckstein slumped in his chair and rubbed his bristly jaw. "Rainbow" was an ultra-secret research project being run out of Dimona. It was part of a joint Israeli-American anti-ballistic missile weapons system developed after the Gulf War, an offshoot of the defunct Star Wars program and essential to justification of the defense budget and continued American support. All of the intelligence branches were tasked with protecting its secrets through high-security vetting, compartmentalization, and a "bodyguard of lies." At the defense minister's weekly progress briefing, Rainbow was top of the list.

"He actually *used* that word?" Baum cringed.

"In Hebrew." Ben-Zion confirmed the worst, while Yudit flipped a page in her record book. She was scribbling like a cub reporter who had been granted an interview with the Dalai Lama.

Baum looked at Uri Badash. "You've started a preliminary investigation on this already, I assume."

"Of course we have. But do you have any idea how many Dimona personnel are linked into *Keshet*?"

"Tens?" Eckstein posed hopefully.

"Hundreds," said Badash. "And the bastard might not be at Dimona proper. Could be someone at Raphael, or IMI." He referred to a national weapons research facility and Israel Military Industries. "And our probe has to be subtle. We don't want to scare the fucker off."

"*If* he exists," Eckstein said doubtfully.

"He exists," said Ben-Zion. Eckstein looked up at the general, who was still not showing all of his hand. "Krumlov would not want to show up here with an empty bluff."

"What do you mean, show up here?" Baum asked.

"His deal is as follows." The general ticked off the points with his fingers. "Krumlov wants to come over to us, but his own people are still after him, plus the Poles, the new Russian Central Intelligence Service, and probably twenty ex-KGB *Smershniks* eager to pick up a few extra rubles for an easy hit in Africa. He can't go near an airport, so he wants us to extract him. He's no fool, and he assumes we will want the falashas, so we can just load him into the same rescue pipeline."

"And what if we tell him we don't *need* any more Ethiopian Jews?" Eckstein offered defiantly. "And he can stick his mole up his ass?"

"As I said, Mr. Eckstein," Ben-Zion continued patiently. "He did not rise to his former position through idiocy. He controls the orphanage and its immediate surroundings, *and* he has already notified the Joint Distribution Committee of the existence of these young refugees. The

Joint is pressuring us to act. If we don't, Krumlov will turn the children over to your flesh hunter, Amin Mobote, and our Czech will make damn sure that AP and UPI hear all about it."

"So," Baum concluded. "Any public relations gains we made with *Solomon* and *Jeremiah* will be buried when everyone finds out we sacrificed fifty kids to a vicious warlord."

"Exactly." The general nodded. "And that's not the end of it."

"Don't tell me," Eckstein grunted. "He wants a million dollars in a Swiss account."

"Actually, it's surprisingly more romantic than that. Krumlov's fiancée was left behind. He wants us to get her out as well."

"*Ma?!* What?!" Eckstein nearly shouted, then added an obscene curse on Krumlov's mother. "*Koos shel ha'ima shelo.*"

"Tell him to send her a fucking airline ticket!" Baum was equally flabbergasted by the Czech's *chutzpah.* "I'll pay!"

"No go," said the general. "His conditions are hard."

"So's my ass," Eckstein spat, and he got up, banged the chair down on the floor tiles, and marched to the door. He had no intention of leaving; he just wanted something hollow to echo with the impact of his palm and he smacked the wood. After a moment, he calmed himself and turned back, his eyes meeting those of Uri Badash. "What are the chances, Uri, that the whole thing is a bluff?"

Badash shook his head regretfully. "Slim, Eytan. The man knows us. He knows that if he's fucking with us, when he gets here we'll just pack him and his girlfriend in a crate and drop them off in Vladivostok."

Eckstein squinted at the GSS man for a moment, then extended a hand to Baum, who slapped his box of cigarettes into Eckstein's palm like a surgical nurse. Eckstein took Baum's lighter and lit up, remembering how often he and his partner had tried to get each other to quit and nearly succeeded; then some operational pressure would trigger the nasty habit once more.

Ben-Zion, who had stopped smoking some years before, responded by bending to plug in the standing fan, which had the effect of lifting Yudit's hair back like a fashion model in a phony "outdoor" studio shoot.

Baum turned to Chernikovsky. "How long have you known about this, Horse?"

The analyst looked to Ben-Zion for permission. The general nodded. "Three days," Horse croaked.

"Long enough," said Baum. "Let's hear it."

Like an accident investigator for an insurance firm, it was Horse's task to estimate damages without tact or remorse. It was an essential though unpopular position in SpecOps, causing him painful bouts of self-hatred. But he was well-heeded and respected for his talents, even though he was known throughout the Department as "Benni Baum's nightmare."

He took off his glasses, rubbed the bridge of his nose, and looked at his knees as he tried to delay offering up a bleak scenario. "Well, best case is easy to imagine. Krumlov is straight, his mole is real. We get him out, turn the traitor, and . . ."

"Horse." Benni cut him off, though he used an uncharacteristically indulgent tone. "We don't pay you to soothe us with fairy tales."

Chernikovsky blushed, nodded, sighed, and got back on track.

"Okay. Middle case. The whole thing is a double play. There *is* a real mole, but he is minor, a plant, developed and run by the Russians or the Czechs just for bait . . ."

"Excuse me." Yudit had stopped recording and was raising a finger like a schoolgirl. "But someone has to clarify for me to get this right." She tapped her pencil on her notebook. "All this chaff about the Russians and the Czechs. Has anyone told them the Cold War's over?"

"The war is over," Horse quickly answered, "but the East Bloc armies and intel services are still in place, and soldiers and agents have to eat. What they used to do for Mother Russia, they now also do on contract, for the Iranians or Saddam or North Korea. They sell off the intelligence they obtain, or take on penetrations for hire."

"Okay, I get it." Yudit returned to her pad.

Itzik frowned at her. "I'm sending you to that course on the splintered Soviet services."

Yudit winced. "I should have kept my big mouth shut."

"It's down at Mossad H.Q. By the *beach.*"

"I'll go." She grinned.

Baum turned to Horse impatiently. *"Nu?"*

"Okay," Horse continued. "So, Krumlov has not really gone to ground, he's a false defector, and they chase him just to make him look genuine. They hope we'll take him in and pick his brain, and blended into his debriefing, maybe months from now, he'll suddenly slip us some kind of unrelated false lead. But it will be significant enough to *us*, and we'll go crazy running it down, while they laugh their asses off and run some other op right under our noses."

"Standard stuff," said Uri Badash. "Like Nosenko and the Americans." Over the years, the Central Intelligence Agency had found itself besieged by false defectors, both during and after the Cold War.

"So, they cook up this mole thing just to establish Krumlov's bona fides?" Ben-Zion rubbed his jaw.

"Possibly." Horse clearly did not want to commit himself to any single theory.

"All right, Horse," said Benni. "We've all played that game before. It's just a chess match. Let's hear something dangerous."

Horse looked at Baum, whom he admired the way a clumsy violinist regards Isaac Stern. He blew out a breath, making his thin lips flap.

"Okay. Worst case, Benni." He took in both Baum and Eckstein with his sad, tired eyes. "It's an ambush. The two of you have many enemies. The Russians, the Iranians, Ahmed Jabril, Islamic Jihad . . . Could be any one of them baiting a trap. So, again, Krumlov is a false defector, but there is no mole. Whoever's handling Krumlov knows you two are running ops in Africa, and that we are soft on the refugee issue. They gamble that you'll be sent back in for this. And then they just kill you, and Krumlov disappears."

Eckstein turned to Baum, eyebrows raised, and both men simultaneously dragged on their cigarettes. The fan blew the smoke in loops around their heads. "Hard to argue with that premise," said Eckstein. "Though I'd love to trash it."

"But it's unlikely," said Benni.

"Really?" Eckstein snorted. "Forget about me. *Your* head would make a nice trophy over a few fireplaces *I* can think of."

"It's the girl, Eytan," Benni offered optimistically. "Krumlov's fiancée. She's the indicator that it's all legitimate. If someone wanted us for organ donors, why send us off to Prague chasing this skirt?"

"I did not say Prague," Ben-Zion cut in. "I said he left her *behind.*"

The two officers frowned at their commander.

"She's in Sarajevo." It seemed almost as if Itzik was suppressing a smile, although his lips twitched a bit and it was hard to discern whether from mirth, guilt, or gas.

"Sarajevo?" Baum mouthed.

"A lot of people die in Sarajevo." Uri Badash frowned. The Balkan war was at the height of its madness, and he was openly uncomfortable with the idea of Eckstein and Baum setting foot in that bloody circus. "Two more wouldn't even make radio news."

"And it's double indemnity," said Horse. "If they miss you in Sarajevo, they get another chance in Ethiopia."

"Nonsense," said Benni. "It is not an ambush. They couldn't be sure that *we* would be tasked." He looked at Ben-Zion and smiled. "Unless the mole is Itzik."

Ben-Zion was not amused. Eckstein took a drag off his cigarette, then stubbed it out on the floor. In response to Ben-Zion's sour expression, he covered the ugly smudge with his sandal.

"I say we take the offensive," Eckstein proposed. "Split this up. Send in a *Mat'kal* snatch team to get Krumlov, while Benni and I go in to get the kids."

"Negative," Ben-Zion snapped. "If this mole is real, Krumlov will only give him up for a villa in Kfar Shmaryahu and a fat retirement plan. But if we kidnap this Czech, he'll clam up like a mafia don." It was hard to argue the point with Itzik, who himself embodied the mob traditions of management. "And besides, elections have been held down there. It's sovereign territory again. We cannot just operate that way."

Eckstein watched his commander, knowing that every operational plan considered by Ben-Zion was first weighed against potential political fallout at home.

"You're going to make a fine prime minister someday, Itzik," said Eckstein with a tight smile. It was not a compliment.

The general glared at his major, and Yudit glanced up from her record book. She almost clucked her tongue, but just slightly shook her head instead, knowing that once again Eckstein had gone too far.

Ben-Zion looked at his watch, then picked up a spotless black briefcase.

"I have to get to another meeting." His tone had gone arctic, and he headed for the door as everyone watched him. "You two have twenty-four hours."

"For what?" Baum inquired, wondering if, given Horse's dark assessment, Itzik wanted them to think it over once more before really committing themselves.

The general turned, his fingers on the door handle. "To assemble a team, establish codes, contacts, transport, backups, and commo procedures. By tomorrow morning, I want you on the way to Sarajevo." He walked out, and the banging door echoed in the sterile room.

Horse clicked off his laptop and Yudit slowly closed her record book. Uri Badash popped a stick of gum in his mouth and slipped off the desk. No one spoke. With the air thick with stale smoke, it was like a mausoleum after a cremation.

"Well." Badash broke the spell. "The Yugoslavians can't make a decent car. But maybe the food's good."

"Yeah." Eckstein shoved his hands in his pockets and walked to the window. "I wonder what they eat in Sarajevo."

Baum moved to Eckstein and dropped a hand on his shoulder. "With the snipers playing human pinball night and day?" He summoned up his jocular side.

"They eat dirt, Eytan. They eat dirt . . ."

2

* * *

MORE THAN ANYTHING on earth, Eytan Eckstein wanted to go home.

He longed for it in instinctive, visceral ways, like a man stranded in a snowstorm, struggling through deadly cold, kept alive by the image of a cabin lantern and smoke drifting from a stone chimney. He needed to return, his heart like the bruised soul of an orphan child, drawn by forces inexplicable to the truth of his birth. He thirsted for the arms of his wife crossed against his back, her breasts pressed to his chest, her hair nestled in his neck. His hands stung with their own emptiness, desperate to feel the brushy oval of his son's head as he trapped the boy's laughter against his belly. He could already sense his bare feet on the cool tiles of his home, every man's private world where he can wander in utter darkness, knowing each step on every stair, the hard corners of furniture that pose no danger, the light switches that need not be touched.

He wanted it so badly that he avoided it for the entire day. For he knew that once he crossed the threshold of his family, it would be impossible to return to the office and function with a clear head.

Eckstein realized that this magnetic pull was a sign of his fading youth, a certain weariness that comes upon aging warriors. This was different than maturity, for he believed that truly mature men did not continue to race cars, or parachute, or play dangerous games of cat and mouse against armed adversaries, all the while calling their child-ish vocations "the job" or "duty." A part of him was still addicted to the work, while a wiser part nagged him with a recurring dream whose significance would have been obvious to any freshman psychology student.

It was always the same, short and clear, though all the dream's characters but himself were faceless. He was in Lebanon again, a young paratroop sergeant, the sound of smattering gunfire beyond a rocky hill sharp and staccato. Around him, men moved quickly in blurs of olive drab through mists of dust and smoke, shouting orders, frantic, and he was being lifted at last onto a canvas stretcher. Yet there was no pain, no hint of wounds, only an enormous peace and flood of relief as he was carried from the field. Forever. To home.

It had not always been so. As a young SpecOps officer, home had been the playing fields of his missions, his bachelor flat merely a place to store books, ignore electric bills, and change into clean clothes—none of which sported Israeli labels. When he married Simona, for a
• long time home became a joyful reward after weeks or months away, but not a quench for loneliness, for his comrades were still his closest family.

But once Oren was born, suddenly the picture shifted, his self-centered life pulled off-balance. It was then that he began to wonder when his obligation to a country, an anonymous populace, an idea, should be rededicated to the sculpting of a single child's soul.

As he found himself alone in his car now, driving hypnotically on a shimmering highway, he faced the fact that the love all soldiers resist had turned him into a coward. Of course he could have reordered his day, spent an hour with Simona, and "crashed" Oren's elementary school before carrying out the rest of Itzik's orders. But then he would have had to tell his wife the truth, that his appearance would be fleet-ing, and in turn she would have forced him to tell the same to their son. He also knew that no matter the tears or disappointment or anger, nothing would change. He would still be going, and he would have faced the workday reverberating with guilt.

No, he would make it easy on himself. Yes, he was a coward.

Benni Baum had elected to stay on in Tel Aviv for a few hours while

Eytan headed back to Special Operations headquarters in Jerusalem. The colonel and major had divided their pre-mission responsibilities, with Baum gathering all relevant intelligence on Sarajevo and Eckstein assembling a team, proper backstopping documentation, transportation, and required equipment.

Jan Krumlov, obnoxiously optimistic regarding Israeli complicity, had provided the embassy in Addis Ababa with a photo and a document describing his fiancée's physical characteristics, her Sarajevan places of residence and employment, and her daily schedule and likely haunts after hours, though it was doubtful she was frequenting bars and discos in a city that was nightly set ablaze by artillery fire. Baum, with Horse in tow, headed over to AMAN's research facility, the largest intelligence department of its kind in the entire Middle East. Once there, he proceeded to bully analysts and field operators of the Slovak desk, arming himself with detail maps, aerial reconnaissance photos culled from NATO allies, the latest updates on the factional fighting and a who's who of the madmen laying waste to the former Yugoslav cultural capital.

Finally, he dug up a Mossad counterpart who had just returned from a very nervous year of deep cover in Sarajevo. Over coffee in the large canteen on the main floor of Beit Sokolov—which is primarily a journalists' hangout below the IDF Spokesman's Office—Baum picked the man's brain for an hour of sotto voce interrogation. He gleaned a wealth of useful information on danger zones, access and escape routes, and the street survival tricks for placating Muslims, Serbs, and Croats alike. However, he was less than heartened when the officer kept shaking his head and interjecting the phrase, "*Al tilech le'sham.* Don't *go* there."

Eckstein, for his part, had a list of tasks that would normally have taken at least three days to accomplish properly. While the extraction of Krumlov's fiancée was neither a snatch nor a rescue, but instead an "escort" from a dangerous environment, it still required proper pre-mission consideration. As a career intelligence officer, he was accustomed to quick action in response to surprise developments in the field, and he had often put off sleep for days on end, functioning on autopilot, then collapsing into a twenty-four-hour slumber that would have

alarmed a coma specialist. In the past he had welcomed these chal-
lenges, thrown himself against the odds with a certain fanatical enthusiasm. But today he was a bit alarmed to discover that his heart was not
in it.

The route that connects the seaside Mediterranean city of Tel Aviv
to the mountainous capital of Jerusalem is a superhighway now, and
Israeli motorists, always flaunting the speed laws, can slice across the
country in an easy half-hour. But Eckstein had opted for a detour, a
delaying tactic, not yet fully cognizant of why he drove *south* toward
Rishon Le-Zion. And as he motored the small Fiesta, windows open,
the wind powdering his sunglasses with cigarette ash and the radio
blaring Shalom Hanoch's bloody tribute to Israeli highway death—
"In Daddy's New Car"—he wondered if he hadn't taken a wrong turn.

Not geographically, no, although for a moment he remembered with
a sour grin those early days as a paratroop recruit and his reputation as
a poor land navigator. Those endless orienteering exercises, usually at
night in the rain, and his comrades would heckle him.

"Eck-shtein! Where the fuck *are* we?"

"How the hell should *I* know? Keep walking. It's a small country."

Since then, and spanning the years of his career in AMAN, he had
often found himself in precarious locations and predicaments of mortal threat, yet it was only of late that he had begun to really wonder.
Had he followed his fated path or forced himself upon it unnaturally?
Was he, as Benni Baum had once suggested, a barefoot dancer drawn to
minefields?

He had wanted to be a doctor once. The idea fed the same well of
hero complex that later pushed him into the airborne corps, then
AMAN and SpecOps. And he had also considered history as a profession, viewing himself as a bespectacled scholar lecturing at Jerusalem
University, writing brilliant texts on Europe, Hitler, and the war that
had engulfed his family. But quite simply, he did not have the *set-
zfleisch*—literal Yiddisch for "sit flesh"—the ability to study, immobilized, for hours on end.

Every option he had not pursued loomed larger now as a regret, for
each represented a lost "normal" life, shimmering like a wispy curtain
of fantasy behind the hard reality that was his existence. For instead,

he had chosen the army, and he accepted now that no practical excuse for his decision held up anymore. Good pension? A medical career's earnings would have superseded that long ago. Excitement? He had had his fill, and now he felt somewhat like a smoke jumper who suddenly realizes his distaste for parachuting and forest fires. Yet it was too late, for wherever a blaze raged, it was still his job to jump in and blot it out.

His career was peppered with acts of "bravery"; the fact that he could not share them with a soul aside from those comrades who had witnessed them did not matter. He waved them off as "duty," things he did because the Service and the Country required them being done. Yet inside, he knew that each act was propelled by simple, personal psychoses. His father was a kind but weak and sickly man, and Eckstein was self-condemned to a life of outwitting and crushing those shameful genes.

Had a single act of his left a fingerprint on Israel's future? Perhaps one—the prevention of the prime minister's assassination by a Palestinian terrorist back in 1986. Yet now in 1993, that politician's successor, Yitzhak Rabin, was at last bringing peace accords to fruition. If not for Eckstein's reckless "courage," perhaps it all would have happened sooner. Well, that kind of dour speculation was a waste.

In the end, however, it was not career paths, promotions, or pensions that troubled him. It was a five-year-old boy called Oren, and he realized that the son he loved above all else needed no hero, no flesh god to worship. He needed a father, close, at home, a man to learn from, someone to guide his schoolwork, dry his tears, hold his hand. He needed so much more than a pang of hope as he returned from school each day: *Maybe Abba will come home tonight.*

Yes, he had made a mistake, taken the wrong path. And here he was, mounting another mission, soon to be out on a limb again, far away. Sarajevo, and then Africa.

On the surface it was less dangerous a project than so many he had tackled. But having made the decision to quit, while unable to summon the courage to do so *right now*, before another hour passed, he was flooded with a foreboding that iced the skin of his arms despite the early summer heat. It was more than the curse of the *pazamnik*—the

short-timer about to be mustered out of the army and growing ever
superstitious. It was the very real vision of Oren, left sad and lonely
and fatherless, with nothing but old photographs and dim memories to
sustain him.

And so he was delaying the passing of this day, hoping to stall the
commencement of one last operation. For he suspected that this time
he might not be coming back alive.

He passed a road sign that said PALMACHIM, which confirmed that he
was indeed behaving like a patient with a terminal illness. He had witnessed the behavior in other men about to embark on deadly ventures,
suddenly propelled back to their hometowns, high schools, the beaches
of their first kisses. He tossed the cigarette butt from the window and
nodded, driving on toward the site of his military birth.

Palmachim was the seaside parachute drop zone of the IDF airborne corps, and the highway leg he was on led to Tel Nof, the airborne
training school itself. The road was bordered by brushy hillocks and
dusty eucalyptus, yet just ahead to the right a perfectly mowed plot of
green grass rose from the roadside like a golf course in the midst of the
Sahara.

Eckstein pulled off the highway onto a gravel drive, rolled to a stop,
and sat listening to the passing traffic swishing behind him and the
starlings chattering in the tall trees ahead. To his left, sprinklers fed
the emerald field as large as a soccer pitch. At the far border of the
field, wide steps of Jerusalem granite led up to a long platform of similar rock, and above that was The Wall, thousands of names etched in
bronze, overlooked by a brace of steel letters—*Swifter Than Eagles,
Braver Than Lions*. To the right, a lofty stone tower was topped by an
iron pair of Israeli parachute wings.

Many ceremonies were held at the *Andarta*, the memorial to fallen
paratroopers. There were always wreaths of wilted flowers propped
against the wall, going brittle in the sun. Memorial services were held
there on the anniversaries of wars, green recruits received their wings
there after their first five parachute jumps. And it seemed that every
other week the old engraver was there with his tools, adding another
name as an honor squad of Red Berets fired their volleys into an
azure sky.

Eckstein got out of the car, his knee suddenly reminding him of its scars, returning him to that bleak winter day of his wounding in Munich and the names and faces of friends lost. They had fallen in Europe, in Asia, in the hills of Lebanon and the wastes of Iraq. The paratroopers had been laid to rest in ceremony, the secret warriors in private anonymity. The combat soldiers' names shone here beneath the sun, while the intelligence officers were listed on marble stones, rankless, in a small forest to the north, appropriately in shadow. But only one of them had served in both worlds, and it was to that name that Eckstein was drawn.

Ettie Denziger had been more to him than a comrade in Special Operations. They had been teamed together for six missions in Europe and North Africa. At that time he had not yet met Simona, and even though department regulations forbade it, he had finally failed to resist the beautiful blond intelligence operative, and she had also surrendered to his desire for her, even though he was her team leader and strictly off limits. With Eytan's wounding and lengthy rehabilitation, they had grown apart as Ettie continued to operate in the field. And then, when *Operation Flute* was again revived as the terror master Amar Kamil returned to Israel seeking revenge, Ettie and Eytan were reunited. So briefly. And then she was killed.

He was sure now as he walked across the empty grass to the wall that had fate been kinder they would have wound up together. Perhaps, too similar in their Germanic backgrounds and brooding characters, it would not have lasted. But to Eckstein the loss was sometimes stunningly acute, and he had learned that the mourning for an unrealized future could be stronger than any other emotional pain. But all in all, he felt the savaging of a wish, for he would never see her as an elderly, sprightly woman, disguising her exploits as fairytales for grandchildren who would never be.

She had begun her army career at Tel Nof as a parachute rigger, one of those robust girls who pack thousands of parachutes, then jump regularly with their own chutes to prove to the airborne boys that their faith in the riggers is well placed. Later, she had volunteered for a transfer to AMAN. But it was not until her death that her file was pulled in SpecOps and her surprising request was revealed. She wished to be buried as a paratrooper, with her airborne comrades on Mount Herzl in Jerusalem. And she wanted her name listed on the wall at the *Andarta.*

It was strictly against SpecOps regulations, but Benni Baum had bullied Ben-Zion until the request was passed up to the *Rosh Aman,* the commanding general of military intelligence. And so, in a silent midnight ceremony, it seemed so many years ago, a flock of "civilians" had gathered here to honor Ettie's last wish.

Eytan moved to the year of her death, raising a finger to the D's, and he stopped and took in a breath, his heart pounding as he saw that her name was not there. He was about to shout, to raise holy hell with whomever had taken it upon himself to disgrace her.

And then he remembered, and he felt the hot blood of shame rise in his cheeks. Ettie Denziger was her *cover* name. It was the false mask by which he had known her for so long, just as she had known him then as Tony Eckhardt, and all the others by their non-Israeli monikers: Peter, Rainer, Mike, and Harry.

His fingers drifted down the bronze like a blind man reading Braille, and there it was.

Shoshani, Tamar. First Lieutenant.

From right to left, he gently brushed the ridges of her engraved remains. And he closed his eyes, remembering her skin, her slim waist beneath a white cotton blouse, small jewels dangling in a mist of perfume beneath her delicate ears. And then he backed away, and he saw all of her, just for a few seconds of memory, and he whispered.

"Lo hikarti o'tach b'chlal."

"I didn't really know you at all."

He headed back to the car.

The relocation of Israeli Military Intelligence's Special Operations Unit to a dilapidated building across from Jerusalem's Central Post Office was supposed to be a temporary measure. Yet it had been nearly nine years since General Itzik Ben-Zion, while still a full colonel, had managed to convince the Chief of Staff that his Tel Aviv digs were too small for his expanding operation, the crumbling old British Mandate walls and windows too easily acoustically targeted, and that the cultural attachés-cum-spies from every foreign embassy in the city practically picnicked outside his rear entrance, tracking his men and women at every opportunity. Itzik, as an astute career builder, had of course waited with his pitch until SpecOps personnel had pulled off a string of successes.

It was a SpecOps team that had pinpointed the nuclear reprocessing plant in Baghdad for targeting by Israeli warplanes. It was a SpecOps officer who had managed to pose as a Red Crescent ambulance driver and actually report from the bloody fronts of the Iran-Iraq war. A SpecOps woman in the guise of an Italian journalist had dined with Yasir Arafat in Beirut before the city crumbled, setting him up for "removal" by a Mossad *kidon* team, the operation called off only at the last minute by the Israeli Cabinet. And it was Itzik's men who had isolated a lone Syrian T-72 tank near Bahamdoun for a spectacular snatch by *Sayeret Mat'kal,* the IDF's General Staff Reconnaissance Unit of elite commandos (it was not Itzik's fault that the actual theft failed). And, of course, Benni Baum and his renegades from Queen's Commando had been ranging across the continents and stunning the general staff with their audacity for nearly ten years. Back then, it was still the golden age of AMAN's special operations, well before Eytan Eckstein killed the wrong man in Munich and nearly brought down the House of Ben-Zion.

And so the Chief of Staff was successfully lobbied and ground was broken for a new SpecOps facility, not far from the Mossad's own training base in Herzliya. However, Itzik had great faith in the incompetence of the Israeli construction trade. It would take them years, and he gleefully relocated to "temporary" quarters in the capital. In Jerusalem, Itzik's operation was far from the prying eyes of his jealous peers in the *Kiria.* His office sat just minutes away from the Knesset, and MKs and cabinet ministers were casually invited over for lunch, then whisked back to their political temples to whisper laudatory remarks about Itzik's secret domain. In Jerusalem, Ben-Zion became king of the hill.

Yet to Eytan Eckstein, no monarch had ever ruled over so bleak a palace. Perhaps it was the location, the comparative architectural splendor of the surroundings. Just a short walk from Zion Square, the spoke of Jerusalem's teaming pedestrian promenades and cafés, a large promontory called the Russian Compound rose up from Yaffo Street. The centerpiece of this sun-bleached hill was a magnificent Orthodox church of pink granite spires and emerald domes. The eastern border of the compound was occupied by the massive Central Magistrate building, while on the western side, the municipal National Police headquarters also impressed, with its towering communications antennae and a constant flow of uniformed cops and muscular detectives. In contrast to the rest, AMAN's SpecOps building, which occupied the southern perimeter, looked like a cross between a Turkish armory and a tuberculosis clinic.

But Eckstein was not really disturbed by such lack of aesthetics. Ever since his first days as a paratroop recruit, when he had reported to Sanure—the airborne basic training base, which resembled a poor man's Foreign Legion outpost—he had learned to suppress the fastidiousness of his German birthright and accept the Israeli disregard for accouterments. Some of the best combat soldiers failed to properly shine their jump boots or press a uniform. The most brilliant and innovative officers he knew had all spent time in military police prisons. And as for army bases, it was almost always the same. The most impressive structures housed rear echelon hordes of lazy clerks, while the ramshackle huts that regularly failed building inspections contained the most dangerous point men in the IDF order of battle.

At any rate, the SpecOps building had come to be called *Ha'ashlaya*—The Illusion—by its occupants. Outside, its ugliness turned up the noses of passersby. Inside, its three floors were crammed with bustling offices of frenetic efficiency; the Weapons, Electronics, and Special Projects workshops, Photo-Reconnaissance Analysis, Intercept and Cipher Analysis, Communications, Research and Investigations, Cover, Documentation, Internal Security, Central Computer and Support, Planning and Logistics, Training, Transport, the *Miznon* (cafeteria), Itzik Ben-Zion's suite of offices and boardroom, and, of course, Lieutenant Colonel Benni Baum's lair as chief of operations, to which Eckstein reluctantly headed now.

In the "submarine chamber" just inside the nondescript entrance, he was greeted by a deceptively beefy, middle-aged security man wearing a civilian rent-a-cop uniform. Shlomo had served as a reservist private under Ben-Zion during the 1973 war and was kept on as one of the general's pets. He was a humorful fellow enjoying the slide toward his army pension, and he grinned at Eckstein's strange garb and softball league T-shirt.

"Long time no see. Did you win the game?"

Despite his mood, Eckstein managed a smile in return. "Pitched a no-hitter." He showed Shlomo his officer's ID card, which the guard glanced at perfunctorily.

"I don't suppose you know the passwords this month."

"Mmmm." Eckstein thought for a moment. He didn't have a clue. "My wife buys grapes from yours at *Machaneh Yehuda?*"

Shlomo laughed. "That happens to be true, but it's not it."

There was a video camera mounted above the secondary steel door, and suddenly a male voice blurted from a tinny speaker.

"You're not getting in without the password."

Eckstein sneered up at the camera. "Bavaria," he snapped.

There was a moment's delay, then the voice chastised him.

"That's your departmental code, *not* the password."

Shlomo spun in his chair and growled angrily, "Oh, for God's sake, Rafi. Let him in, or you can take the *bus* home tonight!"

The disembodied voice grumbled, the door's magnetic lock buzzed, and Eckstein bowed to Shlomo and yanked on the handle.

"Kids." Shlomo shook his head and returned to reading his newspaper.

In most cases, operations on foreign soil required weeks or even months of preparations. Beginning with a general mission sketch, available intelligence on the target area was gathered, and if it was insufficient, operators were dispatched for additional reconnaissance. There followed the crucial phase of personnel selection for the mission team. Once those people had signed on, together they haggled over logistics, equipment, transport, infiltration, and exfiltration, and then vigorously argued the plan of execution until Benni Baum would bang a shoe on his desk Nikita Khruschev style and shout, "*Maspeek!* Enough!

This is how it will run." The shoe, by the way, was not one he wore. It was an old combat boot he kept close at hand like a gavel.

But the extraction of Niki Hašek from Sarajevo and delivery to her fiancé, Jan Krumlov, had to be done quickly, lest the alleged defector get cold feet. And so Eckstein spent the rest of the day in Baum's office playing "Monopoly," an exercise that bore little resemblance to the popular board game, but was a technique devised by Baum to ensure proper planning under pressure.

Rather than the executive suite one might expect of a high-ranking Israeli intelligence officer, Benni Baum's office was a long, uncarpeted rectangle of speckled tiles and gray plaster walls. At one end, the flip-handled entrance door led to the Floor Two hallway. At the other, a tall multipaned window, its glass affixed with suction-cupped oscillators to defeat long-range acoustical readers, framed the majestic Orthodox cathedral across the compound.

Besides a few faded photographs hinting at Baum's military career and his long partnership with Eckstein, nothing spruced up the walls, which were reserved for maps, recon photos, mission manifests, and one large marker board. The clashing furniture and equipment were reminiscent of a bankruptcy sale and included scuffed bookshelves bloated with texts in seven languages, vertical and lateral steel files, two personal computers linked to the mainframe, and a pair of moss-green spin-dial combination safes. Baum's desk was a mahogany monstrosity imported by a colonel of the Royal Green Jackets during the British Mandate, and from its middle, two metal worktables extended end to end, forming a T-shaped structure surrounded by cheap folding chairs.

It was at this conference table that some of AMAN's most brilliant missions had been plotted by an elite group of chain-smoking, coffee-guzzling, argumentative male and female operators of *Kommando Ha'Malkah*—The Queen's Commando. And it was to this caffeine-stained amulet of past luck that Eckstein turned now, hoping it would provide him answers like an old favorite Ouija board. He did not have an office of his own, for in accordance with "Ben-Zion's Rules," *departments* had offices, not *people*. So for now he sat at Benni's desk, wishing the colonel would return from Tel Aviv so they could put their two exhausted heads together and perhaps form one clear-thinking brain.

A large cardboard box sat in the middle of the conference table. It was full of Baum's Monopoly pieces, symbolic toys used as aids when laying out a mission. These visual cues made it simpler to answer the question: "What's missing?"

As team members sat in assigned positions around the table, thumbing file folders stamped *Sodi B'yoter*—Most Secret—Baum would rummage through his Matchbox cars, plastic figurines, and sundry objects, placing some before operators, then pacing, thinking, hiking up his trousers, changing his mind, and switching pieces around like a shell-gamer. If you were handed a Band-Aid box, you would serve as team medic. But just as you accepted the fact that this mission was going to involve bloody gunplay, the Band-Aids would be snatched away and replaced by a miniature Mercedes, a firecracker, and a little wooden duck. Now you would serve as mobile decoy, and you would be using demolitions for a distraction. All of these assignments were, of course, commensurate with your abilities. If you were a lousy shot, Benni would *not* give you the little sniper rifle from the G.I. Joe kit.

Today, however, the most obvious "pieces" missing from the game were the operators themselves. Talented field personnel did not hang around SpecOps headquarters like movie studio contract players awaiting a juicy role. If they were not off on field missions, then they were somewhere in the country attending a course to supplement their talents, or down at AMAN headquarters in Tel Aviv, lending their expertise to one desk or another. And so, until Benni arrived, Eckstein had to go it alone, with the exception of Mack Marcus, one of his favorite officers from Planning and Logistics.

Marcus was a very tall American-born captain with a crop of thick black curls and a Saddam Hussein mustache. While serving as a sergeant with the Givati Brigade in 1982, he had had his right leg shot off in the early days of the war in Lebanon, and following a long and painful recuperation he was granted a lifetime disability. At the ripe old age of twenty-two he could have comfortably retired on a fat IDF pension, but he quickly grew bored with beachcombing and bar-cruising and demanded an opportunity to return to the army.

Hoping to shock Marcus back to reality, a manpower major sent him off to Training Base One for the officers' course. Mack sprinted through the six-month school, prosthesis and all. Thereafter, AMAN was glad to have him, and he wound up in SpecOps, where he and Eckstein recognized in each other the stubborn characters of cripples in denial. They wryly called each other *Rofef*—"Shaky"—and once a year they would drive down to Tel Nof, try to sneak onto a C-130 making a mass parachute drop, and be inevitably caught and turned away by the grinning airborne cadre. Then they would head over to the beach at Palmachim, get buzzed on Maccabi beer, and watch the drop between wolfish whistles at the local bikinis.

"You're still going to need extraction," said Marcus as he set a little white plastic ambulance in the middle of the worktable. "Even if this thing gets you to the airport, that Sarajevo strip is like Beirut International in the old days. Every time a plane lands one side or the other shells the tarmac, just to show who's got the biggest dick."

Eckstein would have smiled, but he was perched on one corner of Baum's desk, engrossed in Niki Hašek's meager file. "I don't want to just rely on paperwork to get her out. We'll make her a critical care case, so we can push her through roadblocks."

"Good idea. If she's half dead the Serbs won't want to gang-rape her, unless they're necrophiliacs."

"That's it, cheer me up," Eckstein mumbled. Then he said, "Oh, shit. She's working out of the Russian embassy. Why the hell couldn't she be a lunch counter girl or some such goddamn thing?"

Marcus rapped his knuckles on the tabletop. "Focus, Eckstein, focus. We're working on extraction." He limped over to Benni's toy box and removed a yellow bucket of Legos so he could get at the esoterica.

"Okay." Eckstein closed the file folder. "So what would you use?"

Marcus came up with a small metal helicopter that Baum had picked up at the Frankfurt airport gift shop. "How about that white chopper the air force brought in after Operation Moonlight?"

Eckstein thought for a moment, experiencing a brief flashback to the Moroccan beach where German terrorist Martina Klump, in an effort to foil an Israeli-Hizbollah prisoner exchange, had jumped from the chopper skids into the waves. In the ensuing chase, he and Benni had crash-landed in a C-47, and he unconsciously touched the small scar where his forehead had impacted with the control panel.

"It's still got the U.N. markings on it," said Mack. "But come to think of it, the United Nations bit's been overused. You guys should go in as press."

"No go." Eckstein shook his head. "Those freaks over there are using reporters for target practice. They just killed a TV producer from New York."

"Natural selection," Marcus scoffed. Military personnel generally despise news people the way cattle ranchers hate horse thieves.

"But the chopper's a good idea," Eckstein added. "Let's have Itzik contact the air force."

"*You* tell him." Marcus pointed a finger.

"No, *you* tell him."

Both men snickered. No one wanted to bear the news of high operational expenses to the general. If time were not a factor, he would probably have them *walk* out over the Balkans.

"At any rate," said Eckstein, "we'll pick her up plainclothes, then switch to Red Cross."

Marcus wagged a finger. "Not Red Cross. Their wagons get held up all the time for the drugs. Pick something classier." The American fished a plastic bag of little trolls from Benni's box. He selected five of them, one wearing a skirt, and set them out on the table before empty chairs, a trio facing a pair. Two of the dolls would represent Eckstein and Baum. The other three were as yet unknown.

"Okay," said Eckstein. "How about that French relief organization?"

"Right." Marcus closed his eyes and snapped his fingers. "What're they called?"

"Uhhh . . . *Médecins Sans Frontières*."

"That's it! Doctors Without Borders."

"Better call the Art Department," said Eckstein, moving back around Benni's desk to one of his telephones. The Art Department was a small group of talented forgers who worked in one of the basement labs. They spent a good deal of time traveling the world, purloining letterheads, business cards, and logos that might be duplicated for later use as cover. "You get onto Documentation."

Marcus nodded and also reached for a phone, then stopped before dialing. "What do I tell them? We don't even have *katamim* yet." He used the acronym for Special Duty Officers. Almost all field operators in SpecOps were at minimum second lieutenants.

"Just tell them we'll have four men and one woman, and you can already give them me and Baum." Field officers each had a limited series of foreign covers that were learned and practiced until second nature. It was Documentation's task to support those covers with an indigenous paper trail. "They can prep for French or Belgian passports, and lots of wallet trash with medical stuff. And tell them not to go home. It'll take all night to fill in the blanks."

Marcus grinned at him, said, "Right, boss," in English, then both men issued their telephone requests in urgent tones and hung up almost simultaneously.

"Say," Mack suddenly said with a frown. "Where you gonna get an ambulance anyway? They don't exactly have a Hertz rent-a-meat-wagon office in Sarajevo."

Just then the door opened and Benni Baum strode in, followed by Horse, Yudit, and a middle-aged major named Danny Romano, who was head of Personnel. Romano, his ever-present unlit pipe jammed between his teeth, was carrying an armload of files—potential candidates for the first phase of *Operation Sorcerer*. He was a modest man, but he knew the operational talents and present whereabouts of every SpecOps field officer by heart. The files were just there so that team leaders could peruse them.

Romano kicked the door closed while Horse moved immediately to one of the PCs and Yudit picked up a phone to cancel a date. Baum dropped a briefcase full of maps and Slovak Desk reports on the table-top, smiled at Mack Marcus, then picked up the plastic ambulance and turned it over as if searching for a microdot.

"We'll steal one on the ground," said Benni, and Eckstein felt a wave of relief, glad to have his partner back in the game. Eytan laced his fingers behind his head and leaned back in Benni's chair.

"Or barring that," Eckstein added, "we'll hot-wire a white panel truck. I already warned the Van Goghs downstairs to start working up some decals."

"*Médecins Sans Frontières.*" Marcus proudly informed Baum of his and Eckstein's cover choice. "But seeing how you're all a pack of fucking thieves, maybe you should use something like *Espions Sans Moralité.*"

Benni Baum raised an eyebrow at the American. "Spies without morals?" He laughed quietly, his Bavarian beer belly shaking with it. "My boy, you are being redundant."

Oren Eckstein saw his father from the perspective of most five-year-old boys, looking skyward to a giant who was really of average height and build. *Abba*'s hands seemed massive, because with only one he could trap both of Oren's wrists together while tickling him with the other. His voice was low, sometimes soothing, often teasing, and could turn quickly to a threatening growl of "*T'aseh et zeh akshav.* Do it *now*," whenever Oren tried to ignore an "order."

Abba did not chatter. On rare occasion, when he actually yelled, the windowpanes rattled and Oren leapt to do as he was told. He could not know, of course, that these unusual explosions caused his father great pains of reverberating guilt.

I'm hardly around. What right do I have to yell?

Abba was a soldier, of which Oren was very, very proud, although he did not understand why his father almost never wore his uniform. Two pair of wrinkled Class Alephs hung in the bedroom closet, with silver paratrooper's wings and a few small medals—campaign ribbons and operational pins—on the left breast, and a single brass "falafel" on each epaulette. A maroon beret was folded through one shoulder flap and a pair of gritty, red-brown boots sat below on the floor.

"Why don't you ever polish your boots, *Abba*?"

"It's the dust of Lebanon." A small smile from the giant. "Can't be cleaned."

Okay. Oren accepts this, not understanding Abba's nostalgia for the simpler days of soldiering.

Once in a great while, Abba appears from his and *Eema*'s room, wearing his uniform and a cynical, crooked smile, offering a "special meeting" as explanation. Despite Oren's pride, Abba disclaims these events as unexciting, his own role as mundane.

"I'm not a fighter anymore."

"But you always say you work at the Ministry of Defense."

"Yes, but it's a big place. Lots of officers doing boring stuff."

"Don't they call you major, *Abba*? Don't they salute you?"

This time, a full belly laugh emanates from Eytan, while Oren's brow furrows beneath his blondish bangs.

"*Salute* me? Never."

"So, what *are* you then?" There is some frustration in the little worshipper's voice, like a disappointed convert in synagogue.

"An accountant."

"An *accountant*? Can't be."

"Yes." And for some reason, Abba's voice darkens. "I settle accounts."

Oren, having inherited the instinct to spot a lie, does not believe Abba, and retreats into his own version of reality, which is actually closer to the unspoken truth. But more and more, the images he paints are less fulfilling. When Eytan is away for any long period, which is frequent, Oren often goes to the closet, staring longingly at the empty uniforms, half wishing that Abba was something else. Maybe a Jerusalem policeman. Home every night, to have dinner together as a family, read him a story, and put him to bed . . .

But tonight, Eckstein had failed again to fulfill his son's wish. He had not left the office until well after eight. Oren would already be sleeping, and although anxious to see Simona, Eytan was equally reluctant to face her. So, hungry and bleary-eyed, he cruised the Fiesta slowly toward the southeast quadrant of the city.

East Talpiot was still one of Jerusalem's most popular neighborhoods, and the Ecksteins were fortunate to have one of the flats in a semicircle of modern buildings that looked out over the Judean desert. On a clear spring day, before the heat shimmered the horizon, you could see a blue-steel strip of the Dead Sea and even the peaks of Jordan and Saudi Arabia beyond. When things were peaceful in the valley below, the Arab shepherds of Sur Bacher walked their sheep through the dusty hills and you could hear the animals' collar bells tinkling back in echoes. When the Palestinians and Israelis were "negotiating," the nights brought fireworks displays of parachute flares and the pop of rubber bullets.

When Eytan and Simona had first rented the third-floor walkup on *Ma'alot El Ram,* it was not long after his lengthy stint in an army hospital for rehabilitation of his leg wounds. He could barely manage normal progress with a cane, and the challenge of so many stairs seemed insurmountable. Yet the apartment was so luxurious, by Israeli standards so rare a find. It was a duplex, with three bedrooms upstairs, a spacious salon and kitchen on the main floor, *two* bathrooms, a wide veranda, and—rarer still—an American-style fireplace for those bone-chilling Jerusalem winter nights. The price was well out of reach for even a full army colonel, but Eytan, only a captain then, was receiving combat and medical bonuses. Simona's salary as a nurse at Hadassah Hospital would also ease the hardship, and he talked her into it. She almost balked, frowning at the stairs and the sweat on his brow after that first climb.

"No," she said. "I can't let you do it."

"*Ye'hieh b'seder.* It'll be all right," he said. "I'll use it as physical therapy."

And indeed the leg had healed, gotten stronger, and he discarded his cane and fought his way back into SpecOps. And for a very long time, the blush of their union and the comforts of their home dulled the pain of separations. But little by little, as with many such marriages between men of military aspirations and "normal" women, Simona matured, and her acceptance of this adventurous life waned. The adventures were his, the waiting was hers, and she longed for an evolution into a mundane, cohesive family existence. For some time now, Eckstein had secretly yearned for the same, yet was unable to give up his quest to become a man he could not quite identify, and then comfortably retire him to the past.

His love for Simona had not changed, and the arrival of Oren had created that special bond that even couples in conflict discover will bind them together, in some format, forever. But Eckstein knew they were also at a crossroads and, unable to see the future for the murky horizon, it frightened him.

He had his apartment keys, but by the time he reached the door he was all in, and he leaned one forearm on the frame and knocked. The door opened and Simona stood there, one hand on a hip, looking not terribly surprised, as if she had been expecting him.

Actually, "expecting" was the key to her appearance and demeanor, for she was four months pregnant and a chemical glow infused the smooth skin of her cheeks, enriching her long black curls and gem-stone-green eyes. She was wearing a sky-blue, long-sleeved shirt from Eytan's wardrobe, and below the shirttails a pair of black leotards. For a moment Eytan thought of an Ice Capades version of a princess Smurf.

"*Erev tov, Moshe.* Good evening, Moses." Her greeting was point-edly sardonic. "I was wondering when you'd finally show."

"How did you know I was back?"

"There were pictures in the papers, Mister Bond."

Eckstein rolled his eyes, turning his head and looking at their *mezuzah* on the doorframe as be blushed.

"The censors blacked your faces," said Simona. "I couldn't be sure about you, but that big ass of Benni's is hard to miss." She was trying to maintain her anger, but it was always diluted by her husband's appear-ance in the flesh.

Eytan smiled crookedly, leaned in, and kissed her. Her mouth remained closed, her eyes open, and she wrinkled her nose.

"*Foo-yah,*" she exclaimed, the Israeli version of *ugh.* "You should have walked through a car wash."

Eytan hugged her, feeling the small pouch of her growing belly against his belt buckle. She squirmed and pushed him away and he walked into the salon, stopping to stare at an open wooden crate piled with new, unfamiliar toys. Through the open doors to the wide veranda the purple scent of bougainvillea wafted in from the flower boxes.

"You could have called," Simona admonished as she closed the apartment door.

"I was going to," Eytan lied. "But I wasn't sure if we weren't going right back out again."

"Smart move. If you were, you'd be risking your life showing up here."

Eytan sighed. *I seem to be risking it on every front*, he thought, then cringed inwardly at his own self-pity. He walked around the back of their Scandinavian couch and slumped into his favorite black rocker, kicked off his borrowed sandals, and put his feet up on a wicker coffee table with a glass top.

Simona went into the kitchen, then came out with an empty glass, a bottle of tonic water, and a slimmer one of the local Wisotsky vodka that smells like jet fuel. She set them on the table. She was not about to actually mix him a drink.

"How's Oren?" The warm tonic fizzed as Eytan opened the bottle and poured.

"Well, let's see." Simona folded her arms and inspected the ceiling. "Yesterday, he was coming home from school and he saw me getting a ride from Doctor Farkash. He asked me if he was my boyfriend."

Eytan looked up over the top of his glass, then lowered it, holding it over his lap.

"Simona," he said. "I'm falling out of love."

She stared at him, waiting.

"With the job," he added.

She began breathing again. "Good," she said brightly. "Because *I* already hate it."

"I know."

"I never really worry about you having an affair," she said. "You only really love the army, and you can't fuck *that*."

This was clearly not going to be easy. But Eytan had stalled all day, and now he had to face his harshest critic and most dangerous opponent.

"This is my last mission."

"*What* is?"

"Why don't you sit down?"

"I'm fine, thank you."

And so he told her about *Operation Sorcerer*, as much as he could, not mentioning Sarajevo or the mole, but about Ethiopia and the fifty children. He emphasized that, over and over. *The children, Simona, the children.* Yet even as she listened, her head began to move, slowly, from side to side. She too cared about children, and about her country and its struggles and the good deeds so rarely composed by its politicians and foisted on men like Eytan, the pains to be borne by their families, their deaths to be forgotten as other foolish men took up the call. Oh, yes, she cared about children, *her* children, and she watched and listened and his words ran through her like so many Shakespearean soliloquies in a school for the deaf and she was excruciatingly unmoved.

Eytan stopped talking when Simona turned and walked to the veranda doorway. Despite the light in the salon, behind her he could see the stars in a pitch-black sky, shimmering as they do only above the sea or desert. She came back to him then, and he saw the slim shining tracks of tears on her cheeks and the spots on the shirt where they had fallen onto her chest. She knelt before the rocker and she pushed his knees apart and came closer, taking his face in her slender fingers, and he felt the clashing of worlds, her supple skin against his unyielding bristle, and her voice was hoarse with liquid.

"*Ani ohevet o'tcha.* I love you," she whispered. "I loved you when I met you, when you were wounded and sad, and I could still see that boy inside trying so hard to be older and brave, and you were so filled with your guilt and your pain and we really needed each other. And I loved you even more later, Eytan, when I saw your strength, that nothing could stop you. Nothing. And it made me feel safe to be with someone so sure, so unbreakable, and sometimes your stubborn blindness made me wonder, but I wanted it." For a moment, Eytan glanced down, ashamed, but she clasped him harder. "It's so clear to me now. You were the hunter. I was the healer. The perfect, impossible match. But I loved you even more after Oren, when he started to become a person, and *he* started to love you, and I saw you again in his eyes."

Eytan sat, not daring to move, watching her eyes, her mouth, hearing the words as if they ushered from another, altered soul deep within her body.

"And I still love you, no less than ever. But it's like I'm a widow now, and our son is half an orphan, and you're only a ghost who comes here to remind us of what we miss, what we deserve. It's almost like you're out there searching for something so huge, but you've forgotten what's really important, right here in your own house."

She closed her eyes, kissed him very briefly, and got to her feet.

"Don't promise me anything. Don't say this is the last mission. You've said it before. Just decide. If it isn't, when you come back we'll start the divorce."

Eytan watched her as she walked to the stairs, her resolve clear in her posture. This was not a bluff. He had wounded her too often, and she was stronger for that, but she would not permit the suffering of their son or the child to come. She started up, then stopped.

"You'd better wake him up and tell him. About your trip. That you're going again."

She took another step. "There's some fresh cheese and bread in the box, and some tomatoes in the fridge." What curled her lips was not a smile.

"I don't cook for transients anymore."

It was some time later, after he had finished his drink and three cigarettes, that Eytan doused the lights and made his way up the stairs, his knee throbbing as it had not done in years. The door to his and Simona's room was ajar, her long, low breathing sliding from the darkness, and he turned away and followed a strip of moonlight to the end of the hallway.

Oren's furniture was of soft, thick pine, the product of a kibbutz factory in Galilee. The lower half of the walls was papered in a thick blue strip of cartoon bears in diving masks and wide-eyed fishes. The shelves were filled with toppling rows of children's books, from the early thin ones of pictures and few words, to all of Dr. Seuss in Hebrew, and now the simple mysteries of first graders. Volcanoes and dinosaurs were slowly taking over, and model airplanes, mostly built by Eytan as Oren "helped" with sloppy gobs of glue, had replaced the big Lego blocks and lumpy clay sculptures. The menagerie of stuffed animals that had once nearly obscured the boy as he slept with them was now piled in a pyramid of fading furs beneath the window.

Oren slept in his bed, which looked something like a tractor packing crate. The fold-down plastic gate that had long kept him from rolling out was gone, and by the glow of a nightlight Eytan saw the long sleeves of his Power Rangers pajamas and his hands clutching a tan quilt covered with biplanes. His fine hair brushed the pillow like silken fur and Eytan wanted to believe that his expression was peaceful, happy, but he knew that all children looked that way, their skin so pure, no furrows yet engraved to reveal the truths.

Eytan leaned into the bed, touched Oren's hair, then bent and brushed it with his nose, taking in the perfume of baby shampoo. He backed up and lowered himself into a wooden rocker, the one that for a long time, before he began "going out" more and more, he had sailed in at night with Oren on his lap, making up fairy tales, or sometimes singing old folk tunes to smooth the reluctant bridge to bed.

He began to rock now, just slightly, his heels on the coarse camel rug, resting his head on the hard wood, watching his son. And he tried very hard to think of a gentle way to wake him, to take in his thrill when his eyes would widen, to be able to finally peel the joyous hug away and explain, somehow, that he would be leaving again.

He worked on it for a long, long time, planning it, discarding the words that would not work, would not heal. And in the middle of it all, he reminded himself to have his Browning Hi-Power pistol shipped by diplomatic courier to the embassy in Addis Ababa, and then dead-dropped to a certain cafe in Bahir Dar. And then he returned again to Oren, and he thought he could do it, had found the words.

And as he fell asleep, in his softball T-shirt and still-clammy fatigues, he made his bold decision . . .

"I'll tell him in the morning."

3

• • •

Bosnia-Herzegovina
April 30

A CEASE-FIRE IN Sarajevo was not a thing to be trusted. Unlike those days of stillness that follow a major earthquake, you could not have faith that Mother Nature would grant some years of mercy to rebuild your shattered home. Yes, there had been no gunfire for sixty-seven hours, but given the weakling nature of such European-brokered arrangements it was more like halftime at a soccer match. Just enough respite to breathe, take water, and recommence the running.

Some days of late-spring storms had blanketed the Balkans in frothy quilts that further enhanced the unnerving silence, and then the sun emerged from a cluster of gray powder-puff clouds above the rough camel humps. Mount Igman glittered, yet it seemed a century since *Sports Illustrated* photographers had snapped Olympic skiers there, and now the few remaining cameramen were just jittery, half-demented combat clickers, for the only thing racing downhill appeared to be the Slavic civilization.

Still, down at the once-bustling Central Market on Marshal Tito Street, a thin line of foolish college hopefuls listened to a crackling transistor and the growling of their own stomachs. A pop station from Zagreb was pumping out Davor Tolja's techno hit *Zločin I Kazna*—"Crime and Punishment"—and they stamped their feet, shared one priceless cigarette like greedy pot smokers, and waited for a rumored smuggler's car with a trunkload of coffee beans.

61 • • •

A young Sarajevan named Stjepan Tomić, black-haired, handsome, and tall, kissed his blond and weather-pinkened fiancée as he held her hands. Then an eighty-one-millimeter mortar shell arced over Grbavica from a battery of bored Serbs, and in keeping with the strange nature of high explosives and shrapnel, it killed six youths but left the comely groom-to-be intact. Stjepan remained standing, still holding his fiancée's hands, but *only* her hands, with the blood running from his shattered eardrums and patches of her flowered nylon dress melted to his old leather flight jacket in smoky scabs.

Thus, the cease-fire ended.

"It will still take these crazy Yugoslavs some hours to get back in the game. Won't be real hellfire until tonight."

Colonel Valery Stepnin paced before a large window on the third floor of the Russian Embassy annex. All of the glass in the Bascarsija section of the Old Town had long since been blown out and he hated the substitute sheets of frosted plastic, because they made him feel like he had cataracts. Yet he still enjoyed the filtered sunlight bathing his thick boxer's face.

"Their fingers are probably still frozen from the snow, have to thaw out a bit." His rumbling voice dripped sarcasm. "Takes a delicate touch, you know, loading all those shells and azimuthing. Fucking fools."

The colonel was the highest-ranking officer of the new Russian Central Intelligence Service assigned to Sarajevo, but he still thought of himself as KGB, that Kafkaesque espionage icon at whose breast he'd been suckled.

"My father worked with these people during the Great Patriotic War," Stepnin muttered. "With Tito and his partisans. He was a tough one, my father, even survived Stalingrad, killed plenty of Waffen SS himself. But he said these Serbian maniacs frightened him. Walked around wearing necklaces of Nazi ears."

The colonel turned from the window to face his adjutant, a young captain, tall and blond and with the rosy face of a soccer player. Neither man wore a uniform, only rough wool trousers and braided brown sweaters. To wear a uniform in Sarajevo was to be a wooden duck in a sniper's arcade.

"What's the body count now anyway, Yuri?" Stepnin asked.

The captain was holding a sheaf of papers, including the embassy's morning briefing.

"Umm, estimates are more than two hundred fifty thousand shells fallen so far. Approximately sixty thousand citizens wounded, eight thousand dead or missing."

Stepnin nodded and walked to his desk. The blotter had been pierced by a late-night errant bullet while he was out having a vodka with his Bulgarian counterpart. He plucked a black cigarette from a brass holder made from a cut-down howitzer shell. The cigarette was a Balkan Sobranie. He lit up with a wooden match.

"Business is booming," Stepnin quipped, though he did not smile. The Russians had no justifiable mandate in Bosnia-Herzegovina. They were not trying to make peace, only rubles. Most of the local weapons, on all sides, were of Soviet manufacture. Someone had to sell the idiots their ammunition. "Very acceptable numbers." He blew out a cloud of heavy coal smoke. "If you're fucking Satan himself."

"Yes, sir." The captain smiled.

Stepnin dropped his muscular form into his wooden office chair, but its reclining spring was worn and he nearly went over backward, only saving himself by jamming the toe of his cavalry boot under his desk.

"*Yup tvoyu mahtt.* Motherfucker," he muttered. He rubbed the bushy gray bristles atop his large head. "So, report to me on the girl."

The captain straightened his shoulders and opened a thin file folder.

"Well, I killed the tap on her private telephone."

"Why?" Stepnin frowned.

"All the private communications services are blown out in her neighborhood."

"Good boy. Waste of money. What's her name again?"

"Hašek. Niki Hašek."

"Ahh, yes. Cute thing down on the first floor."

"Yes, sir."

Stepnin wagged a finger at his adjutant. "And forget about fucking her, Yuri. Her boyfriend's a defector."

"Had not crossed my mind, sir." The captain smiled broadly, then he raised his chin with some pride. "I checked all the annex tapes this morning. She took a foreign call yesterday."

"Really?" Stepnin leaned forward a bit. "Here?"

"Yes, sir."

"From?"

"Africa."

"No!" Stepnin slapped his desktop, then laced his fingers together and set his elbows as if he was going to arm wrestle. *"Tell me."*

"It was in Czech, and very brief, a man's voice."

"Yes? Yes?"

"He said only, *'Ahoj. Šťastnou cestu.'* "

" 'Hello? Have a nice trip?' That's all?"

"That was all."

"That's it!" Stepnin jumped up from his chair. It rolled backward and tipped over with a crash, but he ignored it. "He's coming to get her!" He plucked up a fresh Sobranie and lit it with the stub of the first, then crushed out the butt under a boot. He had given up trying to keep his office tidy. Everything that was breakable had already been smashed. "No, no." He shook his head and snapped his fingers. "He's sending someone *for* her."

"To here?" The captain looked doubtful, confused. "Who would come *here* to get *anyone*?"

"It doesn't matter." Stepnin was waving his heavy arms, pacing behind his desk. "I have my theories."

"And why leave us such a clue? Contacting her at her post . . ."

"Because he had no choice, no other way to reach her." He jabbed a finger at his adjutant. "She still has her watchers, yes?"

"My best men. Twenty-four hours a day."

"Take them off." Stepnin sliced across the air with a bladed hand. "Put Ivan and Burko on her."

Now the captain looked absolutely aghast. "Ivan and Burko?"

"Yes, yes. And tell them *I* said if anything happens to her, if they even let her *pee* by herself, they'll be here till the very end of this fucking war."

Just then a lone mortar shell detonated in the distance, but it was enough to make the plastic window sheets ripple. Stepnin jerked a thumb over his shoulder.

"And from the sound of it, this century may die before that happens."

"Yes, sir . . ." Yuri hesitated, but his colonel kept him on because he was smart and inquisitive, not because he was a yes man. "But, sir. Ivan and Burko? One's a vodkaholic and the other's nerves are shot."

The colonel smiled wryly at his adjutant and cocked his head.

"Tell me, Yuri. In six years have you ever seen me make a tactical error?"

"No, sir."

"Good boy. Now, take care of this and let's go get an early lunch, before the fucking fools shell all the decent cafés to rubble."

It had taken nearly thirty-six frenetic hours before Eckstein's team was finally in position to cross the southwestern border of Bosnia-Herzegovina. Naturally, they were not traveling as a troupe, but zigzagging individually across Europe, all the while ignoring the alarming news flashes hailing from "Radio Zid" in Sarajevo, because nothing would alter their course anyway.

Eckstein was making his own way to Zagreb, the final assembly point before Niki Hašek's "rescue" commenced in earnest. In general he preferred to travel with Baum, an acceptable practice when their cover provided for an appropriate relationship. However, they had recently abandoned this habit after a trip to Rome, where they were joined in the elevator of the La Residenza Hotel by an old Viennese woman who peered at them over her bifocals, found no resemblance between "father and son," and unabashedly announced, *"Spione.* Spies."

"That really spooked me," Eckstein had said the moment he and Baum were alone again. "No pun intended."

"Mich auch," Baum agreed in their native German. "Call it just a lucky guess on her part, but we must be emitting some kind of *odeur d'espionnage.*"

"Guess we'd better travel solo for awhile, Benni. I'll miss your belching and snoring in coach class."

"Flirt with the stewardesses."

In the case of *Operation Sorcerer,* there was a sound tactical reason for all the team members to avoid each other like lepers until the last possible moment. Horse's speculation that Krumlov's gambit might be an ambush still carried weight, and Ben-Zion had insisted they revert to the most paranoid practices of tradecraft, which sometimes seem silly as intelligence officers mature. But the general viewed his operators as very expensive weapons systems. He hated losing them, because it played hell with the budget.

And so, Benni Baum was flying from Tel Aviv to Frankfurt, switching passports from German to French, then doubling back to Croatia. Eckstein had suffered some stomach-churning hours in Vienna, where there should *not* have been snow this late in the year, but a low ceiling of potato soup clouds hammered the tarmac at Schwechat and inside the terminal an announcer kept apologizing for delays to all capitals. He clutched his Croatian Airlines ticket, pacing and chain-smoking on the lower level, praying that the rest of *Sorcerer*'s "magicians" would make the rendezvous on schedule.

The three additional operators had been selected, brought into Jerusalem HQ and thoroughly briefed before departure to all points. However, each of them was enduring the glitches common to military operations.

Serge Maxime had spent the day silently cursing General Ben-Zion, because he had to go all the way to Paris-de-Gaulle before doubling back to Zagreb. And why? Because Documentation wanted to see the most recent French entrance stamp on his passport.

This was in keeping with Ben-Zion's policy of "consolidating operational expenses." In other words, the general was a cheap prick, and Serge was quite sure that even if the prime minister's wife was kidnapped by a band of thugs in Hong Kong, Ben-Zion would task the rescue team with additional chores: "And while you're there, pick up six Sony CD players. They're on sale in Kowloon and the lab needs them for a demolition job."

Serge was the son of French-Moroccan Jews, a very large young man with fiery eyes, a head of black wire-brush curls, and a bushy beard cultivated while serving with a special forces outfit called *Duvdevahn*. These young men all had fluent Arabic and a penchant for deadly force, their mission to infiltrate the Palestinian population on the West Bank, wreaking swift vengeance on Hamas bomb-makers and Red Eagle terrorists. Whenever tasked to AMAN's Special Operations, Serge served as team "offensive weapon." He still held the rank of sergeant major, having repeatedly refused a commission.

"My uncle was in the Foreign Legion," he would mutter cryptically. "Once you're an officer, you lose your self-respect."

Eckstein took no offense at these remarks. His own self-respect, or alternating lack thereof, was usually a reflection of his family life and had little to do with rank.

Gerard Folberg, the second operative on the manifest, was enduring a delay in Athens, the victim of a fate as ridiculous as lost luggage. He had flown from Tel Aviv aboard Olympic Airways (Israeli intelligence agents *never* fly El Al), but he had been forced to check his rather large *Médecins Sans Frontières* medical kit, which had now failed to be regurgitated onto the luggage carousel.

Folberg was a French-born Israeli whom Eckstein had personally vetted for AMAN some seven years before. Recruited as a corporal from the air force's elite Pilot Rescue Unit 996, his trade was leaping into the sea from hovering CH-53Ds and snatching up downed fighter jockeys. This dash of raw nerve, coupled with a foreign background, was the essence that attracted AMAN talent-spotters.

Folberg's designation on *Sorcerer* was as team medic—he had passed so many army medical courses that his abilities matched those of a surgical resident. He had an unflappable, relaxed air about him, a smooth pond compared to the roiling rapids of Serge Maxime's personality, but Eckstein still wondered that seven years with SpecOps had not dulled his bright eyes nor grayed a hair of his sandy head.

However, at the moment Folberg was aging at the approximate rate of one month per minute. The carousel was nearly empty, most of the passengers gone, and when at last his gear bag flopped onto the rubber belt he hugged it and sprinted for the Alitalia counter in a cold sweat. He still had to switch from his French passport to a Belgian forgery, purchase a ticket, and make the flight to Zagreb. He had thirteen minutes . . .

Francie Koln rounded out the team nicely, serving as decoy and communications officer. She had four languages besides Hebrew and a wealth of field experience, although for Eckstein her presence induced some nostalgic pain. Francie had been Ettie Denziger's best friend, and for a long time he avoided working with her. She did not blame Eckstein for the loss—it was clear that he accomplished that self-flagellation without anyone's help. In fact, Francie admired Eckstein, for his brain, his heart, and his talents, and she would not forget that once when her life was in danger in Cairo, he had blown his own cover, flown to that capital, and beaten down the doors of the Israeli embassy until they whisked her off to a safe house.

She was working a "diplomatic" posting in Jordan now, but Eckstein and Baum brought her in on *Sorcerer* because she was a "turn key"—an asset who could be plugged into any mission. Francie had acquired the departmental nickname *Zikkit*—Chameleon—for she could alter her physical attributes in an instant. With her long brown hair bunned, a pair of wire-rimmed spectacles, and a baggy gray shift, she was an Anglican nun. Then, ninety seconds in a closet with a battery-powered curling iron, lipstick, miniskirt, and a Wonder Bra, and she would emerge as an Amsterdam hooker. She was a great fan of the actress Meryl Streep, and she scored well with almost any nine-millimeter pistol.

Francie's trip to Zagreb via Rome and Naples was progressing without logistical hitches, her only complaint being a personal and private one. She had just *nearly* had her first orgasmic experience, with a GSS officer who also worked at the embassy in Jordan. In her profession good lovers, especially *Israeli* ones, were hard to come by, and the idea of perhaps dying in Sarajevo before achieving that sexual summit would be as frustrating as Sir Edmund Hillary failing Everest . . .

At any rate, in Vienna Eckstein was unaware of the specific tribulations of his teammates. The Croatian pilots, who had a reputation for timidity, refused to fly, and the disgusted Austrians finally rolled out their own Tyrolean Air turboprop.

Eckstein sprinted to it as the snow changed to freezing rain, and they took off in total blindness while he examined a deck of emotional cards flipping through his brain: his affinity for and simultaneous rejection of men and machines Germanic; the enraging idea of a mole inside the Israeli weapons program; the disgust at having to service the whims of this alleged Czech defector; pity for fifty starving children in Africa; guilt at having abandoned Simona and Oren. *Again.*

He set it all aside and fell into proper professional mode, focusing only on the first stage of *Sorcerer*. He looked out the window, completely obscured by a remaining lather of de-icing foam as the small plane bounced through the clouds, and he felt rather like a lost sock in a washing machine.

Zagreb was the last civilized way station before one ventured east toward the growing thunder of errant artillery. The long, drab terminal building at the airport reminded Eckstein of the leftover barracks at Dachau, and just inside, off the frozen tarmac, the atmosphere was nearly as dour.

Pockets of anxious U.N. troops waited before a passport control banner stenciled *Kontrola Putovnica*, wearing their hangdog expressions of military impotence as they dragged damp kit bags across the puddled floor. Eckstein joined this throng of trudging Poles, Austrians, and Frenchmen, and a tall Legionnaire wearing lizard camouflage glanced up from a copy of *Soldier of Fortune* and frowned. The Israeli major was a veteran of more combat than any of these young men, but apparently he looked so much the misplaced, pot-smoking tourist for his black motorcycle jacket and blond ponytail.

His French passport was sewn into the lining of his leathers, so he offered Anthony Hearthstone's British document to the man in the glass booth, received a large white visa sticker, shouldered his blue nylon hockey bag, and walked toward Customs . . .

Intelligence agents all have their secret phobias. After all, theirs is a profession that breeds expert liars, spending their careers waiting to be caught. It is a trade that fosters paranoia, so if you were a mentally healthy, well-adjusted, stable soul when you were recruited, you'll be very far from it when you're done.

Some fear the night, for that is usually when you steal, with an amber flashlight in your damp fist and the sweat dribbling down your temples. Some tremble at a handshake, for a rendezvous with an unknown human asset is often the time when blown agents are murdered. Some resist all intimacy, for if you always sleep alone, you are not likely to give yourself away in the throes of a nightmare.

With Eckstein, it was border crossings: customs clerks, immigration computers, suspect profilers, X-ray machines, contraband-sniffing dogs. Even when he traveled for pleasure, which was rare, he always felt as if he was smuggling a kilo of heroin. And when he successfully passed a harmless checkpoint, he breathed again like a prisoner of war who had just breached the wire of a Nazi *stalag*.

Technical Services had assured him that the only weapon he carried was undetectable by X ray, but it was *his* ass on the line, not theirs. Buried in his bag was a pipe smoker's leather pouch, which along with the briar, tamper, and bristle cleaners contained a box of Dr. Perl Junior pipe filters. Inside the foil-lined box, the bottom row of white filter tubes each held a .22-caliber shell with a Teflon-coated bullet.

The pipe itself was a modification of an old Office of Strategic Services weapon circa World War II. You could actually smoke the AMAN version, or, in a last-ditch emergency, remove the pipe stem and insert an armed filter. Doing so had the effect of cocking a spring-loaded firing pin. Thereafter, you held the bowl in the palm of your hand, pointed the mouthpiece at the target, twisted the stem with thumb and forefinger, and bang.

Before his departure from Jerusalem, Eckstein had been somewhat giddy with fatigue when Avi Lahst, the department's aging *Nashak Ha'rashi* (Chief Armorer), had signed him out for the pipe and box of twenty rounds.

"You think I'll actually have time to reload, Avi?" Eckstein had foolishly chuckled. "Why not give me two rounds to use at most?"

"You can use your *dick*, for all I care," the armorer growled as he returned to short-fusing a Russian hand grenade, for God knew what purpose.

"Sorry. Just asking." Pissing off the *nashak* was an unhealthy habit for a soldier.

If Lahst's ingenious little device *was* discovered and confiscated, that would be bad enough. But such a breach in Croatia, especially during wartime, could easily result in being thrown into a cell and forgotten about for a year or so. There were six customs clerks milling about a long examination table, two of them gleefully rifling the camera bags of an agitated American journalist. Eckstein sauntered toward the doorway marked NOTHING TO DECLARE, his heart beating quickly and his ears pricked for a shout of *"Prestati!"*

But no one stopped him.

Inside the main terminal building all of the airline and rental car counters were dark for the dearth of tourism, and in a country rife with war nerves the trapped air was laced with cigarette smoke. He changed some dollars for *kuna* and moved quickly though a pair of filthy glass doors and out onto the sidewalk, where he saw Benni Baum and turned away from him as the colonel hauled himself onto a half-empty bus headed for the city center.

Eckstein waited until the bus pulled away, then hailed a battered cab. As he folded himself into the small taxi, he spotted Francie Koln emerging from the terminal into the gray light of a sodden dusk. Her auburn hair was coal-black now, a thick brown scarf wrapped around her throat. Francie's gaze fell upon him for an instant, then panned away as if he were no more than the invisible ghost of a fresh corpse. It chilled him.

An absurd profession, he decided as his car rumbled off. *Where your best friends ignore you in public, as if you once seduced them into a drunken orgy they'd prefer to forget . . .*

The entire team had to hole up in Zagreb overnight now, which, on the precipice of such a mission, was akin to having your car break down on a highway while your wife gave birth in a hospital just a hundred kilometers down the road. But Baum and Eckstein could not proceed until receiving a final briefing and go-ahead signal from a field agent who had been working in Sarajevo.

He was called "Johann," but only Benni Baum knew his true identity. The elderly German Jew had worked in Berlin for the British S.O.E. throughout World War II, then emigrated to Palestine and continued his profession in service to the fledgling *Haganah*, forerunner of the IDF. Johann was a jolly raconteur of this particular period, during which he had turned against his former employers and caused great mischief to the British C.I.D. in pre-state Israel.

He had officially retired from the Israeli Army in the late 1960s, but

moved back to Europe at the behest of AMAN, fulfilling the odd essential task for which a dapper Continental was most suited. He regarded
Benni Baum as his own private "control," and just two months before,
the colonel had rendezvoused with his old friend in Munich.

"We want you to go into Sarajevo," Baum had muttered as the pair
of aging spies strolled through the freezing Stachus.

"*Warum?* I thought you liked me."

"I do." Baum grinned. "But you know how it is. Once you can't get it
up anymore, you're expendable."

"By that calculation, half the general staff should be shot."

The two men laughed for a while, then Baum returned to business.

"We've intercepted some Iranian commo traffic. They're smuggling
arms to the Muslims in Sarajevo."

"Well, the poor bastards deserve the help . . ."

"Yes, but you know Tehran. They never give without getting. The
whole purpose is to recruit a fresh crop of fanatics. The militia will
hone their skills in Bosnia and wind up on our northern doorstep when
it's all over. We need to keep an eye on this."

"All right. I'll go. But it will cost you."

"Good. I'll tell Ben-Zion."

"*Scheisse.* With him running the show, I'll be lucky to get cab fare."

So Johann had gone into Sarajevo undercover as a relief worker, and
he had already gleaned hard intelligence on Jerusalem's theory. Just
three days ago he had also received a burst transmission from Benni
Baum in Jerusalem, instructing him to monitor Niki Hašek's daily
movements, then make his way to Zagreb and report.

Inside the city, Serge, Gerard, and Francie had all been prebooked
into separate hotels by Mack Marcus. Eckstein and Baum would not be
able to locate them at this stage, which adhered to the precept of
"What I don't know, can't hurt you." If Horse's fears proved out and the
major and colonel were ambushed here, they would fail to appear for
the next leg of the mission and the survivors would withdraw to home.

Such events had occurred more than once in the history of Israeli
Intelligence, hence the markers below some names at the memorial
denoting "*Chah-ser Ba'shetach*"—missing in the field.

The two officers checked into the International Hotel on Miramarska, but at separate times, into separate rooms, on different floors. At 6:00 P.M., Eckstein took the banging old steel elevator to the third floor landing, where he quickly buried a Ziploc bag containing his pipe and "filters" in the sand of a dying corn plant. It was better to risk their unearthing there than have them discovered during a room toss. On the wall behind the plant he found a small chalk mark, the numeral 7. He erased it with his thumb and returned to his room.

At seven o'clock the Croatian night was black and brittle with a windless chill. Eckstein left the hotel, bundled up in long johns, jeans, a speckled wool sweater, and his motorcycle jacket. His riding gloves were double-padded over the knuckles—if need be, he could punch straight into facial bones without worrying about nursing a broken finger.

A meet with an agent on a night like this in a foreign city was the stuff that caused ulcers and early retirement. Even if the contact was a veteran you'd known for half your life, nothing was certain until you walked away alive. It was always possible that he had been caught and turned. It was more than likely he was being tracked. In Eckstein's business, you reevaluated your friendships with each dawn.

Baum left the International just after Eckstein, wearing his worn leather car coat and Tyrolean hat, following his partner at a constant fifty meters. The streets were swollen with slush and the trams swished by like steel serpents as the two men clipped briskly along Miramarska toward the city center. They hurried beneath the rail bridge at Koturaska and into the clusters of high stone apartments. Zagreb, never well lit at any time, was barely aglow due to the energy-sapping war, its dark edifices reminding Eckstein of a graveyard for giants.

Eckstein's pace began to warm him. He unzipped his jacket, but he did not look behind. It was Benni's job to watch *his* back, and so far he had picked up no trackers, or his partner would have uttered two quick sneezes.

He broke onto the great square of Trg bana Jelačića, where crowds of young Croats swarmed between the slow-moving trams and settled like pigeons at the base of a great green horse statue, blowing clouds of tobacco smoke and lung steam into the night. He stopped and lit a cigarette, glancing at a circular newspaper kiosk at the south side of the square.

Johann appeared at precisely 19:30. He was physically much like Baum, except that he still had a full head of gray hair. He wore a jaunty feather in his Munchner hat, and he was leashed to his ever-present German shepherd, Tasha. Eckstein wondered how he schlepped the animal in and out of Sarajevo, not to mention how he kept the starving inhabitants from making a meal of her.

Johann walked to the kiosk, bought a newspaper, left a pack of Croatia Filters on the slate counter, and retreated.

Eckstein tossed his butt away, moved in, bought a copy of *Erotika*, and palmed Johann's cigarettes.

This was the moment when, if the process was being observed, the opposition would pounce, hoping to snatch all parties involved in the "dead drop" as well as whatever was in the box. If such an action occurred, Benni Baum would immediately cry out in pain, drop to the ground, and feign a massive coronary, just enough distraction to give Eckstein and Johann time to bolt. But nothing untoward transpired, and Eckstein turned and followed Johann to the edge of a raucous crowd encircling an impromptu juggler.

"Excuse me." Eckstein raised the cigarette box as he neared Johann's back.

The sprightly gentleman turned, and Tasha spotted Eckstein and her ears pricked up.

"*Bitte?*" said Johann.

"*Deine Zigaretten.*" Eckstein switched to German.

"*Ach, ja.*" Johann looked at the Croatia Filters in Eckstein's hand. "Thank you. But there were only two left. You can smoke them if you wish."

Eckstein nodded and smiled. "Thanks," he said as he lit up, and he glanced down at Johann's dog. She was looking up at him and grinning, wagging her tail. She obviously recognized his scent, even though she had not seen him in over three years. "Tell her to bark," he muttered. "She's too friendly."

"*Bellst du mal, du blöde Hündin,*" Johann ordered. Tasha barked twice.

The two men turned toward the crowd, and Eckstein edged a bit closer as he smoked.

"They're good-looking, these young Croats," he observed.

"*Ja.* The girls remind me of Munich in my younger days."

"I'm originally from Munich myself."

"Your contact instructions are in the box. Don't smoke them."

"I'm trying to quit. What about the Czech girl?"

"Except for a couple of flies, she's clean."

"I miss Munich sometimes. Especially Oktoberfest."

It was okay, then. Niki Hašek had a pair of Russian babysitters, but they were probably just bored watchers assigned to keep her under surveillance. Had someone been laying a trap, there would have been a "box team" on her round the clock, and Johann would have said something like, "She's a sweet girl, with a crowd of bees to prove it."

"Lightly protected," Eckstein murmured. "That's good."

"Lightly?" Johann almost laughed. "They've got her behind a wall of insane warfare. Only a confederacy of idiots would go in and get her."

"Thanks."

Johann took Eckstein's elbow. "Have you seen the cavalry statue, young man? It's magnificent." He walked Eckstein toward the great horse sculpture, glancing aside to see if anyone moved along with them.

"It is quite something," Eckstein agreed. They stopped walking, and Tasha started butting her nose into Eckstein's leg. He gave up ignoring her and bent to ruffle her ears. Johann mimicked his posture and stroked Tasha's fur.

"You may have some additional problems," he said.

"Really?"

"Hizbollah trainees."

Eckstein said nothing for a moment. Adding Iranian-backed fanatical terrorists to the equation was not news he had wanted to hear.

"They've been coming in by the busload," Johann continued. "Two hundred at least, straight from the Bekaa. They'll be shooting at everyone, just to improve their skills."

"Lovely," said Eckstein.

"They're already roaming the streets, looking for blood. Yours and Benni's would make a tasty cocktail."

"She's a fine animal." Eckstein continued petting Tasha, but his enthusiasm for *Sorcerer* had just waned even further. "Anything else?"

"Yes. Be *very* careful."

Eckstein nodded and straightened up from the dog.

"Well, thanks for the cigarettes."

"Bitte." Johann nodded.

The two men did not shake hands. Eckstein had an urge to grab Tasha's ears and kiss her head before he left, but he resisted.

She whimpered as he walked away . . .

Flying in a military helicopter is somewhat like taking a torturous ride inside a giant blender. Unlike the civilian versions that offer waist-coated businessmen comfortable hops from major cities to bustling airports, army choppers have little soundproofing, scant padding, and certainly no pumped-in Beethoven to dull the engine whine. The steel benches bang and rattle, unfettered cargo buckles whip like yo-yo's, and the unmuffled turbines make communication impossible except by shouting. Your entire body trembles from your heels to the top of your skull, as if you're strapped to a vibrating bed in a cheap motel, and the only solace is that the trip is unlikely to last long. These machines are, after all, designed for assault, perhaps an hour of nauseating banks and turns, at the end of which you are likely to witness someone's death.

Eckstein sat on the starboard bench of the white Bell 212, facing outward, as the steel slabs were bolted back to back. Francie Koln gripped the seat immediately to his right, wincing in rhythm as the bucking turbulence bruised her bottom. Serge and Gerard were on the port side, while Benni perched just behind the two pilots, wearing a headset and backseat driving. The pilots' helmets were angled forward as they squinted into a pitch-black night.

"It's like riding a roller coaster through a railway tunnel!" Francie shouted in English. None of the team members had uttered a word of Hebrew since leaving Israel's borders.

"What?" Eckstein cupped an ear.

"I said, I *hate* you," Francie mouthed through a pained grin.

"Ahhh." Eckstein nodded.

Since no one could properly communicate, he took the time to finally decode Johann's contact instruction and the details of Niki Hašek's schedule. From behind the foil lining of the cigarette box, he unfolded a carefully scripted matrix of numbers. Then, he produced a notepad, pencil, and an old Penguin paperback edition of *A Farewell to Arms*, the key to a highly primitive yet secure book code used only by select members of Benni Baum's "family."

He began to decode, cursing as his pencil point jumped around like the needle on a seismograph. In truth, even to him this all seemed like an excess of logistical support for the extraction of a single hundred-pound girl from Sarajevo, yet the chopper was preferable to losing the entire team in a land where one wrong turn off the road to Mostar could have you executed by a gang of trigger-happy gunmen. Still, Ben-Zion had only agreed to the outrageous expense when Baum unkindly reminded him of a frightening mishap in the general's own youth.

"I seem to remember," said Benni, "that you once got lost and wound up in the Gaza Strip, driving a blue Volkswagen with Israeli plates."

"All right," Ben-Zion had huffed. "You can have the fucking helicopter."

In the late morning, the team had linked up at Zagreb's airport, posing as members of *Médecins Sans Frontières* and greeting each other with genuine warmth. They did not wear white lab coats or flaunt latex gloves, but some stethoscopes gleamed from the pockets of their ski parkas. They now all carried cordura gear bags affixed with the MSF decals, barely dry since their printing by Documentation.

A snow-white Dassault Falcon jet, its flanks emblazoned with red crosses, arrived from Marseilles and shortly the team was airborne for Split, a small city on the Adriatic coast. There they waited for dusk, their ears twitching to the echoes of distant artillery, until the sun slid behind the Italian peaks across the sea and the Bell 212 arrived.

Now it buzzed along the high shoreline cliffs and suddenly banked inward at Metkovic, its rushing white belly reflecting off the huge salt ponds of Adriatic water below, from which humped peaks rose like the dorsals of a dragon. The pilots flew nap-of-the-earth, tilting at the labyrinth of craggy hills and then barely missing them, causing Francie to slap her hand over her eyes.

Eckstein memorized Johann's decoded message, destroyed it, unhooked his crash belt, and smeared his face up against the starboard Plexiglas. Near Zitonlislici, a triangle of dim landing lights appeared in an open field astride the frog-green waters of the Rama River, and he reached out, tapped the back of Benni's head, and signaled "down."

The chopper nosed over and dropped 100 meters, then hovered above the landing triangle just long enough for Eckstein to throw the door and haul in two young men dressed in olive coveralls and slinging gym bags. The pair were commandos from the General Staff Reconnaissance Unit—*Sayeret Mat'kal*—the cream of the IDF's most secret and elite special forces. They had flown to Dubrovnik from Naples, picked up a car, Skorpion machine pistols, and ammunition from a local contact, then driven to the predetermined rendezvous point.

One of them, a bushy-bearded wrestler type, settled on his haunches at the rear of the chopper. The other, a white-blond sergeant who looked like a Soviet *Spetznatz*, squeezed himself onto the bench between Eckstein and Francie. He opened his gym bag, removed a pair of identical pocket pagers, and handed one to Eckstein. The major looked at the beeper, noting two small buttons below the readout screen—one green, one red.

"Green," the *Mat'kalnik* yelled in Eckstein's ear.

Eckstein pressed the button and the readout immediately glowed brightly, showing split numbers for latitude and longitude. The device was not a pager at all, but a miniature Global Position System, tracking its earthbound location via a network of American satellites.

"Red," the sergeant yelled again.

Eckstein hit the second button, which had no effect on his own "pager," but immediately activated the second device in the sergeant's hand. The *Mat'kalnik*'s readout now glowed with the same numbers displayed on Eckstein's device, and they shifted in unison as the helicopter's position progressed. Now, wherever Eckstein went, his location could be transmitted to the commandos, who would track him on a detail map of Sarajevo.

The sergeant nodded, and both men switched off their "pagers."

"Don't call us unless you're really in the shit," the commando shouted.

Eckstein smiled and offered a thumbs-up.

When the chopper landed at Sarajevo, the *Mat'kalniks* would remain on board and perform a mock overhaul of the machine. They would only leave the aircraft if Eckstein signaled an emergency from inside the city. If they could not commandeer a vehicle, they would *run* to him over the three-kilometer stretch.

If Eckstein and his team did manage to make it back to the airport but were pursued, the *Mat'kalniks* would stay on the tarmac and fight it out with the pursuers while the chopper got away, then escape and evade from Bosnia-Herzegovina by whatever means possible. If they did not survive, they carried no identification of any kind to mark their corpses as Israeli. No one in Israel would ever hear of their heroism, and their families would be left to weep over small markers on Mt. Herzl. The commandos understood this. Such was the stuff of young volunteers in the special services . . .

The City of Sarajevo lies in the Dinaric Alps, a cluster of once-majestic architectures along a ten-kilometer stretch of the Miljaka River, whose waters festered now with blood and bloated corpses. The airport overlooks the city from the southwest, bulldozed into one of the slopes that once provided lovely picnic spots, before the park tables became reloading benches.

The strip was controlled—or more accurately, nervously inhabited—by French and British paratroops of the United Nations Protection Forces. This title educed ironic smirks all around, for the paras were barely able to protect themselves. The facility lay in a swath of Serb territory, and from the western promontories Bosnian gunners shelled the Serbs, while in turn the Serbs lobbed explosives over the tarmac and into the Muslim suburb of Dobrinja. Whatever fell short, fell on the airport. The terminal had been shelled into rubble, and the tarmac had more holes in it than the dart board of a Scottish pub, which was extremely uninviting for fixed-wing aircraft. Thus, the helicopter.

The blue runway beacons were barely winking up through a thick ground mist when the Bell pilots set down on the south apron of the strip. The doors slid back and Baum and Eckstein led their team across the moonlike tarmac, sidestepping watery shell craters and chunks of blasted concrete. A crisp wind sliced across the flat expanse and Eckstein, clad in a blue anorak, missed his motorcycle jacket, which had been left aboard the chopper. Baum took the "point," quick-marching toward the wreck of the old terminal, his breath blowing in frosty clouds.

"Well, it's quiet," he remarked in English. From somewhere to the east a lone sniper round cracked.

"*Vous gâchez nos chance.* You're spoiling our luck," Gerard warned.

"This is not a matter of luck," said Francie. "It's about skill, and brains."

"I left my brains at home," Serge growled. "Otherwise I would not be here."

"Cut the chatter," Eckstein snapped. "Makes me think you're nervous."

"But we *are* nervous," Francie retorted. "You wouldn't want us any other way."

"Sss!" Ecsktein hissed hard like a snake and they all fell silent. It was true, however. He wanted them fearful, wary, and sharp. But like all soldiers on the cusp of a combat zone, he did not want to hear about it.

He squinted toward the far end of the civilian terminal, where the UNPROFOR compound glowed beneath a string of generator lights, revealing rings of concertina wire, shrapnel-scarred tents, and the armored personnel carriers in which the unlucky troops slept more nights than not. Arrivals and departures were supposed to pass through this main checkpoint, but the formalities of passports and customs inspections had become laughable in this Dante-esque nightmare, and you could slip with ease through the lightly manned gateway at the south corner of the strip.

A pair of British paratroopers were standing next to a railway pole at the edge of the airport road, stamping their feet and cursing their own prime minister for his sense of civic duty. The large Welsh sergeant turned as the quintet of Israelis approached, tilting his blue helmet back and staring at their colorful anoraks, wool caps, and cordura bags.

"What the bloody hell is this, then?" he snarled. "Lost yourselves on the way to a Himalaya trek?"

The second soldier smirked, tapping his fingers on his SA-80 assault rifle. Eckstein unzipped his anorak, revealing the gleaming stems of a stethoscope, and produced his French passport and *Médecins Sans Frontières* ID card.

"I am Doctor Pierre Angulaire," he said in a heavy French accent, then nodded deferentially at Baum. "And this is Doctor Antoine Arbre." Their cover names were loose translations of their own, which is a technique favored by Israeli intelligence services to avoid memory lapses under pressure.

The Welshman jutted his chin toward Serge, Gerard, and Francie. "And that's Winkin', Blinkin', and Nod, *royt?*"

"We must get to the Koševo Hospital, *rapidement.*" Baum pulled a stern expression and waved his papers in the air. "There is a wounded patient to bring out. A *journaliste.*"

The sergeant shrugged and jerked a thumb toward the road.

"Well, mates, you'll have to tramp it a bit down there. But there's a Serb checkpoint and the wankers are unpredictable. If I was you I'd get back in me helo and . . ."

"*Merci, mon ami.*" Baum cut him off, pushed on the railway pole, and marched through, followed quickly by the rest of the team.

"Bloody frogs," the sergeant muttered as the Israelis descended into the misty gloom. "Looking for a war when they could be at the fucking *Folleez Berger.*"

For 200 meters they tramped along in total darkness, guided only by the feel of cracked tar beneath their feet and the knowledge imparted by Baum's Mossad contact. To the left, the airport. To the right, a wide patch of Serb-controlled no-man's land.

Baum, silently counting out his paces, flicked on a Mini Maglite. Eckstein caught up to walk beside him, but the colonel protectively pushed him away. If someone opened fire, it would come toward the light.

Francie suddenly inhaled a gasp as a figure stepped into the road.

Benni stopped short. Serge slipped to the front of the team, one large fist concealing a flick knife.

No one breathed.

A penlight glowed in the mist ahead, and the figure stepped forward, his fists at his hips. He was small, with a square black beard falling over an old NATO field jacket, and he wore navy sweatpants with a white Nike logo, ending in a pair of black Cossack boots. On his head was a Bulgarian infantry cap, with a red star on the upturned brim and side flaps like the ears of a basset hound.

"*Dobrodoslica.*" The little man greeted his "guests" in a rough tobacco voice. With his cap and beard and a pair of coal-black eyes glistening with wariness, he looked somewhat demented. "I am Zoran Kosanović."

Indeed, Johann had referred to him as "The Mad Half-Jew," born and raised in Sarajevo, the son of a Muslim woman from Mostar and the janitor of the city's small Jewish Community Center. Like most Slavic Jews, he was considered a "neutral" by Serbs, Croats, and Muslims alike, and allowed to cross disputed lines with relative impunity.

Kosanović did not know the true identities of his visitors, nor their purpose here. He had only been told by Johann that they were *lansmen* and that he would be well paid to shepherd them.

Baum stepped forward, offering that warm Bavarian smile that could either disarm potential adversaries or frighten the hell out of captives under interrogation.

"I am Doctor Arbre, and this is Doctor Angulaire." He waved at Serge, Gerard, and Francie. "And our assistants."

"Of course." Kosanović smiled, showing a row of gold teeth. In a land of roadside executions and concentration camps, intrigue hardly stirred him. "I will need the crossing money."

Eckstein produced an envelope containing 1,000 deutchmarks, and Kosanović stuffed it into his jacket without inspecting it.

"*Pridruziti se,*" he said and he turned and stepped off the road, unfurling a roll of white wrapping ribbon as he walked. "Do not step off of the tape," he warned. "Mines."

The Israelis fell into a perfect line like obedient kindergartners.

They followed him up a shallow hill of hardened mud and large, strewn-about boulders. From somewhere a parachute flare arced into the sky and popped, and as the sputtering magnesium floated down Eckstein realized that the boulders were concrete chunks of exploded buildings. Up ahead, the flare illuminated a high tangle of razor wire snaking over the rubble from left to right. Kosanović dropped a hand beside his leg and splayed his fingers. The Israelis stopped.

There were four Serb gunmen sitting inside a sandbag emplacement, cleaning Yugoslav M70 assault weapons and a Dragunov sniper rifle. Off to one side, the "officer" of this band leaned on a PKM light machine gun, and as he turned toward Kosanović his glowing cigarette revealed belts of 7.62-millimeter bullets draped over his shoulders like Pancho Villa.

There was no verbal exchange. Kosanović proffered the cash, the officer glanced inside the envelope, then snapped his fingers. One of his men dragged a coil of concertina aside and Kosanović waved to Baum. The Serbs said nothing as the "Frenchmen" passed through, although one of them reached out and squeezed the left cheek of Francie's backside, as if it was no more than a peach hanging from a passing fruit cart. It took every ounce of Serge's self-control not to strangle the man.

On the other side of the berm, the Israelis stopped in unison, their mouths agape. Even to those of them who had seen Beirut in '82, Dobrinja was a shock.

Not a roof, window, or terrace had been left intact in the Muslim suburb. Although many survivors had stubbornly remained, there was no electric power; not a single bulb glowed from a smashed window. At an intersection of crumbled homes and cratered streets, the only unmarred object was a lime-green Volkswagen minivan. Kosanović marched to it and opened the door like a proud livery.

"Belong to Nurija Kizo, Old Town stove maker," he said as Eckstein and company quickly piled inside. "No one shoots at Nurija." He turned the engine over and Eckstein slid into the passenger seat beside him. "*Everyone* need stove."

He maneuvered the van up a shallow road grade strewn with debris, and then they were on a crest overlooking the city in all its tortured glory.

High above to the north, the black humps of the Balkans were covered in patches of creamy clouds against a quilt of stars. Directly below that, on Marshal Tito Way, the entire Sarajevan rail system of red tram cars lay scorched and piled up in the train yard like the abused toys of a spoiled child, and all the buildings exposed to the "Chetnik" side were riddled with every caliber of hole known to modern warfare.

To the east, the university sports stadium looked like a blackened soup bowl, and the lower quadrants of Dobrinja, where the desperate Bosnian Army had repelled the Serb assaults, seemed no worse off than Hiroshima, and no better. Catholic churches and mosques alike were riddled, apartment complexes collapsed. A slim multistory across from the gutted Holiday Inn had one entire wall scraped away, its black apartments gaping at the sky like twenty horrified mouths. Each once-elegant Hapsburg facade was pockmarked and blistered, and between the army and the Chetnik emplacements you could see the two long thoroughfares of Marshal Tito and Putnika, where the inhabitants still lived and breathed as they sprinted through Sniper Alley.

Eckstein's team leaned forward inside the unheated van, shivering as they stared in disbelief through the cracked windshield. Kosanović lit a cigarette as somewhere a machine gun sputtered, and then another, and then came the familiar double boom of a rocket-propelled grenade.

"So, Doctor." He turned his head to look at Benni Baum. "You want hospital?"

Baum looked at his watch. It was 6:52 P.M. At 7:30, Niki Hašek would be leaving her place of work.

"No," said Baum. "The Russian Embassy. And quickly."

Kosanović clucked his tongue and slowly shook his head.

"Well . . ." He looked over at Eckstein. "What about *my* money?"

"You'll get it," said the major. "When we leave."

"You are very smart." The Mad Half-Jew slowly grinned, and he pointed at the city as it began to glow and flash with gunfire. "Because otherwise, I would not go down there tonight."

4

Sarajevo
April 30

NIKITA HAŠEK WAS a jittery Czech, although she strove to hide that pervasive trait, wearing a skein of not-too-offensive insolence to camouflage her disquiet. She was thirty-two, but looked ten years younger, owing much to a waiflike figure that no doubt resulted from a racing metabolism, filterless cigarettes, and a diet of coffee and unfinished meals.

Her short black hair, fine like a chinchilla's coat, fell in spikes across her brow and bounced when she walked. Her eyes were nearly navy blue, her nose puckish, her jaw angular, and her chin sharp as a thumb, and she would have been beautiful except for the expression she wore even when she slept: Wary. Distrustful. Darting.

Most of her wardrobe—slacks, sweaters, shoes, and the occasional miniskirt—were black. She was mostly like a house cat living in an overpopulated flat, pretending that she ruled, striding along proudly, yet starting frightfully at each sudden movement, as if a boot might trample her without warning. If she had had a tail it would have constantly been flicking, probing, like a mine detector.

When she walked out of the Russian Embassy annex on Vasa Miskin Street—precisely at 19:30, as Johann had relayed—Eckstein did not even bother to check her photo for verification. She was one of a kind, and more than her image, Krumlov's description of her body language was instantly confirmed. As she strode across the sidewalk a boy flashed by on a bicycle and she almost leapt into the air, then quickly regained her composure, rolled her eyes for a split second, and carried on.

That was her. There could only be one Niki Hašek.

The night was deep and darker now, and few pedestrians hurried through the streets, for the teenage blood on the cobblestones of the Central Market had not fully congealed since the noon mortar attack, and the fantasies that a Vance-Owen treaty might bring an end to all this had dissolved. Only yesterday a few evening cafés had reopened their doors, though there was scant food to be served along with the local bitter beer and watery coffee. Now a new rumor pervaded, that the Serb snipers on Trebević Mountain had obtained a batch of Soviet night-vision scopes. There would be no moonlit strolls for a while.

"Early to bed, perhaps not dead," a columnist from the irrepressible *Oslobodjenje* newspaper had warned a colleague from *Time.*

Niki zipped her black down ski parka, turned left, then left again, heading toward the river. Eckstein, who was half-hidden in a doorway at the corner of Karadzića, nodded with relief, for she was following her pattern of heading home to Novo Sarajevo. One hundred meters south, Baum and Gerard waited with Kosanović and the minivan near the far end of an alley, and had Niki altered her course, they could only be advised by a runner. Ben-Zion had forbade the team from smuggling any sort of commo gear into a war zone where its capture was a distinct possibility. This did not disturb Benni in the least, who had cut his teeth in the intelligence services when everyone used hand signals, but Eckstein and the rest were of the *Star Trek* generation and they missed their communicators.

Eckstein's nod also had the effect of signaling Francie, who had been pacing out 100 meters back and forth on the south side of Miskin, staying tight to the riddled facades of the buildings so the Russians could not spot her from their plastic-sealed windows above.

Yet, in fact, the Russians already *had* spotted her. Colonel Stepnin's knees were sore from kneeling at the window of his darkened office, a third-generation monocular night scope pressed to his eye. At the end of the scope, the handle of a dental mirror was taped to the lens tube, with the small reflecting glass poking outside through a hole in the window sheeting. By focusing on the mirror and slowly turning it this way and that, Stepnin had picked up this "girl with no place to go," and Eckstein as well.

"Who are they, sir?" Stepnin's adjutant crouched next to the colonel, wishing he could have a peek.

"*Shhh*, Yuri," Stepnin hissed as he increased the magnification. "I can't say. They look European, but it does not matter. Ivan and Burko will take care of them."

The captain shook his head doubtfully. "I'm not so sure, sir . . ."

"Don't be an old woman, Yuri. Just let it play out."

"Yes, sir."

Francie moved quickly now toward the corner to close the gap with Niki, then pulled up short to avoid tumbling into a pair of Russian watchers as they trotted out the annex door and immediately followed Niki's trail. Her "flies" were average-size men, one half a head taller than the other, their Slavic features more suited to Sarajevo than to the villages of Lebanon and Syria, where the Russians look like sharks in a goldfish bowl. With their heavy woolen coats and fur hats they were hardly surreptitious about their task, nor did Niki bother to turn her head to check for them. When you worked for the Russians, you never walked alone.

Francie picked up the pace again, marching after the two watchers. She had chosen a reversible parka for this bit and now she wore the white side out, for such careless fashion is an anomaly to spies and would hopefully dilute suspicion. She had popped a purple baseball cap onto her head, completing the look of a carefree sport.

"Niki! Niki Hašek!" She pushed right between the Russians and trotted toward the Czech girl as Niki, predictably, winced and turned around. Francie caught up, grabbed her elbow, and led her on again, hugging her close and laughing animatedly at nothing.

Ivan, the taller of the two Russians, at first simply uttered a lewd comment to his partner, Burko. But almost immediately he recalled Colonel Stepnin's warning, and his face darkened and he clipped out a pace behind the two girls, with Burko struggling to catch up.

Serge stepped from a doorway across the street from Eckstein and the two Israelis fell in quietly behind the watchers. All three "couples" moved south on Karadzića now, where the stained glass windows of the Orthodox Cathedral had succumbed to concussions and the street was littered with glittering colors as if a gemologist had spilled his life's work. In the distance the silver waters of the Miljaka rushed below Stari Grad, the ruined buildings there jagged and white like broken jaws sitting on a morgue table.

Francie picked up her pace.

The Russians moved faster.

Eckstein and Serge opened their stride, exchanging no words as the major tightened his padded gloves.

He had come to hate this part of the work. He was not an assassin by nature, and a reluctant thug. Even when he had volunteered as point man for the ugliest task, a part of him always prayed that it would be called off. Now he flexed his arm and chest muscles, determined to do the job quickly and effectively, so he would not have to actually kill anyone. But glancing at Serge, he knew that the brooding sergeant harbored no similar self-restraint.

Francie suddenly took a sharp left, leading Niki into the predetermined alleyway. The Russians hesitated for a moment, then Ivan snatched at Burko's sleeve and they also made the turn. Eckstein held Serge back while he checked the corner, then stepped into the mouth of the alley.

It was a very narrow space, barely wide enough for a horse cart. High above, the stars winked into the long black slot and lines of laundry were slung between the roofs. A flapping bedsheet showed jagged shrapnel holes.

The grunt of a mortar tube echoed from somewhere and everyone froze until the shell exploded to the east in Bašćaršija with a hollow bang and a follow-on tumble of bricks. Eckstein squinted down the alleyway, searching in vain for the minivan, but it wasn't there and it didn't matter. Time was up. A full-blown artillery barrage could kick off any second now, and the Russians might snatch Niki up to *protect* her.

"Nikita!" Eckstein shouted. He began to run, Serge matching him step for step. "Nikita!" He waved and tried to grin, but he knew his expression was tight and frozen.

The Russians whirled around. Behind them, Eckstein could see

Francie hustling Niki away, and he ran faster, focusing only on the girls, hoping that the two watchers would remain confused until he and Serge were on them.

It did not work.

The shorter Russian furrowed his brow, then yanked his hands from his coat pockets. Large hands. The taller one took a step back as his instincts fired in his brain, and Eckstein saw him reaching into his coat but left him to Serge and went for the bull.

He punched Burko straight into his nose. It was a good blow, carried right from the shoulder and launched with his full weight, but the man only grunted, took one step back, and anchored himself. Before Eckstein could strike again he caught the flash of knuckles speeding at his stomach, and he tensed his muscles and took it. The stab of pain fueled him, and he raised his left arm across to his right ear and twisted his entire torso, striking down into Burko's cheek with a knife hand that opened flesh over bone and immediately gushed a stream of blood. But the Muscovite was strong and had a good neck and he did not fall, but staggered back against the alley wall with his feet splayed and impact tears streaming down his face.

Eckstein stepped back and kicked him full bore in the groin with his hiking boot. That did it. Burko went fetal.

Eckstein spun around, but Serge had already done his work, straight-knuckling Ivan in the throat and then breaking his gun hand with a violent wrench as the Makarov pistol came out of his coat. The man was already slumped and unconscious, his fur hat gone and his eyes lolling, but Serge had him by the hair and was banging his head against the alley wall, apparently enraged at having nearly been shot.

Eckstein grabbed at Serge's parka and hauled him away, sprinting for the far end of the alley. The minivan was there, its sliding door open and the girls already inside, but Baum had jumped down, perhaps hoping to get in a few licks himself before retirement. And Gerard was poised with his medical kit, perhaps hoping for a few minor wounds.

Eckstein, poisoned with adrenaline and spewing breath, caught a gleam of something in Serge's fist as they reached the Volkswagen. "No souvenirs," he spat as he snatched the Russian pistol from the sergeant's hand, dumped the magazine into his palm, cleared the breech, and boomeranged the gun back into the alley.

Serge shrugged, grinned, and hauled himself into the van. Baum thumped Eckstein on the shoulder, pushed Gerard up into the passenger seat beside Kosanović, and squeezed in beside him.

Eckstein looked down at the pistol magazine, then arced it up into the night, where it bounced on a rooftop and skipped away like a flat stone on a pond. The van was already rolling toward the river and he had to lunge to make it into the side door.

Apparently, Kosanović wanted to get home . . .

Niki Hašek did not speak. She sat on the middle seat, her small hands in black woolen gloves gripping her kneecaps, looking like a child jammed between Serge's lumbering form and Eckstein's lither torso, which still quivered as he willed his nerves to ease. She had clearly been expecting something like this, for she did not exhibit the clamped panic of a hostage. But she was not exactly rapt with joy, either.

Francie and Gerard were in the rear seat, and Francie gently placed a hand on Niki's shoulder, which only made the young woman jolt. Baum turned from the front, laid one thick arm along his seatback, and gave Niki his warmest fatherly smile.

"*Ça va?*" His tone was caring, his inquiry also a signal to all to stick to French.

Niki stared at him through the wisps of her bangs. Benni cocked his head at Eytan. "*Le photo,*" he instructed, and Eckstein reached into his coat, offering Niki the snapshot supplied by Jan Krumlov. It was a black and white and had been taken by Krumlov on the balcony of their flat in Prague. Its passage from camera to Krumlov into the hands of these strangers and back to Niki was meant to serve as reassuring evidence of a throughline, yet Niki nearly cracked the emulsion as she gripped it. She looked at it as if wondering what had happened to *that* young woman, then glanced up at Baum.

"*De mon fiancé,*" she said as if regretting not drawing up a prenuptial agreement.

"*Oui.*" Baum smiled harder. "*Nous savons.* We know."

Serge laughed, and Francie and Gerard also chuckled, and that seemed to cut the ice a bit as Niki smiled slowly.

Kosanović took the Volkswagen west along Stepanovića, the main thoroughfare, completely deserted now. The intervals between distant gunfire were growing shorter—an aggressive boom, a responding crackle—and as he broke out onto Putnika and the exposed range of Sniper Alley, he began to drive as many do in besieged cities, zigzagging with the hope that a wobbling target is a discouraging choice. In fact, it is the opposite, as snipers are generally men of ego. Sure enough, a heavy rifle round sparked off a building stone just meters before the front bumper, but Kosanović raced faster and Eckstein's team began flailing for handholds as the Mad Half-Jew bore down on the smashed-up front of the abandoned Holiday Inn, passed it, took a quick right onto Brodska, then right again between two huge piles of rubble that looked like the entrance to an Egyptian tomb.

The wide black mouth of a subterranean entranceway loomed up ahead as the van bounced down a ramp, and just before they were swallowed by total darkness, Eckstein looked up to see a white slice of posterboard with a warning scrawled in crayon: *Snajper!*

Kosanović stopped the van and switched on the lights, and everyone realized that he had been driving without them. They were in some sort of empty underground parking garage. Collections of rainwater sluiced through the shelled structure above and dripped off the overhead beams like melt from stalactites, and with each vibration of outside ordnance sneezes of dust drifted down like snow flurries.

Baum hopped down from the van and headed directly for the only other vehicle present, a white panel truck parked between two pillars. This was to be the "ambulance" envisioned by Mack Marcus. Slipping *out* of the airport through the pair of bored British paras was all right for entering the city, but regaining entrance to the strip could only be done through one large Serb checkpoint in Nedzarići and the official UNPROFOR airport gate. For that, they would need a full-blown "circus."

Eckstein joined Baum and they walked around the truck like preflight pilots, touching its flanks and inspecting their fingers. It was very clean, as Kosanović had followed Johann's instructions, evidenced by a pile of wet rags and an empty bottle of dish soap on the concrete floor.

"*Mes amis!*" Benni called out to the rest of the troupe. "*Les pochoires.*" He said "stencils," not recalling the word for "decals."

Serge, Gerard, and Francie piled out of the Volkswagen, set their duffels around the panel truck, and went to work. Gerard came up with a pair of boxer shorts and began further polishing the vehicle flanks. Francie and Serge produced short poster tubes and unfurled the long red emblems of *Médicins Sans Frontières*. Gerard turned to assembling two telescoping antennae with suction-cup bottoms and MSF triangular pennants.

Kosanović approached Baum and Eckstein, clearly expecting a compliment for his work.

"*Très bon,*" said Benni, patting the small man on his shoulder.

Kosanović shrugged. "No French."

Eckstein looked over the Sarajevan's head. Niki was standing near, watching the strangers work as she smoked a long cigarette. She shivered.

Eckstein picked up his own duffel, retiring with Baum and Kosanović to a shadowed corner. He opened the bag and removed a large plastic first aid box, popped the catches, and extracted the top drawer of morphine tablets, hemostats, and surgical scissors. Inside the lower compartment was the full uniform of a British UNPROFOR major. It had been steam-compressed by the basement wizards, and Baum began kneading it to get it unfolded while Eckstein stripped off his MSF clothes.

"Do you know how drive to airport?" Kosanović asked as he watched Eckstein struggle into a pair of very stiff camouflage trousers.

"Vaguely," said Baum.

"What?" The small man frowned.

"Tell us again," said Eckstein.

"Out of this place, down Putnika. Go straight, past TV tower and PTT building and left after trains at big cross streets." Kovanović wagged a warning finger. "No go to Stup! *Left* up through Nedzarići."

"Okay," said Eckstein. He was now wearing a British SAS smock, which would deflect unnecessary inquiries from the King's own troops and might explain the length of his hair. Even so, he pulled a black woolen balaclava over his head, then peeled it back to settle around his neck and tucked his ponytail inside.

"I finish here," said Kosanović. Baum and Eckstein turned to him, realizing he was waiting like a bellhop in a hotel room.

"Of course," said Benni as he fished for another envelope, this one containing Kosanović's fee. He handed it over as the Mad Half-Jew grinned.

"You did very well." Eckstein pulled a blue UNPROFOR beret smartly over one brow. "Thank you." He pumped the little man's hand.

"You good too." The Sarajevan tore open the envelope, threw it away, and deftly split the deutschmarks into three small rolls. One went inside his jacket, one beneath his cap, and he bent to stuff the third into his boot. "Good luck." He pointed up at heaven as if that might help, then started for the Volkswagen. He stopped and turned. "When you get to Chetniks at Nedzarići, be *carefully*," he warned. "They laugh and make joke, but they can kiss you, or kill you."

Eckstein nodded, Baum waved, and Kosanović hopped into the minivan and disappeared back into the rubble of his world.

For a moment the garage was dark as a coffin, then someone switched on the panel truck lights. The two officers walked to the truck, where Gerard, Francie, and Serge stood proudly like troops at a vehicle inspection. The ambulance disguise was fine, the decals and pennants affixed, and a blue siren beacon magnetized to the roof.

Baum opened the cargo bay. Francie had unrolled and inflated an olive air mattress and laid it on the floor. The interior was lined with further props from their duffel bags: hastily torn gauze boxes, trays of medicines, canvas-pocketed instrument holders, and a pair of infusion bags on a tripod. There was even a transparent plastic sanitary sack filled with "bloody" bandages.

"*Magnifique*," said Baum as he doffed his overcoat and pulled on a white lab smock. Gerard, Serge, and Francie followed suit, and then Francie produced a small squeeze bottle and stained their coats appropriately with blood spatters.

They all began piling into the panel truck as Eckstein turned to Niki, who had not moved from her spot. She was on her third cigarette and her hand trembled.

"*S'il vous plaît.*" Eckstein gestured at the ambulance.

"You can stop the French," said Niki. "My English is better." She still did not move.

Baum was halfway into the cargo doors. He stopped and got out, sensing trouble.

"You're not French," said Niki. She tossed the cigarette away and folded her arms. Gerard, Serge, and Francie came quietly out of the vehicle.

"All right," said Eckstein in a relaxed, agreeable tone. He put his hands in his uniform pockets and watched the Czech girl, not making a move, as if she was a suicidal jumper on a roof ledge.

"Maybe that one's French." Niki pointed at Gerard. "But not the rest of you. You are Israelis."

No one said a word. The young woman was obviously gripped by fear now, wishing she had never agreed to her fiancé's plot. She needed reassurance, and no one could really do that for her but herself. An artillery shell boomed somewhere, and she winced as a trickle of dust wisped from the ceiling.

"You are certainly not Americans. They make jokes all the time and they all look alike. And you are not Germans or Arabs or anything. You must be Jews. Anyone else would have killed those two Russians."

Eckstein looked at Baum, who shrugged. "I think it's a compliment," said Benni. "I'm not sure."

Eckstein turned back to the trembling woman.

"We're here to help you, Niki." He looked at his watch. "But we have to move now."

"I'm not going," Niki said defiantly.

Eckstein lifted his head. "You're not?"

"Not without my things."

"Which things, my dear?" Baum's voice was as smooth as a psychologist's, and he raised a hand to make sure his team understood the delicate nature of the exchange.

"In my flat. I have things."

Francie stepped forward, ignoring Baum's signal. She was the sort of young woman who did not truck with feminine eccentricities.

"Listen, *Nikita*," she said. "We have to get in the ambulance and make you over into a paitent. A *critical* patient, and there isn't time . . ."

Niki took a step back, her spine curling like a threatened cat.

"I am *not* going with you unless we stop at my flat! I have *things* there, and if you try to force me, when we get to the Serbs I will just scream and scream. I *swear* I will."

Gerard was at Eckstein's side. He touched the major's elbow and Eytan read his thoughts. They could inject the girl and put her out, force her to come along. But at the other end of the line waited Jan Krumlov, and his full cooperation might depend on how his fiancée had been treated here.

Baum waved his thick hands in the air as if dispersing the clouds of unpleasantness.

"Well, my dear. Of course you are right." He smiled his Father Christmas smile. "We *are* Israelis. Sentimental fools, all of us. And if *I* were leaving my house, never to return again, I would not go without certain trinkets from my closet. Even if the atomic bomb was about to fall."

Niki searched him for sincerity, and finding it, nodded.

"Come," said the colonel. "Tell me where you live."

Live was hardly the word to describe Niki Hašek's home environment, for she had survived her half-year in Sarajevo in a high rise in Mojmilo, where Bosnian government troops had managed to push the Serbs off Mojmilo Hill. Still, artillery shellings and sniper attacks were regular events in the neighborhood, and no building remained intact, not to mention the residents. At each multistory dwelling local civil defense groups organized citizen sentries to prevent saboteurs from sneaking into the buildings. Women watched by day and men by night, and once in autumn, during her regular day off, Niki had volunteered to stand guard along with a neighbor's wife. The woman had wandered away just briefly to fetch a newspaper and was immediately killed, along with the kiosk vender, by an artillery shell. Niki had spent nearly a week indoors nursing a bottle of tranquilizers.

Inside her fourth-floor flat it became instantly clear to Eckstein that the "things" for which she had returned could not be of monetary value. The one bedroom space of cinderblock walls had been completely stripped of even the most meager comforts. Central heating had ceased long ago, so a hole had been sledgehammered through one wall, a steel pipe fitted as an improvised chimney, and a Kizo stove attached. Every item of wood, including picture frames, furniture legs, soup ladles, and even clothespins, had been consumed. When the shelling was too fierce for Niki to venture out for more fuel, she had fed the stove with books, pencils, and even parts of her wardrobe—summer dresses lost their charm on bone-chilling Balkan nights.

A pair of hurricane lanterns burning vegetable oil flickered over the bare flat as Eckstein and Baum watched Niki wander back and forth, clutching a small black suitcase like a child who'd decided to run away from home after being chided for spilled milk. The rest of the team was waiting below in the ambulance, and Eckstein kept glancing at his watch and shooting stares at Baum. Across the city the shelling was becoming far too regular, and Eckstein worried that the ambulance might be damaged, or worse. Baum gestured for his major to be patient, pressing his hand in the air as if petting an invisible cat.

Niki's personal rescue of her nostalgia was a strange dance, but it did not take very long. She quickly selected odd items for her suitcase: a few pieces of clothing, a pair of shoes, a handful of costume jewelry, five boxes of cigarettes she had hidden in the bathroom. She kept glancing sideways at the Israeli officers as if embarrassed to have them witness this, and Eckstein suppressed a pang of pity.

She had passed a steel file cabinet a number of times, and at last she produced a key and unlocked it. From inside she withdrew a pile of letters bound in blue ribbon, then a private journal and a small photo album. Finally, she lifted out a slim velvet box. With trembling hands she snapped it open, removing a fine thick fountain pen of black lacquer with a silver clip. The letters and photos went into her suitcase, the pen and journal into her inside jacket pocket.

She turned to Eckstein and Baum, pushed her bangs back from her eyes, and waited.

"Is that it?" Eckstein asked.

"Yes."

Baum held the door as Niki passed through it, while Eckstein caught up behind him and muttered in Hebrew.

"*Bishvil zeh anu mistaknim et ha'tachat?* For this we're risking our asses?"

Baum laughed softly, thumping Eckstein's back as they left.

Serge drove, his large form squeezed behind the wheel of the panel truck, his bearded face close to the windshield as he negotiated the rubble-strewn roads down from Mojmilo and back into the city. Beside him, Eckstein checked his British uniform, smoothed his beret, and, much like a professional actor, focused on getting into character. He summoned up that certain class distinction of the English officer, an air of brooding remoteness, a view of the world from on high. His spine lengthened and he sat more erect.

Across the city, parachute flares arced up from the hills of Velešići, flashing behind the ragged skyline. And as they turned left again on Putnika, a tank shell lanced quickly from Zuć Hill toward Asići, its firing boom reaching the truck as the red dot impacted like a lightning strike and the impact detonation rattled the windows.

In the back of the ambulance Francie worked quickly over Niki's costume change, while Benni and Gerard politely averted their eyes and Baum distracted the girl with anecdotes about his own adventures in Prague. Niki shivered as Francie stripped her of her clothes, stuffed them into her suitcase, bound one of her bare legs in white surgical wrap from thigh to ankle, then soaked the bandages in yellow Betadine and streaks of blood serum. She helped her into a coarse blue hospital smock, laid her down on the air mattress, and covered her with a thermal blanket.

With Niki's modesty intact, Baum and Gerard joined the process. Niki's eyes bugged as Gerard inserted an infusion needle into her wrist. He was not bothered by the bucking ride of the ambulance, having done the same a hundred times in armored personnel carriers and helicopters. Baum wound Niki's forehead with gauze while Francie applied another helping of Betadine to the wrap, then finger-combed Niki's hair with "blood." Gerard snapped a Koševo Hospital bracelet onto her wrist and Francie considered giving her a cosmetic pallor, but the young woman was already pale as a ghost.

"That's it," said Baum as he patted Niki's shoulder. "You are half dead, my dear. Don't speak."

"I have nothing to say," Niki barely whispered.

Not far past the destroyed *Oslobodjenje* newspaper headquarters Serge took the left toward Nedzarići and the airport, slowing for a moment as a squad of Bosnian "Dragons" raced across the road toward Stup, hauling heavy boxes of ammunition that stretched their arms like baboons. He hit the ambulance beacon switch and the blue light began to spin, flashing the truck hood in eerie cobalt stripes.

Eckstein came up with his pipe and the box of filters, twisted off the stem, loaded one round of ammunition, and carefully reset the weapon. Serge looked over at him and shook his head.

"We should have grenades for this," he complained. "Not wind-up toys."

Eytan smiled and tucked the pipe in his mouth, the bullet an inch from his soft palate.

"For God's sake, just don't blow your own head off," said Serge.

"Then don't hit any bumps, old boy," Eckstein replied in his best British lilt.

Small-arms fire began to stutter intensively from the west, and they shortly came upon another huddle of Bosnian Dragons holding the border at Nedzarići. The Bosnians were clutching their weapons and staring nervously off to the right toward the swelling battle, and they hardly glanced at the ambulance as it drove through the lines.

Serge maneuvered across 100 meters of black no-man's land, through three rows of torn concertina, and then the Serb checkpoint appeared between two long walls of earth and a frame of sandbag mounds.

The emplacement appeared abandoned. There were no Serbs to be seen, only rings of swirling smoke. Just beyond, a Yugoslav BMP armored personnel carrier was parked at a crazy angle, short orange flames licking from its commander's hatch. Serge slowed.

"Nobody's home," he said optimistically.

"Then drive through it," Eckstein ordered, although he felt a tingle of nerves clenching his gut.

Serge hit the gas pedal, then a heavy beam of light flashed into the windshield.

"*Zaustaviti!* Stop!" someone shouted, and Serge, having manned more than a few roadblocks himself in Lebanon, hit the brakes, skidded to a halt before the sandbags, and quickly raised his hands off the wheel.

Eckstein squinted through the blinding floodlight. Three figures had appeared atop the earthen mounds, one of them aiming the powerful lamp, and by the scatter of its beam through the heavy smoke he could make out details that slowly sent a chill from his heels to his groin.

They were carrying AK-74 assault rifles, and one of them shouldered a rocket-propelled grenade. They were all bearded and wore no helmets, but had green bandannas tied around their foreheads. They wore woodland camouflage uniforms, such as those left behind by the U.S. Marines in Lebanon.

"*Gott im Himmel.*" Benni Baum's head was poking forward from the van's cargo bay.

"Are they who I *think* they are?" Serge grunted.

"Hizbollah." Eytan's lips barely parted.

It could not have been worse. Outwitting the unpredictable Serbs would have been bad enough, but facing off with these Iranian-backed fanatics was like falling into a bucket of scorpions. They killed without remorse, for if you worshipped Allah, then only Paradise awaited you. If you were an infidel, you did not deserve to breathe anyway. And if you happened to be Israeli . . .

"Don't get out yet," said Baum between clenched teeth. "Let them calm down."

"They look perfectly calm to me," said Serge.

A fourth figure appeared in the shafts of light between the sandbags. He was squatting, yanking the boots off of a corpse.

"So that's where the Serbs went," Eytan whispered.

"It's a fresh kill," said Benni, as if he was watching a nature film about jackals.

"What's going on?" Gerard called from the cargo bay.

"Shut up," Serge hissed.

Eckstein had to make a decision, and he had to make it now. He had a single .22-caliber shell in his goddamn ridiculous pipe and he was facing the kind of men who often assaulted Israeli positions in southern Lebanon in suicidal waves. He slowly reached into his smock pocket, came up with his "beeper," and pressed the green button. The readout glowed with numbers.

Benni observed this with a side glance.

"You are committing us to a firefight," he warned.

"If they let us through, I'll apologize later for the false alarm," said Eckstein. "If they don't, it doesn't matter." He pressed the red transmit button.

"How far to the airport?" Serge asked.

"A kilometer."

"I hope your heroes can run."

"Pozuri!" A harsh voice ordered. Then, in Arabic-accented English, "Get out!"

Eckstein nodded, took the pipe from his mouth, tapped the bowl very lightly, and put it back in his teeth. He opened the door and stepped from the ambulance.

The heavy beam clicked off, but parachute flares were drifting above and he could easily see the Hizbollah leader who stood before him.

The man was half a head taller than Eckstein and very broad at the shoulders. His uniform was caked with mud, and the AK-74 trained at Eytan's stomach was slick with oil. It had been recently fired, he could smell it, and the man's eyes in his coarsely bearded face glistened with the chemical rush of fresh combat.

"Who are you?" The leader's voice was heavy with gun smoke.

"I am Major Ethan Brick, UNPROFOR liaison to foreign relief." Eytan raised his chin and took the pipe from his mouth. "And who might *you* be, my good fellow?"

The Hizbollah leader did not answer, but stretched his neck to peer at the ambulance. Beyond him, the three other fighters had taken up triangular covering positions.

All four of these men were "nitros," as Benni Baum referred to unrested troops overexposed to combat: ready to blow at any second and for no particular reason.

"What is in *truck*?" the leader demanded again.

"I am Doctor Antoine Arbre, *Médecins Sans Frontières*." Baum had hopped to the ground just behind Eckstein. "We have a critical patient here. We must bring her to the airport."

"Airport?" The Muslim fighter smirked very slightly. His lips were cracked and every tooth showing was chipped, as if his mouth had been smashed by a rifle butt. He briefly looked up at the sky. "Nothing is in the air tonight. Except maybe for death." He pointed at the ambulance. "What is in truck?"

"Only our medical supplies and personnel," said Benni.

The Hizbollah leader turned and called out in Lebanese Arabic to his men. Two of them quickly sprinted to the rear of the van, while the fourth man stepped in to cover Serge, who had slowly emerged from the cab.

"Now look here, fellow." Eckstein puffed out his chest. "These people have a helicopter waiting and their patient is in dire straits and they are short on time. I should like to speak to your commanding officer."

The leader turned back to look at Eckstein, and for the first time the Israeli major's heart began to hammer and he tasted the dry film of mortal danger in his gullet. The man's eyes were hollow, his gaze from another world. A world of no rules.

"*My* only commander is God," he said, and somehow he knew that the British officer before him held a secret danger, and his eyes remained unblinking and fixed on Eytan's face.

There was a commotion at the back of the ambulance and then the two fighters appeared, hauling the teams' MSF duffels, stuffed to overflowing with all their medical supplies. Eytan was about to protest, but he felt Benni grip his arm.

"Feel free, *mes amis*," said Baum. "A donation to your cause."

One of the fighters said, *"Sharmutah,"* the Arabic invective for any woman not of Muslim modesty, and their leader said, "Bring her," and Eytan understood and now he knew this was really going to be it. He took the pipe from his mouth and held the bowl in his palm and gripped the stem between his thumb and forefinger.

Sure enough, within seconds the two men had dragged Francie from the ambulance. Her face was white as bone and one of them had her by the collar, and when Gerard jumped out to go after her the other fighter turned and produced a gleaming bayonet and stopped him short.

Serge stared across the vehicle hood at Eckstein, then turned away.

When Eckstein fired the pipe, he would go for Francie's captor, but he knew he was going to die right there on the spot, and Gerard would die as well, for the fourth Hizbollah was in the clear with his assault rifle and would mow them both down with one long burst.

"Leave the woman *be*." Eckstein nearly spat as he jabbed the pipe stem into the Hizbollah leader's chest. He would give it another second, then he would fire the bullet into the man's heart, go for his weapon, take out the farthest fighter, and hope for the best.

The leader glared at him, reached across his assault rifle, slammed the bolt back and placed the barrel against Eckstein's throat.

"I thought you were men of God!" Baum protested even as he knew it was no good and he braced himself for the coming carnage.

"Even men of God have to fuck," one of the other Hizbollah called out, and for just a split second the leader lifted his head to laugh, and Eckstein *moved.*

He jerked to his right, arcing his left hand up inside and chopping the rifle barrel away, and it went off very close to his ear but he twisted his pipe stem and the little weapon fired.

The big Hizbollah snapped back and went down, but it was not from Eckstein's shot. The short bursts of silenced Skorpion machine pistols were flashing from atop the earthen mounds, and even as Serge leapt to Francie and tackled her to the ground the *Mat'kalniks* had already killed the leader and two more fighters with perfect close-range bursts to the spines. The fourth Hizbollah was engaged in a hand-to-hand struggle with Gerard, who had captured his bayonet hand and broken his knee with his boot, but one of the Israeli commandos marched quickly off the berm, took careful aim as he walked, and dropped the man with a single shot to the skull.

The entire melee had lasted only six seconds.

For a long moment, no one moved, the scene a frozen tableau embraced by that howling silence that follows a horrific traffic accident. And then Eckstein, who was reeling and temporarily deaf in his left ear, snapped, "*Zooz!* Move!" in Hebrew.

Serge jumped back into the ambulance and started the engine, hissing "*Oui!*" with relief that it had not been damaged by a wayward bullet. The *Mat'kalniks* ran to quickly check the Hizbollah bodies for signs of life and threat, and finding none, stripped their pockets of any documents that might prove useful to AMAN. Gerard, shaking like an alcoholic with delirium tremors, realized that his thigh had been gouged by the bayonet tip. Yet when he saw Francie, who was on all fours and unable to rise, he ran to her. She climbed up his chest, sobbing as he hugged her, for in ten years of operations she had never been so close, so quickly, to the terror of her own certain death. And then Benni was there, enveloping his two operatives in his arms and shepherding them to the back of the vehicle, where Niki Hašek had lain throughout the entire ordeal, immobilized by fear.

"*Drive,*" Eckstein ordered as he hopped up into the cab, and Serge charged through the sandbag gate, rolling right over a pair of Serb corpses as the *Mat'kalniks* sprinted after the van and dove into the cargo bay.

The final run to the airport took less than ten minutes. There was no other vehicle on the road, and Serge drove the ambulance flat out. No one uttered a word, and Eckstein watched the surrounding hills where shells were lobbing in lazy arcs and exploding in distant copses of forest.

Compared to the Hizbollah roadblock, the UNPROFOR gate at the airport was as troublesome as a bridal shower. A heavy howitzer shell had struck the terminal and most of the UN troops were huddled inside their APCs. Eckstein merely saluted a young French paratrooper, and the soldier raised a gate pole and waved the ambulance through.

Within one minute the team had stripped the vehicle bare, including its MSF decals, and they were all aboard the helicopter. The doors slammed home, the big rotor blades sliced into air laced with cordite, and the Bell lifted off and turned its back on Sarajevo.

Niki, still wrapped in her thermal blanket, watched the city suffer from a window. Gerard began sewing up the gash in his own leg with a suture needle, while Serge sat with an arm around Francie's shoulder, comforting her even as he looked away. Her head rested on his thick arm, her eyes closed, and she made no sound even as her tears dripped onto her knees.

Eckstein slumped against the steel bench back, wiping sweat from his face with his blue beret. Baum, back in place just behind the pilots, smoked in great gulps and sipped from a *Mat'kalnik's* canteen. The two commandos were already asleep, curled up on the steel floor like contented panthers.

They were soon above the clouds, flight-planned for Italy above a quilt of gray cotton, the stars shining brightly above, and even the engine thrum seemed like blessed silence. The copilot turned back to Baum and stretched a microphone to him on a spiral cord.

"It's Ben-Zion. By relay," said the copilot.

Benni took the mike and twisted around to Eckstein.

"Eytan. What the hell is the confirmation code?" He scratched his bald head. "I can't remember."

"Fuck the confirmation code." Eckstein pulled Benni's cigarette from his mouth, took a long drag, and seemed to deflate with exhaustion as he expelled a stream of smoke.

"Just tell him the Czech's in the mail."

5

* * *

North Africa
May 2

"NOTTA TO SMOKE in the aisles please, *signore.*"

The Italian stewardess smiled at Eckstein. She had a slightly off-center front tooth, full lips, and bobbed black hair that reminded him of Isabella Rossellini. Her voice contained no reproach, and she stood there with a full tray of quivering juices in plastic tumblers, as if expecting a clever retort.

Eckstein looked down at the cold pipe in his hand. It was unloaded—both of tobacco and ammunition—the shells having been relegated to his luggage, checked in the belly of the 747.

"Oh, I don't actually smoke it." He returned a modest smile. "It's just a pacifier."

"*Scusi?*"

"I fiddle with it." He twirled the briar with his fingers. "Something to do with my hands."

The stewardess's eyes crinkled as if she had discovered a boy stowaway.

"Does the flying make you nervous?"

"Sometimes. Depends on where I'm flying to."

She laughed then, her foal-brown eyes examining Eckstein's overcast blues.

"I will bring you a drink."

Eckstein nodded his thanks while the stewardess turned to Benni Baum.

105 • • •

"And you, *signore*?"

"Whatever he's having. *Grazie.*"

"*Prego.*"

She smiled again and walked away down the aisle. Eckstein watched her bend to service the passengers, her breasts pressing against seat tops as she leaned over with the tray. He turned to find Baum frowning at him.

"She looks a little like Simona," Eckstein suggested.

"Analogies to your wife are a flimsy defense."

"Well, *you* told me to flirt with the stewardesses."

"As a distraction. In my *absence*."

"You're sounding a bit jealous."

"Only of your youth, my son."

Eckstein grunted. He was feeling anything but young, the accumulated tension of double missions back to back having stretched his reserves. But perhaps, if all went well, within a few days' time he would be returning to Jerusalem. He was more than ready to begin a new course, beat a quick path to an office job, and salvage his leaky marriage.

He and Baum stood beside the forward galley of the Alitalia jet, stretching their legs in the bulkhead space of the emergency exit. Ten rows back in coach class, Niki Hašek sat in the window spot of their triplet seats. Her head was propped on a pillow against the scratched Plexiglas, but her eyes were open and she stared down at the Egyptian Eastern Desert as if wishing she had brought along a parachute. For the first time in the process of escorting her, Eckstein and Baum could finally relax, for she had nowhere to flee.

The past evening and half-day in Rome, rather than a respite between legs of the mission and the flight to Addis Ababa, had instead turned to a depressing vigil for the two intelligence officers. With Francie, Serge, and Gerard already making their separate ways back to Tel Aviv, Eckstein and Baum were left to entertain their Czech jewel. Yet she behaved more like prisoner than princess, despite the spacious suite booked at the Ambasciatori and the generous offer of a shopping spree, new wardrobe and accessories, if you wish, "on the House of David."

Eckstein loved the Italian capital, its stones and statues and scents and atmosphere of *La Dolce Vita,* and he was willing to escort Niki through any distractions that might snap her from her gloom. But she was having none of it.

Granted they had arrived at Fiumicino close to midnight and thoroughly spent, having made the last leg once more aboard the white "MSF" jet, in which they had scrubbed down in the cramped lavatory and reverted back to "civilians." Trudging at last into the hotel lobby, Baum proffered his Hans-Dieter Schmidt German passport and a similarly forged document denoting Niki as his daughter, Nicole. Eckstein had again assumed the role of Anthony Hearthstone and a yawning clerk flipped through the little booklets.

"Schmidt, Schmidt, and Hearthstone." He jotted their particulars in a ledger. "Are you a law firm?"

"No," said Baum. "A dysfunctional family."

Only Eckstein smiled, while Niki perused the lobby as if searching for a rathole and the clerk solemnly nodded, apparently regretting that he had pried.

The suite itself was vast and luxurious, its expense only approved for reasons of security, in that the trio would not be separated by unattached rooms. There was a comfortable salon, kitchenette, three bedrooms, and a wide verandah overlooking the city. Yet even though Niki had just escaped from a posting in hell, she was utterly unreactive to these surroundings. She exhibited no diminishing of her tension, and immediately sat down before the large television, still wearing her coat, feeding blankly from a bowl of mixed nuts and watching a rerun of the Eurovision song festival.

Eckstein and Baum conferred quietly in the kitchen as they broke open a pair of "blond" lagers.

"What's up with her?" Eckstein murmured in German.

Benni shrugged and took a long swig of beer. "Post-traumatic stress?"

"*Unsinn.* Nonsense," Eckstein scoffed. "She's got a first-class escort and all expenses paid to a rendezvous with the love of her life. She should be dancing around here barefoot and guzzling champagne."

Baum glanced over at Niki, who seemed to have consumed all the nuts and was now onto her fingernails.

"That's the fairytale version," he said. "Don't expect her to turn from a shellshocked bug into a carefree butterfly within six hours. She'll come around."

Eckstein also stole a glance at her. He shook his head.

"Something's off. I'm sleeping near the door."

"Suit yourself," said Baum. "I'm going straight from the Jacuzzi to the pillow." He dropped the empty beer bottle into a wastebasket. "Don't wake me unless she turns into a vampire."

Baum walked to Niki, patted her shoulder, and went off to bed, while Eckstein perused the salon, selected a divan, and manhandled it until its back was pushed up against the entrance door. When Niki noticed his strange mime, she stood up and watched him suspiciously.

"For security," Eckstein lied as he punched up a pillow and looked around for a blanket.

"Do you expect the Russians to come for me here?" She folded her arms.

"No more than I expect a visit from the Pope. Just a precaution. Standard procedure."

Yet Niki was not a newcomer to the ways of intelligence professionals. She lifted her nose at him, picked up her valise, stalked off to an empty bedroom, and slammed the door.

"Just like home," Eckstein muttered. Then he brushed his teeth in the kitchen, switched off the lights and the television, curled up at his post, and immediately fell asleep.

Sometime in the night, a cold breeze flicked his eyelashes. He was instantly awake, and as is the habit of all overly trained combat soldiers, he groped for the weapon that had been his bedmate for years. Yet finding no cool frame of rifle or pistol steel, he realized where he was and lay still.

The glass doors to the verandah were open, the heavy brocade curtains drifting like medieval capes above the carpet. He rose and tiptoed to the doors in a sweatshirt and boxers, and for a moment, he just watched.

Niki stood at the iron balustrade, her small head hanging, her elbows on the railing. A cold wind twisted the smoke from a cigarette. She wore only a long blue T-shirt and she was barefoot. Twenty stories below, the predawn street lamps of Rome glittered like fireflies, and in the distance a crescent moon revealed the dome of St. Peter's Basilica.

When she lifted her head and placed one foot on the lower railing, Eckstein cleared his throat. She started a bit, but she did not turn as he came out on the verandah and took up a place by her side, but not too close. He leaned on the balustrade, yet did not look at her.

"It's a beautiful city," he said. "One of the best on Europe."

Niki sniffed, and peripherally he saw her wipe her cheek with her fingers.

"I could not sleep," she whispered.

"I understand," he said.

"You do *not* understand."

Eckstein waited a moment, his silence an admission that of course he was ignorant of her private plight. He sighed.

"Sometimes, Niki, life can change very quickly. Too quickly to swallow. New beginnings are hard."

"Life." She almost spat the word. "It is ending, not beginning."

He looked at her, and suddenly a chill shot through his spine. The blue T-shirt had a large emblem on its front, a red and gold shield, and the cartoon title *Supergirl* embossed in glitter. It struck him that had he woken a minute later she might have decided to "fly."

"Look, Niki," he said, but he did not try to touch her as she tossed her cigarette from the verandah, folded her arms over her chest, and shivered. "I don't know anything about you. But I do know that you've had a very hard time, survived in a terrible place where your friends died and you never knew when it might be your turn. I've been to that place, more than once, and it can do awful things to your mind."

She stared at him, eyes wide and glistening, her expression telling nothing. He stepped away from the rail and beckoned her with a hand.

"Come. I'll make you a stiff drink, and tomorrow it will all look different."

She took a long breath, slowly shook her head, and walked back into the suite. Eckstein found a bottle of Chivas in the bar, mixed two large tumblers with some ice water, and handed her a glass.

"Tomorrow," he toasted as he raised his drink and sipped. Without stopping for a breath, Niki downed her scotch as if it was Orangina, set the empty glass on a counter, and looked at him.

"You are right," she said, and for a moment Eckstein imbued himself with the talents of Freud, until she added, "you don't know anything about me."

With that, she walked off to bed.

Eckstein poured the rest of his drink into the sink and put up a pot of espresso. Then he sat on his perch and smoked an entire pack of Rothmanns, unable to decode the mystery of Niki Hašek even as the sun came up . . .

Shortly after breakfast—a sumptuous room service affair delivered to the glum trio on a silver handcart—Benni Baum reluctantly dressed for a visit to the Israeli Embassy, where he would conduct a brief conversation with Ben-Zion via secure transmission. While Niki showered, Eckstein briefed his partner on the strange nocturnal habits of Czech defectors. She suddenly emerged from the bathroom and Baum's expression of grave concern turned instantly to jolly uncle.

"I have some errands, Nikita," he said. "But you can do whatever suits you. Go on a shopping spree, take in a museum. Perhaps your fiancé would appreciate some fine Italian sport shirts!"

Niki stood there, her head and small frame wrapped in white towels, a silent, miniature Cleopatra.

Baum patted Eckstein's shoulder and muttered as he headed for the door, "Don't let her out of your sight."

But Niki had no touristic intentions in mind, nor the urge to douse her internal turmoil with a credit card and shopping bags full of Armani. Instead, she asked Eckstein to take her to the Trevi Fountain, where she settled on a stone step to ponder her fate. Eckstein removed himself to a newspaper kiosk and read the *Herald Tribune* as he watched her. She came up with her journal and began to write, curiously using a hotel ballpoint rather than her ornate fountain pen. Flocks of pigeons pecked around her, tourists ran and laughed and clicked Minoltas at each other, but Niki remained as alone as a stranded earthling on Mars.

* * *

"Itzik didn't even want me calling from inside the Embassy." Benni described his morning conversation with the general as the jumbo jet banked and he reached out for a bulkhead. "Made me go out and cruise in the ambassador's car and use the Tadiran." He referred to a triplex mobile scrambler of Israeli manufacture.

"So? What crimes have we committed since yesterday?" Eytan asked.

Benni glanced around, reverting to a private code even though the conversation was in Bavarian German.

"He said the Magician made contact again. Must be worried that we won't show up. Offered us an incentive."

Eytan understood that Benni was referring to Jan Krumlov.

"What incentive?"

"A picture of the little creature with the muddy nose. Delivery upon our arrival."

Eytan raised an eyebrow. Krumlov was prepared to turn over a *photo* of the mole? *Before* he was extracted to Israel?

"Makes no bloody sense at all."

"No, it doesn't," Benni agreed.

"What the hell do we need *him* for if he gives us *that?*"

"Exactly."

Just then the stewardess reappeared holding a pair of iced Bloody Marys.

"These are fresh, *signori*," she said with some pride as Baum and Eckstein took the drinks.

"But we are *not* so fresh," said Baum.

"Although we try to be gentlemen," Eckstein added. *"Grazie mille."*

"Prego." She smiled widely at Eckstein. Peripherally, he caught Benni rolling his eyes.

"Lunch will be served soon," said the stewardess.

"We'll drink up and sit." Eckstein glanced at her name tag. "Sophia."

"And what is your name?" she asked.

"Anthony."

"A fine Italian name."

"My grandparents were from Napoli."

She looked surprised and terribly pleased, but another stewardess touched her elbow and she moved away.

"Napoli?" Baum mouthed as he frowned at his partner.

Eytan shrugged. "Munich. Napoli. Same neighborhood." He sipped his drink, immediately flipping back to the subject at hand.

"A photograph? Now why would the fool hand over his ace?"

"Maybe it's a partial," Benni speculated. "Obscured, or only half a face."

"Right," Eytan scoffed. "Maybe it's Lee Harvey Oswald's head on the body of a Hizbollah, holding an RPG and a copy of *Playboy*."

Benni laughed. This was the part of their work that kept sucking them back into the game, the impossible puzzles, the unsolved riddles, the Rubik's Cubes of unmatched clues and faces and snippets of codes that when properly swung together gave these men a rush beyond adrenaline and orgasm.

Benni's smile faded as he looked at his partner and remembered that these were the waning days of his career. After so many years at war, the adventures had begun to blend, too numerous to remember, some too unbelievable to accept as having actually transpired.

He had worked with hundreds of intelligence officers, yet this final partnership with Eckstein had been a near-perfect yin and yang. Yes, technically, he was the superior officer, but Benni's ordered, methodical approach seemed to require Eytan's impulsive instincts as catalyst now. It was more than colonel and major, not much less than father and son, yet Benni could never have worked this way with one of his own sons, ordered one of them to lay down his life if he had to. Still, it was inexplicable; they had done things for each other above and beyond. When Eytan had been wounded and nearly captured in Munich, Benni's only reflex had been to personally extract him. When Benni's Zodiac had been bullet-punctured and set afire, he went into the water nearly without a care, knowing that somehow Eytan's hand would soon reach out for him, his younger smile chastising the old man. He felt something swell in his heart, but combat officers did not speak of such things.

"I'm going to miss it," he said.

"No, you're not." Eytan jabbed the stem of his pipe at the colonel, who instinctively winced, given the implement's dual purpose. "You're going to go gentle into that good night. Just please don't be one of those old pathetic hacks who hang around the office."

"Well, what the hell *am* I going to do?"

"Go into business. Get rich. Write your memoirs."

"For whom?" Benni demanded just a bit too loudly. Former Israeli intelligence officers did not write memoirs, unless the book had a specific tactical purpose and the army censors had been ordered to lay off.

"For the *Ra'mach Hahistori.*" Eytan used a Hebrew acronym for the IDF historian, who worked in a secure library at General Headquarters and collected classified narratives from all the military branches.

"Now there's a literary graveyard."

"All right. So, you'll enjoy your kids," Eytan suggested.

Benni had two sons, one an air force pilot and the other a paratroop officer. His daughter, Ruth, had recently returned to New York to finish a combined master's–Ph.D. psychology program at Columbia University.

"Enjoy them?" Benni challenged. "They'll avoid me like the plague."

"Not Ruth," said Eytan. "I'll bet she comes home after school and joins the family business."

"Over my dead body," Benni growled, yet he suspected that Eytan was right and secretly wished it would be so. His beautiful daughter had been terribly wounded by his absences during her childhood, yet still she had served as an army field intelligence officer during her compulsory service. Soon afterward, a terrible rift had developed between them and she went off to America, but Benni had discovered that his genes were imbedded in her makeup. She was inexorably drawn to the dark profession, her graduate thesis an exploration of terrorist psychology, and during the recent hunt for German terrorist Martina Klump that fascination had nearly cost her her life.

"Oh, yes," Eytan warned. "She'll do it to you, all right. Pay you back in spades, with nasty tight smiles and innocent shrugs."

Benni sighed. Eytan was correct again; they had both witnessed the tradition. The children of intelligence officers were raised in houses full of secrets, with fathers who were professional liars, who missed birthdays and graduations while they ran around the world playing a game whose details they never shared. Quite often their children would grow up and follow in their footsteps, if for no other reason than to exact vengeance. Nothing could balloon the pride of a retired intelligence officer more, or wound him as deeply, as having a child return from an intelligence course or a field mission and gleefully squelch his curiosity. "Don't ask me a *thing*, Abba. I learned how to keep my mouth shut from *you*."

"Exquisite torture," Benni muttered.

"Count on it," said Eytan.

"And Oren?" Benni reminded Eytan that he faced the same dangers with his own son. "You think he'll be different?"

"Are you kidding? If Simona has her way, he'll be a draft dodger and an accountant."

Suddenly Sophia the stewardess was at Benni's elbow, a small crease between her black eyebrows.

"Your daughter," she said, and for a moment Benni wondered, then realized she was referring to Niki.

He and Eytan turned their attention to the rows of passengers. Between the bobbing heads of the European business travelers and the occasional Ethiopian, Niki was nowhere in sight. Her window seat was empty.

Sophia crooked a finger. Benni and Eytan set their drinks in the galley and followed her, squeezing past the rolling meal carts to the rear of the plane. There were four lavatories on their side of the aft section. Three of the folding doors were half open, while the fourth was locked, its IN USE panel glowing.

Sophia stood to one side, a look of pity on her face as Benni leaned one jug ear close to the door. Despite the heavy whine of the engines and the Babylonian chatter of the passengers, he could clearly hear Niki, coughing and vomiting violently into the chemical toilet.

He straightened up and smiled weakly at Sophia.

"The poor thing," he said. "She gets airsick. Ever since she was a young girl."

Sophia nodded sympathetically, then reached back into the aft galley, handed him a damp towlette, and slipped away.

Eytan looked at Benni, slowly shaking his head as the sounds of soft and miserable keening echoed from Niki's hiding place.

Airsick.

The jumbo jet had not yet bounced in a single pocket of turbulence. The flight was as smooth as glass.

6

Addis Ababa
May 2

IT WAS NOT the distant rattle of gunfire that disturbed Eckstein. It was far away and sounded rather like a desultory woodpecker, and although he might have hoped for cheerier omens upon arrival at Bole International, after Sarajevo it was about as worrisome as a head cold to a cancer patient.

The bloody dictator Mengistu was long gone, along with his Soviet armorers, Cuban advisers, and murderous East German–trained security apparatus. Meles Zenawi's provisional government appeared relatively stable, even though challenged by these sporadic attacks of the Oromo Liberation Front and the All Amhara People's Organization. And these gunmen were amateurs next to the professional terrorists of Eckstein's Middle East neighborhood, where the hard men of Islamic Jihad shot straight and true and the suicide bombers of Hamas regarded death as the only respectable outcome of any struggle.

And it was not the famine that unnerved him, still rampant in Ethiopia, yes, but it would not grossly affect Eckstein's stomach, only further wither his soul as witness. And it was not the beggars or the war cripples or the scores of children thin as desert scavenger dogs who, rather than waiting in front of Addis Ababa's government Ghion Hotel for a chance to con a newly arrived journalist, had adopted the tactic of drifting out to the airport in accordance with aircraft arrival schedules. If you were Caucasian, politically liberal, socially conscious, and a newcomer to Ethiopia, the malnourished tagalongs could play your heartstrings like a Stradivarius and empty your pockets of dollars and deutschmarks even before you changed them to birr.

But Eckstein had been here before, as had Baum, and their "Jewish guilt" was not so easily leveraged. Once you risk your life for even a small portion of a pauper population, your need to atone for your middle-class comforts is greatly diminished.

And it was not the climate that squinted Eckstein's eyes as he walked from the bullet-pocked terminal, although the sun was still high and hard in a blank sky and already he felt the challenge to his lungs from the altitude and dearth of oxygen. Ethiopia was a land of physical hardships and slim comforts, with constant risks from dysentery, giardia, malaria, typhoid, bilharzia, and meningitis, as well dangers from jackals both animal and human. Yet he was prepared for all of that and, in fact, hardly considered it.

What bothered Eckstein, and made him stand still for a moment while rapidly reevaluating *Operation Sorcerer*, was the appearance of his chauffeur.

There was a long line of battered taxis at curbside, waiting to earn a U.S. dollar for each of the five kilometers along the Bole Road into the city. Parked among them, and as oblivious to their honking as a battle tank, was a pine-green Land Rover, its lower half caked in red mud, its gray canvas roof laced with so many repair stitches that it looked like the scarred back of a shrapnel victim.

Leaning against the Land Rover's flank was a man whom Eckstein immediately thought to be a Belgian mercenary, and he sensed Baum's posture stiffen, a short intake of air as the colonel also assessed this unexpected equation. Ben-Zion had informed Baum that the trio would be "met," but both officers had pictured a local cab driver equivalent in height and weight to Niki, who now stood obliviously behind them, sipping from a bottle of Pellegrino provided by Alitalia.

The officers were accustomed to hiring their own vehicles while in the field, or, at worst, being escorted by an asset in place. Allowing the opposition to drive was poor operational practice. This man was clearly a hired gun, and the Israelis had not done the hiring.

It was not just the "lizard" camouflage jacket above a pair of black cargo trousers, nor the French MAT-49 submachine gun slung from the man's right shoulder, his thick fingers lightly tapping the pistol grip. His hair was short, reddish-blond, and thick, his wide face covered with sunburned European flesh that seemed double-thick armor from which a flat broken nose barely protruded. He wore a bristling mustache with Fu Manchu corners that nearly reached his jaw like prickly parentheses.

It was the eyes, ice-blue, flat, and scorched of all joy, that led Eckstein to the conclusion that this man had been in Africa too long, long after his government had gone home. And he had probably deserted— the Legion, or the French Regiment des Parachutistes, or the Belgian Commando—because what does a leopard do with himself in Paris or Brussels?

"Hearthstone," the man said very clearly while looking directly at Eckstein, though only his lips moved and there was no hint of decorum in his heavy Belgique accent.

Eckstein nodded. "And you are?"

"Debay, Michel."

Eckstein noted that he clipped it out military-style, the first name merely a suffix. And Debay was surely *not* his true name, though Eckstein was in no position to pass judgment, having attended so many past rendezvous where the first words from his and other men's mouths were always lies.

"*Enchanté.*" Benni Baum stepped forward, although atypically for him, he offered no handshake. "*Vous êtes Français?*"

Debay did not answer, but tapped his trigger grip again, raised his head slightly, and examined Niki Hašek from the crown of her head to the soles of her sneakers. It was not a sexual perusal at all, and he flicked open the door of the Land Rover, but did not hold it for anyone.

"*Belge.*" He finally answered Baum's inquiry.

Trouble, Eckstein decided as they all climbed into the vehicle.

Debay drove, his weapon tucked between his left thigh and his door panel, a blatant sign that he did not trust his passengers. Eckstein sat in the right seat, with Niki behind him and Baum behind Debay, but they had not yet passed the airport perimeter fence when the Belgian stopped the vehicle, turned, and offered something that was supposed to be a smile, its warmth defeated by two chipped teeth no doubt caused by a fist, a rock, or a rifle butt.

"Switch, please," he said to Baum, who immediately understood and complied as he nudged the confused Niki to reverse positions with him. No doubt the Belgian had garroted a victim or two from behind, and he could not drive comfortably unless a bull like Baum was fully visible in his rearview mirror.

From Bole there was only one way to access the rest of the country, and that was directly through the capital. So Eckstein braced himself for the impending assault on his senses, feeling some pity for Niki, who had arrived from exploded Slavic majesty, had a brief glimpse of sanity in Rome, and come straight here to starving African civil strife. He did not know where the Czech defector Krumlov had ensconced himself, but he assumed two facts:

It would *not* be in Addis Ababa, for although the capital was large and bustling, a sea of dark-toned African humanity was no place for a Slav from Prague to attempt to blend in. A team of similar-looking Russian killers would simply have to set up camp outside the ETC office on Jomo Kenyatta, wave Krumlov's photograph and a wad of birr, and they would shortly have a hundred teenage Ethiopian scouts combing the capital for their missing "friend." The second part of his thesis was that wherever Krumlov presently waited, it was a temporary location and nowhere near his base of operations or the fifty orphans in his "care." For all the Czech knew, the arriving Israelis had homing chips sewn into their shoes, the point men of a larger snatch team that would pounce as soon as he revealed himself. He was a professional intelligence officer, and the revelation of his goods for sale would be done with the seductive finesse of a seasoned stripper.

Eckstein rolled back the cuffs of his khaki epauleted shirt, folding them Israeli-style above the elbows. He was once more wearing Anthony Hearthstone's uniform, including blue jeans and a pair of canvas boots for the cooler air of the mountaintop capital. Baum was similarly dressed, although Hans-Dieter Schmidt—ostensibly a pharmaceutical marketer from Munich—did not wear jeans, but a pair of light-green twills. Niki, to no one's surprise, had remained in her mourning shades of black on black.

Eckstein cranked down his window, leaned an elbow there, and watched the city grow as Debay drove along Africa Avenue toward East Central Addis. He did not care for the city aesthetically. It was flat and sprawling, with few of its structures architecturally appealing, and it reminded him of Kuneitra, the disputed Syrian city on the Golan Heights where no one bothered to repair the shell-pocked buildings because eventually one side or the other would bomb the place back to rubble.

But being a closet romantic, he was fascinated by Third World cities, preferring them to ordered London or pristine Geneva. In Addis Ababa, the humanity was the attraction, for a circus without its performers is no more than a large tent. A fresh flock of war cripples had joined the throngs of ragged street urchins, half-naked beggars, wandering madmen, and hawking street vendors and taxi drivers, all verbally assaulting and exhorting the occasional foreigner, providing confusing diversions while the pickpockets dashed in and withdrew like blurs of hummingbirds. Yet the game of survival, despite its noisy fervor, was for the most part harmless and rarely violent, and despite his mood it made Eckstein smile.

He glanced over at Debay, who was honking the horn at a pair of old men taking their time as they crossed before the front fender and tapped their gnarled *dula* walking sticks. The Belgian's battered nose seemed upturned and wrinkled, and Eckstein assumed that like many of the white "hunters" who lived in Africa, he was an incurable racist. For a moment Eckstein played psychologist and analyzed the soldier of fortune with some silent guesses. Father—a drunken Brussels ironworker who had beaten him. Mother—a German-born whore who had walked out on them. Debay himself—a street kid who had turned to crime, chosen army fatigues rather than a prison coverall, and, ultimately insecure and full of self-loathing, had found a niche in the world where he could always feel superior.

Perhaps it was an unfair assessment. But Eckstein had met enough of such men to concoct this temporary résumé, though he would be happy to be proved wrong. If Debay did not actually refer to the Ethiopians as *keffirs,* he would be pleasantly surprised.

"Where are we headed?" Eckstein asked as they encroached even deeper toward the teaming marketplace called the Piazza. Pairs of soldiers of the Ethiopian People's Revolutionary Democratic Movement seemed to be manning each street corner, wearing their rankless fatigues and slinging corroded AK-47s. Some children played on the roadside carcass of a Russian T-62, the tank's turret completely inverted, like the severed head of a mosquito.

"Into the city," Debay finally answered.

"I can see that."

"Then north." The Belgian was as loquacious as Clint Eastwood in a spaghetti western.

Baum leaned forward in an effort to be friendly.

"Would you prefer to speak French?"

Debay shrugged. "It does not matter."

Because even though French is your native language, Eckstein thought derisively, *you're probably half-illiterate in that as well.* He looked long at the Belgian's profile, and eventually Debay felt his gaze and slowly turned his head. Their eyes locked and Eckstein, understanding the basic laws of wolf packs, held Debay's stare until the man had to return his attention to driving.

Eckstein glanced back at Baum, who raised an eyebrow, sat back in his seat, and openly jerked a thumb toward Niki. Turning fully the other way, Eckstein found her crunched up in the far corner of the rear seat, her legs tucked up under her, one foot twitching as she stared out the window. She was clutching her small diary and her heirloom fountain pen to her chest, and despite the tropical breeze wafting into the Land Rover, she looked cold and alone and somehow diminished.

He had seen that look before, and he remembered where, on the faces of the girl parachute riggers at the airborne school when they sat crammed in the belly of a C-130 en route to their first jump. It was pure animal terror, and it made no sense at all . . .

They broke out of the city on the Bahir Dar Road heading north, but for how far and how long only Debay would know. Eckstein had driven this way in his own rental jeep perhaps twenty times, and he knew that it led to Debre Markos—provisional capital of Gojam—as well as to Bahir Dar, the vast waters of Lake Tana, and Tis Abay, the spectacular waterfalls where the Blue Nile mimicked Niagara.

It was already growing dark as they climbed into the eucalyptus-swathed Intoto hills and the high moorlands, and as if in response to the growl of Eckstein's stomach, Debay produced a greasy paper bag from somewhere and dropped it on the seat between them. Inside were four bottles of Talla beer, a canteen of water, and a large slab of *injera*, the spongy Ethiopian pancake bread reminiscent of pita. Debay popped his own bottle of the warm weak beer, while Eckstein and Baum shared the water and torn slabs of the bread. Niki did not even respond to offers of sustenance.

A few pink wisps of the setting sun tinted the rolling grasslands and sprigs of heather, and then they were in total darkness, with only the Land Rover's headlamps reflecting off the cracked tarmac. Debay glanced at a Casio G-Shock watch—the sort of cheap but rugged time-piece a soldier can lose without remorse—and pushed the Land Rover hard, covering forty kilometers uphill in a bit over half an hour. Just before the large town of Chancho he took a left turn onto a wide dirt track, and Eckstein knew he was heading for Durba. But Durba was twenty kilometers on and there was virtually nothing there but a cement factory and a hundred-meter drop into Muga Gorge.

Debay suddenly hit the brakes, spewing up pebbles and a cloud of dust as Eckstein grabbed for a handhold and Baum grunted. Eight pairs of ruby eyes had suddenly appeared from the darkness ahead, and then four gelada baboons, replete with golden leonine manes, waved their black arms and screeched curses before leaping away into the night. For a moment Eckstein thought Debay might have a secret sentimental regard for the animal kingdom, but then he backed up a bit, spun the wheel, and nudged the Land Rover up a hill. He had simply missed his turn.

The small structure atop the promontory appeared in the glow of the vehicle lights. It was a square, two-story Ethiopian Orthodox church, hewn wholly of pink granite that appeared sallow in the wash of tungsten. A stone stairway led to a black doorway, and a row of windows were no more than chiseled Maltese-like crosses.

At one time there had been an ornate parapet of elegant turrets, but the building had served as cover during the sporadic battles for the Shewa province, and the turrets looked like broken teeth protruding from rotten gums. Such a church should have been off limits to night visitors, for the resident priest would guard his *tabot* with his life. This symbolic icon was a replica of one of the tablets given by God to Moses, the original tablet purportedly still resting within the Ark of the Covenant, which according to Ethiopian lore had been spirited from Jerusalem to Axum some centuries before Christ. Yet apparently this tabot and its guardian had moved to more hospitable quarters, for the entire roof of the church had been collapsed by an aerial bomb.

There was no one in sight as Debay killed the engine and switched off the lights. Half a moon had risen just above the mountains of Gojam, and the church turned to purple-gray.

"Hearthstone," said Debay as he placed the MAT-49 on his lap. "You come with me."

Baum made to open his rear door and the Belgian turned his head.

"Just Hearthstone."

Benni saw Eytan nod, and he sighed and closed the door.

Eckstein's rubber cleats crushed soft dust as he got out, looked at the church, and began to walk. But Debay stopped him with a hand on his shoulder, and Eckstein turned to face that sneer that passed for a smile.

"Une formalité," Debay said as he spread his arms as if to perform jumping jacks. Eckstein complied, stretching his own arms as Debay executed a rapid frisk from shirt collar to bootlaces, including the upper inside thighs and small of his back. Eckstein was glad that he had dropped his pipe into his rucksack, for he was sure that had Debay discovered it an ugly confrontation would have ensued.

"Okay," said the Belgian, and Eckstein caught a heavy whiff of onion. Then he turned and walked up the granite steps.

He blinked for a moment in utter darkness. Then a wooden match flared, someone turned the wick wheel of a hurricane lantern, and there in the flickering glow stood Jan Kumlov.

He was a tall and sturdy Czech of about forty-two, every one of his thick blond husky hairs still healthy in his scalp. His pale eyebrows and flat features reminded Eckstein of the late American actor Steve

McQueen, though without the merry glint and wry smile of Hollywood wealth. He wore a blue chambray shirt of the type favored by merchant seaman, scuffed black jeans, and heavy brown mountain boots. His lean form might have suggested an "aggravation diet" from his year on the run, yet he had a relaxed, easy, powerful energy exuding confidence, not flight. This, of course, instantly raised Eckstein's suspicions. Hunted men flick their heads around often, like newly licensed drivers. Eckstein was certain that this man never looked behind him.

The lantern was standing on a broken pillar and Krumlov turned the wick a bit higher, then stepped forward to get a better look at his visitor. Immediately Debay moved to a flanking position, respectfully to one side yet between the two men. He slung the MAT from his shoulder, yet regarded Eckstein like a suspicious referee eyeing a boxer with a foul reputation.

"I am Jan Krumlov." The accent was very smooth, as if he had studied in Montpelier rather than Moscow.

"Anthony Hearthstone."

Neither man yet moved to shake hands, although Krumlov placed his on his hips and smiled slightly, showing a row of perfect Colgate teeth.

"*Hearthstone?*" He examined Eckstein's surprisingly Aryan features. "Why not just use Smith? Since when does Jerusalem send a *goy* on such a mission?"

It was not the first time that Eckstein's semitic bona fides had been called into question, which was one of the reasons he had been recruited by AMAN in the first place.

"Don't judge a Jew by his cover," he said. "I'd drop my trousers for you, but we've only just met."

Krumlov laughed, though it was virtually silent mirth, his mouth open and his head just bobbing a little. Physically, he reminded Eckstein of himself, although considerably more handsome in the architecture of his facial features. As for his character, Eckstein hadn't a genuine clue, although every turncoat, just like any religious convert, was to be instantly suspect.

"I understand you have a photograph for me," Eckstein said.

Krumlov's amusement returned to a thin smile as he shook his head. "Ahhh, that Israeli reputation. No manners, all business."

Eckstein, utterly unapologetic, watched him. Krumlov looked past his shoulder.

"And where is my lovely Nikita?" He raised himself on his toes, fingers splayed outward.

"In the Land Rover with my partner."

"Partner?" Krumlov feigned surprise. "Not fair. Two against one." Then he looked over at his Belgian and chided himself. *"Tu m'excuse, mon ami."* He turned back to Eckstein. "I forgot. With Debay, I am a whole *platoon.*"

Debay did not smile, and neither did Eckstein.

"Please, please, *please.*" Krumlov rubbed his hands together. "I must see her!"

Eckstein chose not to jockey any further for position, and he walked to the door and waved, although after the glare of the lantern he could see nothing outside.

After what seemed like a long hesitation, Niki appeared in the doorway. Her eyes were very wide, the dilated pupils turning her irises to glistening black olives. Long streaks of fresh tears webbed her cheeks, and as Baum stepped up behind her his expression showed that no matter his age, he would never decipher the female of the species.

Eckstein moved aside as Krumlov took a large lunge backward and opened his arms. He shouted something in Czech, which included her name, and Niki closed her eyes and ran to him, still clutching her diary as he enveloped her, kissed the top of her small head over and over, and whispered into her hair as he rocked her.

Baum stepped up into the church and Eckstein watched the tension drain from his colonel's shoulders as he thrust his hands in his pockets and smiled. Benni looked at Eytan as he blew out a long breath of satisfaction.

One half of the deal was done. Package delivered.

Eckstein looked over at the embracing couple, aesthetically a fine pair, like a tall blond duke and his diminutive dark princess. For a moment he had a melancholy flash of himself and Simona in happier days when their reunions were similar. But of course Debay dispelled the illusion with his hovering just behind Krumlov.

Then all at once Niki withdrew from her lover, and Krumlov looked at her quizzically, like a dancer wondering if had trod on his partner's toe. Her right hand rose, her white knuckles vised around her precious black fountain pen, and as her thumb popped the top and the onyx tube went arcing up into the air, Eckstein saw it. A thick steel needle protruding from the pen, glistening in the light of the lantern, flashing as she drew her hand back behind her head for the strike.

Eytan lunged, hearing Benni grunt and knowing that the range was too far, yet he targeted her elbow as he launched himself in an explosion of hope that his speed might foil her kill.

But his effort was superfluous, as Debay was much faster.

The Belgian drew a nine-millimeter FN pistol from his waistband, dropped his wrist on Krumlov's shoulder, and shot Niki point-blank between the eyes.

PART TWO

MERCENARIES

●   ●   ●

White men's wars are fought on the edges of Africa—
you can carry a machine gun three hundred miles inland
from the sea and you are still on the edge of it.

—Beryl Markham,
West with the Night

7

WHEN THE SUN rose in the east above the mountains of Welo, you could not see Lake Tana from Durba, for although vaster than the Sea of Galilee, it lay far to the north behind a hundred peaks. Yet if you had been here before, its vision stained your soul like a Saharan oasis, and you could feel it, smell the mist curling from the endless burnished steel of flat water, see the pink flamingoes tiptoeing into cool lapping waves of dawn, sense the breeze sweeping the night mosquitos away as the tongues of leopards touched the pearly liquid.

Yet on this dawn the placid vision flitted only briefly through Eckstein's imagination and was gone, instantly replaced by simmering rage and the truth before his bloodshot eyes as he leaned outside against the cold rear wall of the church and smoked, watching.

On the rocky cap of the hill stood a lone, flat-topped acacia tree, its sharp black fingertips glowing red in the rising light. To the right, Debay's shirtless torso glistened as he filled Niki's fresh grave with an entrenching tool. The *chink, chink, chink* of the spade striking rock set Eckstein's teeth grinding, yet his black emotions were not directed at the Belgian, for much like a loyal rottweiler the man had only done what he was fed to do. There was a sense of quiet dignity in his motions, the caring of the soldier for his fallen enemy, the warrior's respect witnessed over and over in places like Gettysburg, Normandy,

Ammunition Hill, and Suez. There was no arrogance left in Eckstein's heart with which to judge the man, for once as a paratroop lieutenant in Lebanon his platoon had ambushed a pair of Palestinian terrorists, then dragged their bloating bodies to a village square and left them there as a warning.

But Jan Krumlov was another story altogether. He sat nearby on a large rock, his elbows on his knees, his fingers in his blond hair, watching Niki's grave as if she might spring from it at any moment like a magician's assistant. And although Eckstein was not sure why, all of his curdling fury was directed at the Czech defector, and he could not mobilize his feet to console him.

Benni Baum, always the more mature of the partnership, accepted the task instead. He came back from having urinated somewhere, stopped, look at Eckstein, and then at Krumlov's bent back. He squared his burly shoulders and went to him.

Krumlov did not look up as Baum squatted beside him on his haunches. Witnesses were usually surprised to see a portly, middle-aged colonel so limber, yet Baum could outrun boys half his age.

"I am sorry for your loss," he said, as if Niki had been taken by a rapid meningitis. He gazed out over the Shewa as the rising sun seemed to set the fringed hills ablaze and the reedy whistle of a shepherd's *washint* flute rose from a valley.

Krumlov raised his head, steepled his fingers together, and pressed them to his swollen lips.

"And I am sorry for your trouble." The Czech's voice was full of liquid, yet even in his shock he acknowledged the efforts of the two Israelis. He knew the game, knew what it was like to plan a dangerous mission, execute it, risk life and limb to bring the "trophy" home, and then discover it was useless, spoiled, smashed.

Yet for a moment, Baum thought that Krumlov meant the deal was off. Still, he spoke carefully.

"The amount of effort is irrelevant now. It was part of the arrangement."

Baum came up with a pack of cigarettes. This time they were du Maurier, for he was not partial to a particular brand and smoked any box that attracted his eye. He offered the burgundy pack to Krumlov, who declined by just briefly closing his eyes, as if he were a priest and the cigarettes pornography.

"The arrangement," said Krumlov, "has not changed."

Baum lit up, taking care to exhibit no outward relief. Krumlov flinched as Debay's shovel sparked against a slab of shale. The Belgian muttered something and carried on.

"At any rate," Krumlov sighed, "Niki's attempt should tell you that what I have is the real thing."

"It does," said Baum, although that was not wholly true.

"Yet, as a professional, you still have a hundred doubts."

"At least."

Krumlov nodded. Niki's journal was lying next to his foot and he picked it up. He sat up straighter, gathering some strength, and placed the notebook and his hands on his knees and looked at the Israeli.

"What is your name?"

"Schmidt." Baum glanced at the journal and quickly looked away, as if it was a woman's cleavage at a cocktail party.

"No. Your real name."

"I could give you another, but why force me to lie again?"

Krumlov pouted a bit, then picked up a pebble and flicked it from his thumb. He looked up as a large lammergeyer vulture wheeled overhead, then he watched the scavenger warily.

"I have given you *my* real name," he said.

"You had to, so we could run background on you. You knew that."

Krumlov shook his head, but the gesture was not argumentative, just melancholy.

"You see why I have tired of this nonsense?"

"Yes," said Baum. "Actually, I am about to retire myself. You can only do it for so long and then one day it hits you. So foolish. For what?" Benni could lie to match any man's sentiments and soul. In truth, he still loved it all and was only retiring because he owed it to his long-suffering wife, Maya. If it was up to him, he would die in the field of old age.

Krumlov suddenly turned to him, his eyes glistening.

"I knew she couldn't do it, Schmidt. In my heart, I knew it. She wanted to come along, to be with me, be a part of it. But even though she was young she was still old Soviet school. Do you know what I mean?"

Baum sighed and nodded. He was at his best playing father confessor, even though with some interrogations his Dracula worked better. Here he was a sponge for another man's torment.

"It's strange how it has seemed to skip generations," Krumlov continued. "First, you had the old-line Stalinists. Then there was my age group, the baby boomers of the Cold War, plodding along for the fun of it. And then we got this crop of children like Niki, searchers, fanatics for causes without hope."

Baum suppressed a painful smirk, thinking how some philosophical Israeli officers described their own security services similarly.

"It was all my fault," Krumlov confessed bitterly. "She was a fine professional. Not a field person, no, but a talented analyst. I thought I'd convinced her to follow my lead, go over with me, live happily ever after, you know? But I suppose once I was gone, she couldn't bear it. She must have told them and they turned her back. She has aging parents in Prague. Maybe they threatened them, blackmailed her into killing me. We still do that in our neck of the woods, you know."

God forgive us, we still do it in ours, too, Baum admitted silently.

"It was not your fault." The Israeli touched Krumlov's shoulder, but he gripped it just for a moment and withdrew. "If a man leaps from a sinking ship, and in the process offers to save another soul, and instead she tries to *drown* him, well . . ."

Krumlov looked at him, a thankful expression, then he plucked one of Baum's cigarettes from his pack. Baum lit it for him and the Czech eased some of his burden while the Israeli colonel recorded as much as he could in his brain and Debay went on burying Krumlov's past, and perhaps his future.

"As I am sure you know, I was with Czech Counterintelligence. Like your own GSS, or *Shabak*, as you call it. But you in Jerusalem, you are your own men, while *we* worked for the Russians, with the Russians, *around* the damned Russians . . ."

Krumlov was a career officer, a lieutenant colonel like Baum. They were his men who had crouched for a year in the gray water tower across from Vaclav Havel's office in Prague. It was an embarrassment to post professional officers 'round the clock to surveil a *playwright.* The man was already being published in thirty countries, about to "bring down the house" with pencil and notebook. What did those slabby Muscovites think? That he was broadcasting nuclear secrets on a shortwave? Either kill him or leave him be. You see, there was no dignity in the work anymore.

However, even as Czechoslovakia moved toward freedom from the Soviets and on to its "velvet divorce"—a split into two republics—there *were* things worth protecting. Commerce.

The mile-long ZTS plant in Martin still manufactured Soviet-designed T-72 tanks, mostly for the Syrians. With a purchase order for 250 of the steel dragons at over $1 million apiece, they were essential to the economy. Krumlov had an entire counterintelligence team working at the factory to guard the secrets of the technical gear. Not that anyone cared if the Syrians were incinerated inside their tanks, but the Americans and Israelis were constantly trying to penetrate the factory, and if the Arab customers discovered a breach they might cancel the contract.

When a Syrian delegation headed by an armored corps general came to inspect the assembly line, Krumlov had them all placed on seven by twenty-four surveillance. Not for fear that they might try to acquire Czech military secrets, but because the Damascus contingent was going on to a trade fair in Prague. The chief of the ZTS factory was an old Krumlov family friend, and he wanted to be sure to underbid any potential competition. This did not, of course, appear in Krumlov's reports to his superiors.

Satisfied with his shiny new tanks, the Syrian general went home and the delegation, now headed by a Colonel Faraj Salameh from Syrian Air Force Intelligence, carried on to Prague. Krumlov ran the surveillance operation himself, laying on photo reconnaissance and acoustic monitoring (the ZTS manager was about to endure the weddings of *two* daughters and could not afford to take chances with his livelihood).

It was there in the capital, late one night near the Charles Bridge, its promenade of sculpted saints dusted with snow and the waters of the Vltava below steaming with draining bathwater from the Old Town, that Colonel Salameh met the Israeli whom Krumlov would come to call "Bluebeard."

The two men walked and talked, and Krumlov, who had wandered out to his team after a late dinner with Niki, joined the chilly surveillance in a joyful indulgence of field nostalgia. Krumlov's team did not understand the conversation they recorded with long-range shotgun microphones, although they also shot ample infrared photographs and got the whole thing from handshake to *"Ciao."* Back at headquarters, the team was stunned to confirm Krumlov's guess, that the conversation was in Israeli *Hebrew*, the translator's eyes bugging behind his spectacles as he revealed that "Bluebeard" was an employee of the Israeli nuclear facility at Dimona, and that he was negotiating the sale of *blueprints*.

Much like Eckstein, and all professional intelligence officers, Krumlov had a distaste for turncoats. In the past, when they were Czechs, he had snatched them up and hurled them into cells like child molesters. Yet something clicked inside him then, the sure knowledge that for all his years of service the political winds would soon blow him into retirement with a pathetic pension and a "second" career as a newspaper vendor. And an idea surfaced, like the certainty coming upon a man whose wife has long denied him her bed, and suddenly there in his hotel room stands a buxom blond bar girl wearing nothing but a pearl choker.

Irreversible.

He immediately clamped a double Top Secret gag order on his team, the translator, and the acoustical enhancement technicians. He dragged a secretary and a legal clerk out of bed and made everyone sign the triplicate forms, stamped the file *Genesis*, and locked it in his safe.

He went home to his flat to think. For two hours he sat by an open window, smoking his grandfather's favorite pipe as a cold wind ruffled the white curtains, watching Prague dawn, a city devoid of any surviving Krumlovs but himself, smiling at Niki as she slept in the moonlight, her limbs occasionally jerking with fits and starts, wary even in her slumber.

And at the end of those two hours, Krumlov was nodding, although not with fatigue.

"It took me four months to make my move, Schmidt." Krumlov stabbed out the du Maurier on the toe of his own boot, as if wishing he were barefoot and could inflict pain on himself. "I knew I was going to do it, but I had to have proof, something hard to offer your people."

Baum's mind flicked back over the Czech's story. There was a large piece missing—his true motivation for defecting. A man does not forfeit his life and homeland due to dour speculations of a boring retirement.

"But you had photographs of Salameh and this 'Bluebeard,' as you call him," said Benni.

"I had photographs of Salameh meeting an *Israeli*," Krumlov corrected. "For all I knew, the man was a bankrupt Tel Aviv taxi driver trying to sell off blueprints of the new bus terminal."

Fair enough. The histories of worldwide intelligence services were replete with self-important "paper merchants," bogus spies trying to make a killing with worthless not-so-secrets.

"I wanted whatever proof Bluebeard was offering of his own bona fides. But I was not about to track him back to Be'er Sheva and toss his flat."

Wise move, thought Baum. *We would have had you at the airport.*

"Salameh was easier. Back and forth to Europe. He showed up in Prague again, picked up a dead drop from Bluebeard, and was silly enough to take the train to Vienna. And as the Americans say, *bingo*."

Baum instantly had an image of Krumlov chatting up the Syrian in the dining car, waiting for the precise moment when one of his Prague beauties stepped in for the diversion. There would have been at least three more personnel working the temporary switch of Salameh's briefcase for an identical one, performing a rapid "UPS"—an uncontested physical search—taking photographs in a train lavatory and then reversing the entire procedure. He wanted to scream, "So, show me what you have already, goddamn you!" But he kept his calm, superbly, for waiting well was the greatest asset of any good intelligence officer.

"So, I convinced her to come with me." Krumlov whispered now, staring again at Niki's dusty grave. "Or thought that I had." He dropped his head, a thick lock of blond hair drifting over his brow. "I suppose every betrayal has its price. But she was so young . . ."

His voice trailed off. Baum watched as Debay, having finished his grim task, folded up his entrenching tool. The Belgian swigged water from a canteen, then poured a puddle into his palm and smeared it over the muscle and red hair of his chest. There was a puckered bullet scar just to the left of his navel. He picked up his submachine gun, walked to Krumlov, stopped, and looked down at his employer, his eyes never taking in Baum at all.

"If you wish, Colonel," said Debay, pronouncing it *coh-loh-nelle.* "I will leave you the Land Rover. I can walk back to Addis."

Krumlov raised his head, a look of confusion.

"Addis? We are not going to Addis."

"*We*, Colonel?" Debay straightened his shoulders, his posture pure DeGaulle. "Do you wish me to stay with you?" He cocked his head toward the grave. "After this?"

Krumlov almost smiled.

"Ask the Jews, Michel." The Czech glanced at Baum, then back at his bodyguard. "In their tradition, if a man saves another man's life, he is responsible for that life forever. Isn't that correct, Schmidt?"

Benni had hoped for a moment that Debay might actually leave, but it was clear that the killing had only further bonded dog and master.

"Correct," he admitted.

"Fill up the petrol tank with the jerry can," Krumlov ordered the Belgian. "It's a long drive and I'd prefer not to stop."

Debay nearly saluted, but he just bobbed his head and went off.

"Another minute, please," Krumlov murmured, and Baum understood that he needed to make his peace with Niki.

Baum got up and walked back to the church, finding Eckstein still at his post, a pile of cigarette butts smeared around his boots like spent shell casings.

"Well?" Eckstein's tone was full of scorn. "Have you heard the whole fairytale?"

Baum raised a palm. Over the years, this gesture of patient father soothing the obstreperous son's temper had become tradition.

"Delicately, Eytan," Benni whispered. "The man has had a loss."

Eckstein blew out an exasperated lungful of sour air.

"All right," he said.

"We're all having a bad morning," said Baum.

"Right. Maybe we just need some coffee."

"Oh, yes. We're not jumpy enough."

Eytan almost smirked, but his anger smothered it. "So, what does he say?"

"Simple stuff. She was going along, but they turned her back on him."

"Right. And what do you think's in that journal of hers?"

"Love letters?"

"Sure." Eckstein, inherently a sentimental man, kept empathy at arm's length. "You tell me, Herr Schmidt. Why do you send a killer after a defector?"

"She was not a killer."

"Okay. An amateur with a kill order."

"To prevent the defection."

"Or?"

"To make a false defector look genuine." Benni patiently recited chapter and verse from the AMAN "manual" that was passed down verbally like tribal campfire legend through generations of officers.

"Right. So you arm-twist some nervous girl who you *know* isn't going to pull it off."

"But she nearly *did*, Mr. Hearthstone."

Eytan waved the notion away.

"Nearly doesn't count, and her handlers probably gambled that she'd fail, or knew that Krumlov was protected. Or for all we know Debay is one of them, too, part of the whole setup. Krumlov is selling us a bag of tricks. You think there was shellfish toxin in that needle? I'll bet it was saltwater."

Eckstein's vehemence was raising his voice, but suddenly he stopped talking. He was looking over Benni's shoulder, and Baum turned to see Debay standing down the hill below the church. The Belgian was beside the Land Rover, and in his left hand he held a wild rabbit aloft like a freshly caught trout. Where and how he had snared it, neither Baum nor Eckstein could guess, but the little animal was clearly dead and in Debay's other hand he held Niki's murderous fountain pen. He tossed the rabbit into the back of the vehicle.

Eckstein looked at Baum and blinked. "So? If I was right all the time, you couldn't feel so superior."

Baum smiled. "You might still be right. But they'll determine that on the other side."

Eckstein nodded. At times he forgot that his task as a military officer was to follow orders and let his commanders work out the conclusions and deal with the morality issues.

"Mr. Hearthstone."

Benni and Eytan turned to the sound of Krumlov's voice. He walked to them slowly from the oblong pile of earth and jagged rocks.

"I must thank you," said the Czech. "For attempting to save my life."

"It was reflex," Eytan said, too quickly.

"He is modest," said Benni, wanting to add, *and as impolite as an El Al stewardess.*

"Perhaps," said Krumlov. "Well, we should go."

Eytan put his fists on his hips, thoroughly disgusted with all the politesse on the heels of Niki's "murder." The image of her head snapping back with Debay's perfectly placed gunshot kept flicking before his eyes, and he knew he would hold Krumlov responsible no matter the outcome.

"I hate to bring up business," said Eckstein.

"Yes," said Krumlov as if reluctantly remembering a debt. "The photograph."

He lifted his chambray shirt, and there, tucked into his waistband, was a plastic envelope. He must have been keeping it there for a very long time, for the skin of his stomach was red and peeling in a roughly rectangular patch. He handed it over.

Eytan carefully tore the seal and removed a single glossy black-and-white photograph. Benni moved closer to him, and they both stared down at a posed portrait.

But it was not of a single individual. It was of *eleven* people, seven men and four women. They were clearly Israelis by their jeans and sandals and rolled-up shirt sleeves and Ray-Ban sunglasses hanging from neck lanyards, and there, fuzzy but unmistakable in the background, was the reactor dome of Dimona. They were some sort of technician team, on a lunch break no doubt, holding cans of Cokes and with greasy sandwich wrappers open on a nearby cement picnic table.

Almost comically, Baum and Eckstein looked up at Krumlov simultaneously. He smiled thinly.

"As you can see, that *is* Dimona."

Eckstein tasted bile in his throat, the anger welling up from deep within his bowels, and as he dropped his hands to his sides he felt them twitching, unsure whether to ball into fists or strike out like vise grips and tear out the man's glottis.

"Which man is it?" He demanded hoarsely.

"Or which woman?" Baum added. His sympathy had also expired.

Krumlov observed their tones turning from amity to adversarial, and he quickly became the cold professional again, his demeanor that of the big boy with the key to the toy chest.

"All in good time, gentlemen." He looked at Eckstein. "As Mr. Hearthstone said, we've only just met."

"*When?*" Eckstein asked through clenched teeth.

Krumlov shrugged. "Down the line a bit. Perhaps after some trust has been won, by both sides."

On the hill below the church, the Land Rover engine came to life and Krumlov turned toward the sound. Benni stopped the Czech with a hand on his elbow.

"You just thanked this man for risking his life for yours," he reminded as he cocked his head at Eytan. A vehicle door slammed, and they all knew it was Debay getting out of the Land Rover, having seen a hand on his master.

"Yes," Krumlov acknowledged. "But as he said, it was reflex."

"*When?*" Eytan demanded again.

Krumlov looked at Baum, then at Eckstein, his lips moving into an ironic smirk.

"When?" He thought for a moment. "Maybe I'll point out your mole, Mr. Hearthstone, when Schmidt here tells me his real name."

Eckstein and Baum exchanged looks. Eytan had not overheard the conversation between Benni and the defector, but he quickly guessed at the common banter between adversarial spies, and without speaking the partners performed the same calculations. Benni was retiring, Eytan was coming in from the field after this one. It didn't matter anymore, to hell with tradecraft. If they could have the mole's identity *right now*, then maybe it could be encoded and relayed to Jerusalem and within two days they'd have Krumlov and the falasha kids in the air and bound for Tel Aviv. Eckstein just blinked a "go ahead" to Baum. The colonel turned to Krumlov and took a long breath.

"It's Baum." Benni nearly choked as he said it, but he got it out even though it burned his throat like a regurgitation of lava. "My name is Lieutenant Colonel Benjamin Baum."

Krumlov smiled tightly and slowly shook his head, like a school-teacher scoffing at the prank of two clumsy students.

"As I said, Mr. Hearthstone. When Schmidt tells me his *real* name."

And he walked off to the Land Rover, leaving Eytan and Benni with mouths ajar, stunned to discover that the truth was the most worthless tool of their trade.

8

. . .

Amhara
May 3

THE WAY TO the Gojam province was very long, and very beautiful, and very silent. The Land Rover carried four men of such swollen personal histories that each could have regaled the rest with enthralling tales of a hundred adventures, yet the irony of such men is that, by nature and necessity, they are not raconteurs. And so, although forced to keep each other's company, they were distinctively apart, and alone.

As the sun climbed higher it burned the mountains and wadis once again, and the meager rains had not yet come to Ethiopia, so there were no quilts of sudden yellow wildflowers in the valleys, and the small bursts of trees and scrub on the craggy summits looked like singed hair on an old man's head. High above, the vultures wheeled in a merciless pewter sky and below from the steep ravines the boy shepherds coaxed their mules laden with piles of craggy sticks for firewood.

Eckstein had seen it all before, and saw none of it now, and he yearned to arrive at wherever they were going, to escape this bucking capsule so thick with thoughts that he could swear they formed a cloud to match the one of yellow dust that rolled in through the windows, kicked up by the Land Rover's large cleated tires.

Debay drove, his weapon near at hand, while Krumlov sat beside him, his fingers folded around Niki's journal between his knees as he stared through the gritty windshield, his entire posture cramped as if

143 . . .

he struggled to keep his emotions from bursting forth like a geyser. Eytan sat behind the Czech, with Benni next to him, and at one point they exchanged looks as Krumlov squeezed his eyes with thumb and forefinger, slumped a bit, and his back shuddered.

Debay glanced once at his master, then quickly looked away again as Krumlov wiped his eyes on his sleeve. The Belgian could kill a man, but to see one weep or offer him solace was another matter, and Eckstein cringed inwardly at the idea that these were the sorts of comradeships he had fallen upon in the waning days of his career. And suddenly he felt a terrible pain for Krumlov and his murdered love and a life and a past burned beyond recovery or recognition, for he remembered his own suffering after the death of Ettie Denziger, then imagined for an instant, with stunning fear, how he would feel if he lost Simona or Oren, and he swallowed hard and swept it away and spoke.

"Unless you've got another jerry can, Debay," he said to the driver, "or unless we're almost there, you're going to need petrol."

Eytan's voice, the first that had been heard in nearly an hour, snapped Krumlov from his mourning and he sat erect as if coming awake and looked at the gas gauge.

"Yes, Michel," he said hoarsely. "The station at Debre Markos."

"Fiche, I think, *mon colonel*," the Belgian corrected, and Eckstein was satisfied that at least the mercenary knew his way around the *weyna dega*, the rough highlands where amateurs could quickly find themselves without water or transport, hopelessly dehydrating beside a luxury vehicle with an empty gas tank and a blown-out radiator.

Fiche was the last stop for supplies before crossing the Blue Nile Gorge, a slash in the earth one kilometer deep and as wide as America's Grand Canyon. Crossing was done by way of a very slim roadway constructed by failed Italian conquerors on a series of viaducts, and not recommended for victims of vertigo. The descent, crossing of the Nile, and ascent into Gojam could often take three hours, and if your vehicle ran dry and you had the misfortune of being followed by an EPRDF convoy, the impatient troops would likely roll your downed steed over the side. They *might* let you get out first.

And so they stretched their legs at a roadside canteen in Fiche, and while Debay filled up the tank and his jerry can and checked the radi-

ator, Krumlov walked off to the edge of a precipice and squinted out over the cruel countryside. A gaggle of teenage boys immediately chased after him, shouting, *"Ato! Ato!"* But he lifted one hand in a gesture of regal dismissal, muttered, *"Hid,"* and they skulked away. His posture and his use of colloquial Amharic were apparently dissuasive.

For the first time in a long time, Eckstein's knee ached, and he concluded that the old wound had transformed itself into something of a soothsayer. Rather than reacting to changes in the weather, it inflamed in the presence of questionable circumstances. He did not mention it to Baum, but as the two men flanked an outdoor table of old railroad ties on oil drums and shared a bowl of *wat* and two warm cans of Pepsi, Eckstein remained standing, and Baum knew why.

Eytan looked around. They were alone, and he cocked his head toward Debay, now paying off the old canteen proprietor next to a rusty gas dispenser. The Belgian pulled a roll of antacid tablets from his pocket and popped two into his mouth. Eckstein had seen his stomach wounds. The medicine was not for nerves.

"Atah choshev sh'hoo hayachid? You think he's the only one?" he muttered in Hebrew.

Benni understood. Eytan was wondering if Krumlov had more such men in his employ.

"Not the only one," said Benni between mouthfuls of the thick, spicy stew. "There will be more gunslingers at the ranch."

"And what's Debay expecting at the end of all this?"

"Cash?" Baum shrugged. "Or maybe he also dreams of a life in the promised land."

"As what?" Eytan scoffed.

"A brigade commander?" Benni offered sarcastically. Tens of foreign soldiers came to Israel each year, some of them with considerable rank and experience, dreaming of leading battalions of Israeli troops like the flip side of T. E. Lawrence. They were always shocked to discover that they would be shipped off to a three-month Hebrew *ulpan* course and then start off as buck privates like every other conscript.

But Eckstein did not find this funny at all. Debay was a danger to the mission, and any man like him multiplied the risk. Since 1981 there had been no less than eight covert missions to extract Ethiopian

Jews, and all of them had considerable frameworks of AMAN officers, Mossad agents, naval commandos, or *sayeret* recon troops. With a flock of only fifty children, perhaps he and Benni could handle it alone, yet Krumlov's bodyguard contingent loomed as a potentially opposing equation.

Mercenaries were generally brutal men motivated by money. To neutralize them, you needed equally brutal men foolishly driven by idealism.

"We're going to need support," Eytan muttered.

"I know it," said Benni, and the Land Rover engine turned over and coughed, like a prison guard forbidding conspiratorial whispers among the inmates. Eytan and Benni strode to it without enthusiasm.

The blazing African sun was finally spent by the time the Land Rover crested its last rise in Gojam, yet still the mountains glowed like the tongs of a blacksmith, and the journey had taken its toll. Even Debay was sore throughout his warrior's physique, and the older bones of Krumlov, Baum, and Eckstein were bruised from a thousand jolts of the slamming undercarriage. Their shirts were stiff with dried sweat, their hair and eyebrows encrusted with dust like the frozen mustaches of arctic explorers, and the vehicle's windows had been thrown open to the roiling filth when at last no one could stand the stench. Yet when Krumlov's orphanage came into view, Benni, who was most pained despite the cushion of his girth, forgot his suffering and whispered, "Please stop."

The remains of an Emperor Fasil summer castle sprawled before them on a flat plateau of starving grass. The ancient stones formed a perfect horseshoe, with a pair of crumbling turreted fortresses bracing the mouth. From them, walled passageways led back to the body of the palace, whose quadrants were high towers capped by perfect granite domes.

The buttresses and slotted battlements had not survived a thousand years of weather and strife wholly intact, yet they retained their majesty, especially in a land of thatched roofs. But it was not the castle itself that mesmerized Baum, for he had seen much loftier cities of gold and emeralds. It was the barbed wire, rows of it in concertina girding the horseshoe like seaweed washed upon the Belgian gates of Normandy, and the pull-aside gate of razor wire, and the crackling campfires, not for pots of stew but only weak soups and sallow teas, and mostly for burning infested rags of the newly dead, the sweet stench of toasted sweat drifting over the castle walls.

And it was the rutted ground imprinted with the bare heel marks of small feet, the distant clicks and whistles of children playing in a graveyard, the *punt, punt* of an old threadbare soccer ball being kicked by scabbed toes salved with motor oil for want of iodine. And most of all, it was the armed men at the wire, their sun-slickened faces gleaming under cocked berets, their camouflaged sleeves rolled to the elbows and sinewed arms rippling over assault rifles.

And for the briefest moment, but for oh so long, he was a child again on Cyprus after the war, in a British internment camp, his father dead and his mother gasping to the frightening chorus of others succumbing to the cholera, and other children fading quickly as he looked on and wondered when, if ever, freedom, while the British paras scowled and dreamed of Southampton and suns of home.

And in that instant Baum knew, as Eckstein already did, that this was not about Krumlov or the hide-and-seek of a duplicitous mole. It was about children, and when the first pair of hungry eyes fell on him, the objective would be clear, his and Eckstein's fates sealed.

Debay, who had stopped the Land Rover at Baum's request, turned to look at the Israeli colonel, who was leaning forward and squinting through the filthy windshield at the savage reincarnation of his past. Baum hardly breathed. "All right," he finally said, and Debay put the machine in gear, and as the vehicle rolled forward again, Eytan touched Benni's shoulder.

A very large young man in a leopard camouflage smock dragged aside a coil of concertina and the Land Rover trundled into the compound. Immediately a small cloud of burry-headed children in worn shorts and T-shirts swarmed toward the truck, and it rattled with their tapping fingers on the windows. Their noses smeared the dusty glass, their fevered eyes peered inside, yet seeing no fresh boxes of supplies they just as quickly fluttered away like a flock of disappointed pigeons.

Debay opened his door and hopped down while his passengers painfully unfolded themselves from the vehicle, and even as Baum and Eckstein squinted to take in their surroundings, the sun breathed its last gasp and Krumlov's orphanage faded beneath an instant curtain of royal blue night. Now the scattered fires bathed the compound in flickering yellow light, but Eckstein could still pick out the forms of those that had succumbed that very day, small heaps covered in empty burlap provision sacks, and more than anything he wanted just to sleep now and face the misery on another day.

"Herr Colonel." The large young gate guard was offering Krumlov a ragged salute and a strangely warm smile, given the environment. Krumlov nodded at him.

"Bernd." He returned the greeting. "How many today?"

"Only sree." The guard offered the casualty count in a heavy Berliner accent. "We will bury them tonight."

Benni looked at Krumlov. "At that rate, your fifty children will be only a handful by the time we get them out."

"Fifty?" The large German mercenary almost laughed. "We have well over seventy here, and more come even as these die."

Eckstein gnashed his teeth as he stared at Krumlov. Their relationship had begun badly enough, but now it was clear that the Czech was a truth-twister of the first order. But then again, what else could spies expect of each other?

"When I first made contact, it *was* fifty." Krumlov shrugged. "I do not control the suffering in Africa. Your God does that."

"Our God is clearly an absentee landlord," Benni muttered as he looked around. He and Eytan shared the same cynical sentiments regarding religion. Their patriotic fervor had little to do with Judaism.

"You are the Israelis, then?" Bernd asked with a touch of childish wonder, as if he was meeting film stars. Eckstein noticed that he was slinging an Uzi submachine gun, a standard of the Bundeswehr. He also noted that field security was a misnomer here; his and Benni's covers had been blown before they had even set foot in the mission area.

"*Ich heise Schmidt.*" Benni introduced himself in Bavarian, which furrowed Bernd's brow.

"Hearthstone," Eytan offered curtly. Bernd nodded as if trying not to click his heels.

"And I'm Manchester." The small knot of men turned to a new voice. Another armed man had appeared from the dark, and he walked directly to Bernd and stood beside him. He was short and muscular, with a bristly mustache, a jauntily cocked maroon beret, and a British para smock caked with dust. A Sterling submachine gun was slung over his back and he held a burning Rothmann in his fingers, Bogart-style. He saluted in that stiff-palmed, springy gesture common to the Brits. "Andrew Manchester, formerly sergeant major in the employ of Her Majesty's Two Para." He dropped his hand and grinned a grin that almost made the Israelis squint. "Presently in the employ of question-able intellects."

Manchester looked up at his partner, Bernd smiled down at him. "And for some reason," the Englishman said, "people refer to us two chaps as Frick and Frack."

Eckstein caught Debay's disapproving frown at the antics of these two men, and he and Baum quickly recalculated their first impressions of Krumlov's hired killers. It appeared that the "opposition" might not be as drastic as they'd anticipated.

"A pleasure," said Eytan.

"We're hardly that, sir," Manchester retorted. "But we are endurable."

Eytan managed a smirk, while Manchester came to his tiptoes and peered over at the Land Rover's windows expectantly. "And where, pray tell, is the missus?" He looked over at Krumlov with a mischie-vous glint in his eyes. Apparently the entire camp had been expecting the arrival of Niki Hašek. "We've got the party hats and horns . . ."

The British merc stopped in mid-sentence, seeing the flat pallor that washed over Krumlov's face and the way Debay cleared his throat and looked away toward the fires of the compound. A profound stillness engulfed the group, and while Eckstein did not feel it was his responsi-bility to comfort anyone, Baum chose to defuse the moment and leave the full explanations to those responsible.

"She did not make it," he said.

Manchester and Bernd glanced at each other, but the Brit decided that Niki had simply stood Krumlov up. Nothing less predictable nor more harmful than a female whim. "Bloody women," he grumbled.

Debay hefted his submachine gun and walked off into the darkness of the compound. Krumlov watched him, then turned his gaze to his own boots. Manchester, clearly uncomfortable with the pitfalls of male-female strife, quickly changed the subject and jerked a thumb toward the entrance gate of razor wire.

"Colonel," he said to Krumlov, "that bleeding Feldheim hasn't brought in the foodstuffs or the meds."

Krumlov frowned. "He was supposed to be here yesterday, Andrew. Has he made contact?"

"He is down at the U.N. checkpoint," said Bernd. "Probably drinking a lager and munching *Sacher torte*."

"The prick," Manchester added. Eckstein and Baum turned to Krumlov for an explanation.

"Rolf Feldheim," said the Czech. "The United Nations commander in these provinces, an Austrian bastard of the first order. He is supposed to supply us regularly, but we often have to bribe him."

"With what?" Eckstein asked.

"With whatever my good men can steal." Krumlov cocked his head at Bernd and Manchester.

"It's a Robin Hood thing." Manchester shrugged without apology.

"He wants you to come down there, Herr Colonel," said Bernd with a tone of resentment that anyone should order his master about.

"As soon as you arrive, he said," Manchester added. "But just say the word, Colonel, and we'll go down there and shoot that Nazi wanker and take everything he's got."

"Please, Andrew." Krumlov raised a palm. "Your loyalty is appreciated, but an act like that would be our last in this country. It is Feldheim's game board, we must play by his rules." The Czech turned to the huge German. "Bernd, go fetch Debay before he drinks himself into a stupor. I'll wait for him outside the gate."

The German nodded and went off to find the Belgian, while Manchester moved to drag aside the concertina. Krumlov pulled himself up into the Land Rover and turned it over, then spoke to Eckstein and Baum before he shut the door.

"I will return soon. You should get to know the children." He turned the heavy vehicle around and rolled it out of the compound, while Debay came trotting across the dark dust and hopped into the Land Rover as it roared off and down into an invisible valley.

Baum and Eckstein looked at each other, then off across the miserable compound of silent death interspersed with trickling laughter. "That's the last thing I want to do," said Eckstein.

Baum understood too well, but he lifted his gear bag and jutted his large jaw toward the main edifice of the castle hulking at the horseshoe's head in the dark. "Come," he said. "We'll set up and take a head count, fluid as that may be."

"All right," Eckstein sighed and also hefted his bag. "Then we should break out a map, draw up a rough plan, and think about contacting Ben-Zion."

"Fine." Benni smiled. "But let's wait until we can wake the bastard from a wet dream."

Eytan expelled a short laugh and the pair began to walk, but they immediately stopped in their tracks as some sort of ghostly vision appeared from out of the darkness.

Was it a woman, or a witch? Was she real, or a mirage born of the day's heat and lack of sustenance?

She was well over two meters in height and her long black hair sprang over the shoulders of a white shroud as she emerged from the shadows. She appeared to be floating above the ground, although her gait was staggering, as if she were impaired somehow, and her teeth flashed in the flickering firelight and a small cloud of the starving children surrounded her and ran with her and laughed as they darted like minnows.

Both Eckstein's and Baum's mouths were open, as at first they each thought of some biblical spirit. And then, as she spotted them and stopped, they nearly blushed with their foolishness. The woman was walking on some sort of makeshift stilts, like a circus clown, her billowing soiled sheet covering the sticks and offering the illusion of antigravity. She hopped down, gathered the stilts like crutches, swept off the sheet, and looked at the Israelis. The children scattered away as she approached.

"Bonsoir," she said, and seeing the stunned expressions of the two strangers, she switched to English. "Are you the two new men?"

"Babes in the woods," Eckstein heard himself whisper.

"Pardon?" Her brow furrowed as she stepped closer, now at her normal height, somewhat shorter than Baum. She had a wide forehead

from which her thick hair was swept back and behind small ears, and her black eyebrows were arched above glistening blue eyes, a very small nose, and bow lips unenhanced by any makeup. She wore an overlarge Sorbonne sweatshirt above scuffed blue jeans and running shoes that had been white long ago. There was no telling about her figure, for the clothes seemed to belong to someone else, someone much larger, but her arms were slim and her hands very small.

"Yes, we are the new men," said Baum. "Schmidt and Hearthstone."

"It sounds like a Swiss bank." She smiled, showing very white teeth, then quickly tucked the smile away as if it was only a cool handshake. "I am Dominique Forelle." Her French accent carried a heat of its own. She looked around past Eckstein and Baum at the concertina gate now guarded again by Bernd and Manchester, then glanced down at the tire ruts left by the Land Rover. "Where is Jan?"

"He had to go to a rendezvous," said Eckstein.

This seemed to confuse the young Frenchwoman further. "And Nikita?" She lifted one palm. "Where is she?"

Once again Baum and Eckstein were caught in a quandary, unable to decide whether to tell the truth or leave that to Krumlov himself. It was clear that this strange assortment of foreigners was intertwined in almost a familial way, and with Niki's death the Israelis felt like intruders at a wake. Eckstein sighed and looked at Dominique, her natural beauty making her seem out of place in this camp of hard men and suffering children. Was she Krumlov's niece? An associate from his espionage past? A sometime lover, willing to step aside as his true love returned?

"I am a nurse," she said as if responding to Eckstein's private speculations. "Jan recruited me from Doctors Without Borders."

"What a coincidence," Eckstein muttered.

"Niki will not be coming," said Baum, yet he offered nothing further.

"Oh, *mon Dieu.*" Dominique put a hand to her mouth. "The poor man. Jan was so excited . . ."

Niki's demise suddenly hurled Eckstein into a darker despair, as he understood that Krumlov's mourning was even more genuine, and the Czech's ability to forgive Debay even more stunning.

"Itegue Dominique! Itegue Dominique!" A child's voice cried out

from the darkness, intriguing Eckstein further, as the Amharic title means "Empress." A pair of small hands flung themselves around her legs and she smiled and turned as the head of young boy peeked out from behind her. She sank her fingers into the short bristle of his scalp.

"This is Addisu Mangasha," said Dominique. The boy's saucer eyes peered from behind her baggy jeans. "We call him Adi." He slipped his small form from cover and Eckstein took in a breath, knowing that Baum was also trying to suppress a similar pang.

Addisu Mangasha was the African shadow of Eckstein's own son, Oren, a thin frame of featherweight bones who could just as well have been Eckstein's offspring, barring genes and a thousand years of unnatural selection. For in truth, the Ethiopian Jews, whether or not the lost biblical tribe of legend, were certainly closer in color and culture to the ancient Israelites than any sabra such as Eckstein, his blood thinned and flesh blanched by centuries of European winters and the occasional Nordic rape.

Eckstein knew immediately that at first his combatant's instincts would attempt to keep him distant from Adi. He had learned from operational years that to get close was to lose focus. When you went in to extract an agent or an asset, you viewed that human as fragile cargo and nothing more. Like a heart in a freeze box slated for transplant, just get it on the plane. Don't love it, for God's sake.

But Eckstein was aging, preparing himself for his own "extraction" from the Service, and that hard border of professional detachment was beginning to blur. You kept your heart hard for the sake of your career, your future, your next mission. Now, in the twilight of that career, he was surrendering to the thaw.

"This is Mr. Hearthstone, Adi," said Dominique. "And Mr. Schmidt."

Adi's gaze remained fixed on Eytan.

"How old is he?" Eckstein asked, trying to think of the boy as nothing more than another sheep in the flock.

"He is eight."

As if to confirm this, Adi held up four fingers of each hand. He had the body of a five- or six-year-old boy. He wore frayed, cut-off jean shorts, a baggy pair donated by some relief worker, scrunched at his nothing waist with a bootlace. Above that was an incongruous T-shirt sporting the logo for a nonexistent Hard Rock Cafe—Jerusalem. On his feet, rubber sandals cut from a tire. His head was shaved close to bald, his face all eyes, huge and round like one of those kitsch paintings of tearful chidren on velvet. He had milk-white teeth, and Eckstein wondered how he kept them.

"He is a Mura," Dominique added, and Adi frowned when he heard the word.

During *Operation Solomon*, in preparation for that mission, census takers had first roamed Ethiopia, noting the families of Jewish descent in towns and villages far and wide. These became the selected 14,000, members of *Beta Yisrael*—The House of Israel.

But there were other Ethiopian Jews, descendants of the Beta who had converted or assimilated. In their own eyes they had every right to join the exodus, but *Solomon* had to draw a line, a cutoff point. They were the *Falasha Mura*, and for the time being, they were left waiting at the gates of paradise in African purgatory.

"His parents died in Gondar during the rebellion," Dominque explained as she petted the boy's head. "He was raised by his grand-parents. They were selected for the airlifts, but as you know, only the children of Beta were allowed on." Her eyes darkened, as if she collectively accused Eckstein and Baum of collusion in this misery. "No grandchildren."

Eckstein knew these stories too well. Adi had been left behind with a promise, "You're next."

"Next" had not come, not in two years, but apparently Adi's fixed gaze upon Eckstein was the assessment of a hopeful heart, and the boy knew. This man was here to take Adi to the Promised Land and back to the bosom of his family. The tall blond man with the ponytail looked like the Israeli Jews he remembered. Perhaps Eckstein's cover could fool a hundred adults of intentions pure or perverse, but not Adi.

He suddenly stepped from behind Dominique, marched right up to "Anthony Hearthstone," grinned widely, and stuck out a hand as thin as the paw of a rhesus monkey.

"Shalom!" he croaked drily.

Eckstein stared at the wide, glistening eyes while Benni Baum burst into laughter.

"And hullo to you, too," Eckstein managed as he gently clasped the boy's hand, afraid that it might snap. Adi smiled even more broadly.

"That is a lovely British accent." Dominique regarded Eckstein as if he was an immature teenager. "But I somehow think it is practiced."

Eytan was thankful for the darkness, as he felt the heat of a blush rising, yet the night failed to protect him from Dominique's intensity as she stepped closer and looked up into his face, searching his eyes.

"I have prayed for someone to come and save these children, Mr. Hearthstone. Someone to lead them from this wilderness to a better place." Her eyes glistened and her lips nearly trembled with emotion, and Eckstein wanted to look away but he could not. "I have hoped for a Moses," she said. "Are you, perhaps, that man?"

Eckstein fumbled for a glib reply, yet without another word, Dominique took Adi's fingers and strode off toward the castle. Adi kept glancing back over his shoulder and grinning until the pair was engulfed in shadow.

Eckstein expelled a long breath and Baum said nothing for a moment. Having worked together for so long, they no longer needed to verbalize their obvious and similar reactions in the field. Their silent thoughts were broken by Manchester's voice.

"She's a bloody enigma, wrapped in a mystery, and the London *Times* crossword's easier to figure out."

The Israelis turned to the Englishman, whose face was aglow in the spark of another cigarette.

"Every chap goes soft on her at first," the Brit continued wistfully. "And you can see why. But she's not for any man. At least, not for any *living* man."

Eckstein frowned. "There's a puzzle right there, Mr. Manchester. Care to decode?"

"Please, sir. Just call me Andrew, or Sergeant, if you're feeling sociable." Baum smiled, liking the burly little Brit even more. Manchester jutted his chin off after Dominique. "Colonel Krumlov knew her from before. But he warned us when he brought her in. She's very professional, and very, very untouchable. Something to do with a once-in-a-lifetime love in gay *Paris.*"

Eckstein nodded. He had known a few men and women for whom one lost love was all they ever needed or wanted. They could survive the rest of their lives on a memory, taking sustenance only from their sated hearts.

"Don't have the details, mind you. But I can say it's a bleeding waste. Saw her once bathing down at Lake Tana . . ." The mercenary raised one hand as if swearing on a bible. "I was on sentry duty, chaps." He grinned mischievously. "Only doing my job."

"Of course," said Baum.

"Don't know how she does it," said Manchester.

"Does what?" Eckstein asked.

"Keeps those feeble little things alive." The Brit plucked his cigarette from his mouth and swept a gesture over the camp, making red arcs in the night. "Most of the time she can't get any medical supplies, and the food's hardly a few sacks of grain. I think the survivors carry on for her smile, like they don't want to snuff it and let her down."

Eckstein turned to look after the departed Dominique, wondering as well, but just then the roar of a vehicle engine echoed from the valley. Manchester immediately unslung his Sterling, cocked it, and strode quickly toward the concertina. Headlights glowed up from below the plateau and Bernd's silhouette also readied his Uzi.

The Land Rover reappeared at the gate and the mercenary pair reslung their weapons, hauling the razor wire aside. It stopped just before Baum and Eckstein, who shielded their eyes from the headlight glare until Debay doused the engine. Krumlov climbed wearily from the cab and walked to the Israelis. He was smoking and his face was haggard and drawn.

"I'll see him indicted for war crimes one day," the Czech growled.

"Feldheim?" Baum surmised.

"Uncooperative?" Eckstein's voice dripped sarcasm, for he harbored a special disdain for all members of the United Nations. "I'm stunned."

"Worse." Krumlov threw his cigarette to the ground and crushed it as if the U.N. officer were under his boot. "He won't hand over the supplies, but he blames it on Amin Mobote."

Baum and Eckstein exchanged looks at the mention of the warlord who had nearly foiled their most recent mission to rescue Ethiopian Jews.

"Claims he can't get a convoy through unless Mobote approves it. And of course, Mobote won't approve it unless he gets a hefty payoff from you." Krumlov looked directly at Baum.

"From me?" Baum touched his own chest, then patted his pockets. "I assure you, my salary would only make him laugh."

"From your government." Krumlov failed to smile.

"How much?" Eckstein asked, though his tone was full of suspicion. He was sure that this Rolf Feldheim intended to pocket a percentage of any such arrangement, but he would not be surprised if Krumlov would also benefit somehow.

"One million," Krumlov sighed. "U.S. dollars."

"A *million*?" Benni's eyes bugged. "For a truckload of rice and antibiotics?"

"And safe passage."

"Ahh, there's the rub," said Eckstein without humor. "We pay them off and they don't kill us all on the way to an extraction point."

Krumlov nodded, but he only glanced briefly at Eckstein, then looked off across the encampment. "I assure you, these children will not survive any journey of significance."

"And I assure *you*," Baum retorted, "that our superiors will not be blackmailed by some terrorist fringe."

"Well," Krumlov shrugged. "They will need food and supplies and treatments." He folded his arms and regarded the two Israelis with a challenge. "If you must go the hard way, then the mission is entirely up to you."

Baum and Eckstein looked long and hard at the Czech, then at each other.

"It always is," Eckstein offered.

"So what else is new?" Baum concurred, and he clapped Eckstein on the shoulder.

They lifted their gear bags and headed off toward one of the campfires, where they would forgo sleep, confer long into the early hours, and make a plan . . .

9

*   *   *

Bahir Dar
May 4

MAJOR ROLF GERHARD Fedlheim cursed the year of his birth, for
he had come into this world ten years after the Third Reich ceased to
exist.

His father had been an *Oberst* in the Waffen SS, his uncle a deco-
rated Luftwaffe ME-109 pilot, and little Rolf was raised on the laps of
nostalgic veterans drinking lagers in Viennese *gasthäuser* and whisper-
ing about the glories stolen by the Allies and Jews. As he grew, it
became clear that neither the German nor Austrian armies would be
allowed to recover their destinies and once more rape Europe or lay
waste to Russia—at least not in this century. Yet Rolf nurtured the fantasy that perhaps, if he was patient, he too would one day command a
battalion of *panzer* striking across the burning fields of Poland. And so
he studied well in *Gymnasium*, was a star student of history, strutted to
right-wing political party meetings, and quit university in favor of
officer's bars in the Austrian army.

However, no matter how much Rolf prayed to the spirit of Wagner
for one more glorious struggle, said test of Teutonic manhood never
did present itself, and he became an embittered commander of a border infantry battalion, defending the southern Hungarian line against
God knew what. In the late twentieth century, the closest an Austrian
officer could come to combat was serving with the United Nations

peacekeeping forces in various hot spots of the world, and Rolf was forced to sit on the sidelines in his blue helmet and snow-white command car, watching Third World natives spill each other's blood in Lebanon, Yugoslavia, and Afghanistan. In twenty years of service, he had never fired a shot in anger, and had barely chambered a round in self-defense.

His ancestors would *not* have been proud of him. For while they had become genuine war heroes, ultimately the embittered young Feldheim had become a thief.

Africa was the siren call to his darker spirit, a ravaged continent where demand was a flood and supply a trickle, a place where an officer on a pathetic salary could increase his own personal coffers with no more than the nod of his head. U.N. relief crates tumbled off the cargo ramps of supply aircraft, but they rarely made it to designated storage houses for proper and equitable distribution. A hundred representatives of village mayors, overworked hospitals, and refugee camps qeued up daily to receive their meager share, but between each bag of rice and a hungry mouth stood Major Feldheim, and his sense of charity was linked directly to his wallet.

Feldheim, of course, was self-delusional regarding his chosen role as a corrupt relief broker. Such was the game played out around the world where famine was rife and pragmatic men held the cards. He simply viewed the process as Darwinian, with those who had the means to effect their survival most worthy of it, while he certainly deserved to draw a certain "combat pay," given that neither the U.N. nor the Austrian government sufficiently compensated an officer for living in this black hellhole. The association he had struck up with the Oromo warlord Amin Mobote was merely an extension of his pragmatism. Mobote would provide the opportunity to make a killing, so that finally Feldheim could go home, muster out of his ersatz army, retire to a villa in Salzburg, and dabble in something harmless, like the illicit art trade.

At the southern side of the Bahir Dar Airport terminal, the sun beat mercilessly on the walls of Feldheim's white Quonset hut, making the corrugated steel painful to the touch and the air inside a burden to breathe. There was an air conditioner that could be powered off a gasoline generator, but Feldheim preferred the windows thrown open to the hot wind and the roar of aircraft engines and the whine of mules braying. He enjoyed his perch at a large metal desk, the sweat stains in the armpits of his khaki blouse, the small fan blowing cigarette smoke into his squint. He liked his post, for it fulfilled his fantasies of Tunisia after Rommel had cut an armored swath across North Africa.

The airport was a small oasis of semimodern technology amidst a desert of barefoot natives, mule-drawn carts, and Chinese bicycles. It stood removed from the town at the end of a ten-kilometer dirt road, still rutted with shell craters, the occasional burned-out hulk of a Russian-made BMP, and clusters of huge blue-headed vultures who flapped their wings and seemed to gossip as they tore the parched flesh from brown cow carcasses. The Ethiopian Airways flights were still irregular, so the military held the field, and barely disguised Russian pilots and mechanics shimmered like ghosts as they trotted across the melting tarmac to service MiG fighters and Hind helicopters.

Outside the rust-red door of Feldheim's hut a long line of customers wound across the dust, along one thinly shaded wall of the terminal, and out into the weather-cracked parking lot. They carried empty burlap sacks or wide woven baskets of red and yellow and green straw, and the lucky ones had pack mules in tow and there was even one pair of donkeys bridled to a wooden cart. The Ethiopians waited well and patiently and in silence, flicking the green bottle flies from their eyes. Some of them had walked as many as a hundred kilometers through the Gojam province, and not one of them wore a pair of shoes.

"*Yigbu,*" Feldheim called out from inside the hut.

The door opened and a tall woman slipped inside, bending to remove her head basket as large as a wash tub. She was draped in a muslin smock from her neck to her knees, cinched with a purple rope at the waist. Her hair was a cap of ink-black ringlets, her wide eyes and long lashes set into aquiline Ethiopian features, her skin like unmarred chocolate butter.

Feldheim looked up from his desktop, his expression unchanging from that of the patient bureaucrat.

"*Tenestalegn,*" he greeted her.

"*Selam.*" She dipped her head.

He placed his burning cigarette in a metal ashtray and slightly flared his nostrils to take in her wild scent of pure dried sweat. The glow of her mahogany skin set the flesh of his inner thighs tingling.

"Please." He gestured at a metal chair. The woman shyly laced her fingers behind her back and declined by looking at the floor.

Feldheim smiled at her subservience. The Austrian was decidedly non-Aryan in appearance, his black hair and brows giving him a nearly Mediterranean look, which most probably fueled his disdain for those of color. He examined the woman from her toes to her throat.

Once a month, he would fly down to Addis and indulge himself in the prostitutes at the Hard Luck Café. The most beautiful whores in all of Africa sold their wares there, and you could have yourself a Nordic blonde or a flame-red Circassian, but the major always favored a pair of local stunners who shunned soap. Their pungent bodies inflated his lust as he imagined himself a powerful slave owner in colonial America.

"What is your request?"

The woman produced a flimsy sheet of wrinkled paper and set it on the desk. Feldheim opened it, reading the careful English script from the *alaka*, the village elder of Dengel Ber.

"Three bags of rice, one of maize?" Feldheim inquired.

"Yes, please." The woman nodded.

Such bags were very heavy, fifteen kilos apiece, but Feldheim had no doubt that she would carry them in her head basket without complaint. She had a powerful, sinewy neck. He liked strong necks. He liked to grip them from behind.

"Do you have the release fee?"

"Excuse me?" A furrow formed between the woman's eyebrows.

"The *asrat*." The word meant "agricultural tax," an ugly term from the days of the fiefdoms. "It is twenty birr, five birr per bag."

The woman's hands began to tremble. "I . . . I did not know."

"Everyone must pay the release fee." Feldheim picked up his cigarette and sucked in some smoke. "It is the law."

"But I do not have this." She touched her breast bone through the muslin smock.

"I am sorry. You will have to go back to Dengel Ber and get it."

"It is forty kilometers."

Feldheim sat back in his chair, shrugged and lifted his hands.

"I will be here when you return."

He smiled apologetically. The woman offered no further protest, but just picked up her basket and left. Such was life in Africa.

There was, of course, no such thing as a "release fee" for U.N. supplies. Feldheim had made it up, along with perfect documentation to cover himself should inquiries ever be made. An Italian forger in Asmera had created the order on "official" U.N. stationery, and over a year ago Feldheim had mailed it to his own post in Ethiopia while on leave in Vienna. Thereafter, he had opened an account at the Commercial Bank of Ethiopia in Addis, and once a month, while indulging his lust in the capital, he would deposit an attaché case full of birr. He never touched the proceeds, only let them accumulate, and he did nothing to conceal the collection of fees, going so far as to complain about the order to his noncommissioned officers and angrily wave the paper in disgust.

If a superior should arrive to question the practice, he could safely click his heels and claim, "I was only following orders." But, given the rampant corruption within the entire U.N. relief structure, that was unlikely to happen, and when it was all over he would be leaving Africa with a substantial bank check in U.S. dollars.

As long as Ethiopia stayed hungry, his account would grow, but despite the constant flow of beggars it would never be enough for a luxurious retirement. His true nest egg would come from the Czech Jan Krumlov, his flock of Jewish orphans, and a sentimental Israeli government. It was a financial *coup de grâce* that would require all of his tactical brilliance.

"*Yigbu.*"

Another Ethiopian entered, this time an elderly man wearing a soiled *shama* and carrying a curled mule whip. Feldheim recognized him from previous visits, the white-haired elder knew the routine, and no words were exchanged at all.

The old one produced a request for thirty bags of maize and placed a stack of 150 birr on the desk. Feldheim stamped a release form and sent him off to the cargo hangar, where his soldiers were unloading a C-130 just arrived from Berlin.

The cash went into a locked strongbox. Feldheim's adjusted bank balance went into his head.

"*Yigbu.*"

The door opened once again as Feldheim turned to signing a stack of leave orders for some of his men. The door was quietly closed.

He glanced up at his new customer, a very large man by any standard. His bare calves were very thick below the cuffs of billowing brown pantaloons, and above he wore a threadbare, stained gray suit-coat. His white *shama* was draped across his trunk like a bandolier, but it had also been pulled up to cover his head like a burnoose. Strangely, he wore cheap plastic sunglasses and carried a *dula* walking stick, which he clearly did not need. He looked about as starved as a professional wrestler.

"What is your request?" Feldheim returned to his paperwork.

There was no reply, and Feldheim looked up again as the man removed his sunglasses and swept the *shama* from his head. He was completely bald and almost blue-black, his wide eyes somewhat Mongolian and the flared nose that of a bull. There was a pair of lightning tattoos at each rippling temple beside his sharp eyebrows, and a long bullet scar along his left cheek.

It was the Oromo warlord Amin Mobote, and Feldheim's hands gripped the edge of his desk and his spine stiffened. He immediately thought of the Beretta .380 pistol in his drawer, then just as quickly realized that such a puny caliber would hardly faze the giant if his intention was to snap Feldheim's neck.

Mobote smiled slightly, showing large ivory teeth, and he raised a brow.

"You summoned me, Major." His voice was a volcanic rumble. "So why do you go so pale?"

Feldheim willed his shoulders to drop and forced a smile of his own.

"Because you always appear like a ghost, and where I least expect you, Colonel." Feldheim did not like the fact that Mobote held a rank higher than his own, but a warlord could call himself "king" if he wished. "And those clothes . . ." He gestured at the frayed suitcoat.

Mobote looked down at himself.

"Well, it is very dangerous for me in these provinces."

"It is dangerous for you anywhere north of Bale."

The Oromos were a southern tribe and considered themselves the orphans of Ethiopia. A string of governments had ignored their needs, and they were the last to receive benefits, welfare, agricultural assistance, or education. They were genetically larger and stronger than the Amharic peoples, but regarded as tribal farmers of low intellect. Their bids for independence were largely ignored, but Mobote was the first of their warriors to make the Oromos a force to be reckoned with. He would take his rebels far and wide and risk his own life for an official nod of recognition.

"And where are your men?" Feldheim asked.

"I should not tell you." Mobote frowned. "It is poor security."

"But we are partners, Colonel. Are we not?"

"You are our financier. Does that make me your servant?"

Feldheim shrugged and lit up a cigarette, taking care to hold his hand very steady.

"It makes you nothing, Colonel, if you wish to cancel the arrangement."

Mobote nodded, accepting once again that every liberation had its price. He looked at the metal chair and moved to sit. His wide back completely obscured it.

"They are in Kunzula, in the forest. And they are hungry."

"Well, then." Feldheim immediately picked up a fresh release form and began to write. "Thirty bags of rice, thirty of maize. Five jerry cans of water. Will that do, for now?"

"Yes."

"But even a man like you cannot carry such a burden alone." The Austrian smiled as he wrote.

"No."

"I will send a vehicle. My men will leave the supplies at the southern tree line tonight, on the azimuth between Kunzula and Yismala."

"Thank you."

"Do not thank me." Feldheim put down his pen and stamped the form. "I am your partner."

The idea of such a liaison made Mobote conscious of a knot in his stomach, but at times one had to lie down with snakes.

"Why did you wish to see me, Major Feldheim?"

The Austrian rose and walked to one wall of the hut, where a large laminated map of the country was taped to the tin. The plastic corners of the map were curled from the heat. He tapped a spot with his pen.

"The Czech and his Jewish orphans are here in the mountains near Dengla, at the ruins of the Fasil. They are sick and starving. I met with him yesterday. I offered to help."

Mobote raised his wide chin. "And your offer had conditions."

"Of course." Feldheim ignored the tone of Mobote's comment and continued perusing the map. "Krumlov has contacted the Israelis and offered up the *falasha* children, but he wants to go with them."

"Why would he want to do that?"

"There is a price on his head." Feldheim turned from the map, one hand behind his back and his cigarette held between his other thumb and forefinger. "I am sure you know how that feels."

Mobote folded his large arms. "But *I* would not flee from my home."

"This is not his home. He is a traitor of some sort and has already *quit* his home, and to an educated European Africa is no more than a place to suffer a bad sunburn and endure mediocre beer . . . I hope I have not offended you."

Mobote said nothing, but he was imagining Feldheim hung from a game warden's fence and slit open from sternum to pubis like a poacher.

"Perhaps he thinks he will live as a hero in Israel," Feldheim speculated. "If he brings these waifs out safely."

"A true hero does not survive his struggles," said Mobote.

"Really?" Feldheim tried to suppress his amusement. "Only the good die young? I believe that was a Billy Joel hit."

"A what?"

"Never mind." Feldeim waved his cigarette. "In any case, I offered to intercede with you on their behalf."

"I do not understand."

"I am afraid I made you the villain, Colonel. I told the Czech that you would allow me to deliver the supplies, and you would guarantee his and the orphans' safe passage, in exchange for one million dollars from the Israeli government."

It took a moment for Mobote to grasp the role he'd been given, but as he took it all in his face seemed to purple and he rose from his chair and clenched his fists.

"I would not do this!" he roared and the walls of the Quonset rattled and Feldheim backed up and slipped behind his desk. "I would not hold children for money!"

"You would not?" Feldheim asked with all the composure he could muster.

"Never!"

"*Wirklich?* Really?" Feldheim slurred in his native Viennese. "And what was that incident last month in Eritrea? You attacked the Israelis then without such righteousness . . ."

"It was not about *them*. It was to show that we *also* deserve a province and it was not for money!"

"So noble, Colonel? Tell me, how much is the liberation of the Oromo worth?"

"It is *not* a thing of money." The muscles at Mobote's neck bulged like a ship's hawsers.

"How will you buy more guns, ammunition, medical supplies, communications?"

"We *have* these things."

"You have *nothing*," Feldheim snapped as he calculated his margin of safety for a verbal counterstrike. "You hide in the forests because you are nearly out of ammunition, and you must come to *me* and beg for *food*." He took a beat, marching about as the humiliation hit home. "Can your people eat your political slogans? Do you think liberation is built on dreams? It requires power, and that means money, and who will give it to you? What country? What king? Who cares about the Oromo but *you*, Colonel? And who can supply you with the means to an end but *me*?"

Somewhat like a naive child who had been thrashed for his stupidity, Mobote stood there, slowly deflating. His eyes flashed at Feldheim, his nostrils puffing, but he moved to sit in the chair again and looked at his knees and slowly whispered as if convincing himself.

"We need more guns . . . ammunition . . . supplies."

"Yes." Feldheim nodded briskly. "And believe me, a million dollars is nothing to these Israelis. It does not even buy a single battle tank, and their money comes from the Americans at any rate. To them, it is an annoyance fee. To you, it could mean a country."

Mobote was not yet able to look at Feldheim. When he finally spoke, his voice seemed to have dropped a full octave. "What is it you want me to do?"

Feldheim squared his shoulders and walked back to the map. "I want you to apply pressure."

"Explain, Major," Mobote said quietly. "In plain English, without hints."

"Take your men to the Czech's orphanage and lay siege. I will add some ammunition to your supply delivery. Let no one and nothing in or out until Krumlov sends a messenger and agrees to your terms."

"*My* terms."

"Yes, Colonel. They shall be *your* terms, *your* conditions," said Feldheim. "The man with the power sets the rules of the game." He mistakenly assumed that Mobote would miss the double entendre.

The African waited, but there was nothing more. "That is all?" he asked.

"For now." Feldheim pushed the supply release form across his desk.

Mobote rose, took the form, wrapped the burnoose around his great bald head, and replaced his sunglasses. He picked up his *dula*, walked to the door, and turned.

"And if the siege does not work, Major Feldheim?"

"Then you will attack, Colonel Mobote." The Austrian raised a clenched fist. *"Attack."*

10

THE STEEL OF Eckstein's pistol was cold as an icicle against the small of his back, but nestled there where he had tucked it into his jeans it gave some comfort as he stood alone in a black wadi southeast of Lake Tana. Like a cowboy of the American Old West, as an Israeli he had been raised to handle a gun, respect it, and use it cautiously, yet without hesitation if necessary. And hailing as he did from a "rough neighborhood," he did not regard a weapon as a symbol of virility, nor an option to be disputed by vote-seeking lawmakers. It was simply an extension of his person, and without it, he felt rather like a fashionable woman without her purse.

He stared up into the night sky and shivered, despite the olive wool pullover and his New York Yankees baseball cap turned bill-backward and jammed onto his head. It was well past midnight and the African earth had long surrendered its warmth, but the tremble he felt was more empathic, for the man who would soon fall to him from 16,000 feet was about to experience a bone-chilling shock of altitude freeze much harsher than Eckstein's mild discomfort.

He rubbed his arms briskly, then squinted at the luminescent dial of his black Breitling. It was five minutes to midnight, nearly forty-eight hours since he and Baum had first set foot in Krumlov's orphanage, and he had spent most of that time on the wild roads of the Rift.

On the first morning he had nearly come to blows with Debay over possession of the Land Rover, but Baum had impressed upon Krumlov that Eckstein's operational priorities were key, and by nature of the profession, private. So, as Debay grumbled and his trigger finger twitched, Eckstein had left them all behind and traveled to Bahir Dar.

His prearranged "mailbox" was a small roadside café on the outskirts of the lake, the young proprietor having served the photographer Anthony Hearthstone in his previous travels. In this instance, another stranger had first arrived from Addis some days ago and paid the boy well to keep safe a shallow wooden cigar box. The lid was glued shut, and when Eckstein arrived to recover it he was pleased to find it untampered with, its considerable weight assuring him that his Browning Hi-Power had indeed made safe passage from Jerusalem. He rewarded the smiling teenager behind the rickety counter with a further quintet of American presidents, then sat down at a dusty old table and slowly sipped a warm Pepsi until the boy left the café to service a battered Volkswagen at the gas pumps.

Eckstein produced a folding knife, pried the cigar box open, and slipped his pistol and spare magazine into his camera bag. He then placed Krumlov's dubious mole photo into the box, carefully warmed the dried glue with a cigarette lighter until he was able to reseal the lid, and set the box back on the café counter. The same resident AMAN agent who had delivered the box would shortly return from Addis Ababa to recover it. He sat down again and began encoding a message to Horse at SpecOps headquarters.

Although the technical world of modern espionage is replete with impressive gadgets such as high-speed burst transmitters and satcom transponders, Eckstein and Baum harbored idiosyncratic tastes when it came to secret transmissions. Some of the most primitive methods were still the most secure, and unbeknownst to their superiors such as General Ben-Zion, they often resorted to a simple one-time pad or book code in the field.

Both Baum and Eckstein, as well as select members of their "family," always carried identical dog-eared copies of the Penguin edition of Hemingway's *A Farewell to Arms*. When separated, they would communicate by encoding and decoding messages using the same page of the book. You wrote out your communication in English, located those same letters in a given passage, then devised a numbered matrix to indicate each letter by line and position. By prearrangement, they would also further encrypt through multiplication and indicate the page number with a prefix. However, when together in the field, it would have been a tradecraft sin for them both to carry a copy of the paperback, so Baum had left his in the nervous fingers of Horse in Jerusalem.

Eckstein rang up Horse from the counter boy's old rotary telephone, reversing the charges. He greeted the jumpy Russian in English, then claimed that, as a harried photographer, he required that the "office" immediately overnight a packet of negatives to be worked on in the field. The list of negative numbers Eckstein recited was, of course, his encoded demand for immediate mission support.

"I . . . I don't think we can do this so quickly," Horse protested even as he decrypted with a calculator.

"Just give it to the boss," Eckstein insisted, meaning Ben-Zion himself.

"I can't. I mean, I *will*, but you know him, he won't . . ."

"And don't take no for an answer. Tell him if he wants me to bring home the Pulitzer, he has to send the film."

"The Pulitzer?"

"Just do it. He'll scream at you for a while, but you'll live."

"Scream? He might *shoot* me."

Eckstein hung up on him. It was the only way to handle Horse's insecurities, and this sort of unilateral demand from the field was the only way to secure Ben-Zion's compliance. An actual discussion with the general would have resulted in all sorts of refusals and recriminations.

His message, of course, had nothing whatsoever to do with film. And it was also the sort of thing that would require General Staff approval. But there still existed in the Israeli Army a time-honored tradition regarding men in the field—the soldier in harm's way had the right to request any manner of logistical support, and get it.

Eckstein not only wanted the required medical supplies for the children, but a doctor as well. If they would be expected to survive any sort of overland trek to an extraction point, they would have to be examined, treated, and nourished. However, the luxury of waiting for a tropical disease specialist to arrive by normal methods did not exist. He would have to be selected from the ranks of the army, and arrive from the sky.

Although it was practice in the Israeli Army for robust field surgeons to accompany elite troops on the most dangerous missions, there were perhaps only five such men in the entire country who were not only parachute-qualified, but also able to execute a HALO—High-Altitude Low-Opening—drop. They had begun their military careers as volunteers to the top commando units, such as Sayeret Matkal, the Naval Commandos, or Paratroop Recon. With numerous secret and hair-raising missions under their belts, they mustered out and went through university and medical school.

Yet eventually, these men discovered that they were more at home in enemy territory than in the emergency ward of Hadassah Hospital, and they returned to these elite IDF units as career medical officers. It was common to find the names of such surgeons among the roster of those killed in action after a particularly bloody cross-border operation. The morning copy of *Ma'ariv* would display a black-bordered collage of young faces, and among them the more mature thirtysomething doctor gone to his grave as well.

Eckstein did not summon this sort of talent lightly. In the course of his career he had come to know all of the potential candidates, as the same men volunteered time and again for the most harrowing endeavors. He had specified the hour and exact coordinates for the drop, and although he did not know who would arrive from the black heaven like an armored Daedalus, he had no doubt that the man would be the best of the best.

Once more he scanned the flat bowl of the wadi, satisfied that he had chosen the best possible terrain for a blind drop zone. The area reminded him of the moonlike landscape of northern Sinai, with its large pools of hard-packed grit, pale gray beneath the starlight. The wadi was dotted with thistle bunches throwing prickly shadows like sea urchins, but any parachutist would rather suffer an ass full of thorns than a broken femur on slabs of granite. He squinted toward the rising hills and the few flickering lights of Bahir Dar, six kilometers to the northwest and 500 meters higher. Then, just to be sure, he removed his "pager" global positioning system from his pocket and once more double-checked the coordinates he had scouted before making contact with Jerusalem.

The green dot of his watch's second hand swept past twelve, and Eckstein strode across the wadi, producing a Zippo lighter from his pocket. For a daylight parachutist, you marked the drop zone with colored panels and popped a smoke grenade as a wind indicator. At night, you had to indicate both wind and target area with a triangle of beacons. He had no mini-strobes as part of his kit, so he had relied on the traditional IDF markers utilized since the old days of the *Haganah*.

From the café in Bahir Dar, he had taken three empty lima bean cans, filled them with sand, fashioned three thick wicks from a torn burlap sack, and soaked each can throughout with petrol. Then, he had tested the wind and laid out these *guznikim* in an oblong triangle. Now he quick-marched from can to can, igniting the wicks, then took up a position off to one side.

He squinted up into the black sky, his ears pricking up like a German shepherd, though he knew that he would not hear the engines of the fat-bellied Arava special operations aircraft that should, at that very moment, be cutting its power more than four kilometers above. Now, with the beacons lit and the surgeon exiting the aircraft into the frozen night, he knew that this was the most vulnerable window of the operation. If the insertion had been compromised by some unknown factor, any opposition would be about to pounce. Still staring up at the sky, Eckstein slipped the Hi-Power from the small of his back, cocked the slide as quietly as he could, and held the pistol alongside his leg.

He imagined the doctor now, flat on his belly and hurtling through the blackness, glancing at his wrist altimeter as the needle spun the meters away, and he felt the raging wind flapping his jumpsuit and slapping his face, for he had done it himself too many times. He could do nothing to help the man now, so his thoughts turned to yesterday's return to Krumlov's orphanage, where Benni Baum had managed to procure him an old Renault jeep to replace Krumlov's precious Land Rover. The jeep sat now nearby in the lee of the wadi, half-concealed by brush.

He had spent half the next day in the compound before setting out again for the return trip to the drop zone, a day in which Adi had taken his hand and proudly escorted him on a tour of the miserable enclave. Like many Ethiopian children, Adi had a firm grasp of English, peppered with Amharic expressions. Most of all, he spoke of Dominique, in tones of love and admiration, and Eckstein was surprised that the child was privy to her secrets.

"She is very old," said Adi as he led Eckstein toward the camp's "recreation area." This was nothing more than a patch of ground shaded by an old army poncho on broom poles, beneath which some of the small girls were weaving colored straw into figures that looked like voodoo dolls. Their hands were so emaciated that Eckstein had to look away.

"She is?" Eckstein smiled, remembering how Oren's concept of age also blurred with anyone beyond high school.

"Oh, yes." Adi held up all of his fingers twice, then one hand and one extra finger. "How old is that?"

"Twenty-six."

"You see? Very old." Pairs of other children kept trying to join Adi and Eytan on their rounds, fascinated by the tall blond *faranji*, but Adi possessively shooed them away.

"Then I guess I'm *really* old," said Eckstein.

"You? Yes, but I think you are like Dominique's prince was."

"Her prince?"

"She tells to me stories before I sleep. What are they called?"

"Fairytales?"

"Yes!" Adi nodded vigorously. "About castles and princesses." He raised a finger like a wise old sage. "But *I* know they are sometimes about *her*."

"You're a smart boy, aren't you, Adi?"

"I will go to school someday in Israel and I will be *very* smart."

From Adi's stories, Eckstein understood that Dominique had been in love with an older man in Paris. Many of the details were missing, but he gathered that she and her lover had been somehow unable to cement their relationship, and the beautiful young woman had entered a self-imposed nunnery of her own soul. The sad tale made him think now of his own life, and how we so often fashion our own tragedies, and of Simona and Oren, waiting there in Jerusalem for a husband and father who had also chosen repetitive exile, perhaps atoning for some kind of psychological sin of which he was barely aware.

He shook it off now as he distinctly heard the distant snap and rushing billow of a parachute exploding from its container. It was less than a thousand meters above and to the northwest, and he squinted there, although he expected to see nothing yet. The canopy would be the blue-black nylon of the XL-Cloud design, and the surgeon's jump coverall would be equally dark. He waited, then thought he saw the glinting steel of a harness D-ring passing above as the parachutist swept over the landing triangle and turned back into the wind. And all at once he was there, like a small bat dangling from the risers, and the form grew larger and came sweeping in from the northwest, jump boots crossed at the ankles and black gloves working the nylon riser toggles. The goggled face loomed from the night and Eckstein instinctively stepped back as he heard the man whisper a curse and come speeding across the moonscape just a meter above the ground.

The jumper lifted his feet as he passed, yanked the brakes hard, stalled, and plowed up a plume of sand as he disappeared behind a clump of thistle. There was a resounding thump and a grunt as he impacted ungracefully with the ground. Eckstein looked around, then marched briskly toward the impact area even as the large HALO canopy fluttered and deflated.

He came upon a rather comical mime, as the parachute had enshrouded its master, who was silently punching at it like a cat smothered in a silk bedsheet. Then a gust of wind swept it to one side, where it snared on a hedgerow of thistle and wavered there like a beached jellyfish. The surgeon came to his feet and muttered as he struggled to free himself from the harness.

"*Hara shel n'chitah.* What a shitty landing."

"*Lo rah, mitzidi.* Not bad, in my opinion." Eckstein smiled.

The surgeon spun on Eckstein, instinctively reaching for a thigh holster, but then he immediately realized that his Hebrew invective had been answered in kind and his arms relaxed. He was clad head to foot in a black jump coverall, a cork-lined Snoopy helmet on his head and old-fashioned, rubber-rimmed goggles. He looked like The Phantom of comic book legend, and he swept off the goggles and squinted at his "ground crew."

"Eckstein?"

"Hearthstone, in these parts," Eckstein answered in English.

"Okay." The surgeon offered a callused hand. "I'm Motti Rotbard."

"Got a cover name?"

"Max." The surgeon squatted slightly and rubbed his knees.

"Good enough. How was the ride?"

"Fucking freezing, and I didn't spot your *guznikim* until about five hundred meters."

"Sorry." Eckstein shrugged. "Best I could do." He stepped a bit closer to the doctor, examining his face as the man removed his helmet, revealing stiff black curls, heavy eyebrows, and light eyes. "I know you. Aren't you at Tel Nof?" Eckstein asked, meaning the IDF airborne school.

"That's right." Max nodded. "And I know you, too. You're the spook with the shot-up knee, always trying to sneak onto one of our jump planes."

Eckstein laughed quietly. "That's me."

"Idiot." Max grinned. "At my age I already hate this nonsense, and you still think it's fun."

"Maybe I need a shrink more than a surgeon."

The parachute canopy was threatening to billow up and fly away as a gust of wind swept across the flat plain. Eckstein gestured at it.

"Let's bury your chute and get moving."

"Bury it?" The doctor frowned. "Ben-Zion told me to pack it up and bring it back."

"That's because he's a cheap bastard," Eckstein scoffed. "If he wants it back he can come down here and haul it out himself." He produced his small folding knife from his belt and moved off to free the chute from the thistle. Max was wearing an assault vest over his coverall, and he also came up with a parachute knife, shrugged, and followed along.

"Well, you're commander in the field."

They spent some time on their knees digging a square hole, then Eckstein expertly folded the chute and risers into its container and laid it inside.

"Where's all the supplies?" he asked as they covered the hole with sand, then began to further camouflage it with rocks and brush.

"I dropped the gear bag at about two hundred meters."

Eckstein stopped working and looked up, alarmed. "You dropped it?" The gear bag would have been hanging below the surgeon's harness on a rope as he glided, but dropping it from 200 meters would have destroyed all of the fragile supplies. Max reached out and patted Eckstein's shoulder.

"It had a cargo chute on it, and an infrared beacon. You think they let any idiot go through med school?" He rose to his feet, slipped a small night scope from the chest pocket of his vest, placed the scope to one eye, and scanned the wadi. "And there it is," he said, pointing off.

Eckstein kicked some more dirt over the fresh grave of the parachute, then smoothed the area with his hands and got up.

"Ahhh," said Max as he looked at the XL-Cloud's tomb and quoted from a famous book of Hebrew poetry. "*A Canopy in the Desert.*"

"Abba Kovner." Eckstein named the author.

"An educated man? Since when does Ben-Zion hire scholars?"

"He doesn't. We conceal our intelligence so he won't feel threatened."

Max chuckled and the two men went off to find the gear bag.

In Africa, there is no gentle slip from dusk to night, nor languid rising of the sun at dawn. Here it is as if the world is flat, like a vast sea of thirsty brush on shallow waves of desert, and rather than a gradual transition from night to day, the light suddenly rushes into the sky like a tidal wave of glowing neon.

Eckstein and Max had recovered the gear bag and carried it to the concealed jeep, and Max had pulled a plastic bag from the large satchel and changed from his commando coverall into a pair of jeans and a plaid flannel farmer's shirt. By the time Eckstein coaxed the Renault back up to the Bahir Dar road and set out along the rim of Lake Tana, the flat blue shell of dawn was already tinting the steel plate of the waters below. Enormous flocks of flamingos fluttered down to the shores like settling swarms of pink butterflies, and Eckstein had to brake more than once as small herds of bony bushbuck antelope suddenly appeared and loped across the empty road.

Driving a standard shift always brought the ache back to Eckstein's knee with the constant braking and clutching, but he was pleased to be at the wheel of the old green field car with its tattered tan canvas roof. Baum had somehow managed to acquire the jeep in the middle of nowhere, enlisting Manchester's aid to lead him from the compound on a scavenger hunt, and Eckstein smiled as he imagined the bulky colonel bribing some local surveyor to temporarily "rent" his transport. Yet his smile faded as he drove further on, for Max, who had been rather jolly and loquacious after his hair-raising arrival, now sat in the passenger seat and stared silently out at the passing landscape. Something was on the surgeon's mind.

"I assume Ben-Zion briefed you on *Sorcerer.*" Eckstein broke the silence, which consisted of the wind flapping through the open windows and the roar of the jeep engine and its tires over splintered tarmac.

Max nodded, still looking out his window at the marvels of Tana.

"About the children," Eckstein prodded. "And one adult we have to extract along with them." The rules of compartmentalization were such that the doctor should only have been privy to facts he needed to know, and nothing about Krumlov or the mole hunt. Had his parachute jump gone awry and he had been captured by Ethiopian troops or a band of rebels, he would have been able to reveal nothing more than scant details.

The doctor turned toward Eckstein, pulled a pack of Marlboros from his pocket, and offered one up. Eckstein declined. Max lit up and sighed.

"I know everything."

"You don't say."

"Yes. The general had to give it all over."

"He hates that. He's a secrecy junkie."

"Right. Which should tell you something."

It did indeed. There was no reason to brief Max fully on Krumlov and his defection and the information he was offering, unless the doctor was also serving as a messenger bearing bad tidings. Ben-Zion's field messages to Eckstein and Baum were often tainted with some sort of devious twist, especially if they were behaving as the insubordinate bastards he so resented.

"You're not going to like it," said Max.

"I rarely do. No need to be shy."

Max smirked sadly as he shifted more toward Eckstein, who glanced over at the surgeon's expression and stiffened at its melancholy.

"I used to be one of you boys," said Max. "An intellectual killer." He used the Hebrew word *egdachan*, which means gunman and is rather distasteful, as it suggests the mindless assassin. "That's why I went over to medicine. When I was a kid I shot first and didn't think much about it. Then I decided that saving our own wounded was just as courageous as killing the enemy, and made for better nightmares."

"Okay, so what's the message?" Eckstein asked impatiently, wishing he had also chosen medicine as a career path.

Max smoked and squinted through the windshield.

"This Czech, Jan Krumlov."

"Yes?"

"He's not to come out alive."

Eckstein drove, although his vision began to blur with a building rage and his knuckles on the Renault's steering wheel were going white. The words echoed in his brain, *He's not to come out alive*, but he hoped, prayed, that somehow Max had misunderstood or miscommunicated. It could not be that after all this, AMAN wanted Krumlov killed. He forced his heart to calm, his questions measured and even.

"What do you mean?"

"You know what I mean." Max continued to stare forward, his expression that of a man revealing to his friend that his wife is cheating on him.

"It's a kill order?"

"Come on, Hearthstone. It's not like you've never heard one before," Max scoffed. "You're not a virgin and we don't work for the Pope . . ."

But Eckstein suddenly slammed on the brakes and the jeep skidded and sprayed up loose stone as he pulled over to the side of the road. Max threw a hand against the dashboard to keep from being bounced around the vehicle, and Eckstein pounded the steering wheel with a fist and spun on him.

"*Koos shel ha'ima shel koolchem!* You're mothers' cunts, all of you!"

He spat, roping Max in with the entire demented Israeli intelligence community. "Are you all out of your fucking minds?!"

Eckstein's frustration had been welling up since Sarajevo and Niki's death and the impossible wrenching images of the starving children, children surviving only due to Krumlov's care, whatever the Czech's true motives.

"Do you have any idea what we've been through so far to get that fucking Czech defector prepped for extraction?" he spat. "We were fucking shelled and shot at from one end of that Balkan shithole to the other, just so we could deliver Krumlov's fiancée to him, and *then* we finally get her here and she tries to kill him and we all wind up cleaning her blood and brains off our faces! And *now* you're telling me that the supposed *key* to the security of our biggest weapons program has to be tossed into a dumpster like some unwanted bastard infant in the Bronx?!"

He was shouting, and his arms were shaking and he could feel his face burning cherry-red with the rage, and he knew it was unprofessional as hell and he didn't care. He should have turned down the mission. He knew better. Anything like this that Ben-Zion sent you on was bound to be a cluster fuck from the jumpoff.

Max, of course, was a bit surprised at Eckstein's emotion, yet unintimidated. He sat in his seat and watched the tormented major, understanding exactly what Eckstein was going through. His voice was calm and measured as he spoke.

"I think you're shooting the messenger," he said with the sympathy of a psychologist. "Not that I blame you."

Eckstein made to reply, but he found his ire overtaken by disgust and he burst from the Renault and the door slammed against its hinges as he hopped down and limped toward the hood of the jeep. He pounded the metal once with a fist, and a flock of black-headed siskin fluttered away from a nearby bush. Then he stood there seething, looking out over the African dawn.

Max got out of the jeep and quietly joined Eckstein, standing across from him on the other side of the engine compartment. He placed his box of cigarettes on the hood, and without turning Eckstein took the Marlboros and lit one up with his own lighter. He did not apologize for his outburst. It wasn't necessary.

the game,

an-
as

hoarsely. "Let's hear this twisted logic."

tions in Jerusalem," said Max. "They've
ne they already have."

"

meeting about your mission. Joint intel-
the routine. Mossad spilled the beans."

barely breathed. Mossad worked closely with
abak, but highly sensitive operations were not always
ween services unless absolutely necessary.

here *is* a mole inside *Project Keshet*, but he's already been turned.
Mossad caught him two years ago and they've been playing him back,
without bothering to tell AMAN or Shabak, of course."

Eckstein took a long drag off the cigarette, the smoke keeping him
even as he watched it taken away by the dawn breeze. It was standard
stuff, catching a spy and then making him pretend to his masters that
he was still fully functional, while you fed him a mixed bag of harmless truths and deadly lies to be passed on. But in this case it didn't
make sense.

"Then why the hell did Itzik send us out here?"

"He didn't know about Mossad's boy till after you left. Maybe, at
first, they all wanted to see what Krumlov had, but then the handlers
panicked."

"But Krumlov won't even talk until he's in Tel Aviv, and I only just
dead-dropped one piece of evidence."

"They got cold feet. They're afraid that he's going to get off the
plane at Ben Gurion, and then blow the *same* man who's already been
doubled."

Eckstein sighed and slowly nodded. He understood, and Max needed
to say no more. As it stood, Mossad already had a mole in play as a double agent, every intelligence service's dream and a very rare commod-
ity. *Keshet* was a joint operation along with the Americans, so the CIA
was probably privy to the ruse and insisting that the mole's false product keep being fed to the shattered Soviet Bloc, or the Syrians or who-
ever was the "end-user." Now, if a Czech defector who knew the mole's
identity were to make Israeli shores, then the Israelis and Americans
could no longer pretend not to know about the spy and the entire gambit would be blown.

It was simple. It was nothing new. It was the way o
pathetic and cruel.

Krumlov could not reach Israel.

Krumlov could not come out of Africa alive.

Eckstein tossed his cigarette to the road and covered it with his
vas boot, grinding and suffocating the burning embers until there v
nothing left, just the way his own foolish concepts of honor and hand
shakes and a man's word were consistently crushed by the realities of
his chosen vocation. He did not look at Max as he slipped his still trembling hands into his pockets and squinted off into another morning of
impossible choices.

"I hate this fucking job," he muttered, and he turned and got back
into the jeep.

11

* * *

GENERAL ITZIK BEN-ZION was a man of a hundred faces.

Most of them were variations on a theme: expressions of disapproval, frowns of distaste, squinting interrogations as to the veracity of any intelligence officer's claims, and a selection of tight-lipped displays of barely contained rage. There were a couple of smiles in his repertoire, but they never surfaced in the office. He saved them for his grown children, yet even they were shocked when his lips parted to reveal his teeth, reserving judgment in the same way an animal trainer watches a domesticated tiger.

Certainly the one expression, including tone of voice and posture, that Itzik never allowed anyone to witness was a slack-jawed nod of subservience. And if you were unfortunate enough to be in a room with him when he was forced by circumstance to sublimate his will, it was a frightening experience bound to have dire repercussions, and you never wanted to witness it again.

"Yes, Commander."

He sat gritting his teeth behind his enormous mahogany desk in the far corner of an office that had once served as a conference room. Three large windows were lined with double-thick soundproof Perspex and slat blinds. The wall behind the desk displayed countless plaques and laminated platitudes from various branches of the army, as well as posed photographs of the general and a Who's Who of Israeli politicians. A large glass table held a small forest of statuettes and trophies, the Israeli Army's traditional gifts in lieu of medals, which are considered immodest and unfitting for the socialist nature of the State.

The long wall across from the windows was covered with operational maps and color-coded pennants, and before that sat a couch, a coffee table, and a number of hard-backed chairs. There were no bookshelves in the room. Like the head of a Hollywood studio, Itzik himself did not read books. Subordinate officers performed that task and then briefed him with trembling oral summaries.

Ben-Zion's desk was neatly ordered with operational files and mission reports, as well as three separate telephones, including a multiplex Tadiran scrambler. At the moment he sat stiffly in his black leather chair, one hand holding a black earpiece to his head, while the other rested on his desktop, tendons rippling across a closed fist.

"*Ken, Hamefaked.* Yes, Commander." He nodded again into the phone, and as he repeated the response that most likely no one had heard him utter since he was an inductee a quarter-century before, he raised his eyes and looked across the room at Horse.

The small Russian analyst was sitting on the couch, and the general's expression shot him through with fear as he prayed that Ben-Zion's conversation would go on forever, so that he could not vent his rage on the nearest target. Yudit was perched on a nearby chair, chewing a pen and unperturbed by her boss's suffering, rather like the patient daughter of a mafia don. Uri Badash stood with his hands in the pockets of his jeans, perusing the map wall as if he'd discovered a new country.

"Yes, Commander. I'll do that . . ." Itzik stopped talking, then winced, looked at the telephone as if it had short-circuited in his ear, and slowly replaced it in its cradle. He raised his palms, placed them on the desk, and slowly came to his full height. Sunlight lanced through the slat blinds and pierced his salt-and-pepper curls as he turned toward Jerusalem and muttered.

"Being yelled at like a fucking schoolboy by *Rosh Aman.*" He meant the chief of Army intelligence, one of the very few general officers, along with the chief of staff, who was unimpressed by Itzik's stature or credentials and demanded only performance. Itzik laughed once, an ugly sound. He turned back to his desk, spotted a heavy file drawer half open, and suddenly kicked it shut with all his might, the sound echoing in the room like a gunshot.

"I'm being screamed at by my commander like some fucking recruit!" he yelled. Horse stiffened as if he'd been whipped and clenched his bladder, while Yudit looked up and Uri Badash turned from the map wall. "Do you believe this?!" Itzik railed. "Do you *believe* this?!"

To Horse's panic and dismay, the general advanced on him, jabbing a finger, and the analyst began to slowly shake his head as if begging not to be executed.

"It's them," the general yelled. "That fucking Eckstein and Baum!" Horse continued to deny his complicity with his wagging chin. After all, he hadn't given *birth* to them. "I issue an order and those two take it under advisement like some communist cell! What the hell are they doing down there?!"

"Itzik." Yudit's tone was soft and measured and patient. "It's not Horse's fault. You know those two have minds of their own."

"And he can *read* their minds!" The general spun on her even as he continued gesturing at Horse, although she held his gaze courageously and frowned her disapproval. "He knows exactly what they're thinking and what they're up to!"

"I . . . I *don't*, sir," Horse croaked. "I really don't."

"Leave him be," said Badash.

"You stay out of this." The general spat at the Shabak officer as if the man was interfering in family affairs. "It's Shabak that gets us into all this shit, with its fucking security checks and mole hunts and paranoia."

"Apparently even paranoids have enemies," Badash responded.

But Ben-Zion seemed not to hear him, and he turned back on Horse, although his vehemence had been somewhat dispelled and was now only a seethe.

"All I can tell you is that those two had better be barbecuing that damned Czech as we speak, or it'll be my ass and yours and all of our careers and our fucking pensions."

"That's such a noble concern," Yudit offered sarcastically. The general looked at her and wagged a threatening finger.

"I'm warning you, my dear. I'm warning you. You can be replaced."

"Of course." Yudit rolled her eyes. "I'm sure there's at least one other crazy female in the entire army who'd put up with you for more than a day."

As always, her demeanor completely deflated the general's tirade, and he threw up a surrendering hand and marched back to his desk. He rummaged uselessly through some files for a moment, still growling. "I want to talk to those bastards voice to voice. Right now. We sent that surgeon in with a satcom, right?" He looked up as no one responded. "Right?"

"Yes, sir." Horse found his voice again, barely.

"Well? Get me a commo man in here!"

Yudit got up from her chair and walked to a telephone, ringing up *Kesher*, the communications center, and quietly relaying the general's order. The general stared at Horse for a long moment, then gestured at a slip of decoded transmission sitting on the analyst's lap. It was another short and infuriating message from Eckstein, relayed by telephone from the café in Bahir Dar, shortly after the major had picked up Max. The paper was stained with sweat prints.

"Read that damned thing to me again."

Horse lifted the paper and it fluttered in his hands like a dying butterfly.

"Reception fine." He looked up at Ben-Zion. "I guess that means the surgeon arrived okay."

"I know what it means, for God's sake. Go on."

Horse continued reading Eytan's response to Itzik's distasteful order.

"Regarding your request. . . ."

"*Request*," Itzik huffed.

"We will not be able to ship the smaller items without the cooperation of the customs broker."

"Sounds like they can't get the children out without Krumlov's help," Yudit translated as she moved back to her chair.

"I know what it means, goddamnit!" Itzik yelled. "Those insubordinate bastards think they can manipulate me? Pull on my heartstrings? Since when do I have heartstrings?!"

"None that I recall," said Badash.

"I issue a kill order and they treat it like a suggestion from a lonely hearts' club!"

"Well, sir," Horse croaked bravely.

"What?!"

"It's . . . it's just that they are probably a bit confused, and maybe frustrated. After all, the objective of *Sorcerer* was to get Krumlov back here alive. And also they extracted that poor Czech girl and . . ."

"The objective of *Sorcerer* is to protect the Keshet project at all costs! When that meant having Krumlov unearth his mole, he was getting a first-class ticket. But now that it means keeping him from blowing two years of playback, he's *expendable*. Is that clear?"

"Horse isn't protesting, Itzik," Yudit interjected. "He's just explaining."

"And who are you?" The general's voice rose again in hopeless defense. "Mother Teresa?"

A knock at the door kept the exchange from escalating, but before Itzik could respond it swung shyly open, revealing a uniformed technical sergeant from the communications center. Itzik put his fists to his hips and barked at the noncom.

"I want a relay to that mobile satcom in Africa."

"It's already set up, sir," the sergeant responded. "We'll patch it through to your desk." The young man looked at his watch. "But there's a fixed time for transmissions. Eight more minutes."

"Don't keep me waiting." Itzik huffed and sat down in his chair, as if only he was permitted to control the movement of sun and stars

"Okay." The sergeant shrugged, caught a smile from Yudit, and slipped back through the door. "We'll buzz you." His voice echoed in the hallway.

Itzik muttered something, and the room fell silent as he shuffled some papers on his desk. He glanced up and frowned at Uri Badash, who had moved to the glass table of trophies and was finger-dusting a bronze free-fall parachutist mounted on a wooden pedestal.

"You know," Badash began quietly as his counterintelligence instincts hooked on a speculation. "I wonder . . ."

"Wonder out loud," Itzik growled as he slipped a sheet of paper into his shredder.

"Is it possible that Krumlov's mole is *not* the same man as Mossad's double?"

Horse winced, for of course he had already been considering this possibility, but had decided to keep his mouth shut. When facing Ben-Zion's ego, survival was the better part of valor. Itzik stopped fidgeting with his files and squinted at the Shabak officer.

"What do you mean?"

"Is it possible that there are two such individuals? One that we have, and one that we don't?"

"Are you out of your mind, Uri?" The general jabbed a finger into his own temple. "*Two* moles?"

"Think about it, Itzik. An elaborate decoy play. The Mossad people said it wasn't easy snaring the first man, but it wasn't that complex, either. He made mistakes, small ones, yes, but all the same. Maybe he was a giveaway, a sacrifice. Once we had him, we stopped looking. Now Krumlov comes at us with the real thing, and all we can think about is saving our phony pipeline."

"Now *there's* a scary thought," Yudit whispered.

"Oh, for God's sake!" Itzik slapped a thick file and raised his large hands to heaven. "I'm surrounded by fantasists! A second mole? And the first one's just bait? Uri, you've been reading too much Ludlum."

Badash furrowed his brow. "Who's Ludlum?" He was not a man given to recreational reading, and what he did read was limited to true crime books and motorcycle magazines.

"Never mind." Ben-Zion waved him off disgustedly.

Badash shrugged, and having nothing better to do while they waited out the remaining minutes, he reached into his shirt pocket for a pack of Time.

"Don't do that." Itzik pointed at the cigarettes. "I'm on the verge of starting up again."

Badash sighed and put the box away. A beige scrambler telephone on Itzik's desk warbled and the general snatched it up.

"Yes, patch him," he snapped into the phone, then held it away from his ear until the sharp whine of a satellite relay was quickly adjusted by someone in *Kesher*. Eckstein and Max were apparently on a windy hilltop somewhere, having stopped en route back to the orphanage.

Itzik looked up at his office guests while he waited, gathering an expression of "Now we'll see who's boss." Then he quickly focused on the voice coming through the earpiece.

"Yes, it's me, Mr. Hearthstone," he growled. "Your nemesis." He waited a moment, then rolled his eyes. "Yes, the transmission's secure! Except for your little fan club sitting here with me." Horse looked at his scuffed shoes. "Now make your pitch, so I can demolish it quickly."

Ben-Zion listened for a while, although halfway through Eytan's briefing of the situation in the field, the general got up and began to pace as far as the telephone cord would allow. He was already gesturing with a fist as his face flushed and he cut Eckstein off.

"Now you listen to *me*, Hearthstone. Despite all the propaganda emanating from the Jewish Agency, not every branch of this government is a fucking charity organization! It's high time that you and Colonel Santa Claus left your bleeding hearts at home and started thinking like professionals." Eckstein was apparently protesting, but the general only paused for breath. "I don't *care* about them! That's right! This project is not *about* them. Someone else will tend to that later, and if not, to hell with the bad PR. Now just follow my orders and do what you were trained to do or we'll all wind up selling fruit in Machaneh Yehuda! *Out!*" And he cut off transmission by slamming down the phone.

No one in the room moved while they waited for Itzik to calm himself. Yet the general was no longer agitated. In fact, a small smirk had crossed his lips, a hint of satisfaction. After all, he had done all he could, relayed his commander's demands as clearly as possible, and there were witnesses. He looked at the door as someone knocked hesitantly.

"*Kaness,*" he barked.

A courier entered the room. He was in plain clothes and slinging a canvas map case. The armpits of his checkered shirt were ringed with sweat and his longish hair was tangled, as if he'd been driving madly with the window open.

"It's a delivery from the Kiria, via Africa," he said. "Someone has to sign."

Yudit got up and retrieved a clipboard from the courier, while the young man opened his map case and extracted Eckstein's cigar box.

She scribbled her signature, took the box, and walked it over to Itzik's desk. The courier backed out of the office.

Itzik looked at the cigar box, but he made no move to touch it. It had been double-sealed at the embassy in Addis Ababa with something that looked like a detective's evidence tape. This indicated that an embassy sapper had already X-rayed the container and approved its passage by diplomatic pouch via commercial air carrier. The Israeli intelligence services had made a tradition of blowing up opposition members by remote control, so they were doubly suspicious of such special deliveries, even when they originated with their own operatives.

"If it hadn't already been checked," said Itzik as Yudit, Horse, and Badash gathered around, "I'd call the bomb squad in here."

"Eckstein wouldn't try to kill you," said Yudit. "He'd be afraid of hurting one of us."

"Very funny," the general snorted. He opened a drawer and came up with a pristine bayonet, sliced through the tape, and pried the box open.

The black-and-white photo originally supplied by Bluebeard to Colonel Salameh, then copied by Krumlov, lay there alone, its picnicking entourage offering their tired smiles as if challenging the observers to a game of Guess Who?

"Speaking of funny," Badash muttered.

"Are we supposed to guess?" Yudit speculated.

But Itzik was not disturbed by the presentation of so many options. He had been at this game a very long time.

"Well, Krumlov's no fool," he said. "I wouldn't expect him to just give over the man's name and passport number."

"It is a teaser," said Horse. "Just to whet our appetites."

Itzik lifted the photo and turned it over. Eckstein's handwriting appeared in light pencil.

Not first-generation. A photographic copy of original delivered by "Bluebeard" (Czech designation) to Syrian handler (A.F. Col. Faraj Salameh), intercepted briefly by K.

"So, it's second-generation." Itzik nodded, all intelligence officer now and his ego in check.

"Or third," said Horse.

"Why third?" Badash asked.

"Well, if Krumlov intercepted the original photograph, then he would have taken a picture of it and put it back. But he wouldn't turn over that copy to us. He'd make a duplicate off his negative, or take another photo of the copy."

The other members of the huddle looked at the small Russian appreciatively, in response to which he blushed and removed his glasses to clean them.

"Remind me to not scream at you so much, Horse," Itzik muttered, a backhanded compliment that actually made the analyst smile.

"Could that name 'Bluebeard' be descriptive?" Yudit asked.

"Highly unlikely," said Horse. "It would be a random selection from an StB computer, the same way we do it."

"Horse, run the file on this Salameh immediately," Itzik snapped.

Horse fumbled to get up from the couch.

"Not *now*." The general rolled his eyes, leaving Horse in midair. "*Nu*, Uri?" Itzik looked at the Shabak officer. "Which bastard is it?"

Badash walked to a black briefcase he had deposited on the couch, spun the combination, and removed a file envelope marked *Sodi Beyoter*—Most Secret. He returned to the desk as he unwrapped the clasp thread, but his expression already foretold what he expected to find.

He slipped a Mossad interrogation photo from the envelope and laid it on Itzik's desk next to the Dimona group shot. This was the mole the civilian intelligence agency had already unearthed and turned back on his handlers. The photo was split—a full frontal and a profile of a dark-skinned man in his early thirties, with a code designation in Hebrew and a series of numbers below, much like a convict layout.

The three men and Yudit crowded into Ben-Zion's side of the desk, all peering down at the two photographs, moving their heads back and forth like observers at a tennis match. After a short while, they stopped. Itzik came to his full height, placed his hands on his hips, and whispered at the ceiling.

"Shit."

Yudit looked up at her boss. "He's not in the picture, is he?"

The general sighed and shook his head.

"Mossad's mole is *not* in Krumlov's photo," Badash confirmed. "Right, Horse?"

The little Russian looked carefully again at both photographs. "Correct," he barely croaked, but he was watching Ben-Zion as if the general was an unpredictable junkyard dog.

"Which means. . . ." Yudit said.

But Itzik had turned away from his desk and was once more at his picture window. He had split the blinds with a finger and was squinting at nothing down on Yaffo Road.

"Which means," he began, and already you could hear the bile rising in his throat. "That if Krumlov is not just playing with us, and he has sent us a photo that really includes his mole . . ." He trailed off.

"There are two moles," Badash concluded.

"Which is what Eckstein and Baum believe," said Yudit. "Why they want him brought out alive."

Itzik said nothing. His mind was churning, flipping through the options, none of which were appealing. If Krumlov did in fact hold the key to a second mole, and that man was one of the people in his group photo, then the Czech's death would probably seal that secret forever. Krumlov's flight from Czechoslovakia would have already resulted in a flash message to that agent, and he would have gone inactive for now, laying low. Picking him out of the crowd without Krumlov's aid might prove impossible.

On the other hand, if Krumlov's photo was merely a phony enticement, then he might arrive in Israel and triumphantly announce that his mole was indeed the one already featured in the Mossad file. In that event, the mole's playback would immediately become useless.

Eckstein and Baum knew this. They had already worked it out. Just relaying Krumlov's photo back to Israel had placed Itzik in the conundrum of having to make a career-altering decision.

"I really hate those two." The general whispered as he shook his head. "I really do."

12

• • •

Gojam
May 6

A TRIO OF armed sentries embraced the battered road just one kilometer from Krumlov's castle, and as Eckstein gunned the jeep over the last crest before the plateau his headlights caught the glint of gun metal in the distance and his breath caught in his throat. He and Max had ridden most of the long day and into the night in silence, for the brief satcom discourse with Ben-Zion had only served to keep Eckstein's fury at a low simmer. Now the order to assassinate the Czech receded quickly into a nonissue as the simple matter of survival preempted all other thoughts and actions.

The road dropped down from the crest and then wandered like a scaly serpent's tail through a long bowl of scrub and rock, finally thinning as it rose again over a shallow grade and slipped into the concertina perimeter of the castle ruins. Dim fires glowed from within the Fasil walls beyond, but Eckstein knew that Krumlov's mercenaries had no line of sight to the dark men who had obviously been posted in the depression to foil entrance or exit. Instinctively he hesitated, braking the jeep as he tried to assess the situation.

"Don't stop moving," Max said flatly from the passenger seat.

Eckstein nodded and immediately released the brakes. If the sentries sensed hesitation in the vehicle's approach, they would quickly cock their weapons. He coasted over the rise, put the rumbling jeep into low gear, and began to pick his way along the road, buying the precious minutes that could alter a simple twist of fate. He and Max automatically fell into the habits ingrained as field combat officers.

"Assessment." Max said as he shifted forward in his seat. "Who are they?"

"Probably Amin Mobote's rebels, but I can't tell yet." Eckstein squinted through the gritty windshield, but he did not alter his posture. "Sit back. Look bored."

Max nodded and forced himself into a casual lean against the seat, even though his leg muscles were already bunching. "Guess the range."

"About half a kilometer."

"Brief me quick."

"They're ragtag, but deadly," said Eckstein. "Usually wear old army fatigues, no ranks, black berets, carry AKs or H&Ks. They've picked up the kaffiyeh fashion from watching Arafat on TV, but they only use them as scarves."

"I'm spotting something like that around their necks," said Max.

"That's it, then. Mobote's muscle. Fuck."

"Can we talk our way through?"

"Negative. I'm sure they have orders now, no personnel or supplies in or out."

"Goddamnit." Max grumbled curses as he began to reach for the pistol tucked behind the small of his back. "I swore I wasn't going to ever do this again."

"Don't *move*." Eckstein spat. "These people work the night, they'll spot you drawing even at half a klick through headlight glare."

"Fucking great." Max hissed as he returned his hand to his knee. "I'm not even chambered."

"Neither am I."

"Absurd. Two impotent Jews in the fucking Wild West."

Eckstein grimaced as he gripped the wheel and shifted, for he knew exactly what Max meant. The Israeli code of arms held that you never chambered a round in your weapon until absolutely necessary. Almost everyone in Israel carried a gun, and the risk of an accidental discharge was very real to the populace. Therefore, even the most professional gunmen learned to draw their weapons, cock the slides, aim, and fire within a second. Granted, in a split-second gunfight you could lose your life over this precaution, but it was better than dropping your pistol in a supermarket and killing your neighbor's teenager.

The jeep began to climb the long shallow grade toward the sentry point. Eckstein could clearly see the three rebels now unslinging their AK-47s from their necks and gripping them aggressively. One of them stepped into the middle of the road and began to wave a flashlight over the cracked macadam, a signal to slow and halt, while the other two flanked the shoulders.

"What are you carrying?" Max whispered now through clenched teeth.

"A Hi-Power."

"Me too. What kind of ammo?"

"Hollow point."

Max shot Eckstein a curious glance. Hollow point ammunition was extremely deadly, exploding inside its target and shredding flesh and bone.

"I used to load standard metal jacket," Eckstein explained quickly, "until I saw one go through a guy and shatter a flower vase."

"You're worried about the furniture?"

"I'm worried about bystanders."

"Well," Max huffed. "There are no bystanders *here.*"

At fifty meters from the rebels, Eckstein casually reached for a soiled white oil rag atop the dashboard. He slowed as he rolled down his window, stuck his hand out, and waved his surrender pennant. The rebel in the road, clearly the roadblock commander, responded with something like a sneer, then crooked a finger at the jeep and summoned it on.

"He's got balls, standing in the road like that," said Max.

"He's also got a loaded AK."

"Can you bluff us through?"

"They're not going to let us through. At best they'll turn us away, but if they make us get out for a weapons search or they spot the satcom and the medicines, we're finished."

"Shit," Max hissed. He slowly wiped his right palm on his jeans.

Like an Olympic sprinter just before a medal race, Eckstein's years of experience and training began to take over. The sections of his mind reserved for sorrow, regret, and moral hesitation began to shut down, and what was left was a healthy dose of fear that surged adrenaline to its proper posts. He was a man about to be mugged in a filthy alleyway, and he could not afford to indulge the past nor hope for a future. He could only prepare, and rely on his wits and reflexes.

"Just go for it when I do," said Eckstein as his mind raced over a lightning tactical plan. "Pop your door handle first so your man has to step back, but stay in the car."

"*Ruth,*" Max snapped, using the IDF colloquial for "Roger." He paused for a moment. "Tell my kids I loved them."

Eckstein took in a breath, slashed the image of his son from his mind's eye, and tried to slow his racing heart. "Tell mine the same."

He stopped the jeep just two meters from the rebel in the road. He left his hand and the rag outside the window as he put the clutch in and held it there while he shifted into first, just idling. The two flanking rebels approached the sides of the car. Their uniforms looked as if they had not been washed in months, their kaffiyeh scarves nearly gray with sweat and their black faces shone like oiled teak wood. Eckstein stuck his head out the window and grinned.

"Hullo, mates."

There was no response, except for the rebel leader standing in the headlight glare, who just cocked his chin and snapped his head back, a clear order to exit the vehicle. Eckstein heard Max's window rolling down and the surgeon began to babble a distraction.

"We are paying a visit to the orphan children up the road." Max's hand moved to the door handle; he flipped it down and applied pressure to the metal with his knee as his right fingers moved toward his back. "You know, conditions are very terrible in these parts. Very, very bad . . ."

Eckstein's sentry was clearly young and unnerved, his finger on the trigger of his assault rifle. It would be very hard to beat him to the draw, since he was already drawn. The Israeli major suddenly faltered, searching rapidly for another way out, perhaps some appealing tale, a joke, a ruse, something to buy time, something to prevent the inevitable. But it all flashed by like so much fantasy and then he knew what had to happen and he hated it but he just could not think about that now.

"Get out!" the rebel leader barked suddenly in a deep African accent. At the same time, both flanking sentries turned their heads to him and Eckstein did not need to signal Max. There would be no other such chance.

Eckstein dropped his rag as he snatched his Hi-Power from behind his back with his right hand. He felt his left fingers gripping the vertical grooves of the slide and he realized he had never cocked a pistol with so much strength. And then the barrel seemed to jab through the open window under its own power and he pulled the trigger and the flash blinded him in the night as the rebel just outside flew back as if he'd been sledgehammered in the chest.

Eckstein fired again, even as he heard Max's pistol exploding over and over inside the cab, the ring of his spent shells careening off metal somewhere. And then he was stamping on the gas and releasing the clutch pedal and just grabbing the wheel with his free left hand, and he saw the horrified face of the rebel leader as the man tried to jump back.

But it was too late for him. The jeep bumper smashed into his thighs and he snapped forward like a rag doll, his forehead banging off the hood with a sickening thud before he flipped back onto the road and Eckstein ran right over him. The jeep lurched up on the left side and Eckstein winced as the wheels trundled over flesh and bone, and then the cleats bit tar and sprayed up pebbles and they were roaring up the hill for the castle.

The gunshots echoed away in the small valley, and then there was silence, except for the roar of the jeep engine.

Eckstein glanced over at Max, who was sitting there holding his pistol with both hands between his knees. He was hunched over as if he had a stomach wound.

"*Nifgata?* Are you hit?" Eckstein did not realize he was shouting. The gunfire had temporarily deafened him.

No answer.

"Max!"

"No." Max slowly shook his head. He looked up at Eckstein. His eyes were filled and glistening. "You all right?"

Eckstein was as far from all right as he could possibly be, but he was not wounded. He glanced around the jeep cab and spotted a pair of bullet holes in the canvas top just between himself and Max. Apparently someone had gotten off some AK rounds before he died, but in the hell of a vicious gunfight one rarely notices these things until afterward.

"I'm all right," Eckstein whispered as he swiped a stinging dollop of sweat from one eye. He realized that he was still gripping his pistol as he drove, and he thumbed the safety on and rid himself of it, dropping it on the console.

Max recovered, smeared the sweat from his brow with his sleeve, and twisted in his seat. He peered through the rolled-up rear window flap. The three small corpses lay back there in a rough triangle of limbs askew and mouths agape. Death had long ceased to impact his surgeon's professionalism, but killing again caused him a wave of nausea. He slumped in the seat and took in great gulps of air.

"Well," he whispered. "Now we've done it."

"Right." Eckstein was thinking the very same thing. "That should bring on half of Africa. Not that we had a choice."

"We could have just turned around."

"And then?" Eckstein understood Max's churn of guilt, so he let him find his own way.

"I know. They'd have called in a whole platoon and hunted us down and got us with a rocket-propelled grenade."

"Right."

Max thought about his own conclusions for a moment, then began to accept his and Eckstein's survival as sufficient justification.

"Well, Ben-Zion will he happy," he mumbled. "At least he'll know you haven't gone soft."

"Yeah. A body count always makes that prick smile, as long as it's good for his record."

The castle suddenly rose before them as they crested the last rise in the road. Eckstein knew that the gunfire had been heard and that Krumlov's mercs would be jumpy and primed for action. He glanced at Max.

"Take your pistol by the barrel and hold it outside the window."

Max hesitated. "How do we know the rebels haven't already taken over the camp?"

"If they have, they'll kill us. If they haven't, Krumlov's men will kill us. Unless they're damn sure we're disarmed."

Max cleared his weapon and quickly extended it, butt first, outside the window, and Eckstein did the same. They stopped in a spray of dust and pebbles just before the high curls of concertina, but the powdered air bounced the headlight glare back at them and they could see nothing out ahead.

"You there!" It was Manchester's voice, loud and cockney and threatening. "Douse your bloody lights or we'll shoot your fucking heads off!"

Eckstein hit the headlight switch, and he and Max settled into blackness.

"Ahhh," he sighed grimly. "There's no place like home . . ."

Krumlov's orphanage was hardly a summer camp, yet in the ensuing minutes after Eckstein's jeep was allowed through the gate, the place took on the surreal qualities of such a recreational facility, albeit in an African purgatory of disease and misplaced hope. The night was balmy and thick, and while the "camp counselors" gathered in a huddle just inside the mouth of the horseshoe, the children continued their makeshift games, the strong ones scampering about and giggling, oblivious to the impending doom that was all too real to the adults.

For a full ten minutes, Eckstein and Max endured a harsh critique of their actions. The source of the invective was, not surprisingly, Dominique. The nurse was furious that her children had suddenly been jeopardized twofold, and she refused to accept the logic that the two Israelis had no choice but to open fire.

"You might have at least tried *talking* to them first." She stood with her arms folded across her Sorbonne sweat shirt, her eyes wide and blazing, her mouth pursed in disgust.

"We *did* try," said Max, but he found his voice curiously subdued, as if he had suddenly been transported back to kindergarten and was suffering the reprobation of his teacher. He had only just met the young woman, but there was an air of moral strength emanating through her striking features and he despaired in a wash of shame.

Eckstein said nothing. He took no pride in the killings, but he had already been over it fifty times in his head and concluded that other options were nonexistent. Yet he absorbed Dominique's anger as if it was a punishment deserved, and he found himself strangely transfixed by her. As she hissed at him he suddenly pictured her engaged in a domestic conflict with a lover, and what followed were erotic images that made him blush and he swept them from his mind, wondering what the hell was wrong with him.

"You clearly did not try hard enough!" She spat. "Now they will certainly come here *en masse*. Isn't it enough that these poor things are starving and sick? Did you have to subject them to an armed assault as well?!"

She focused all of her ire on Eckstein and seemed to ignore Max's complicity, and it was, strangely, as if Eckstein had constantly disappointed her in the past and now this was the culmination of it all.

"I trusted you." She pointed directly up at his face. "I had faith, that you would *care* for these children."

"I do care," he tried to respond, but she ran right over him.

"That you would be clever, and careful. Yet you walk around this place with your hand in that little boy's, giving him hope, and then that same hand draws a pistol without *thinking*."

"I thought very hard, Dominique."

"I called you Moses." She put her hands on her hips and stabbed her chin at him. "Perhaps it should have been *Caligula*."

"Enough, Dominique!" Krumlov suddenly waved a hand before her face, as if trying to snap her from her inappropriate rage. She twisted her head to him, her eyes still wide and burning, and he lowered his voice. "Enough. These men are professionals, they were forced to make a rapid and difficult decision. We shall respect *your* decisions when it comes to the children. But if combat is at hand, you will leave it to the soldiers."

She raised her hands and made to answer the Czech, but then she took in a long breath, looked at the ground, and whispered, "*Oui*, Jan. *D'accord.*" And she turned and strode away.

The group of men let out a collective sigh of relief. Eckstein stood there slowly shaking his head, and Baum smirked at him.

"It always heartens me to see you fail so miserably with a woman."

Eckstein nodded weakly in return. "We should take away her stethoscope and give her a gun," he said.

"She would only use it on us," Krumlov commented.

"Pardon my insolence, sirs," said Manchester, who was standing there fidgeting with his Sterling submachine gun. "But we should set up. The buggers might show any minute and I've left Bernd alone at the wire."

"Yes." Krumlov nodded. Eckstein noted that in the past two days the Czech seemed to have aged, his boyish good looks having suffered the strains of mourning Niki. Baum had told him that he had spotted the Czech more than once, off and alone and reading from Niki's journal. Krumlov turned to Benni. "You are the ranking field officer, Colonel Baum. I leave it to you."

Benni realized that the Czech had chosen to address him by his real name, apparently accepting it as bona fide for now.

"All right." Benni hitched up his trousers. "What have we got for arms and ammunition?"

"Bernd and I've got our SMGs," said Manchester. "Plenty of rounds, one crate of frags."

"That's it?" Eckstein asked.

"We've also got a captured RPG." Manchester shrugged an embarrassment. "But I'm afraid the thing's had a vasectomy."

"No rockets?" said Eckstein.

"Sorry," said Manchester. An RPG without projectiles was nothing but a steel tube, no more lethal than a bassoon.

"I have a MAG," offered Debay. He meant a Belgian light machine gun.

The group turned to the mercenary, who was standing outside the huddle and looking up at the roof of the center hall of the castle, the head of the horseshoe.

"How many rounds?" Eckstein inquired hopefully.

Debay counted ammo boxes on his thick fingers. "Maybe eight hundred."

"Can you get up there?" Benni pointed up to the roof.

"Of course," the Belgian snorted.

"All right, then." Benni bent to the earth and pulled a pen from his pocket. Someone produced a flashlight, and he drew a rough overhead sketch of the compound in the dirt. "Manchester and Bernd will hold the wire out front. Debay will set up on the roof and cover the walls." He looked up at Eckstein. "Mr. Hearthstone, you and I and Jan will stand mobile with pistols, back here inside the horseshoe. We will respond to support any approach. Max, you will please help Dominique get all of the children inside the main building and stay with them there."

Max pointed off to the Land Rover, which was parked in the lee of one of the crumbling side walls. "What about that and the jeep?" he suggested. "We could use them for a breakout."

Krumlov bridled at the suggestion. "And who will be chosen to leave, dear Doctor? We have many children here. Shall we select only ten or twenty, perhaps by short straws?"

Benni looked up at the Czech, surprised to hear a tone of concern for the orphans. "I don't think our doctor was suggesting that, Colonel."

"I meant as a diversion, sir," Max confirmed to Krumlov. "Some of us would have to volunteer to drive, alone. The drivers would probably be chased down and killed, but it would buy time for a back-door escape."

Krumlov looked at Max, then touched his fingertips together like a monk. "My apologies."

"No need," said Max.

"Israelis do not leave the weak to the wolves, Jan," Benni added. "Especially not children." He sighed, pressed his palms to his knees, and stood up, perusing the huddle of men. It was a thin plan, so few combatants to cover so much area, and they all knew it. "That's it, then. To your posts."

"When they come," said Krumlov. "They will come like the Mexicans at the Alamo."

Benni dusted off his hands and lifted them. "Then we will pray that history does not repeat itself. Now, move please. It might not happen for days, or it might happen within the hour."

"Tally ho." Manchester hefted his Sterling and marched off like one of the Queen's own guards toward the gate. Debay shook his head as if he was in the company of glib amateurs, and he headed off to wherever he had stored his precious cache of heavy firepower. Krumlov put his hands on his hips and slowly turned, perusing his meager fiefdom.

"Well." He sighed. "I suppose I should go make amends with my nurse. Hers will be the most difficult task." He turned to Max. "Shall you join me, Doctor?"

"Certainly," Max nodded. "I'll just get the medicines." As Krumlov strode away, the Israeli surgeon lifted an eyebrow at Eckstein, who pursed his lips and nodded with a frown as if being nagged by Simona to perform an unseemly domestic task.

"What was that all about?" Benni asked when he and Eckstein were alone.

"What was what?" Eckstein was squinting off toward the entrance gate of razor wire, where Manchester and Bernd were performing the standard preparations of soldiers about to suffer an assault. The large German was piling broken stones into small mounds for firing positions, while Manchester loaded spare weapons magazines and checked the heads on fragmentation grenades.

"That little eyebrow thing that you usually receive from stewardesses."

Eckstein did not laugh. His back was turned to Benni and he kept his voice low and spoke in Hebrew.

"You know who Max is?"

"A special ops surgeon, ex-*Mat'kalnik*. I've seen him at Tel Nof."

"He showed up with an order from Ben-Zion."

Benni felt his shoulders bunch in reflex to Eytan's tone and the mention of an order from the general. "Which is?"

Eckstein turned to him. "We're to say *kaddish* for Jan, here in Africa."

Kaddish was the Hebrew prayer for the dead, but no matter how poetically you phrased it, it was obviously a kill order. Yet in so many years of service Benni had long ceased to be surprised by such turns of events, alliances, or moralities. However, he already sensed from the roiling conflict in Eckstein's posture that the major was not at all convinced of the order's validity.

"It must have been a cabinet-level decision," said Benni. He searched his pockets for a cigarette, found one battered Rothmann in a crumpled box, and lit up. "But the reasoning had better be sound. I'm not so sure we can pull this off without him."

"You're taking this very well," Eckstein said sarcastically, but Benni was also used to his major's personal tortures when it came to the "wet work." He had just killed two men, and they were not his first, but thankfully his young partner had not yet lost his soul and Benni was actually relieved each time he witnessed Eytan's quandaries.

"Just give me the facts, Eytan. Then, if need be, I'll salve your conscience."

Eckstein sighed, found a cigarette for himself, and relayed the alleged logic behind Krumlov's impending doom, as well as the details of his own failed protests to Ben-Zion. When he was done, he expected Benni to agree that the decision was reflexive and ill-considered, but Baum gave him no satisfaction. It was not his job to pave Eckstein's path to redemption. Benni's curriculum vitae was replete with enough mortal sins of his own.

"Sounds sound to me."

"Oh, really? And what if he really has the goods? Suppose there is a second mole in that photo? Who's going to pick him out for us?"

"I suppose we'll leave that to Shabak." Benni shrugged. "Or maybe we can shake it out of him first."

"Water torture, Benni?" Eytan's voice was filled with disgust. "Matches under his fingernails? Or should we just put a gun to Dominique's head and make her kneel in front of him?"

"Look, Eytan . . ." Benni stepped forward and placed a hand on Eckstein's shoulder, but the major shook it off.

"I'm not doing it, Benni. I'm *not*."

"*Look*, Eytan." Benni dropped his hand on Eckstein's shoulder again, but this time he gripped him hard and fixed him with that gaze that had often made captured terrorists foul themselves. "I've heard all this before. Every time you're briefed for a hard assignment you always whine and resist and struggle with your demons until I remind you who you are and you remember and then you accept it. This time I'd like to cut to the chase, if you don't mind. We're under assault in fucking Africa and we just don't have the time."

Eckstein was about to resist further, but he knew that Benni was right. It was just a mental game, a way to be able to tell himself that at least he was a *reluctant* assassin. He slumped a little until Benni relaxed his grip, then he took a long drag off the cigarette and looked up at the stars.

"I just don't want to end my career this way."

"But it's not about your career. Is it? We're protecting the plans for an anti-ballistic missile system. If the Syrians get them, the Russians get them. If the Russians get them, they sell them off to the Chinese. Then the Chinese just modify the rockets they're selling to Baghdad, make them corkscrew or some goddamn thing so nothing can knock them out of the sky, and the next time Saddam gets a hard-on Tel Aviv is *fucked*."

"Exactly! So, suppose he's genuine? Suppose it turns out that his information was fine, and we've just tossed him in the grave for nothing?"

"And suppose he's still working for the opposition? Suppose it's all a ruse and you wind up escorting him and his poison back into the bosom of your own family? You talk about ending your career with a distasteful deed? Do you really want to be remembered as a pathetically emotional officer who opened the gates for the Trojan Horse?"

Eckstein thought about all of this long and hard. He looked out across the darkened compound, at the small fires being extinguished by Debay's boots and handfuls of earth from the mercenary's callused hands. He thought about Krumlov and Niki and the way the Czech, no matter what he was or had done before or really harbored in his soul, showed genuine concern for the children and their nurse, even though he was using them and his secrets for his own safe passage. It was true that Eckstein had always twisted himself into emotional knots at the precipice of any mission that required the spilling of blood, but in the end he had followed orders, and God alone knew how many mourners still cursed the unknown face that was his own. And now he might play this hunch incorrectly and deliver a virus to the body of his country, but he could live with that. What he could not do was to kill again. Not this way.

"Well, I'm not going to do it," he said quietly to Benni as he shook his head. "My gut tells me he's clean. I won't be a the killer of a prophet."

Benni smoked, squinting through the dark haze at his major. He could execute the order himself, but where would that leave Eckstein? Insubordinate? Disgraced? Primed for court-martial, or worse? And what if he was right, his instincts on the mark? Their careers were nearly over. Would they exit apart, one stage right, one stage left? Benni had his own grown sons of whom he was sufficiently proud, yet his chest swelled with Eytan's integrity no less than if the man was his own flesh and blood.

He decided to respect his decision and stand by him as equal partner, as they had always done for each other.

"Fine," he said. "So you won't be the prophet's murderer. But just be prepared, my son, because you may discover that you've become the devil's shepherd."

"I felt my ears burning, gentlemen." It was Krumlov's voice, and Benni and Eytan spun to him, having been so engrossed in his fate that they did not sense his approach. "Not that I comprehend a word of Hebrew."

Benni smiled, but without his eyes. A good intelligence officer could speak your language fluently and not give it away for years. The American chiefs of station in Israel were like that, cornering you at their farewell embassy barbecues and suddenly breaking into stunning Tel Aviv street Hebrew over a Texas drawl.

"Well, Jan, you are correct," said Benni. "We were discussing a delicate situation."

Eytan stiffened, but said nothing. He did not know where Benni was going with this, but he knew when to stand fast and observe, carefully.

"The situation is certainly delicate," Krumlov agreed. "Deadly might be a more accurate description."

"Yes," Eckstein muttered. "Deadly."

The Czech looked at him and his thick eyebrows furrowed. His blond hair was matted with African dust, and sweat rivulets had made strange tracks along his tanned cheeks like trails of tears.

"I'm going to lay it out straight for you, Jan," said Benni. He looked over at Eckstein, locking his eyes for a moment, and Eckstein trusted him as always and nodded imperceptibly.

"First of all, allow me to introduce Major Eytan Eckstein. It is not a cover name." The gesture was meant as a trust-buyer, but it had no effect and Krumlov just glanced at Eckstein and waited. Benni carried on. "Second, Jerusalem has not purchased your product."

The vocabulary was the same throughout all intelligence services. Benni meant that his commanders did not believe Krumlov's story about the mole. The Czech nodded, sighed, and looked around for a place to sit. He backed up and lowered himself onto a large rock, letting his legs splay like a child's, and he pulled a pack of cigarettes from his stained shirt pocket, and Eckstein wondered if all soldiers and spies were intent on self-destruction.

"I am not surprised," said Jan as his match flared and he looked up at the two Israelis. "They only have half the picture, so to speak. But when I am there and can actually point out to them . . ."

"You will not be there." Benni cut him off curtly. Eckstein looked at his colonel. Now he was lost, he had no idea where Baum was going with this. Krumlov stopped halfway through a drag on his cigarette.

"What do you mean?"

"You are not going to Israel, Colonel Krumlov," said Benni in his darkest tone of finality. "We have orders."

The Czech's face twisted, the muscles around his mouth contorting, and he pressed his hands to his knees and stood up. "That is foolish." He tried to control his trembling voice. "Then they will *never* know what I know."

"They will," said Benni. "One way or the other. But you will not be coming out with us. You will not set foot on Israeli soil."

"Damn you!" Krumlov jabbed his burning cigarette at Benni's face. "What the hell happened?! You mean to tell me that you've gone through all this for nothing? You expect me to survive all this, knowing that I could have left Niki comfortably in her Balkan hellhole, but at least *alive*? You don't want the vital information that can save your own country? We had an agreement!"

"Jerusalem's 'agreements' shift like the winds of a desert *hamsin*," said Benni, "in case you haven't been reading the papers."

Krumlov stood there quaking, but he put his fists to his hips and rooted himself like a marble statue. "You cannot stop me. I'll go without you."

Benni cocked an eyebrow and turned to Eckstein. "Tell him," he said.

Eckstein hesitated for a split second, but then he just gave in to Benni's ploy, even though he had not yet worked it out. "We've been ordered to eliminate you."

Krumlov's mouth fell open, and he cocked his head forward as if he could not possibly have heard correctly. "What?" he whispered.

"Yes," said Benni. "But we can also offer a deal."

This should be interesting, Eckstein thought. It was like writing a soap opera via modem with a distant partner and never knowing where he was going to take the plot.

"*What* deal? Why the hell do they want me dead, for God's sake?"

"You know I can't tell you that," said Benni. "But it does not have to happen. You will just tell us which person in your photo is Bluebeard, and you will help us get the children out of here. In turn, we will become pathetically incompetent as you escape from Africa."

Both Eckstein and Krumlov looked at Baum as if the burly colonel had just conjured a unicorn out of thin air. *Brilliant*, Eckstein thought, *and so simple. Why the hell didn't I come up with that?* Jerusalem would have the information they needed, and then Shabak could do with it as it wished. Krumlov would have his life, and if he was smart and took Dominique with him, he might have quite a nice life after all. So what if it wouldn't be on the beaches of Netanya?

But Eckstein started as, inexplicably, Krumlov slapped himself on the forehead and began to laugh. Benni and Eytan watched the Czech as his body convulsed with it and he arched his head back at the star-filled night. He sucked in a stream of smoke and blew it into the blackness.

"Oh, you fools!" He had trouble producing the words through a sour laugh that sounded like sobs. "You damned ignorant fools!"

He reached into his trouser pocket and Eckstein's fingers twitched toward his pistol, but the Czech threw something to the ground at Benni's feet.

"Pick it up, Baum."

Benni looked down. It was Niki's blood-spattered journal.

"You've watched it and wanted it, haven't you? Now *pick it up*."

Benni bent and retrieved the notebook. Yes, he had wondered if the journal held some vital secret, some key to Bluebeard or the Czech's true motives for defecting.

"Do you read Czech?" Krumlov sneered.

"Slowly," Benni said. "It takes me time."

"Well, you can borrow it. It's fine reading, pages and pages of love letters to me. She wrote every day, Baum." He nearly choked with the image of it. *"Every day."*

Eytan was barely breathing, for watching the flood of Krumlov's grief was immeasurable torture.

"But just read the last page, Baum. Just those three lines."

Benni slowly opened the journal. The pages were crowded with very fine script. He turned to the final page, but Krumlov already knew it by rote and he saved Baum the trouble.

"I loved you with all my heart, Jan," he recited in a hoarse whisper. *"And I must come to you to kill you, my love. But I will not try until I am sure to fail."* His voice deserted him as the tears streamed down his face.

Benni slowly lowered the notebook. "We are so sorry," he said.

Krumlov waved it off furiously. "You see? She committed *suicide* for me. She only tried to do what she was forced to do when she was sure that someone like Michel Debay would stop her. And do you know why? Because Niki knew the truth, she knew my dream, she wanted me to have it."

The Czech began to pace back and forth, gesticulating wildly and giving full voice to his own bitterness.

"You think I'm just some Slavic salesman of secondhand secrets? You think all I care about is a villa on the Mediterranean and a big-breasted sabra girlfriend? That's what you think this is all about? I'm like the old white hunter tired of the chase and looking to settle in the velt among the pretty brown natives, *right*?"

Eckstein and Baum just watched him, transfixed like an audience to a televised moon landing. He stopped pacing and turned on them, jabbing right and left fingers toward the chests of the two Israelis.

"I am no less than you are, my secret friends," Krumlov hissed. "No less. My father was a Czech partisan during the war, and when he came out half alive the communists made him a general. A *general*, a rank that none of us will ever see, I assure you. And all throughout my fine

Catholic childhood, which was itself suppressed by the party, I wanted nothing more than to be like him, a hero of the state, an StB officer *par excellence*. And it never occurred to me that my beautiful blond Polish mother was anything other than what they both claimed, an immigrant from Warsaw who had found her white knight on his sweaty mount in 1945. I never *imagined* that the terrible scar on her forearm might be a self-inflicted wound to conceal her tormented past. But it wasn't until *after* his death that I discovered the truth. She was an immigrant, all right. A refugee, and he had found her half dead in a ditch while she was trying to *walk* to Prague. From *Auschwitz*."

Krumlov was trembling now, his whole body resounding with twitches of emotion, and Benni and Eytan found themselves also trembling as they listened, knowing what was coming, not believing it, but believing every word of it. Krumlov stopped shouting and his voice grew quiet, but it was another voice, full of liquid and the blood of his torn heart.

"Oh, I will tell you who your mole is, my friends," he whispered. "But I will tell you in Jerusalem." He hurled his glowing cigarette to their feet like the gauntlet of an enraged knight. "You see, I am a Jew. Just like *you*."

And he turned and disappeared into the night of the doomed camp.

PART THREE

SAVIORS

• • •

They showed you a statue and told you to pray,
They built you a temple and locked you away,
But they never told you the price that you pay,
For things that you might have done . . .
Only the good die young.

—Billy Joel

13

Vienna
May 7

ECKSTEIN HAD ALWAYS loved Vienna, but he did not understand what the hell he was doing there.

He stood alone in the huge public park called the *Prater*, its greenery lush and its sodden black trees glistening while a steady drizzle fogged the cool summer air, and he put a hand to his forehead and gathered his brows together, trying to remember. There had been a satcom contact from General Ben-Zion, some sort of argument in which Eckstein insisted on a face-to-face before he would carry out the general's latest orders. And, of course, Itzik had refused.

Yet here he was, in the warm and elegant Austrian capital of Beethoven, *Sacher torte* and *Anschluss*, and he could only surmise that it had all finally gotten to his overworked brain. Too much pressure, too many years of plotting and planning, double-think, and self-examination after the fact. Something had finally short-circuited up there and he had actually lost two days of travel from Africa to Europe. He could not remember leaving the orphanage, making his way to Addis Ababa, or flying out of the continent.

But when he looked down at his own clothes, he was still wearing his filthy jeans and sweat-stained bush shirt. He felt the rain matting his hair and he reached up to wring out his crusty ponytail like a twisted washcloth, and suddenly he wanted to be rid of it, cover or no cover. *Enough*, he decided. He was finally going to amputate the damned thing, and he grinned inwardly and nodded, remembering a jolly barber he knew in the First District not far from St. Stephan's Platz.

He was standing on a wide macadam walkway at the entrance to the Prater's gigantic amusement park, and suddenly General Ben-Zion appeared from a glass-walled *Biergarten,* curiously licking a large ice cream cone, something of which Eckstein had never seen the officer partake. Eckstein was alarmed, for Itzik was in full dress uniform as if he had just come from a diplomatic function at the local Israeli Embassy or a classical concert at the Stattsoper. Even as he approached, the general resumed a heated conversation that Eckstein did not recall having engaged in at all.

"Look," said Itzik in basso English as he stamped to a stop in front of his major. "We're not going 'round and 'round on this like that fucking giant wheel." He threw a thumb over his shoulder and Eckstein followed the gesture, spotting the Prater's Ferris wheel nearby, the largest in the world. Instead of simple open metal seats, each carriage was an enclosed windowed room the size of a small rail car, and the massive wheel itself towered above all of Vienna's buildings. "Enough talk," Itzik continued. "I've heard all of your arguments, and now I want you to get back on a plane and carry out your orders."

"I always carry out my orders, Itzik," said Eckstein, even as he felt the resentment rising and tried to control it.

"*Chantareesh.* Bullshit." Itzik looked down as a large droplet of chocolate ice cream fell onto his pristine boot. He appeared to debate wiping it off, then decided that bending before his subordinate might demonstrate weakness. "You and Baum think you're God's moral editors, changing every letter and word until it suits your fairytale view of politics."

"The equations have changed, Itzik." Eckstein tried to ignore the insults and stick to the facts.

"They have *not* changed."

"The man's motivation is clear. He's a Jew, he finally wants to come home, and without him I doubt we can get the children out of there."

"Oh, *spare* me," Itzik growled. "Who the hell says he's a Jew? And even if he is, that's all the more reason to suspect his motivation *and* his product. And as for the orphans, we're not holding an ingathering of the exiles here, not in this case."

"In *case* you've forgotten, General," Eckstein snapped, "that's *exactly* what the army's prime directive is supposed to be, in a dead heat with national defense."

Itzik apparently sensed that, just as with Baum, if he engaged the colonel's protégé here in a battle of wits he was going to come up short. As a delaying tactic he walked the sloppy cone over to a trash can, disposed of it, and came back smashing his palms together like cymbals. Then he stepped right back up to Eckstein and jabbed a finger in his face from his considerable height.

"You *will* do your duty, Eckstein."

"What duty?" Eckstein could not be cowed, and he balled his fists and jammed them to his hips. "I'm quitting right after this one, and I'm not going down in AMAN history as some brainless killer who abandoned a flock of helpless black Jews just because our government is run by racist whites."

"What the hell are you talking about?" Itzik finally gave full voice to his fury, and a young Austrian couple passing nearby glanced at him and giggled. "We already got *thousands* of black refugees out of that stinking pit. You're not fucking *Martin Luther King*. Now follow your orders and finish off Krumlov!"

"If you want to kill someone," Eckstein shouted right back as he jerked a thumb in the vague direction of Tel Aviv, "why don't you just knock off that fucking traitor you already have?" He was alarmed at his own indiscretion, having this row *en clair* in the middle of a public foreign park, but he couldn't help himself and he went on. "If the prick has an 'accident,' then the Americans can't complain, *can* they?"

Something in Eckstein's suggestion brought Itzik up short, and his mouth just worked for a moment while his brain scrolled through the strategic options. It was actually a sound idea, eliminating the source of all the trouble in the first place. The "secret" of Mossad's turned mole was already known by so many parties that it was highly doubtful his playback channel was still secure. He was rather like a diamond heirloom at the crux of a family feud—if someone suddenly hurled it into a river, the argument would become moot. But the general quickly shook off the thought, because he knew that his own superiors would sense that this new tack was a result of his inability to get Eckstein and Baum to follow his orders.

Personally, he did not want Krumlov to die, and in fact he suspected more and more that one of the people in the Czech's photo really was a second mole, which was why he had Horse working on it with the lab boys around the clock. But no matter what, that dubious character from Prague, Jew or no Jew, was not setting foot alive on Israeli soil unless the order from On High was retracted. And Itzik would be the last one to ask for such a reprieve.

"I'm warning you, Eckstein." The general lowered his voice again to give emphasis, still wagging his finger at his major's nose. "If you show up in Tel Aviv with that *StB-nik*, he'll disappear within two hours and you'll wind up pulling a long, uncomfortable stint in Prison Six."

"And if I do," Eckstein sneered. "I suspect that you and I will be roommates."

Itzik pursed his lips hard. Eckstein was on the mark, of course. In the Israeli army, when subordinates fell from grace, their commanders usually took the dive as well. The general folded his arms and squinted off across the park, as if he had finally realized that this was a public place and such a discussion should not be held here.

"All right, Eckstein," he sighed in barely a whisper. "What do you want? What the *hell* do you want?"

"If I can't bring Krumlov out, send me a team of *mat'kalniks*. At least then I'll be sure to get the kids out."

"You want me to order up a commando mission to lead you out of Africa like Little Bo Peep? Is that all?"

But Eckstein could not be baited by having his ego pricked. "You'll have to pull strings with the air force, too. We'll need a quck pickup from a hot landing zone."

Itzik considered this for a long moment. "Okay, *kibalti*." He agreed to the demands even as he shook his large head. "But pass this message along to Baum. I'm sure this was all his idea."

"I'm all ears."

"Tell him he successfully blackmailed me, but I'll be filing his refusal of orders in writing. So if he had any dreams of staying on and getting my job, he can forget it."

Eckstein had to struggle not to smirk. The last thing Benni wanted was Ben-Zion's job. "I'm sure he'll appreciate that."

"To hell with both of you," said the general, and he jutted his chin over Eckstein's shoulder. "Here's your wife. Maybe she'll talk some sense into you."

Eckstein was momentarily stunned, then he quickly spun around, and there indeed was Simona, marching briskly toward him along the walkway. His mouth fell comically open, for Simona had Oren in tow and when the little boy spotted his father he broke from her grasp and sprinted through a train of puddles with his arms whirling in a blur.

For a moment Eckstein twisted his head around, perhaps to nod a thanks to the general he usually regarded as a peer of Machiavelli, but Itzik was gone and all at once Oren smacked into his father and nearly bowled him over.

"Abba! Abba!" The bouncing child crushed his father's waist in a bear-like grip as Eckstein regained his balance. He wanted to say something to his son, to explode with joy at seeing him, at feeling his adoration, but nothing would emerge from his mouth and he just bent and kissed the boy's sun-bleached head over and over.

He looked up and watched as Simona approached, her face so smooth and tan and her teeth grinning wide and white. She tossed her black curls behind one ear and hurried, and Eytan saw that suddenly she was very, very pregnant, much farther along than she should have been. How had that happened? Had he lost *more* than two days in his brain-damaged reverie? Had he lost half a year? It didn't make sense, but he didn't care. It was strange, she was wearing all black: a fashionable black spring coat over a black maternity dress and black flats on her small feet. Other things about her were different, her eyes more blue now than green, her lips fuller than ever.

Before he knew it, she had slipped a hand around his neck and he felt the fine leather of her black gloves and she kissed him hard and he could taste *hummus* when there should have been *wienerschnitzel* on her tongue.

"Ani ohevet ot'cha. I love you," she whispered into his mouth.

"How?" He gently took her shoulders and pushed her away, staring at her glowing face. "How did you get here?"

"How did *you* get here?" She grinned at his foolish expression.

He actually did not know how he had gotten there, but he said, "By plane."

"Well?" Simona threw up her gloved hands. "By plane!"

Eckstein embraced her as she dropped her hands on his shoulders and kissed him again. Her lips were warm and soft and moist, and as she drew them away from his and he opened his eyes, he watched her cock her head to one side and grin playfully. He felt the hardness of her growing belly, like an overinflated beach ball, and her breasts had blossomed and she was suffused with that hormonal glow and all at once he wanted her. But he looked down at his filthy clothes pressed against her pristine fashions and he was ashamed.

"*Sla'chee li, Mona. Ani masree-ach.* Forgive me, Mona. I stink."

"It's all right." She smiled. "I'm used to it. Besides, you can't smell anything in a dream."

"Right." He nodded.

Of course, it was all just a dream. He knew that. But as the full realization hit him, he began to panic, tottering on the edge of wakefulness and resisting it with all his subconscious strength. He did not know what lay on the other side of this gift, this brief interlude of love and peace, but whatever it was, he was not going back there, not yet.

"I'm just here to remind you of what waits for you at home." Unlike the recent past, Simona's tone held no reproach. "They should issue some sort of mini-video player to all you field agents," she suggested mischievously. "Then you could just spend a minute with your family when things get ugly out there."

"But we'd never take any risks," Eckstein said.

"Exactly."

"*Abba! Eema!*" Oren had had quite enough of his parents' intimacies, and he was running around them in a tight circle, tracing a finger along their waistlines. "I want to go play in *luna pahrk*!" He used the Israeli term for an amusement park. "Hurry up or I'll turn you both into butter!"

Eckstein shot a hand out and snatched Oren by the back of the neck, and the boy giggled and squirmed as his father drew all three of them into a family hug. They stood there for a moment, a warm huddle of smiles in the foggy drizzle, and then Simona placed her hands on Eytan's chest and pushed away with a smile.

"I'm going clothes shopping in the *Innenstadt,*" she said. "Spend some time with your son."

"More black?" Eckstein gestured at her dress.

"It's my color, for now." Her tone was still very light, and she kissed him briefly and stepped away. Eckstein looked down at his son and offered the boy his hand, and Oren made a small leap into the air and began to drag his father toward the amusement park. Eckstein glanced back over his shoulder, but Simona was gone.

"So, where are you, *Abba?*" Oren asked as Eckstein tried to keep up with him.

"Africa."

"And how long will you be *here?*"

"As long as I can." Eckstein was straining to stay with the dream. He loathed a return to the deaths and the hunger and the moral quandaries. He thought breifly of Adi, the boy who was Oren's frail shadow. "Maybe you can help me, Oren."

"Really?"

"I have a problem. A decision to make."

"Tell me the story," Oren said with gleeful enthusiasm, just like on those rare occasions when his father was home to put him to bed with fairytales.

And Eckstein told his son the story, all of it, not as if he was simplifying the details of betrayal and murder and extortion for a child, but as if he was in a debriefing session. The tale was rather long, and as he told it Oren pointed out a strange Viennese food cart and Eckstein bought him a waxed paper bag full of sweet radish curls that had been sliced off the large fruit on a sort of lathe.

"Go on," Oren said as they walked and he munched on the white ringlets, and Eckstein went on until he had come right up to the part where he had to make a decision about Krumlov and the mole and the orphans.

When he was done, he sighed and brushed droplets of cool rain from his forehead and back over his matted hair. He suddenly felt Oren tugging his hand, stopping him on the walkway, and when he looked down his son stood in a pool of sunlight, his blond bangs dry and sparkling, his face beatific.

"But it's so simple, *Abba*," Oren said as he shook his head, wondering why he should suddenly be wiser than the man he adored and admired above all the biblical kings. "It's the children." He spread his arms wide and lifted his small palms to the sky. "The children are good. You must save the children. Nothing else really matters. Right, *Abba*?"

Eytan stared at his child and he felt his throat thickening, the wetness in the corners of his eyes. *How did I lose this?* He wondered. *Where have I been?*

"Well?" Oren placed his small fists on his hips, mimicking one of his father's stern gestures.

"Right," Eytan whispered. He took in a long breath and looked up at the sky, and there before them was the huge Ferris wheel. It was just rolling to a stop, one large car settling itself on the platform, disgorging a crowd of laughing teens.

"Hey!" Eytan barked. "Let's go for a ride!"

"No." Oren's expression instantly darkened and he shook his head.

"Come on," Eytan coaxed. "It's the biggest one in the world."

Oren came to his father and hugged him hard, burying his face in his belly, refusing to look. "It's too high."

"Nothing can happen." Eytan petted his head.

"Yes it can. We could fall."

"No. Really."

"Really? No one has ever died on a Ferris wheel?"

"Well . . . I suppose a few people have. But . . ."

The boy lifted his face, his frightened gaze locking his father's eyes to his own.

"Why would you want to risk that, *Abba*?" he asked. "When everything you have is right here on the ground . . . ?"

Eckstein was momentarily stumped by the question, the boy's reedy voice echoing over and over in his brain. *Why would you want to risk that, Abba?* His mouth worked to make a reply, but there was no way to tell a child that something on earth might be more important than a father's love for his son, and he suffered a twisting blade of emotion in his heart as all the false objectives of his life and career came hurtling toward him and shattered like so many idols of salt. He tried to dredge up an answer, but all at once Oren's expectant face wavered and faded and Eckstein could see nothing but a deep, thick darkness . . .

A black chill snaked from his ankles and up through his thighs and into his belly, and he reached up to swipe the rain from his forehead again, but he found the liquid warm and slick and realized it was sweat. He was lying on his back, and although he stretched his eyelids wide he could see absolutely nothing and he thought he had gone blind. He heard himself keening, and then he felt a small hand on his shoulder and he was fully awake.

Dominique knelt on the cold stone floor beside him. Her face showed no real empathy; rather, it was the expression of a patient nurse in a hospice. He looked around and realized he was in her makeshift clinic, the main room of the castle where she had gathered her children for the night. He and the other men had retired there in shifts, one by one, to rest on a pile of burlap sacks.

"You were having a nightmare," said Dominique. "I was afraid you would wake them." She glanced around at the tiny heaps of huddled arms and legs, her children curled together in small mounds like trembling puppies. Max had obviously attended to them all, for two of the children were wrapped in cocoons of silver thermal blankets with infusion bags hanging from portable monopods.

"Thank you," Eckstein whispered. "I'm all right."

His mind strove to replay his dream before he lost it altogether, the images of his wife and son that he wished he could tuck away in his wallet like cheap department store photos. But they quickly faded as he realized that his conversation with Ben-Zion had been real, another argument via the satcom that had taken place just before he went off to snatch an hour's nap. He slowly sat up and shook his head, feeling dizzy, his mouth dry. Dominique handed him a plastic canteen, and he nodded and sipped the warm water with its foul polyurethane taste.

He closed the canteen and immediately felt for his pistol, and when he found the cool steel where he had tucked it next to his thigh he

calmed down a bit and managed a tight smile. Dominique sat down
on the crumbled floor. She drew her legs up and dropped her small
wrists on her knees, and as Eckstein squinted at her he realized that
Simona's new features in his dream had been borrowed from the
French girl's face.

"Of what were you dreaming, Mr. Hearthstone?" she asked in a low
whisper.

Eckstein hesitated, fumbling in his damp pocket for his cigarettes.
He lit one up and in the brief flare of his lighter saw that Dominique
was frowning at him.

"That is so bad for the health," she said.

He looked at her carefully, wondering that she could be so naive.
They were all going to die here in this country, he knew that now, and
even a three-pack-a-day habit wouldn't make a damn bit of difference.

"My name is Eytan," he said. "Eytan Eckstein."

Something like a wry smile crossed her full lips, as if she had heard
the confession of a mischievous child. *"A-tahnne,"* she pronounced in
her lilting accent. "It is a nice name, like the French name Étienne."

"Yes, well, it's mine and I guess it will do." He paused for a moment.
He wanted to tell her about his dream, yet he was a private man by
personality and profession, and confiding in strangers was far from
habit. But his well of secrets had long overflowed and it all seemed like
so much nonsense now. "I was dreaming about my wife and son," he
said. "And about Krumlov and my superior officers."

Dominique laced her fingers together and looked out through the
broken doorway of the room.

"And are you happily married?" she asked, not as if she cared about
his status, but wondering herself how such comfort might feel.

"A man who is never home can be easily pleased with his marriage,"
he sighed. "My wife calls me a ghost. I'm afraid she's right."

Dominique turned her head back to him. "I must apologize to you,
Eytan. For my anger."

"There's no need."

"No, there *is* need. You are not here to save souls. You are here to
save lives, and I do understand that. I sometimes have, how do you say,
a temper?"

"Got one myself."

"I was very upset about the death of Nikita and Jan's loss, and then these things happened in the valley, but I know it was not your fault." She looked at him as if she could not reveal all of her impressions without baring too much. "I think your appearance reminded me of some things."

Eytan just watched her, unsure if she meant his arrival or his looks.

"At times we meet someone," she continued, "and they remind us of the past and other sadness and these things bubble up, but it is not their fault. Do you understand?"

"I think so."

She searched his face for a moment, then said very directly, "Jan is a good man."

"Is he?"

She lifted a hand from her knee and waved it as if brushing off an annoying fly. "I am sure your superiors do not think so, yet I know him well."

"Where did you meet?"

"In the Balkans. His service was there and I was with a relief organization."

Eckstein nodded, waiting, expecting to hear perhaps that the two had become lovers, at least for that time. She seemed to know what he was thinking.

"No," she said. "We were never lovers. Perhaps he wanted to bed me, but when he learned my story he stopped. He has been like a father."

"It must be quite a story," Eckstein said gently, as if he was not probing at all. He had learned the subtler gifts of interrogation from Baum.

"It is just a story of broken love." Dominique shrugged. "Perhaps like your own. Nothing special."

"They are all special," said Eckstein, thinking of Ettie Denziger and what might have been.

Dominique sighed wearily, as if she had told the tale too many times and each time it pained her anew. But then she began to relay it, like a fable with lessons to be shared by all victims of love and loss.

"I was nineteen years old, in Paris." She laced her fingers and again squinted out through the doorless opening of the castle. "I fell in love with a man twice my age. But no," she emphasized as she briefly wagged a finger. "He was not, how do you say, a lecher? We were simply thrown together and he was wonderful and I was young and wounded and he gave me everything I needed then."

"And you, him," Eckstein said.

"*Oui*. And I gave him the same. I wanted desperately to marry him, but he was wise and insisted that we wait, that I was too young, that I would grow tired of him and want my youth and my young life and a younger man."

"And did you?"

"No, I never did, but I thought he must know better and so I left him and I tried. And when I came back to him, it was too late."

Eckstein probed no further. He knew that she would tell the rest in her good time.

"His family hated me." She slowly shook her head, remembering. "They thought I was very bad for him and that I would hurt him. But it was not so." She paused for a moment, and in the glow of his cigarette as he took a slow drag Eckstein could see the glisten in her eyes. Yet she did not cry, only gathered herself for the rest and went on. "He died very suddenly. All at once he was very ill and it did not take long. He wanted me to go on and to live and love again, but I swore that I would not, that I would rejoin him in time, with my own death, whenever that would be."

Eytan felt a constriction in his throat, a terrible sadness for such a young life frozen for eternity. He chose his next words carefully and barely whispered them.

"But he did not want that, Dominique. Isn't it a waste?"

She turned to him, and he thought he might have angered her with his challenge, but she only smiled weakly.

"What is a waste, Eytan Eckstein? What is a waste? Is it not a waste that you travel the world fighting for something that will go its own way with or without you? Is it not a waste that somewhere you have a love and a wife and a child, yet you may die here in this place and be forgotten by everyone except them?"

There was no reply to be made except the most painful affirmative, so Eckstein just watched her in silence.

"I am twenty-six years old now," she continued. "And I am not a saint. I have had other lovers, though without love. I miss that one true thing, yes, but it is all right because I know there cannot be something more in the world than what I had. That kind of love comes only once, and even though I was young I knew that then." She raised her chin a bit. "But I am not here to die. I am here to help these children, so that they can grow and perhaps find such a love, which is all there is in life. Yet I am also not afraid to die, because I believe in another life after this one, and in that life I will be with him again forever, as we should have been."

She stopped talking as something stirred in the large room, and Eckstein watched her move quickly to the side of a small girl who lay on her back, moaning in her sleep. Dominique touched the girl's forehead and Eckstein could see the bone white of her hand against the small black brow glistening with fever. The nurse opened a canteen and lifted the girl's head and helped her drink, then soothed her in French and covered her with a muslin sheet.

Eckstein wanted to run, to jump up and flee from this hell of despair, to escape back to his home in Jerusalem and lock himself away with Simona and Oren and never come out again until there was a final peace in the world. But he knew that, as with Dominique's love, it was an illusion, something that would never be.

He shook his head and squinted at the luminous dial of his watch. His rest period was over and he was grateful to have a reason to leave, and as he stubbed out his cigarette, picked up his pistol, and came to his feet, he heard the first shot.

It was distant, perhaps a probe or a sniper or even Bernd too jumpy at the wire, but it froze Eckstein like a hunted doe. He flicked his eyes toward Dominique, unsure if he was in fact awake and had really heard anything at all, but her eyes told him he was fully within the reality of the moment. From a darkened corner of the large room Max suddenly leapt forward from where he had fallen into an exhausted slumber after tending to the sickly for four hours. He was cocking his Hi-Power and swiping sleep from his eyes with his sleeve.

"*Atkafah?* An attack?" he snapped at Eckstein, but before Eytan could reply a sudden flurry of gunshots echoed from somewhere close outside the camp and both men smashed into each other as they charged the open doorway.

They skidded into the pitch-black compound, twisting their heads around madly, ears wide open and scanning like sonar, for the firing had died for a moment. And then it came again, long bursts of automatic concussions mingled with the erratic pulls of single shots. It was coming from the mouth of the horseshoe, where Bernd and Manchester were holding the wire, and then they could see the star flashes outside in the shallow valley throwing the razor wire and the two mercenaries' positions into brief and sharp silhouette. Baum suddenly appeared, trundling by at full tilt and waving to Eckstein.

"*Kadima!* The fools are trying a full frontal!"

Baum was closely followed by Krumlov, who had somehow acquired a pair of Makarov pistols and was sprinting with them in his fists like an old-time American sheriff.

"Don't be so sure!" Eckstein yelled at his partner. "It might be a feint." And as Baum's thick form sprang over the earth toward the razor wire, the colonel waved his arms at the berms on both sides of the compound.

"Then cover the flanks," he yelled, and Eckstein and Max looked at each other, then immediately split up, each of them leaping to climb the piles of broken castle stones that formed the legs of the horseshoes.

Eckstein rent his jeans and the skin of his shins as he scrambled up the left berm, but he felt nothing and barely heard the growing gunfire above the ragged rasping from his own lungs. At the top, he flopped onto his belly over a painful pile of jagged building blocks and squinted out into the valley.

They were there all right, but as Baum had said, they were mounting a ridiculous frontal attempt, with no flanking action or suppressing fire. Perhaps it was plain foolishness, poor training, or bravado, but all in all over twenty rebels were leapfrogging up through the black valley, firing their AKs toward the mouth of the horseshoe and yelling like banshees. In response, Eckstein could hear Bernd and Manchester returning short, conservative bursts from their Uzi and Sterling, and as every fourth round was a tracer, the red streamers lanced out toward the rebels and sparked off of stones, making a strange web pattern of ugly lightning that bounced up into the night.

Eckstein came to his feet, for he could not possibly crawl fast enough over the ragged stones, and he clumsily hopped from rock to rock, making his way along the battlement toward the main gate. He winced as Debay suddenly opened up with the MAG from behind and above, and he looked back to see the Belgian prone on the roof of the castle, carefully aiming defilading fire down and just over the heads of his comrades. The heavy 7.62 caliber rounds made long red lines like laser beams, and the thunder of the MAG and its ringing shell casings obliterated all of the other gunfire and yelling that were erupting in the camp below. Baum and Krumlov had reached the main gate, but having nothing more than handguns, they had taken up positions behind the crumbled stone gate sides, waiting until the rebels closed and they could be really useful. Eckstein glanced across the compound, and between Debay's tracer streams he could make out Max moving forward on the same plane as himself.

He reached the tower at the end of the berm, but it was no longer an architectural form at all, its square body collapsed long ago into a peaked pile of rubble. Eckstein slid partway down the slanted formation, found a footing, and lay partially on his left side. He extended his quaking arms between two large broken blocks and gripped his pistol two-handed, squinting to find a target out there in the night.

But before he could fire, the rebels suddenly lay down en masse, perhaps 100 meters out. They ceased their fire and rolled into the best covering positions they could find, and for a moment the echoes of gunshots died away and Eckstein could clearly hear the men of his recent kinship breathing and cursing, and the metallic clinks as they checked their weapons and reloaded.

"Come on, you bloody fuckers," Manchester hissed hoarsely. "Let's give ya a taste of the Queen's own armaments."

It was strange to hear the Brit suddenly so chauvinistic regarding the origin of his personal weapon, but Eckstein knew that the merc was just shit-scared and pumped up on adrenaline.

"*Ja, kommt hier, ihr Schweine!*" Bernd yelled more forcefully.

There was an endless delay of silence while the gun smoke that had been spewed drifted clear and away on a light gust of predawn breeze. Yet Eckstein held no illusions that the rebels had had a change of heart and would withdraw. They had no doubt found their dead comrades in

the road not far down the valley, and they would be wanting the blood
of the murderers and nothing would deter them.

He unlocked his elbows to allow his muscle tremors to settle, and he
looked down to check the defensive perimeter below. Nearest to him
was Baum, peeking from behind Eckstein's perch, his pistol at the
ready. To Baum's right, Bernd lay behind a pile of stones, poking his
Uzi through the razor wire, with Manchester in a similar position five
meters hence. Krumlov mirrored Baum's stance across the thick
strands of concertina at the far gate, and above him Max crouched atop
the second crumbled gate tower.

"They are preparing to take us," Baum said.

"How do you know?" Krumlov whispered.

"It is the silence before the violence." Max's voice echoed from the
darkness.

"Think they've got heavy weapons?" Eckstein wondered aloud.

"They'd be suppressing us with them if they had, luv," Manchester said.

"But there is an RPG out there," Bernd snorted. "I can smell it."

"Never argue with a German nose," Baum agreed.

"Das stimmt, Herr Oberst." Bernd pulled a grenade from the pocket
of his smock.

"Do not fire until I do," Baum ordered. "Then quickly, and
together."

Eckstein tried to adjust his position for more comfort. Sweat had
beaded on his forehead and was gathering in his eyebrows, and a muscle in his back had drawn itself into a painful knot between his shoulder blades. For a moment he wondered how Dominique was faring
back in the castle keep with the children, but he decided that Jan had
probably given her a pistol of her own. That, along with her stoic view
of death and afterlife, would make her more dangerous than any of
these men.

A thick quilt of high clouds had slid in to obscure the stars, and now
Eckstein could see nothing of the dark valley or Mobote's men. Yet
suddenly there was a long rustle, like a large snake sliding through a
dry wheat field, and he knew the sounds of soldiers coming quickly to
their feet, their weapons slings clinking and ammunition pouches
bouncing.

Someone out there yelled hoarsely and the attack began, one assault rifle firing first, then a long string of the barrels opening up as the rebels came on at a running crouch. Green tracers flicked out from the darkness and smashed into the castle stones, and Eckstein hunched low and tried to steady the triangle of his tritium night sights, aiming just behind one flashing rebel gun barrel. He waited for Benni's signal, knowing Baum would want his men to open up together and with everything they had, and he waited and waited and his entire body began to quake and he cringed inside and felt as if he would explode if Baum did not let them fly already.

"Now!" Baum yelled, and everyone in his firing line opened up, sub-machine guns, pistols, Debay's MAG. Eckstein started pulling his trig-ger, and as soon as he did so he was instantly deafened by his own gunfire, his ears stuffed as if with wet cotton, his wrists bucking and his eyes squinting against the sun-white bursts from his own barrel.

He heard thin yells from the rebels, some of fury, some of horror and pain, and he fired carefully and precisely and only at sure targets, albeit ghostlike shadows that leaped and staggered quickly forward. He winced hard when a huge flash exploded thirty meters out from the front gate, and he glanced down quickly to see Bernd standing to his full height, hurling hand grenades while Manchester covered him with long bursts from his Sterling. Just beyond them, Krumlov was fir-ing both his Makarovs and above him Eckstein could see the flashes from Max's pistol on the far berm. Then Benni came into view, step-ping from cover and nudging closer to Bernd, covering the *grenadier* from his left flank.

Eckstein's pistol slide locked back, which was not good, since he only had two more full clips in his pockets. "Magazine!" he yelled, a reflex of his training, and he quickly thumbed the slide release, caught the empty clip, tucked it into his pants, and came up with a fresh load. For some reason, Debay's MAG had stopped firing, and Eckstein glanced back to see the big Belgian leaping from the castle roof and down onto the far battlement. The MAG was a very heavy tool, yet Debay hefted it like a plastic toy and sprinted forward along the crumbled battle-ment with the grace of Gene Kelly.

The surviving rebels continued their rush, although their momen-tum was waning, and Eckstein opened up again. Bernd's grenades were taking their toll, but the enemy AK-47s were powerful and unceasing, the heavy Russian rounds cracking through the air and sparking off of every abutment. Peripherally Eckstein saw Max slam backward onto his rump, and then the surgeon toppled forward onto the ground just outside the wire. Eckstein twisted and immediately began to slide down from his perch, but Krumlov was faster.

The Czech snatched at the razor wire and hauled back on the concertina, opening it just enough to slip through, and Eckstein could not hear what he was yelling as he leaped out, firing both pistols. The sight was stunning, enough to root Eckstein's eyes to the scene as Krumlov emptied his right-hand pistol, tucked it into his belt, grabbed the fallen Max by his shirt collar, and dragged him back through the wire into the compound.

Debay suddenly appeared, jumping from the battlement berm with his MAG, and as he hit ground he yelled, "RPG!" Everyone slammed himself down as the launching boom of the Russian rocket blasted from somewhere out front, and then the secondary explosion erupted inside the compound. A gout of flame threw the encampment into harsh daylight as the Land Rover's petrol tank exploded, and for a moment both defenders and attackers paused as if someone in the game had suddenly changed all the rules of engagement.

"My fucking auto!" Debay roared as he came to his feet, locked the MAG to his hip, and opened up like a madman through the wire.

"It is now or never, comrades!" Baum yelled, and Eckstein understood that his colonel was about to engage them in the traditional Israeli army tactic: When outnumbered and outgunned, *attack*. As quickly as he could, Eckstein slid down the last tower slabs and crashed to the ground next to Baum. The colonel lept to the concertina and dragged it wide open and Bernd hurled one more grenade and gathered his Uzi, and Baum howled, "Follow me!" and burst through the gate.

They charged in line abreast, instinctively matching each other's pace, for they were all combat-trained and this dance of death was their common language, with Debay and his MAG at the point, all running forward and firing and screaming obscenities. Eckstein could see little beyond the barrel of his pistol, but that was always how it was in combat, nothing more ordered or visible or defined than the full-speed wreck of two commuter trains. The AK barrels exploded back at them through the night, but you could not think about that now, you just had to charge and run and shoot at everything that moved, and hope that when you finally overran them you wouldn't be left standing there alone while the enemy laughed at you and blew you to kingdom come.

And all at once it was over. Debay had halted and stopped firing, and Benni was shortly beside him and Manchester too, though the Brit let off one last burst at nothing. Eckstein found himself at the left flank of his ragged line, his pistol empty again, his breath ragged and tearing at his parched lungs. Down in the valley he could see the few fleeing forms of the last rebels as they sprinted away into darkness, and he did not look down at the nearby scattered torn bodies of their comrades.

He suddenly felt the adrenaline nausea, slick in his throat, and he bent over his knees and regurgitated a stream of boiling liquid, then wiped his mouth on his sleeve and stood up. Debay still had his MAG trained into the valley, but Baum and Manchester were looking back at the gate.

Bernd lay on his face in the dirt, halfway between the concertina and where they had all halted. Krumlov was kneeling over the large German, but he did not bother to touch him, and he lifted his face and looked directly at Manchester.

The Brit moaned from deep within his heart and ran to his friend. But everyone else seemed to already know that this pair's days and nights of jolly banter were over . . .

They lay Bernd's body down inside the compound, not far from the wounded Max, who had taken an AK round in the hip. That in itself might have been a survivable wound, but the tumbling bullet had exited from his opposite shoulder. He was breathing liquidly, half propped up in Dominique's lap. The French nurse looked up at Baum as the Israeli colonel approached, and he could tell by her eyes that it would not be long.

Manchester sat upon the ground next to his German comrade, his eyes blank, a trickle of blood from a small scalp wound dripping off the end of his nose. Debay remained outside the compound, having checked the rebel corpses and cursed at the dearth of usable ammunition, and he lay prone next to his MAG and waited. Eckstein and Krumlov joined Baum in a small huddle around the wounded surgeon. Max squinted up at Krumlov.

"You are a very strong man." Max tried to smile at the Czech. "I am not light and you dragged me like a rag doll." He coughed hard and it pained everyone to hear it. "Thank you."

"Don't thank me," said Krumlov. "It was reflex." And he caught Eckstein's eye.

The children had begun to venture out from the castle keep. They stood in small groups, but well back, not daring to come closer and disturb the adults in their strange doings. Benni jutted his chin at them.

"We must get them out of here. Now."

Krumlov looked over at the still burning Land Rover, then gestured at the jeep. "How?" he wondered. The tires and engine compartment of the Renault had been shredded by Russian rounds.

"On foot," said Baum. "We'll split them into two groups and head overland."

"*Ce n'est pas possible,*" Dominique protested. "They will not survive such a trek."

"They will not survive here," Max wheezed, and she held him as another terrible cough racked his lungs. "Take all the medicines," he managed. "Use the aspirins only for fever . . . the Lomotils for dysentery . . . half a pill and spaced . . . And take as much water as you can."

"That we shall," said Benni as he slowly rose to his feet.

Max stiffened, and no one moved as his body quivered and he dealt with his pain and the internal floods that were quickly drowning him. He relaxed then and took in some heavy breaths, and when he managed to speak his voice came from very far away.

"And Eckstein," he whispered as he tried to raise a hand. Eckstein moved to him quickly and dropped to one knee. He took Max's hand in his own and the grip was still powerful, but only for an instant. Max managed to flick his narrow gaze from Eckstein to Krumlov, and then back again.

"*Kach oto ha'baita,*" he whispered to Eckstein in their mother tongue. "Take him home . . ."

And then he died.

14

Kunzula
May 8

MAJOR FELDHEIM HAD agreed to meet Amin Mobote with the dawn, but as he watched the arrows of early light piercing the high leaves of the forest trees, he realized that he had come to despise each sunrise. In the past twenty years he had seen nearly all of them, for such was the primitive life of an army officer, and he could well survive without the glint of morning dew or the cheery chirp of a starling ever again.

He already longed to be free from the shackles of his structured existence, to wake late beside a Bavarian blonde, to wander into the vast study of his *Schloss Feldheim* that would soon come to be and sip *schwarzer Kaffee* while wearing a silken bathrobe. Yet the major did not realize that this premature fantasy was actually a danger to him, for he had already begun to shed some of his strategic acumen. He had become somewhat like an actor playing a strutting role, and a thespian rarely senses any true risk in his performance.

With the arrogance of a duelist who feels he is unmatched, Feldhiem waited for the warlord in the dry forest just south of Lake Tana. The Austrian's armored command car was easy to spot, its glistening white flanks spraying off shafts of sunlight through the brittle summer brush crackling against peeling tree barks. Dust rose from an inch of ground talc as Mobote and two bodyguards hiked up a long hill and joined Feldheim in a patch of lukewarm shadow that would have to do for true shade.

Mobote now wore an Italian camouflage smock, the sleeves sliced off to reveal his large biceps and rippling forearms, and hanging from his thick garrison belt was a Colt .45 automatic with pearl grips. Even though his present cease-fire with the fledgling Addis government appeared to be holding, he usually only moved by night, and this rendezvous was again a discomfiting exception. He was not wearing the traditional kaffiyeh around his neck, as the white scarf might only tempt an ambitious EPRDF sniper.

Mobote stopped beside Feldheim's vehicle, placed one combat boot on a rock, and assumed a Fidel-like pose. He had endured a night of battle and his large eyes were shiny and shot through with pink exhaustion, and the stench of sweat and cordite wafted from his uniform. His large hands were stiff with oozing blisters, for he had led the burial party for his fallen men. He no longer resembled the Mobote who had appeared at Bahir Dar, a beggar at Feldheim's kitchen door.

Feldheim examined his visitor, yet he took no pains to offer respect and continued sitting in the open command car door.

"Akami alaguma?" the Austrian asked after the warlord's health in standard Oromigna.

"Galatama," Mobote replied, unimpressed and squinting at Feldheim as if he was indeed a desert python.

"So, how many did you sacrifice?" Feldheim shifted in his seat, pulled some cigarettes from the command car cab, and lit up without offering any to the Africans. Mobote frowned at the Austrian's field mufti, pristine khaki shorts and crisply ironed blouse, while the guerrilla's own uniform was caked with the dried drool and blood of others and chafed his hide wherever it made contact.

"Three on the road, seven more in the attack," said Mobote.

"Very good." Feldheim nodded, holding his cigarette in his best Eric von Stroheim mannerism. "Now we have black Africans killed by Israeli Jews. That should prove valuable in our under-the-table bargaining."

"It was not so one-sided." Mobote bridled and swelled his chest. "I believe my men killed at least two of them as well."

"Really? I am impressed."

"My warriors did not die for a tactical game of your enjoyment,

Major Feldheim," Mobote snarled as he worked to suppress his disgust. His fingers tapped the pearl handle of his automatic, and Feldheim glanced at the weapon.

"Of course not, Colonel. But it was a very important first stage of the process." The Austrian pointed up through the trees. "They will be rewarded in heaven."

"They were rewarded here on earth by their brides," Mobote said. "But now their brides are widows."

Feldheim looked at the African for a moment, then he understood and nodded. "Then their widows will also be rewarded. A piece of the pie."

"The pie . . ."

"*Life* insurance, so to speak."

"*Death* benefits, you mean."

"Yes."

Feldheim crushed his cigarette under a crisp canvas boot, then hopped down from the command car and came up with a short stick like a riding crop. Mobote failed to take in the cliché, for he had never been exposed to the Germanic penchant for muscled horses and whips. The Austrian squatted over the powdery earth, swept some dry leaves aside, and began to sketch with the stick.

"This is their camp, the castle, which I assume they have already left."

"Yes," said Mobote as he looked down. "They have escaped in two groups, one north and one north east."

"They will want to extract the Czech," said Feldheim. "But Ethiopia is an Israeli ally of sorts, and they will not violate her airspace."

Mobote frowned. "Please be more simple, Major. I have little patience this day."

"They cannot walk all the way to the sea. They will need an aircraft to get out." Feldheim drew a line due north from Krumlov's defunct orphange to the Eritrean border above Gondar. "They will try to cross the border, where they will feel safe to bring in an airplane."

Mobote slowly squatted before the Austrian and squinted at his crude sketch.

"But it does not make sense. The Israelis have fewer relations with the Eritreans."

"Which is why they will not care about violating her."

"Yes." Mobote understood and nodded slowly. "Then it is simple. We can take all of the them, including the children, long before they reach that place."

Feldheim stood up and brushed off his hands. He smiled somewhat.

"I am sure you could, but I have a new plan for you."

Mobote looked up. "What do you mean?"

"You do not need to take the children."

A cloud descended over Mobote's face. He had ordered an attack on the orphanage and lost some of his best men, and now this European was shrugging it off on a whim. The warlord fingered the long bullet scar in his left cheek, something he did whenever his anger was about to overflow. He rose to his considerable height.

"Are you telling me we attacked for nothing?"

"Not at all." Feldheim wagged a finger quickly. "You attacked to drive them out, and you succeeded brilliantly. We had no intention of actually killing them all."

"We . . ." Mobote snorted.

"And I thought it all out again last night, and it suddenly came to me," said Feldheim in rapid staccato as he began to pace, kicking up dust and slapping the stick against his thigh. "The Israeli government *might* pay a million for those disgusting waifs. Or they might not. But it would be a long negotiation, and it might backfire."

"How backfire?"

Feldheim turned to the Oromo and explained in the tone of a superior intellect. "The Israelis are pathetic when it comes to public relations. They could discover a cure for cancer and make it look like a medical fiasco."

Mobote nodded, for he was actually well-versed in global politics and quite familiar with the shenanigans of Middle Eastern nations.

"But." Feldheim raised a finger high. "If you did manage to capture the children and hold them for ransom, the Jews might find a way to draw in the international community. Announcing that the OLF has taken sickly children hostage could result in total rejection of your cause. Any Oromo bid for independence would be scoffed at."

"This is what I feared." Mobote's expression instantly darkened again. "This would not be good."

"No. It would not. However, there are more valuable jewels hidden in this dung heap."

"Go on."

"As I told you before, there is a price on Krumlov's head. It is not terribly large, but both the Russian Intelligence Service and the StB want him dead. However, this is certainly not just because he deserted his motherland or his service. And it appears the Israelis are attempting to save him. He possesses vital information of some sort. His value as a prisoner might be a good deal higher than that of his corpse."

"Now I begin to see," said Mobote. "You want to capture him alive."

"Correct. But he is only the sapphire. The diamonds are even more valuable." Feldheim walked to the command car and extracted a manila envelope from the front seat. He unwound the clasp and handed it to Mobote. "As U.N. commander in the area, it is within my power to request surveillance of suspicious personnel. Those were taken at the Addis airport a few days ago."

Mobote reached into the envelope and removed a set of grainy black-and-white glossies. He looked at them for a long moment, then summoned one of his bodyguards, a noncom in his guerrilla unit. The sergeant nodded quickly at the photos and mumbled something in Oromigna.

"The bald one and the blond one," said Mobote. "They are the two men who arrived at Krumlov's compound five days ago. But they are not the corpses we unearthed. They have gone."

"Yes," said Feldheim. "And here is the key, where knowledge is power. You see, it is a well-known fact that the Israeli army will do almost anything to recover a missing, captured, or even killed soldier from the field of battle. It is foolhardy emotionalism, but there it is. They have exchanged hundreds of Palestinian prisoners for the corpse of a single private. Over the years they have spent countless millions on commando missions and secret bribes to bring back a pilot-navigator shot down over Lebanon in 1986. Everyone knows that he rots in a prison in Tehran, but still they keep trying."

"So," said Mobote. "You want me to take these men as well."

"Yes. How many troops do you have?"

"Nearly one hundred."

"Good. Split them up and follow these mad pied pipers. Take some pieces out of them if you must, but make sure they do not escape. You must bring me Krumlov alive, and at least one of these two men."

"And then?"

"Within weeks, you will have enough money for all the supplies and weapons you require. And I will have what *I* require to quit this game forever. Fair enough?"

Mobote thought about this for a moment as he stared at the surveillance photos of Eckstein and Baum. It was distasteful, kidnapping and ransom, but such were the fortunes of war. And as the Austrian had pointed out, one could not put a moral price on liberation.

"It is agreed," he said, and he extended a large encrusted hand. Feldheim looked at the guerrilla's paw, cringing at its film of blood and fluids and thinking of the diseases rife in Africa. But he swallowed his distaste and sealed their pact with a firm handshake.

"As I said," Feldheim smiled. "The Israelis might pay a million for these pathetic children. But they will certainly pay ten times that for the return of one of their intelligence agents."

"This may be difficult," Mobote warned. "They fought hard, and they will fight hard again. We will take one, but he may be damaged."

With that, the warlord turned from Feldheim and cocked his head at his men. The trio began to descend into the forest.

"Do not worry, Colonel Mobote," Feldheim called out as he pulled a handkerchief from his pocket and briskly cleaned his palms. "The Jews will pay to get him back, even if he is nothing but a charred skull and a bag of bones."

Mobote stopped and turned, squinting carefully at his "partner."

"I am not worried, Major," he said. "I will leave that emotion to you."

And he was gone with his men into Kunzula.

15

WHEN YOU HAVE walked more than thirty kilometers in the mountains, the pain becomes your friend. As your body begins to fail, drained of water, your muscles twitching, your lungs as dry as summer straw, pain is the foe you must defeat, and the ally of your stubborn soul. If you cannot stop, it is the beast that prods you on, the only sense remaining as your vision blurs with liquid salt, your tongue tasteless and caked with dust, your hearing filled with nothing but the hammer of your own heart and rasping breath.

Yet there is comfort in the familiar, and if such treks are part and parcel of your profession, then the stages of suffering are as welcome as a monk's self-flagellation. You already know that your shirt will soak to blackness, and wherever a strap or harness presses you it will soon be outlined in waves of dried white salt. If you have not been able to Band-Aid your nipples, they will soon chafe and bleed into the cloth, and wherever your belt cinches your trousers, the flesh of your waist will be sawed away as if by sandpaper. If you have not been able to powder your groin, after a thousand steps your testicles and inner thighs will compete to flower heat pimples. The blisters on your feet and ankles fill your socks with bloody fluids, but you dare not remove your canvas boots, for you'll never get them on again. If you do rest, you remain erect and keep moving to deceive the muscles of your screaming legs. Otherwise, your calves will ball into cramping fists, crippling you with spasms that cannot be relieved except by two other men with very strong hands. You must never, ever lie down.

Eckstein had, of course, walked much farther than this. As a paratroop officer he had led platoons of men for ninety grueling kilometers, tortures lasting over twenty-four hours from the armor base at Julis to the Western Wall in Jerusalem. He could no longer count the stretcher drills he had suffered as a noncom, the fully loaded combat marches through Sinai as a recruit. Yet with each of these events, traditional factors guaranteed success. There was the peer pressure, for a man could not fail his comrades and demand to be carried. And then there was the momentum, for such forced marches were conducted at a brisk rate just short of a jog.

But tonight, in Africa, Eckstein wondered if he would make it. There were no peers to spur his machismo, and speed was out of the question, because his comrades were children.

The departure from Krumlov's orphanage had been relatively uneventful. While Dominique had carefully divided the children into two groups of equal physical strength, the men had quickly buried Max and Bernd. And then by the light of the burning vehicles, Baum and Eckstein had spead their map and chosen route distances, times, and a hopeful rendezvous. The main battery of the satcom was dying and the spare had taken a bullet, but they managed to make one final coordinate contact and then it was finished and they were off before first light.

Eckstein, Dominique, and Debay had thirty-two children in tow, and at first the way was easy, all of it downhill toward Wonbera. The children's wanting bellies were full of waht, rice, and weak tea, quickly prepared by their nurse, and with the change of venue and a new adventure they were energized and gleeful, nearly skipping ahead of the dour adults into the cool valleys before dawn. By a mad stroke of luck, a farmer driving a tractor and towing a long flatbed of hay had stopped to offer the strange troupe a lift, and all through the day they had ridden along the banks of the Blue Nile to the foot of the mountains that rose to Guba. But there the farmer reached his home, and with dusk the trek began in earnest.

Now they had been at it for over six hours, all of it uphill, the joy of hope stillborn and sucked out of them. Eckstein was at the point, bent forward and pressing down on his own knees to force each painful thrust upward. He had fashioned a backpack from a burlap sack, with leg holes at the bottom and slits at the top through which he had thrust his shoulders. Inside was the sleeping form of Dvora Yohanni, a seven-year old girl who could not have weighed forty pounds, her sandaled feet bouncing beside his waist and her forehead thumping against his upper spine. To counter her weight, his own rucksack was hung before his chest. By day he had completely covered his head in a fallen rebel's kaffiyeh, and Bernd's Uzi and ammunition remained in the pack. Now the scarf was wrapped around his throat and the Uzi slung from his neck, and he rested one fist on the cool steel while with his other hand he gripped Adi's fingers and pulled the boy along beside him.

Just behind Eckstein, Dominique also carried a sickly child in a makeshift ruck, and Eckstein was amazed that the French girl had not faltered or complained even once. Below, the remaining children fell away in a ragged line, with Debay bringing up the rear, striding along with his MAT-49 in one hand and the largest child of the pack riding him piggyback. The Belgian had joined this group on Krumlov's orders, reluctantly leaving his master's side, but he was silent and powerful, a human pack mule, and with each kilometer he would quickly switch to another child until all of them had been able to rest against his muscled torso and ride his strength.

But still, it was not the kind of progress that would spell success. There was no rhythm to it and often the children faltered, swaying and coughing, sometimes sitting down without warning, and Eckstein would be forced to stop and wait until the line formed again and they went on. It was demoralizing, the sort of forced march that happened after a battle, when the objective was only to move the wounded quickly enough to ensure their survival. Yet here there would be no extraction force waiting, no field hospital, no flight of helicopters ready to pluck them all back to safety. There was only the mountains and the hours, and perhaps a rendezvous with Benni, if they were very lucky, on another day.

The night was wide and thick and cool, and Eckstein moved in a swirling froth of steam emanating from his own skin as the broiling moisture of his body evaporated from his pores. It was as if he was atop the peaks of a planetary world, the black mountains arching into a sky full of stars so bright that the dwarf bushes and sharp rocks cast hard shadows onto the paths plowed by goats and wind. With each new crest, he stopped to take azimuth readings with his compass, then adjusted his trajectory and carried on. He tried not to look back into the bowl of valleys behind, for he already knew that they were followed, but he could not make quicker progress and watching the rebels close the distance would do nothing but raise his anxiety. Early on, Debay had jogged to his side, touched his elbow, and thrown a thumb over his shoulder. Eckstein had come up with Max's night scope, swept the foot of the mountains, and found the glint of gun steel in the distance. Checking again every hour had revealed their pursuers maintaining the range, like coyotes stalking a wounded buck. It was unnerving, but not terribly threatening—for now. When Eckstein chose to rest for the night, which would have to be soon, he would discover the enemy's true intentions.

"I am tired, Eytan."

Adi's whisper startled Eckstein, for with treks like these he often slipped into a semi-meditative state that removed him from the physical realities of his body. Also, none of the children had spoken for hours. In the daylight they had been encouraged to sing and laugh and Dominique had told them stories to burn away the kilometers. But with nightfall Eckstein and Debay had to be stern and force their silence. Night combat discipline was a difficult concept for Ethiopian children, or any children not Israeli. But the exhaustion had finally hit home and they no longer made noise, except to whimper occasionally like tired puppies.

"*Ishee*," Eytan whispered in return, using the common Amharic expression of reassurance. "We will stop soon." He felt Adi tug at his hand and he looked down to find the boy's eyes wide with a question.

"Are you not tired?" Adi wondered.

"Yes. I am."

"You carry so much things. *And* Dvora Yohanni. You are very strong."

"I am not so strong. But I am very stubborn."

"Stub-born?" Adi tried to pronounce the word.

"*Ahiya.* Donkey," Eytan said.

Adi nodded and fell silent again, while Eytan squinted up ahead to a peak at the far side of a razorback ridge. On the eastern side of the summit three small structures stood out as pale blocks against the star-studded blackness. Eckstein did not need to take another azimuth reading. He knew that this was his objective for the night, a cluster of shepherd's shelters that had been built long ago as a signal relay site for the armies of Melanik.

"Eytan?" Adi whispered again.

"Yes?"

"Can you tell me about Jerusalem?"

It was strange, for the small buildings on the side of the peak had also made Eckstein think briefly of his home. Perhaps Adi had seen pictures of the city in a book, or been told stories about Israel's capital by the Israelis who had come before and failed to rescue him from his purgatory. For a moment he could see the circles of stone edifices that ringed the Judean hills, and he could smell the sweet perfume of pine mixed with desert dust.

"There is no other city like it," Eytan whispered. "It is like one giant stone castle on the top of a mountain, and the mountain is very green and soft. The sky is almost always blue, and when the sun sets at the end of the day the whole city glows pink and gold and silver. At night, the towers of the castle touch the moon and the stars." Eytan's words gushed forward without plan or thought, and he realized his own homesickness and how he suppressed it.

"Is God always there, Eytan?" Adi asked. "In Jersusalem?"

"God is always there," Eytan replied. *And the Devil, too,* he added silently, thinking of the insane religious fanatics stoning cars on Shabbat, the clashes of rioting Palestinians and the border police on the Temple Mount, the gunfights between terrorists and citizens in the promenade on Ben Yehuda. Yes, Jerusalem was a wondrous and gorgeous city, full of angels and demons.

"And will I be a *faranji* there too?" Adi asked.

The word meant "foreigner," and it was clear that Adi had never in his young life felt at home, as if he truly belonged to any place or any-one. His only dream was to live in a land where an unnamed cloak of comfort would welcome him with maternal arms. No one he knew had ever returned from Israel to tell him the truth, that the falashas, once rescued from their hell in Africa and spirited to the promised land, still faced incredible hardships at the bottom of the Israeli food and immi-grant chain. They were black, undereducated, warm, naive, and kind, and they found themselves struggling upward through a sea of cynical Middle Eastern spartans.

But Eckstein was not about to shatter Adi's hope with harsh reality, nor sully his dream with the truth. There was no point to it, for he was unconvinced that any of them would make it as far as the Eritrean bor-der, let alone to the shores of Tel Aviv.

"You will be a king, Adi," he said. "Like Solomon." And he could hear rather than see the boy smile . . .

The trio of stone huts sat on a small cut in the mountainside, forming a triangle on the shallow plateau. It was a perfect defensive resting place, for the only approach was frontal, as the sides of the peak were nearly vertical walls of sharp granite and slipperly shale. The thatched roofs of the structures had been worn away by wind and weather, offering peeks at the stars through wide and broken slats of twigs and straw. There were no windows, only crude doorless openings, and the front of the lower hut had been somehow blown out as if by a satchel charge, leaving a half-moon, gaping mouth. Together with the two huts above on the grade, this left the impression of a crudely sculpted face on the isle of Tiki, with the upper huts forming high wide eyes and the lower an endless scream.

Eckstein squatted a few meters down the slope before the first hut, his elbows resting on his knees, Max's night scope in his hands. The wind was swift and cool at this height, and although it made hearing the warning rustle of an assault impossible, he was satisfied that who-ever was in pursuit had chosen to rest in kind. They were out there on another peak, perhaps two kilometers back, and they had arrogantly lit a campfire and warmed themselves and cooked by it. It was after

2:00 A.M., and Eckstein had held the first watch and was secure that he and Debay could maintain the vigil in shifts. They all would live another night, at least.

Most of the children had been bedded down in the western hut above, after a meal of brown flour and beans mixed with the tepid water from Debay's jerry can. Dominique had asked for water to wash herself, and although Debay had balked at using the precious liquid for anything but sustenance, Eckstein had reminded him that they would have to find more of it tomorrow anyway or be finished. He filled a canteen for her and she went off, taking Adi with her to the eastern hut to rest.

He reached down now for the cap of the jerry can and watched the stars flicker in the water there as he sipped. Then he unbuttoned his shirt, took it off, and poured a palmful of water into his hand and smeared it over his face and arched his head back and shivered as it sluiced off his chin and onto his chest. He remembered how once as a paratroop recruit on a fifty-kilometer forced march, he had opened his canteen and poured half of it onto his head, an infraction for which his sergeant had made him haul a full jerry can around on his back for a week. But there was no one to admonish him here for sins of the field, and he raised the cap in a toast to the spirits of all hardened noncoms and finished off the water in a gulp.

He waited another minute while the wind dried his skin and took his own smell away from him, and then he pulled the shirt back on, its fabric stiff with salt and sweat but no longer damp. He pocketed the night scope, picked up Bernd's Uzi, and walked back up to the first hut and Debay.

The Belgian was not sleeping. Eckstein found him sitting in a corner of the stone hut, the MAT-49 submachine gun across his lap, his legs splayed. There was not enough ammunition for the MAG light machine gun to make it worth hauling, so he had left it behind. Starlight filtered through the torn roof, striping a pile of five empty cans of Tala beer, which were apparently as important to Debay's kit as bullets. The mercenary sipped from his sixth can as he watched Eckstein for a moment, decided the Israeli was not a threat tonight, and looked up through the slats of thatch into the night sky, squinting.

"I am going to hell, Hearthstone," he said.

Eytan thought the Belgian meant a lack of structured exercise and too much alcohol intake.

"Cut down on the beer," he suggested as he helped himself to an unopened can and slid down another wall, sighing as he popped the tab. The Tala was warm as urine, but it was liquid.

Debay snorted. "This?" He frowned at his own can and crushed it, the aluminum crackling under his calloused fingers. "*Merde.* I could drink a hundred of them and still fuck like a teenager."

"I'm sure you could." Eckstein sipped, thinking of how poor a beer drinker he was himself. A couple of Maccabees and he was usually ready for a nap.

Debay tossed the can aside and lifted the submachine gun from his thighs. Eckstein instinctively stiffened, his fingers twitching toward the Uzi near his knee, but the Belgian removed the MAT magazine and began to field-strip the weapon by rote. His eyes were bloodshot, but they focused through the blasted gap of the front wall and down into the valleys, flicking with a vigilance of their own as his hands continued their work, unattached to his vision.

"No. I mean to *hell*," he said. "Fire and . . . how do you say?"

"Brimstone."

"*Oua.*" The Belgian version of *Oui.*

Debay pulled a camouflage-patterned handkerchief from his jacket pocket, snapped it open, and spread it on the dirt floor, laying the MAT receiver and bolt down.

"Do you believe in hell, Hearthstone?"

"Do I?"

"All of you. *Les Juifs.*"

Eckstein came up with his Rothmanns and offered one to Debay, who looked at the box and grunted. Eckstein lit up.

"Well, not really." He shrugged. "Not in hellfire and damnation and all of that. The Old Testament says we'll be rewarded or punished here on earth. Nothing specific about an afterlife."

Debay nodded, coming up with a small screwdriver and a strip of flannel gun cloth. He wrapped the tip of the tool and began to preen each crevice of the weapon receiver.

"I killed a priest," he said.

Eckstein stopped in mid-drag, lowering his cigarette, holding the burning end above his lap. So that was it. That was the cancer eating at the man's soul. Yes, it was true that he'd been gut-shot; Eckstein had seen the puckered scars around his belly when he dug Niki's grave shirtless. And he had also seen the Belgian peeling off stomach tablets from a roll and popping them like candy. But apparently they were not a part of his medical kit to soothe a damaged intestine. Somewhere inside he was a religious man, and his sin ulcerated him.

"It was in Angola," said Debay. "Ten years ago. I worked for those South African bastards."

He was not a simple racist. He hated everyone impartially, and he usually focused on the blacks to justify what he had done.

"They said he was a terrorist. But he was not. He gave them food and water, when they came to him, when they were wounded by us, or running. We were very angry. You know, you hunt and hunt, weeks in the fucking bush. Then you finally bring down an animal and some *fou* finds it before you finish it, patches it up, sets it free. You know?"

Eckstein said nothing. Debay stripped the ammunition from the magazine and began polishing each round.

"I volunteered to do it. The father had a little parish, a small white house. Stucco, I think you call it. He drove an old black Renault. It was *très difficile* to get to it. They protected him always. But I was good. Three hours crawling to the house, putting the charge under the car. Ignition wired. Simple."

Eckstein flicked his hand and suppressed a grunt as the ash burned his fingers. Debay seemed not to notice.

"We watched, from the bush. Binoculars. It was the next morning. I was happy when he came out. Then, a woman came too, a *noir,* with a child. They all got into the car."

Debay did not describe the rest. He just nodded over and over as he cleaned an already spotless weapon.

"So," he finally said as he snapped the MAT back together, the bolt echoing in the hut as it rang home. "Do *you* believe in hell?"

Eckstein shook his head. "No."

Debay grunted, as if to say, "What do *you* know about it?"

Eckstein had killed too, but not *that* way, and no *bystanders*, thank God. Mistakes? Oh, yes. But women and children? Not yet. Not ever.

Yes, he thought. *There is a hell, my friend. I've been to it and you live in it. And if there is a place like that after death, where you smolder inside the inferno of your own guilt for a thousand years . . . You're going there, God help you.*

Debay got up and slung his MAT.

"Well, maybe you Jews are right." One corner of his mouth turned up. "The Chosen People. Maybe God tells you the truth, and lies to the rest of us." He stepped into the gaping mouth of the hut, then stopped and spoke without turning. "I will take the watch until dawn. You can go to sleep. I do not sleep."

He walked off to be with himself, alone. And Eckstein was, for the moment, very grateful to be the man he was, wanting as that might be.

He slowly shook his head as he finished off the can of Tala, and his muscles ached and bunched in his calves as he stood up shakily. He picked up the Uzi and slung his ruck over his shoulder. There was no reason for him to move, for he could well have rested right where he was. Yet at the moment his greatest sense of discomfort came from the possibility that Debay might wake him. Not to change the guard, but to confess some other horrific sin of his past, and Eckstein wanted nothing more than to escape such realities, if only for a few hours . . .

Dominique lay on a coarse mattress of damp hay, alone in the eastern hut but for Adi, who was curled up in a darkened corner and sleeping soundly. She had covered him with one of the burlap bags used as a makeshift sling for carrying the smaller children, and then she had finally removed her sneakers and socks, wincing as the wool was torn from her blisters.

After some time in the cool night air, her feet no longer hurt and the muscles of her legs were calming, and she lay there in her jeans and the wrinkled white nurse's blouse she had donned after washing as best she could. Her fingers were laced behind her head and she allowed her eyes to flutter, the stars above flickering between her lashes. She knew that they were all very close to death, for she had seen Eytan and

Debay peering back into the valley during their trek, and she could tell by the way they glanced at each other as only troubled warriors do. Yet she was not afraid for herself, only for the children, and there was no choice but to leave it to these men.

Debay was nothing but a machine, a hating thing, useful now in the way a vicious dog might be welcome at the right time. Eckstein was something different, but also useful to her now, for in age and form and temperament he reminded her so much of her dead lover. She felt the warmth slide through her body, and as always before she slept, she thought of Étienne.

Dominique did not fear her body the way some nuns and nurses did who had not always been sisters of an order, and who remembered sexual pleasure the way alcoholics remember the sting of gin. Although she had sworn a loyalty of love to Étienne, she was not a nun and she had long ago decided that it would not do to suppress forever that which God deemed natural. She and Étienne had had a fiery and spontaneous sex life, full of wildness and gentleness, at times candlelight and wine, at times near violent frenzies in semi-public places. He was gone, but you did not flick your biology off like an oil burner switch.

However, to tempt herself and others as little as possible, she often wore an expression of blank disinterest, raising it like a motorcross caution flag at all hints of pleasures of the flesh. Her nearly lavender eyes, framed by uncombed long tangles of coarse black hair, went blank and unblinking, examining each potential seducer from a face that seemed of alabaster. Men often assumed with their pricked egos that she must be a lesbian, while women deduced that she was heterosexual and wounded, which was closer to the truth.

She took some pains with her costume, never wearing anything, since Étienne, that even hinted at her cleavage, nor any bra that would further flatter her young breasts. She knew that if a certain type of man, one physically like Étienne—strong and blond with a good smile—were able to glance down at her open chest, she might feel his lips again and want that memory too badly.

She had thrown every bathing suit away.

And so, from the neck down, she was colorless, wrinkled, and baggy. Yet in a special pouch, carried tucked in her military-style duffel, she kept one set of the lingerie she had shared with him, and whenever she felt sure and secure, locked at night behind a proper door or even a knotted tent flap, she would shed her uniform and dress in satin.

That was all gone now, in this cold night in this high place, but she lay quietly and remembered how she had pleasured herself, although never alone. Always with him, his image, her memory, feeling his arms, his chest, his hips, his warm lips upon her, their thrusting. She never used an object of any kind, for he was alive, warm and trembling, and he lived within her fingers and they served as every part of him that still reached out for her. And her fingers somehow detached themselves from her own arm, and they became his gentleness or his violent hunger, and she always came, for him. She would not stop until she arched, shuddered, and cried out his name in a whisper.

More than once, she wept afterward as she lay there breathing, or quickly folded the lingerie, hid it away, and donned a T-shirt and jeans and curled into sleep. But that was how she had kept herself for him. She had played both parts, and they had remained, in the dark, together.

Yet tonight, she would not find that refuge in this open place, and she realized with fear as sleep refused her that her struggle to keep the past alive might fail. If she survived, she might have to face the fact that she was changing. And if she changed, her purity for Étienne might fade. She began to hope that she would die, and as she felt the wetness come to her eyes, she suddenly started and sat up to find Eytan Eckstein standing in the open doorway of the hut.

"I am sorry." His silhouette whispered in the dark. "I did not mean to wake you."

Dominique quickly brushed her fingertips across her eyes. "It is all right," she whispered in return. "I did not sleep."

He stood for a moment, his ruck in one hand and the Uzi in the other, as if awaiting permission to cross the threshold of a lady's chambers. His head turned and he jutted his chin at Adi's fetal form.

"How is he?"

"Very fine," said Dominique. "Very strong."

"Yes." Eytan shifted his feet. "I was going to sleep in the other hut, but the rest of them are a tangle of legs and arms." He smiled slightly and shrugged, and Dominique crossed her legs and pointed at the hay.

"You may rest here."

"Thank you."

Eckstein gently laid the ruck and weapon near the entrance of the hut, then he found a place in the shadows and sat some distance from her. He looked out the doorway of the hut into the stark mountains and valleys below, and he thought about how throughout his life he had always sought the hard way, the highest height, the most forbidden alleyways, the battlefields farthest from help and home. The foolishness of youth had stayed with him for many years, and he had always survived without so much as a nod of thanks to fate and good fortune. But tonight he felt a tremor of loss, a conviction that at last he had bricked himself behind a wall from which there was no escape. What surrounded him now, this wind and this hut and this woman and this sleeping child, were his companions at the end of the road.

He drew up his knees and rested his elbows there, and he touched his hair and felt its length and the gathered ponytail that seemed so foolish now. His flesh and soul were exposed tonight, and no false documents or pocket litter or fashionable coif would suffice as cover.

"That hair must be uncomfortable to you," Dominique whispered, still conscious of Adi's sleep. She touched the black curls that fell from her head across her shoulders. "My own certainly is."

"Yes," said Eckstein. "I'm finished with it, but I don't think I'll find a barber here."

Dominique leaned to one side and rummaged in her rucksack. She came up with a large plastic box emblazoned with a red cross, and from inside she extracted a pair of scissors that gleamed in the starlight as she snapped their jaws together.

"What is that story in your Bible?" she asked. "Samson and . . ."

"Delilah." Eckstein looked at her and he smiled at her cocked head and the hint of mischief in her eyes. "She cut off Samson's hair and took his strength. But I guess there's no danger in that here, because I don't have any left."

Dominique came to her knees and walked on them to Eckstein, and she slipped behind his back and he did not move as he felt her close, her head perched above his, her fingers touching his ponytail, then gripping it.

"Are you certain?" she asked.

"Please," he replied after a moment. "Cut away."

He closed his eyes as he heard the blades closing on his hair, a sound like a surgeon's shears slicing through tendons, and he strangely felt as if his past was being amputated by the fingers of a female spirit sent to release him from some unspoken burden. She reached out and held his severed tail before his eyes like a trophy, but he did not look at it.

"Don't stop there," he whispered.

"The rest is not very long."

"It can be shorter."

She used her small fingers as a comb and the clipping sound was a comfort, and he felt the matted tufts dropping onto his shirt back and shoulders. She was gentle and slow and careful, and somehow he knew that her aesthetic sense was fine enough, for certainly she had clipped the ends of sutures from the wounds of children who trusted her. After a while she stopped, and he opened his eyes and she was still behind him.

"I think you should remove your shirt," she said.

Eckstein said nothing, but he certainly felt the thump of his heart and ignored it as he unbuttoned the stained khaki. He heard her opening her plastic canteen and then there was water in his hair and it dripped onto his shoulders and stung the chafing wounds there from his rucksack and weapons sling. And then her hands were working through his hair and brushing the soiled tufts from his back and he shivered.

She crawled around from behind and sat before him on her heels. She looked at the top of his head and moved some of the wet strands this way and that, and then she put her hands in her lap and nodded.

"It is very good," she said and she smiled a bit. "I am immodest."

"Thank you." His voice was barely audible.

She looked at his head for a moment, her eyes lowered to his chest, then rose again to his face, and as her fingers drifted to his chin he felt as if she was looking at someone else. Her face blurred as she leaned toward him, and then her lips were brushing his and one of her hands gripped the back of his neck and all at once they were on their knees, pressing their faces to each other, their lips open and tongues entwined and their breaths coming quickly as they suddenly strove to suck in each other's life.

She held his face so hard, her hands pressing against his ears, and she kissed his mouth and his cheeks and his eyes and his forehead, and then she flicked her fingers to her blouse and tried to unbutton the top button. He brushed her hand away as he helped her, quickly opening the shirt and pulling it from her shoulders, and in the darkness he could not see her body or her breasts but they both gasped as they gripped each other's backs and pressed themselves together and crushed the cushion of her chest between them like a cherished pillow.

They stripped each other quickly and in silence, cognizant of Adi's sleeping form, yet not really caring that he might wake to witness their frenzy, and their lips and tongues remained entwined until they fell together to the straw and found their fingers locked, their knuckles white with strength, their mouths tasting cool skin laced with brine. She pushed his head to her nipples and arched into his mouth as she reached down to grip him, and he wanted badly to descend and taste her, to bury his face in her, but she wrapped her legs around his waist and forced their bodies together, and as they joined they groaned into each other's ears. Somehow, in their wanting for it to last, they rocked together for a long time, each holding back from fear of facing the other side of this abyss when it was over. And at last, as their bodies were heated and slick and their hands burrowed in each other's hair, they came together in a frozen embrace of sorrow. Yet Eytan felt no guilt about Simona, for she was there. And Dominique did not betray Étienne, for she was with him.

They never spoke. But trembling, together and alone, they dressed again. And when they lay down, their breaths recaptured, they stayed immobile for a long while and stared at the stars. Side by side, their hands touched only once, a long firm grip, more like a farewell than anything else.

And when at last they slept, they did not embrace, but turned their backs close to one another for warmth, with no more romance than that of two sergeants seeking comfort in a winter tent . . .

16

*   *   *

Tel Nof, Israel
May 9

THE COMMANDER OF the Israel Defense Forces parachute school despised cigarette smoke, precisely because he had quit his two-pack-a-day habit just six months before, and there is no one more fanatic or rigid than a reformed addict. But the Israeli Army is an extremely difficult environment in which to refrain from tobacco, fried foods, or beautiful young women, and Colonel Zev Carmon was considering early retirement before the constant temptation to sin against his health and morals would do him in.

However, this evening he would have to endure, for an emergency briefing to salvage AMAN's *Operation Sorcerer* was underway in his office. Clouds of cigarette smoke laced the foul atmosphere, bowls of greasy french fries sat on his long table, and General Itzik Ben-Zion's secretary was a stunner. Carmon was tempted to don opaque sunglasses and a gas mask.

Given that special operations often involved aircraft, parachute drops, and fast helicopters, it was common for the Tel Nof commander to host the teams of officers sending men into harm's way. This evening, Carmon's long office, roughly the size of a freight car and up on the second floor of the base's concrete HQ, was choked to the throat. Ben-Zion was there, along with his blue-jeaned minions, including that strange little brain they all called *Horse.* He had also brought along Mack Marcus, the crazy one-legged American who was constantly trying to board a C-130 for one more static line drop. The colonel in command of the Air Force Special Operations Squadron was there, the major in command of Zev's own *Samanim*, or Pathfinder battalion, as well, and Lt. Colonel Shaul Nimrodi had been summoned from retirement because he was the best man ever from *Anaf Ha'tasa*—the Air Delivery Wing.

The commander of *Sayeret Mat'kal* was present in his usual guise—wrinkled fatigues with no rank or insignia of any kind, worn sandals on his feet, and a distinct odor of kibbutz cow dung. Uri Badash had shown up from Shabak, which made this operation a curious mix of soldiers, civilians, and spies, yet no one had thought to invite Mossad, which was fine with Zev, as it reduced the arrogance quotient somewhat. And of course they had all dragged along their own intelligence officers and personal attachés, which was annoyingly distracting because the latter were all young women selected for both beauty *and* brains. The phones were ringing off the wall, combat jets kept up window-rattling takeoffs from the adjacent air force base, and Field Security had locked the doors and taken up posts wearing their Ray-Bans and Brownings.

It was a fucking circus. Just another day in the Israeli Army.

"*Hevreh, hevreh.* Comrades, comrades. Please stop yelling." Carmon raised his palms from his position at the head of his T-shaped desk and conference table. Although the session was taking place in his office, he was more or less a polite host rather than the commander of the operation. That role fell to Itzik Ben-Zion, who at present was leaning across the table and having a heated discussion with the commander of Air Force SpecOps. "The smoke's killing me, I've got a splitting headache, and my best field surgeon's in Ethiopa." Zev did not yet know that the man of whom he spoke, Motti "Max" Rotbard, had been killed in action and already buried in the green hills of Africa.

Ben-Zion shot Carmon a look that could have curled a tire iron, but he did not pull rank on the paratroop colonel. He feared that Zev might remind him in public that they had been high school peers, and that the handsome, red-headed Carmon had often snatched Itzik's girlfriends from under his nose.

Itzik took a breath and settled back down, but he continued to address the air force commander across the table, albeit in a more controlled tone.

"Look, Dani. I'm simply saying that you'll have to have another C-130 ready to go in as soon as my people set up a landing zone."

"Don't nag me, Itzik." The air force colonel jutted his chin aggressively. "The first unit's not even halfway there yet." He turned to his squadron intel officer. "Where are they now, Avner?"

An air force captain stood up and leaned over a long relief map that had been rolled down the length of the table and secured with full ashtrays. "Should be approaching latitude sixteen degrees, right here." And he pointed to a spot over the Red Sea just north of the Eritrean coast.

"I wish I could have put just one man in there to mark the drop," said the Pathfinder major as he shook his head and peeled an orange.

"My people don't need a marked DZ," the wrinkled *Mat'kal* commander scoffed. "They could spot a tampon string in a Moroccan brothel." He glanced around the room and grinned. "Sorry, girls."

Yudit looked up from her steno pad and rolled her eyes.

"Don't be such an arrogant prick, Yossi," Lt. Colonel Nimrodi chided the commando leader. He was a small, very muscular man who looked like the French actor Jean-Paul Belmondo, and he chain-smoked Marlboros from an onyx holder. "I seem to remember you trying to HALO into Iraq and nearly landing in fucking Afghanistan. Your heros will make the target, but only because we force them to use those pocket GPSs. And I'm not sure they have enough brains to operate them."

The *Mat'kal* commander smirked and sarcastically saluted Nimrodi.

"And something else, Itzik," said the air force commander as he wagged a warning finger at Ben-Zion. "Splitting the operation up like this is very risky. We can violate their air space once and get away with it, but when we send in the second aircraft—maybe tomorrow, maybe not for three days—what then? They'll put a Strella right up our ass."

"Oh, please," Itzik grumbled. "The Eritreans don't have any shoulder-fired missiles. They barely have bolt-action rifles."

"Excuse me." Mack Marcus raised a finger, instantly receiving a threatening glare from Ben-Zion. "You're right, the Eritreans don't have shit. But the rebels, especially Mobote's people, have lots of scary toys."

"Another country heard from?" Itzik snapped at the American-born officer. "You're Planning and Logistics, Marcus, not field ordnance intel."

"I'm a war cripple." Marcus smiled and shrugged. "I'm allowed to be brilliant and well-informed and speak out of turn."

When the laughter died down, Zev Carmon leaned across his desk.

"So, tell me, Itzik. Who *do* you have on the ground out there?"

Ben-Zion looked around the room as if hesitant to reveal the identities of his field agents. But at these ranks everyone would soon know everything anyway.

"Baum and Eckstein," he said quietly.

Shaul Nimrodi stiffened and inhaled sharply on his cigarette. Benni Baum had been a very close friend for many years. They had spilled blood together, some of it their own. And Eckstein was like a son to Baum. He stood up and bent over the map, quickly locating the rendezvous point and measuring distances. He turned to the Air Force SpecOps commander.

"Fuel up that second C-130, Dani. Put the crew on alert and cancel all leaves. And get the pilots in here for a re-routing."

"You're giving me orders now, Shaul?" the air force colonel bridled.

"Do it. Or I'll soon be having a talk with your wife."

The air force commander flushed with anger, but he said nothing. The two young air force women present focused on their notepads, and Itzik smirked and folded his arms.

Zev Carmon coughed and waved a cloud of smoke away from his face.

"And you think Baum and Eckstein are going to make it, Itzik? Get all these sick kids *plus* your defector to the LZ in one piece?"

"They'll make it," Itzik replied without overt enthusiasm. "And the defector's not coming out."

The entire room fell to complete silence. All fidgeting and smoking and nibbling on fries and fruit stopped in mid-motion as everyone turned to stare at the AMAN SpecOps commander. But Itzik was not about to elaborate further, and he simply returned their gazes with the smoldering glow of his black eyes.

"Then what the hell is this all about?" the air force colonel demanded. He pushed his chair back and stood up and waved his arms in the air. "Planes, fuel, pilots, *Mat'kalniks,* and cabinet approval? For what? Two men and a bunch of waifs who could have walked to a beach and been picked up by a fucking fishing boat?"

"That's none of your business." Uri Badash spoke for the first time, but from where he sat in a shadowed corner of the room, his authority boomed like a cannon. "This operation reflects on many security issues that have nothing to do with the army." Badash reached into his pocket for his own cigarette pack and lit up, then languidly waved the burning stick like Claude Rains in an old black-and-white war film. "And now, if this part of the briefing is finished, I'll ask everyone who is not AMAN to leave." He nodded in the direction of Carmon. "With the exception of Colonels Carmon and Nimrodi, of course. We are guests in their living room."

"And exactly who the fuck do you think you are?" the air force colonel spat.

Badash blew out a smoke ring and watched it wander toward the ceiling like the halo of a disgraced angel.

"I am the man who approves your security clearance, Colonel."

The air force officer instantly understood that he was dealing with the upper echelons of Shabak. His fingers tapped the table, then he mumbled, "And they say we inherited nothing from the Germans." He cocked his head at his subordinates and everyone began to gather his or her files, maps, and canvas briefcases.

Within a minute, the office had cleared of all but Itzik, Horse, Yudit, Marcus, Badash, and the two paratroop colonels. Zev Carmon rubbed his forehead and stared at his conference table, which looked like the aftermath of a high school pool party with its empty Coke cans, bowls of grape stems and orange peels, and still-whisping ashtrays. He looked up at Ben-Zion and gestured at Nimrodi.

"You know, Itzik . . . Shaul and I can leave, too. We won't be offended and I need the fresh air."

"Don't be ridiculous," said Itzik. "You kept your mouths shut before Entebbe, so I'm not terribly worried."

Carmon shrugged and Nimrodi smiled widely around his onyx holder. Ben-Zion opened a Coke can and looked at Uri Badash, who had moved to the center of the conference table next to Horse. The analyst had been helping Badash with his subtle investigation of the mole candidates from Dimona, pulling their military files from the AMAN mainframe and searching for any anomalies that might break the case.

"So, Badash," said Itzik as he wiped his mouth. "You've had the services of my genius here 'round the clock. Is there a second rat in the woodpile or not?"

Badash placed a hard black briefcase on the table and opened it, while Horse fidgeted nervously with the worn clasp of his own canvas case and tried not to meet his commander's eyes. Badash came up with eleven thick file folders, each corresponding to the seven men and four women in Krumlov's photo. It was clear that many Shabak analysts and counterintelligence officers had been poring over the documents, for they were dog-eared, finger-soiled, and marked with coffee cup rings. He dropped the pile on the table and its weight made a resounding and ominous thud.

"Well, if there is a mole," said the Shabak officer, "we don't have a shred of hard evidence yet."

"*Atah retzini?* Are you serious, Uri?" Ben-Zion demanded incredulously.

"Did he say *mole?*" Nimrodi whispered to Zev Carmon.

"Quiet, Shaul," Carmon murmured in reply. "We're just 'Death from Above,' remember? These poor fools have to use their brains."

"Look, Itzik," said Badash. "We've been running a very delicate counterintel op here. If any one of these people smells an investigation, they'll tell each other about it and our potential mole will shut down like Mea Sharim on Shabbat. Each of them passed the original security clearance with flying colors, and they've all passed the annual checkup at Dimona. We've been running our most experienced tracker teams on eight of them twenty-four by seven, and believe me, not one of them has even glanced at a copy of *Pravda.* The other three are on leave, two of them abroad."

"You let these Dimona people travel overseas?" Nimrodi interrupted.

"Yes. With restrictions," said Badash.

"*You* know more secrets than Fidel Casto's chauffeur," Carmon said to Nimrodi. "And no one stops you from flitting around the world like Hugh Hefner."

"Exactly." Nimrodi grinned. "I'm a playboy, not a spy."

"Maybe you'll just have to round them all up and lean on them," Mack Marcus suggested to Badash.

"Who are you?" Badash scoffed. "Saddam Hussein?"

"You noticed the resemblance." Marcus stroked his moustache.

But Itzik was in no mood for the playful banter of the officers' boys club. He got up from the table and walked to Zev Carmon's bookcase full of military trophies, many of them presented by the visiting officers of foreign airborne units. He picked up a bronze statue from the 82nd Airborne and examined it.

"Uri," he said quietly. "You've got to find that mole, all by yourselves, without any help from Krumlov. The decision has been made. He's not coming out."

"Well, it's a stupid decision and I'm ready to scream at the idiot who made it."

"The idiot sits in the prime minister's office, and you know damned well that no one but his wife screams at him with any success."

"Excuse me, Itzik," Horse whispered.

"And what's more," Itzik ignored Horse and continued, "it's the correct decision. If Krumlov is a plant, then we'll be completely humiliated by bringing him in."

"Excuse me," Horse tried again, just a bit louder as he raised a trembling finger.

"And worse than that," Itzik carried on. "Jerusalem answers to Washington on this one, and even *I* don't have a clue as to what's been promised over *that* hot line."

"Itzik!" Yudit suddenly yelled, and everyone turned their heads to her and fell silent as schoolboys being scolded by a nanny. She opened a hand and extended it toward Horse. "Raphael is trying to say something."

Itzik glowered at her, but she just raised an eyebrow at him, and Nimrodi and Carmon worked to hide their grins while they both wondered if Itzik was sleeping with her. The general turned his attention to Horse.

"Yes?"

"Ummm." Horse cleared his throat. "I believe we already have the answer."

"You do," Itzik stated flatly.

"Well, uh, yes. I've been thinking about it, I mean, while we were sitting here. I mean, I've been thinking about it for a long time, but you know, it just sort of became clear . . ."

"*Out* with it, Horse," Itzik snapped.

The little Russian fumbled with the clasp of his case and removed the envelope that contained the original group photo from Krumlov. He slipped it out and stared at it, more as a way to focus on something other than his commander's eyes.

"Well, I believe that Krumlov has already given us the answer. It must have been part of his plan all along. You see, he could not have known for sure that he would actually survive to make it to Israel. After all, there is an active wet order out on him, and he has been living quite out on the edge in Africa . . ."

"So?" Badash demanded impatiently.

"Shhh," Itzik silenced him. "Go on, Horse."

"Remember," Horse continued, "that Krumlov also wanted us to bring out his fiancée. He expected her to come with him to Israel. But he also must have known that *he* might be killed, while *she* might survive and wind up here alone. He would have wanted us to care for her well, even in his absence. When he gave Eckstein the photo, he was giving us all the information we needed. The answer is somehow right here in the photograph. I am certain of it."

Horse laid the photo down, adjusted his glasses, and folded his fingers together. Badash cocked his head at Horse and looked at Ben-Zion.

"I'm supposed to be the counterintelligence genius," he said. "But this guy's really good."

"Yes, he is," said Yudit.

Ben-Zion pointed a long finger at his secretary.

"Yudit, take my car and this Einstein and his picture and get him back to the lab in Jerusalem right now. And use my cell phone and tell the basement not to go home. They'll be working all night."

Yudit stared at her commander, but she did not move.

"*Bevakashah.* Please," Itzik added.

"Yes, Commander," said the comely young woman, and she got up and took Horse by the hand and the nervous analyst could not leave with her fast enough. When the field security officers had sealed the door from outside again, the remaining five men remained silent for a moment. Finally, Zev Carmon spoke up.

"Itzik, just who is that weird little man?"

"Horse?" The general sighed. "He's my worst nightmare." He walked to one of Carmon's windows and stared out at the distant airborne training field, where a battalion of recruits were marching with dummy parachutes across the blazing sand pits toward the thirty-foot tower. "But sometimes," he added, "the only truth is in our dreams . . ."

17

• • •

FOR THE FIRST time ever in the more than half-century of his harrowing life, Benjamin Baum was about to surrender to failure. His
breath was coming in long, harsh rasps, each inhale filled with the
scorching grit of African dust, each exhale expelled with despair as the
high mountain oxygen failed to support his hefty frame. From the kaffiyeh draped over his large bald head, to the cotton of his khaki shirt, to
his coarse dungarees and woolen socks and canvas boots, every centimeter of fabric was soaked through with coagulating sweat and
grinding salt. His unmanicured toenails had sliced into their fleshy
neighbors over kilometers of craggy rock and brush, so he knew that
the liquid squishing in his soles was his own blood, and the bulbous
knees that had seen him through so many weekend soccer matches
finally felt as if they were about to burst.

It was over. He had come to the end of his strength and he knew it.

He struggled up another long grade of jagged rock and slippery
pebbles, his teeth grinding and his lips pursed over them to hide his
grimace, his nostrils flaring like a bull to take in whatever sustenance
the failing day might offer. In his right callused paw he gripped the
small black hand of a boy called Yona, in his left the pencil-thin wrist
of a slip of a girl called Esther, and each of these children pulled along
another, and these next two as well, so that all in all Benni was hauling
the weight of six children in addition to his own girth.

Krumlov was back behind him on the mountain path, doing the same. And below, Manchester was climbing backwards, nudging the remainder of the children along like a stubborn sheepdog as he trained his Sterling back into the valleys, where the rebels were closing fast. They had been at this since dawn, from their resting place in the valley near Dangla and on to the heights of Mount Beleya, where they were to meet Eckstein and Dominique and Debay, if that trio and their wards had survived this murder, which Benni doubted. He was a stubborn powerhouse of a man and uninjured in the legs, while Eckstein had a half-crippled knee and the French girl was young and determined but hardly a mountaineer. There was no point to any of it anymore. He felt the despair roll over him like a tidal wave and he decided that he was just not going to make it.

"We cannnot do it anymore, Mister Benni," the little boy Yona croaked in a voice full of dust. "We cannot."

"Yes you can." Benni gripped his hand tighter and stamped down angrily on the unforgiving earth and pulled his train of children along even harder. "I am old and tired and fat and *I* can do it!" he lied. "I can continue on until the moon is high and the air is cool and we come to fine fresh water. *You* are strong African children, so certainly you can do better than I."

"Yes," said Esther from Benni's left. "Don't whine, Yona."

"I am not whining!"

"Then walk and be quiet. What would your father say?"

The little boy pursed his lips. "My father is dead."

"But he is watching you," Esther chided. "And he wants you to help Mister Benni and walk all the way to Israel if you must."

Yona tugged at Benni's hand and his eyes bugged. "Do we have to walk all the way to Israel, Mister Benni?"

"No, Yona," Baum rasped, the pain hard in his lungs and the sweat stinging his sunburned eyelids. "But Esther is right. We must walk until we can rest, and we must think of our fathers and find strength."

"You see?" Esther's pride swelled with her own wisdom and her gait became springy for a moment.

And Benni suddenly felt shame as indeed he thought of his own father, an image that had spurred him on through all the trials of his life. His father had died in Dachau and his mother in a DP camp, and he was very small when he was taken from them. But he remembered his father's stubborn Germanic nature, and some of his last words: "Remember, my Benjamin. When life is very hard, think nothing but of putting one foot in front of the other, and soon you will come to a better place."

"*Einen besseren Ort*," Benni whispered aloud now. "A better place . . ." And he pressed on toward the summit of the final climb, trying to ignore the screams of his muscles and ligaments and the parched desert of his mouth and throat.

He heard the trod of boot soles on the slippery wash of pebbles behind, and suddenly Manchester was at his shoulder, breathing steadily yet with the wheeze of an overburdened horse. The Brit had shed his camouflage blouse and rolled it into his pack, and he was wearing a soaked olive T-shirt over his fatigue pants and a dark bandanna wrapped around his forehead. He was bent under the weight of his full combat pack, and his Sterling was slung from his neck.

"How much farther, Colonel?" Manchester asked as he marched briskly along.

"That next summit."

"Are you sure?"

Benni shot him a look.

"Begging the colonel's pardon, but the bloody wankers are closing again."

"Well, hold them off."

A large pack of rebels had been biting at their heels throughout the day. They would maintain their distance, then suddenly rush forward until Manchester gave them a short burst with his Sterling. The range was too far and he never hit them, but they would desist for a while and then resume the game.

"I shall do that, sir. But I'm running a bit low on ammo."

Benni pulled Max's Hi-Power from his waistband and handed it over.

"If you run out, use this. And when the pistol's out, try hurling curses."

"Right, sir." Manchester grinned, saluted smartly, and jogged away. Benni's bravado instantly deflated and he resumed grinding his teeth.

"I don't know about you, Colonel Baum. But I am just about done." Krumlov's voice barely reached out to Benni from behind, a hoarse gasp suppressed by the rising winds of dusk.

"*Ich auch*," Benni agreed in German, which he knew Krumlov would understand, while the children would not. "But we must make the rendezvous."

"And then?"

"And then . . . we will be there."

Something like a bitter laugh fluttered out to Benni from Krumlov's throat. Baum realized that this must be even harder for a Czech raised in the cool greenery of Europe, while at least he had the benefit of growing up in the desert hills of Jerusalem.

"They are toying with us, you know," said Krumlov, and Benni knew he meant the rebels. "They are driving us on exactly where they want us to go."

"No. They are driving us on exactly to where *we* want to go."

But it certainly seemed like a classic squeeze play, the rebels trying to herd them into a position they favored, as if another force was waiting to complete the ambush and finish them off. Yet Benni and Eytan had set the coordinates with Ben-Zion and there could be no diversion from the rendezvous if there was to be any hope of escape at all.

"And do you think Eckstein will be there?" Krumlov wondered.

Benni did not immediately reply. For the first time in their fifteen years as partners, he wondered if Eckstein had finally committed himself to one mission too many. He knew now that they should not have taken the assignment. They had just returned from Africa when Ben-Zion sprang it on them, and they were feeling too arrogant and successful and prideful. He knew now that such things were best left to younger men, and he should not have let Eckstein go back in and he certainly should not have come along for one last stab at glory. He felt terribly guilty, like an old boxing coach who goads a burnt-out pugilist into one more fight, just to experience the vicarious victory.

And yet, in those fifteen years of working together, Eckstein had never blown off a meet. If they linked up successfully tonight, then they would get out of this alive. And then, back home, Benni would pull all of Eytan's field clearances and shred them and chain the boy to a desk forever.

"He will be there," Benni said, more as a prayer to himself than anything else.

He pressed on and squinted into the northern escarpments, where the flat cap of the summit on which they were to rendezvous loomed a bit larger, but still so far. He wanted to take the folded map from his pocket and run one more navigation check, but he dared not let go of the children's hands, for they might collapse on the spot and he would never get them up again and he knew he could not carry even the lightest of them now. The water was gone, the jerry can that Manchester had hauled without complaint finished off during their last brief rest stop. It had been much too long since their last intake of liquid, and the children's swollen lips were dry and cracked and slitted and he dared not look at them or the pity in his soul would be too much.

The brutal sun was finally falling into the west and up ahead the steep grade on which they climbed wandered to the right of a volcanic thrust of sharp shale. The path was falling into shadow there, so Benni made that his next mental objective, the simple shade that might cool all their flesh enough to make the final leg possible. A gunshot from behind made him wince, but he knew it was just Manchester doing his best to discourage the pursuing jackals and he pulled the children along harder.

From Krumlov's small troupe Benni then heard the cry of a child, and it grew into a long sob and a seething wail and he turned his head to see the Czech stopped on the grade. The last child in his line, a very tiny boy wearing an oversized T-shirt and ragged pantaloons and sandals made of an old tire, had sat himself down and was bobbing and crying over his swollen feet. Manchester's gunshot had done it, as it almost always did, shocking the children into the horrible reality of their plight. At least one of them would always begin to cry as the sonic bang echoed off the surrounding mountains, yet up until now they had been successfully cajoled and coaxed back into the fray.

But now it was not going to work any longer. "We are almost there," had been repeated too often, and now it just seemed to all of them like a cruel lie. It was like driving from Jerusalem to Eilat with your toddler kids in the backseat, and eventually all the promises and road games and jokes and songs ran dry, and there was nothing left but kilometers of blank desert road and they would go dead silent for a while but inevitably begin to keen.

Krumlov looked up the grade at Benni with utter despair in his eyes, but Baum could do nothing for him. The Czech walked back to the little boy, picked him up from the ground, and tucked him under his arm like a paper sack of groceries. And Benni turned and gnashed his teeth and went on.

Half an hour later, barely able to make his swollen knees pump out one more step, they were less than fifty meters from the top of the rendezvous summit. By this point, nearly all of the children were weeping or whining like wounded animals, an infectious anguish that had spread through the ranks, and no kind of encouragement could quell it. Baum searched the surrounding paths and ascents for a sign, any sign at all, that Eytan had arrived. He looked for a posted piece of cloth on a stick, a wisp of signal smoke, perhaps even the green glow from Eckstein's pocket GPS, although he doubted now that a *Mat'kal* team would arrive in time to receive the major's signal. But there was absolutely nothing, only the chill of the night winds now making him feverish and half-delirious, and he was mumbling curses to himself like an amateur explorer lost in Sinai.

He stopped and released the hands of Yona and Esther, and the children quickly collapsed where they were and began to rock like mourners over their blistered feet. Below, Krumlov also stopped, and Benni was not terribly shocked to see the Czech slowly crumple to his knees, the little boy still tucked under his arm, and Krumlov sat back on his heels and looked up at Benni with a plea in his eyes that Baum was certain begged for a merciful execution right here and now. Manchester stood well back on the grade, looking up and slowly shaking his head.

Baum turned and made for the summit, feeling so terribly light now without his burden of children, but still in the racks of bone and ligament torture. He used both hands to press down on his knees and pumped himself along like an old well handle on a farm. And finally he rose to the cap of the summit and stood there, half bent over, looking out across a magnificent panorama of harsh mountains and scrub trees and up into a sky where the vultures were already wheeling so hopefully.

For some reason, his eyes dropped from the purpling heavens and down the other side of the mountain.

And there, tilting his head back and looking up at him with an inverted smirk, sat Eckstein on a flat rock. Debay stood off to one side cradling his submachine gun, while Dominique had gathered her ragged children into a half-circle and was playing a makeshift game of pebble jacks with them.

"*Zeh haya yafeh* . . . It would be nice," said Eckstein in Hebrew, "if you'd try to be on time once in a while, Benni."

And Baum could not help himself. He sank to the earth and put his trembling hands on his thighs, and even while he grinned so hard he felt the skin at his lips cracking like charred coal, he cried . . .

The joy of reunion was brief and quickly ran bitter, for it was rather like two groups of battered firefighters linking up in the midst of an uncontrollable brush blaze. The small plateau below the summit's cap was a half-circle of wind-shorn bushes and hardpack, and the adults had gathered the children tightly in the center to provide the only comfort available, each other's bodily warmth. Dominique moved slowly among them, petting their feverish foreheads and stroking their trembling, bony backs, and she lied to them in French and Amharic about how they would soon be rescued and fly away to a land of gentle warmth and fine fruits and the comfort of their lost families.

Her arms and legs ached terribly with the strains of climbing and the muscle tremors of dehydration, yet she focused on her task and did not rest, and only once did she make eye contact with Eytan. He thought that perhaps her expression was that of acknowledgment, that together they had helped each other remember what it was that made survival worth the effort. Yet she held his gaze for only a moment and then turned away, and he decided that she might as well have been cursing him for bringing her hope in this hopeless place.

Like the professional soldiers that they were, Debay and Manchester had greeted each other with nods, held a brief discussion about small unit tactics, and without awaiting orders from anyone set up a defensive perimeter. It was a nearly impossible task for only two men, but Manchester lay himself down prone at the edge of the plateau facing west, while Debay climbed back up to the summit and covered the eastern approach. They had divided up the remaining grenades and ammunition, and the inventory was so paltry that they did not remark on it at all as they went off to make their last stands.

Krumlov, Baum, and Eckstein stood in the lee of the summit at the eastern side of the plateau, their heads bowed and their flesh quivering in the cool mountain winds. They had shed all of their packs and satchels, yet their ruined muscles were unrelieved by the unburdening. Eckstein's Uzi was slung from his shoulder, Baum again had his pistol in his belt, and Krumlov's twin Makarovs dangled from the Czech's drooping hands. The night was nearly upon them now, just a sliver of pink remaining in the western peaks, and as always with the surrender of heat in desert climes the air grew thin again and carried even the smallest sounds from far and wide. In the valleys below, the careless trod of rebel footsteps on loose stones echoed ominously, and frequently the rebels called out to each other arrogantly.

"We are nearly out of ammunition," said Benni.

"I don't think it much matters, Colonel," said Krumlov. "If the patient is terminally ill, even a truckload of medicine is irrelevant."

"Speaking of which," said Eckstein as he turned and watched Dominique work her comforts, "she must be out of Max's supplies. Otherwise she'd be administering them, just to boost the children's morale."

Baum watched Eckstein watch Dominique. He knew his partner very well, every look and nuance, and of course he noted that Eytan's hair had been freshly shorn by delicate fingers, but he did not comment because it certainly did not matter. The lip of combat was a precipice upon which strange things happened between people, and he had been there himself more than once and the mores of normal civilization did not apply.

"Manchester and Michel are very fine soldiers," said Krumlov. "But even with us to back them up they cannot cover every angle. Mobote's men will soon be upon us. They may wait until dawn, but only to catch us when we are most weak. It is certainly their game and they will play it as they see fit."

Eckstein turned his head back to the two men.

"We could try to break out in hour or so, when it's fully dark."

"And then what?" Benni asked. "Even if we can burst through their thinnest line, the rest will be on us like wolves. These kids can barely move anymore, not to mention sprinting downhill like mountain goats."

No one was offering much comfort here. They were silent for a moment.

"Perhaps it is time to give it up," Krumlov suggested with a sigh.

Baum and Eckstein looked at each other.

"You might be a fine prize, Jan," said Benni. "And worth caretaking as a prisoner. But Eckstein and I, well, we'd wind up in Benghazi. Or worse, Tehran." The images of Israeli air force navigator Ron Arad came too easily. His Phantom F-4 had exploded over Lebanon in 1986 and he had survived the ejection and parachute jump, only to be sold to the highest terrorist bidder. For years the Israelis had offered huge bribes for his return, mounted commando raids to kidnap his kidnappers, begged and pleaded and threatened, all to no avail. "The idea of rotting in an Iranian dungeon does not appeal to my concept of comfortable retirement," Benni added.

"And what about them?" Eckstein gestured once more at the huddled children and Dominique. "Maybe they'll take the children alive and sell them off as slaves. But what do you think they'll do with her?"

And of course, Benni immediately knew that something had indeed passed between his partner and the beautiful nurse. It was in Eckstein's voice, the cold failure to address her by name. But he was right, she would be tortured and raped and passed back and forth as a fine European female plaything.

"Yes." Krumlov nodded. "I would rather shoot her myself . . ."

Eckstein and Baum again exchanged looks, and each knew what the other was thinking. Here on this high place in these desert mountains, it was all too reminiscent of Massada, the giant plateau in the Judean desert where in A.D. 70 a band of nine hundred Jewish rebels had chosen to commit mass suicide rather than be taken alive by the Roman legions. And there were more modern examples of such desperation, secrets still closely held by the Israeli army. During the Yom Kippur War of 1973 a squad of Israeli soldiers, surrounded in an emplacement on the Golan Heights, had saved their last bullets for each other rather than be taken alive by Syrian commandos.

Again a flood of despair washed over Benni, but he tried to dispel it by focusing on more trivial matters.

"Well, at any rate, we don't know how long we will be here," he said. "One of us should forage for food. Maybe even a wild animal or prickly fruit of some kind."

Eckstein expelled something like a short laugh, but his mood could not really be swayed by these incidental issues.

"I wouldn't worry about the menu if I were you, General Custer."

Benni made to retort, but he just nodded and found himself frowning bitterly at the absurdity of it all.

From somewhere in the western valleys came a heavy pop, and then a *whoosh* into the sky like tearing newspaper, and the three men turned their heads to it and froze. They immediately knew what it was, a military parachute flare, the sort of handheld tube you slammed down onto your knee or a rock to fire it off. It was designed to demoralize the enemy, the ball of magnesium igniting high over his head and floating slowly down, throwing his positions into harsh relief and exposing him like a cockroach in a Caesar salad.

They watched the rocket arc into the sky, and they squinted hard as it flashed and then cruelly illuminated the entire plateau. Eckstein looked over at the huddle of children, over sixty small heads arched back and their bugged eyes staring up at the bright swaying star. Eckstein heard the reedy voice of Adi call to him.

"What is that, Eytan?"

"Fireworks, Adi," he replied. "It must be some sort of holiday."

He felt Benni's hand grip his elbow, for they both knew that a parachute flare was the precurser to an assault.

"You there!" A deep voice echoed from the distance somewhere below. Krumlov looked at Baum and Eckstein, and then Benni sighed and began to walk to the western lip of the plateau. Eckstein and Krumlov followed, and the three men stopped beside Manchester, who was lying prone with his Sterling and checking his remaining, paltry magazines. Benni reached out and pressed on Krumlov's shoulder, and all three of them lowered themselves to their haunches to provide something less of a target for snipers.

"You there!" the voice called out again. It was a deep tone with a heavy African accent, gravelly as if its owner smoked too many filter-less cigarettes. "I am Amin Mobote of the Oromo Liberation Front, and I have many men with me. Many, many men."

"Good for you," Eckstein mumbled.

"Release your weapons and come down to us and you will not be harmed."

Benni rubbed his jaw and considered his options. He squinted down into the craggy valleys, but even with the light of the flare he could not make out any specific human forms, for they had all certainly taken to good cover before the rocket was fired. Manchester, however, still had fine young eyes and could make out the glints of steel gun barrels.

"There's a whole bloody herd of them, Colonel," he said. "They've spread out into three formations and they'll take us even if we knock half of them off."

"Perhaps they will take the children first," Krumlov suggested. "Peacefully. Then we can stay here and fight it out as men."

"But we are not all men," Eckstein reminded him.

Still, Benni thought, if indeed the children could be spared some-how . . . He came to his feet and Eckstein watched him and held his breath.

"Colonel Mobote!" Benni called. He did not really know if the rebel leader held any sort of rank, but flattery certainly could not hurt at this point. "Will you take the children off first? And will you swear as an officer not to harm them?"

There was no immediate reply. Krumlov looked at Benni and frowned in confusion. "If we release the children, Colonel Baum, he will certainly hold them as hostages until we surrender."

Benni raised a hand, requesting patience. "Let's see."

Mobote's voice echoed out again.

"I will agree to take the children off first," he called. "But you must know that I will execute them if you do not then surrender."

Eckstein raised an eyebrow. "Well, at least he's honest."

There was no preventing the children from hearing this exchange, and they immediately began to whisper among themselves, and some of them began to cry. Benni turned his head to watch Dominique as she shushed her orphans and tried to assuage them, and he heard the rattle of stones and saw Debay sliding down from the summit. The Belgian cocked his MAT and marched briskly across the plateau to join Manchester, and Benni knew that he had absolutely no options. To guarantee the children's survival, they would all have to surrender. And to surrender meant the failure of *Operation Sorcerer*. Krumlov's mole might never be unearthed, and he and Eckstein would become no more than anonymous headstones in the Intelligence Memorial grave-yard. After all their years of work, that would be their legacy.

No, not tonight. Not this way.

"I am afraid we have no deal," he called out to Mobote. "You will have to come and get us."

He squatted again and looked around the half-moon lip of the plateau, but there was no need to hand out assignments. Krumlov moved off to the far left flank with his pistols, and Manchester and Debay, having the heaviest firepower, split up and took up proper positions at the mid-flanks. Baum looked at Eckstein, and the two men said nothing and shook hands, and Baum moved to the center of the half-moon, while Eckstein went off to the take the far right flank.

Eckstein lay down on the hardpack with his Uzi. He removed the magazine, checked that the bullets were seated, then tapped the spine of the metal rectangle against his palm, more out of superstition than proper ammunition alignment. He had two more magazines in his pockets, but he doubted that they were full and he did not want to know.

"Eytan."

He turned his head and found Dominique kneeling next to him. Her eyes were liquid and her hair trembled around her face, and she put a hand on his shoulder.

"Please, Eytan" she said. "Save one bullet for me. I will not be taken by them."

After a moment, he nodded. "Neither will I," he said, and he reached to his shoulder and covered her fingers with his own, and then she slipped away and was gone.

He turned back to squint into the valley, and he heard the rustle of the rebels preparing themselves, weapons bolts ringing home, gunsling rattles. He thought of Simona then, and how he had failed her, and he thought that she would be better off now. She would finally have what she needed, she would find a real man, a man who worked at Bank Leumi and hated the army and would come home to her every night and be happy to be there. She would mourn, yes, but she too would know that she was better off.

And then he thought of Oren and he felt his heart throbbing. Oren would not be better off. Oren would be alone forever, no matter who came into Simona's life. And he would have a little brother or sister and he would not ever be able to share it with them, he would not be able to explain why his father was gone or what it was that was so important that *Abba* had left him. The images of his shattered son were suddenly so powerful that the fury with himself rose and with that came tears of bitterness.

To leave him alone, oh no, oh God. What have I done?

Three more parachute flares suddenly arced up into the night. It was starting, and Eckstein swiped his sleeve across his eyes and gripped his weapon and felt his body tighten like an electrified snake.

Then all at once another sound came from the north. It was a heavy, plunking cough, and he knew that sound too well, the firing of a projectile, and the fear gripped his bowels. They had mortars. They would shell them first into oblivion, just as good infantry should do to an entrenched position. It would be all over in minutes.

But the shell did not explode on the plateau. Instead, it exploded down in the valley. *Are they so stupid that they've fired on themselves?* he wondered. Then another mortar bomb burst among the rebels, and another, and suddenly a light machine gun opened up from somewhere close by. But it too was not trained on the plateau, but into the rebel enclave, and its tracers reached out red and quick and punched all across the first line of Mobote's men.

Eckstein did not understand. He foolishly came to his knees, riveted by the scene of at least four weapons striking out from the night and spitting their death into the rebel assault. He could hear Mobote's men shouting, he could see their shadows scrambling for cover, running off down the mountainside. Rifle grenades flashed among them and tracers slit into their ranks, and he flicked his head around and found Benni also on his knees, staring.

But Baum *did* understand. Baum was grinning, and he slapped the top of his bald head with his hand as if he'd witnessed a biblical miracle. Short of ammunition and tactically wise, Manchester and Debay resisted the urge to join in the rout and just watched, while Krumlov scrambled his way over to Baum carrying a look of utter amazement.

It was over quickly. Perhaps the murderous fire had lasted for all of three full minutes, but it was enough to make Mobote and his men think they had encountered en entire EPRDF battalion. They hurried away into the night, and for another full two minutes there was nothing but silence and wind.

"*Lo lirot, hevreh.* Don't fire, comrades," a youthful voice called out in Hebrew.

Eckstein rolled to his side and watched incredulously as four young men climbed over the northern lip of the plateau. They were all dark-skinned, with shaggy hair and bright eyes and the muscular torsos of the finest field operators. They wore baggy blue jeans and dark farm shirts and combat boots, and they carried many kilos of ammunition, grenades, various automatic weapons, a Minimi light machine gun, and even a fifty-two-millimeter mortar and an RPG. They wore olive headbands like ninjas and they had hardly broken a sweat. They were clearly commandos from *Sayeret Mat'kal,* and they had parachuted in somewhere and made it to the rendezvous point at the behest of General Itzik Ben-Zion.

The lead commando was a black youth who looked like one of the Ethiopian orphans grown into a man. He spotted Eytan, pointed at him, and grinned.

"Eckstein," he said simply, as if he had studied a photograph of the major and successfully identified him. "And Baum," he added as Benni suddenly recovered ten years of his life and marched quickly to grip the boy's shoulders.

Krumlov, Manchester, and Debay slowly gathered to approach the commandos, but they could do no more than stare, as if the Israelis must be ghosts. Eckstein got up and joined Benni at his side.

"I don't have to tell you how glad we are to see you," said Eckstein.

"If I were you," said the commando leader, "I'd be glad to see me, too. We picked up your signal only half an hour ago." He bent over slightly and bounced on the balls of his feet, which made his heavy web gear shift to his comfort. He was carrying a Galil sniper rifle with a night scope and many magazines of 7.62-millimeter ammunition. "But we should get going," he added. "They might have an observation post around here, and if they realize there's only four of us they'll be back."

The commando leader turned and called out to his men in Hebrew, issuing orders to check ammunition and gear and break out the water and field rations for the children. Benni touched the young man on the arm.

"I'm afraid it's not that simple," he said. "Eritrea is still very far off, and I don't think these kids will make it no matter what treats we give them."

"We're not going to Eritrea," said the *Mat'kalnik*. He opened a plastic canteen and offered the water to Benni, but Baum saw Dominique standing behind Eckstein and he reached around and pushed it into her hand.

"We're not?" Eckstein raised an eyebrow.

"No. We're going to the Sudan. It's much closer. Just a few more kilometers that way." He pointed off to the west.

"The Sudan?" Benni looked stunned. Violating Eritrea was bad enough, but the Sudanese hosted every violent and fanatic anti-Western guerrilla movement of record. "But it's a terrorist state."

The *Mat'kalnik* popped a stick of gum into his mouth and grinned.

"And what's this, Colonel Baum?" he asked. "The Garden of Eden?"

18

•   •   •

Jerusalem
May 10

THE YOUNG ISRAELIS who worked in AMAN's Special Operations basement laboratories were a pale, surly, and cynical lot, for much like cosmonauts sentenced to interminable periods aboard a space station, their nights and days were indistinguishable. They had no set hours and they simply labored until the labor was done, and often one assignment would fall on the heels of another, so that their exposure to the fine weather of the world outside was limited to half an hour's meal break at the promenade on Ben-Yehuda Street. And then it was back to the dungeons.

Most of these young men and women held officers' ranks and advanced degrees in photography, computer science, physics, or chemical engineering, and they had signed on with Military Intelligence for the long run, secure careers in their fields of choice and the guarantee of a substantial pension when they mustered out. Yet after a couple of years the exotica of supporting intelligence operations wore off, for they were never privy to the full purpose or results of their work, and there was certainly no such thing as overtime in the Israeli Army. None of them were going to get rich doing this, but many of them would certainly go half-blind, and their social lives were less than pathetic.

However, the laboratories themselves were certainly some of the

281   •   •   •

most sophisticated in the entire country. There were supercomputers, nuclear auto-analyzers, satellite ultra-high-frequency communications centers, and laser benches that would have been the envy of Livermore. Of course, all of these "toy rooms" existed on the same level as the armory and ordnance labs, which was why the whole floor was buried ten meters below the street level and reinforced by a meter-thick shell of steel-reinforced concrete. Everyone secretly disdained the armorers and explosive ordnance personnel, yet treated them with false smiles and respect, for if one of them sneezed at the wrong time the entire SpecOps building would probably dissolve into a pile of smoking rubble. Thus, the basement floor was commonly referred to as *Ha'Kever,* The Tomb, for if you tried to stay there for your full twenty years you would most certainly succumb to a death of either the body or spirit.

"Horse, you are driving us crazy," Rafi Simkovich complained. He was a twenty-seven-year-old photoanalysis expert and had just spent two full days processing high-altitude reconnaissance of an Iraqi chemical plant. He had been walking out the door to finally go home to his enraged wife in Gilo when the word had come down from Ben-Zion to stay on in support of *Operation Sorcerer.* "There's simply nothing here."

Simkovich was bent over a long bench that ran the length of the photoanalysis lab, staring down through the curved glass of a huge round magnifier mounted on a corrugated neck, below which sat Krumlov's photo of his "candidates" clipped into a metal brace. Behind Simkovich another long table was bolted to the bare concrete wall, and upon that sat four state-of-the-art IBMs, one of which was currently being pecked at by Rina Harari, a pretty, sallow-skinned blonde doomed to constantly renew prescriptions of her black-rimmed spectacles.

"Look at it again, Rafi," Horse instructed. This was his element now, and Ben-Zion was not around to belittle or berate him, and he was determined to crack the mystery of Krumlov's traitor or expire right here in The Tomb tonight. Horse paced back and forth beside the central bench, rubbing his forehead and fogging up his glasses with exhalations. Yudit had taken a place at one of the computers, but she was flipping through a copy of *Vogue* rather than participating in a puzzle beyond her ken. Uri Badash was perched on a rolling office chair, chain-smoking and squashing the butts on the speckled tile floor as he reread every file in his briefcase. And Mack Marcus did not need to be there at all, but he was unmarried and unfettered by any serious relationship at home, so he sat atop a wooden bar stool and massaged the stump of his severed leg, while his artifical limb lay on the floor like the aftermath of a mannequin mishap.

"Rafi's right, Horse," Rina muttered as she continued to squint at her monitor. "It's just a photograph of a photograph, and there just aren't any secret messages or codes or God knows what hocus-pocus you're imagining."

Horse blushed, but he did not respond. Rina's tone wounded him, not so much for its critical analysis of his theory, but because he had a secret crush on her and his efforts were certainly failing to impress. In truth, his own faith in his hunch was beginning to fade, for he had expected that at least some kind of physical anomoly would be revealed by in-depth inspection of the picture.

Simkovich had first run the photograph through a high-resolution scanner. Then, Rina had digitized it and begun an inspection of every centimeter. While her search did reveal in fact that it was not first generation, but a photograph of a photograph, nothing appeared to indicate that the photo had been altered in any way. The background of Dimona was real, none of the candidates had been shifted or altered, there were no heads carefully pasted on unmatched bodies or the like. No one in the photo was holding a microscopic sign that said, "It's me!"

Then Simkovich had taken the print into his next-door photo lab, where they all peered at it under infrared light, then watched as a laser wash revealed no anomalies on the surface or the back, aside from Eckstein's penciled notations. After that, a technician from Documentation came in and carefully exposed the photo to test strips of sixteen different compounds designed to bring out the inks of secret writing. Nothing had come up. And finally, under great protest from Simkovich, who was exhausted and hungry and fed up, Horse had made him rephotograph each face in the portrait individually. Another technician was still in the darkroom, blowing them up.

"Maybe it's simpler, Raphael," Yudit offered to Horse as she sniffed at a sample of Calvin Klein perfume glued into her copy of *Vogue*. "Maybe you take all the first letters of all the first names of the candidates, put them together and they spell out the culprit's identity."

"That's cute, Yudit," Marcus snorted as he rubbed his stump. "But I doubt our delivery boy even knew the identities of all these people." He was careful not to mention Krumlov by name in mixed company. "He probably doesn't even know the real name of his traitor."

"We've already done it," Badash muttered from his chair.

"What?" Marcus looked surprised.

"We tried it. We took all their names and even their military ID numbers and gave it all to Codes and Ciphers. Just in case." He held up a hand and formed a big fat zero with his fingers.

"Well, that was my only stab at brilliance," said Yudit, and she resumed her reading.

"The Dirty Dozen minus one," Simkovich sighed as he looked up from his magnifier to the far wall of the lab. There was a very large cork board mounted there, and each of the eleven head shots from Uri Badash's official files had been pinned up next to one another in a line. "Except that, at least according to our silly little wild goose chase here, they're all clean."

"They are *not* all clean," Horse protested in a fierce tone that surprised everyone. "One of them is it, and we shall find him."

"You're being obsessive-compulsive, Horse." Yudit turned and smiled at him. "But I like that in a man."

"So do I," Rina murmured. "They keep the house really clean."

The lab door opened and Simkovich's technician stormed in with a large yellow box marked Kodak. He dropped the box on the central table and put his hands to his hips.

"There, Rafi. Can I go home now?"

"You can go home when I say you can go home. Go get some coffee."

"I've already had six cups."

"Then go take a piss."

The technician muttered a curse and walked out.

Horse opened the box, revealing eleven more blow-ups, these having been made with a high-resolution macro lens and large-format film to keep the grain down, and shot directly off of Krumlov's photo.

"Let's tack them up," said Horse as he divided the still-damp prints.

Yudit got up to help him as Mack Marcus tossed her a box of push pins, and together Horse and Yudit began to match each new photo to its mate on the cork board. The renewed activity was a respite for Yudit, and she became a bit silly and animated as she tried to marry the faces and pin the new ones below the old.

"It's like a television game show," she chirped. "I'll take 'Spies and Counterspies' for one hundred, Alex."

When they were done, everyone in the room gathered in back of the central workbench and gazed across to the cork board. The faces, of course, all matched. Some of the angles and poses and haircuts were a bit different, but essentially they were identical in every way. No one had acquired a nose ring or a neck tattoo or a stylish punk buzz cut, as these things were forbidden to nuclear workers with high-security clearances.

After a full five minutes, Simkovich finally threw up his hands. "All right. I'm going home. Just tell Itzik we're fucking incompetent." He stalked to his desk and began to stuff his burn bag with some loose papers from the blotter.

But Horse had not yet surrendered. He did not know Jan Krumlov, nor did he care very much about the Czech's personal or professional motives, nor whether he was a saint or a devil. But Eckstein and Baum were out there in Africa, and what Horse did or failed to do tonight might make all the difference in their mission. And their lives.

He crossed from the bench to the cork board, and he stood for a very long time before each pair of photographs, looking down, then up, then down again. And only when he was absolutely certain that nothing in the comparison stood out as peculiar did he move on.

Halfway across the row of images, he stopped, and except for the strange bobbing of his head, his body was still as an ice sculpture.

"I'm *going*, Horse," Simkovich snapped as he hefted his briefcase and clutched the burn bag stuffed with classified documents. "I'm *going*."

Horse slowly raised a finger, and something in his posture, the way his shoulders hunched hard, stopped Simkovich in his tracks. Everyone watched as Horse's finger slowly drew across the air.

He was standing before a pair of shots of a young man in his late twenties. The Dimona candidate was dark-skinned, with curly black hair and a full beard. The beard was very thick and not well-manicured, and in both photographs it rose across his face and threatened his cheekbones. Horse's finger moved to the lower photograph of the man and settled on a spot just below his left eye.

"What is that?" he whispered.

Badash moved in closer. Mack Marcus, still sans his artificial limb, placed one hand on the wall and hopped in beside Uri. Yudit peered over their shoulders while Rina turned from her monitor.

Badash squinted past the trembling tip of Horse's finger.

"It looks like a mark of some kind."

Horse lifted his finger to the second image above, pointing to the same spot on the upper photograph.

"It's not in that one," said Yudit.

"It's a pencil mark or a pen mark, for God's sake," Simkovich snorted as he slammed his briefcase down on his bench. "We probably made it while we were handling the damn thing."

Horse ignored him. "Rina?" he said over his shoulder. "Is it in the original?"

Rina turned back to her computer and immediately began to scan her digitized image of Krumlov's group photo. "I wouldn't have missed that," she said, but her tone belied her conviction. Everyone continued to stare at the pair of photos while she pecked away at her keyboard and drove her mouse.

"Yes," she whispered after a long moment. "It's there. I guess I saw it but I didn't think anything of it. It's not a microdot or anything. It's just a mark . . ."

Like a flock of geese fleeing after a gunshot, Horse, Yudit, Badash, and Marcus all split away from the cork board and quickly regrouped behind Rina's chair. She had enlarged just the relevant section of a single face, and now only the corner of a dark eye and a cheekbone and some wild strands of beard hair filled a window of her monitor in black and white. And there, just below the eye, was the unmistakable black speck, about the size of the tip of a crayon in relation to the face.

"Give me two hundred percent," said Simkovich, who had now joined the group behind Rina and given up on going home.

Rina moved her mouse, zeroed in on her target, and clicked twice. The screen blurred for a moment and then the image reappeared, but this time it was just the corner of the eye and some skin and the black dot, about the size of a chocolate chip. The mark was strange, for it was not uniform and had sort of a swirl to it, as if it had been made with a felt pen.

Horse restrained his hope from taking wing, but he could not stop his heart from beating a bit faster and he felt the prickle of sweat on his balding head. "Mack," he whispered without turning. "Tell me again. It's *not* in the photo from Uri's file."

Marcus hopped back around the central table to the cork board. "Negative," he said after a moment. "It's not in the top one."

Rina worked her keyboard and a glowing green line swept across the image like a beach wave. "It has no altitude," she whispered. "So if it's a mark, it was made on the original, *before* it was copied."

"And if it's not in our Shabak file photo," said Badash, "then it has to have been added afterward, to this group picture."

"Unless it's just a spilled drop of something," Simkovich guessed. "Or it could be something that grew on his face, like a sun freckle."

"It can't be a birthmark," said Yudit. "You're only born once."

"No. It cannot be a birthmark," Horse whispered, yet his voice was very strange now and everyone turned to look at him. "But it *was* deliberate." He was trembling all over and sweat had beaded on his brow, and as he turned and looked across the room at Mack Marcus he held on to Yudit's elbow to steady himself. She winced with the power of his grip.

"What do *you* call such a thing, Mack?" Horse prodded, even though he already knew the answer and that was why he trembled so.

And Marcus, who had now gone quite pale, faced the entourage and placed both hands on the central table to support himself. He nodded and shook his head all at once as he tried to control his voice.

"In English, my comrade?" the American-born officer said. "You call it a *mole* . . ."

19

Almahel
May 10

MAJOR EYTAN ECKSTEIN and Colonel Benjamin Baum ran, for their own lives and for the lives of those they led.

The two men should have been in a recovery ward at Hadassah Hospital in Jerusalem, for between them they shared more than ninety years on earth, yet less than a total of seven hours sleep over the past three days, and their sustenance level and calorie intake was far below that required of middle-aged adults, let alone field combatants on a brutal African mountain sprint. They had been exposed to stress levels that would cause a Formula One racing driver to pull into the pits and quit, and their brains had long ceased to function at the required tactical levels and their bodies had passed the stages where pain should be heeded as an alarm indicator. The only thing that kept them going was their own egos, for they were Israeli intelligence officers and special operators, and to complain or fail was simply not in their lexicon.

Eytan and Benni loped along on point, focusing hard in the dark to keep from falling over ambushes of jagged rock and thorny brush as they led their enlarged troupe of ten adults and sixty-eight children. The four *Mat'kal* commandos had quickly watered the children with sips from their canteens and fed them with energy wafers supplied by the IDF medical corps, and then the column was off, rapidly descending from the summit at Abu-Mendi and into the western valleys toward the Sudan. Benni had warned that this would not be enough sustenance to carry them far, but the young commando officer had only smiled and led the troup briefly off its course. His parachute drop had included a large supply container, which he and his men had secreted in a rock cluster before engaging the OLF rebels, and when it was found and opened the orphans and adults fell upon it like Mexican revelers on a Christmas piñata. And then they were on the run again.

With renewed strength and hope, they hurried down and into the wadis before the ridges that would rise again and challenge them at the border of Sudan. The appearance of the commandos had brought more than food and water, it had delivered faith and optimism, and even the most damaged leg muscles could pump out a few more impossible kilometers on that kind of ethereal fuel. However, the commandos also carried a timetable that could not be scorned, for already a second aircraft was en route to its designated landing zone in the no-man's land between the Sudan and Ethiopia, and if its crew did not immediately spot the proper designator on the ground it would not even circle once before returning for home.

The *Mat'kalniks* always prepared meticulously for any mission, and knowing that their cargo would include sickly children, they had brought along collapsible aluminum poles and modified parachute gear containers. Now the two pair of commandos jogged along sequentially, the poles stretched between their shoulders. Beneath the poles five of the most sickly children lay sleeping in the suspended gear bags, swinging like trussed lambs en route to a county fair. The commandos, used to hauling full stretcher loads of wounded comrades and all of their combat gear, barely grunted under the strain of a few kilos of slim bones and flesh. The rest of the children snaked along in a wavy line, guarded on the flanks by Manchester and Debay and prodded by Krumlov, with Dominique weaving between her bleating little patients and constantly counting heads.

The presence of the commandos had lifted Eytan's spirit from his flatline of despair, their strength and grins a challenge to his age, a reminder of what he had once been and needed to be again, just for a few more hours. He himself had been a fine paratroop officer, but these boys were of another ilk altogether. Their unit was an ultrasecret force of anonymous warriors, answering only to the chief of staff himself. Their "ancestors" had pulled off the Entebbe Raid, the elimination of Black September terror masters in the heart of Beirut, and the kidnapping of Hizbollah's Sheik Obeid from his living room in Lebanon's Jibjit. Yet the names of their heroes and the details of their exploits were never mentioned in the Israeli press, and the army psychologists considered them all to be semi-psychotic. No matter how long they lived—and many went to their graves without seeing their twenty-fifth year—they would never speak of their adventures to a single soul. What sort of man chooses a spectacular profession, the details of which he can share only with a mirror?

The *Mat'kal* officer, a captain called Karni, was indeed the son of Ethiopian immigrants to Israel. He was tall and lean, with skin the color of Nutella, a small sharp nose, black eyes that glittered with mischief, and the gnarled hair of a Rastafarian. His first sergeant was a blond kibbutznik who had obviously had his hair and eyebrows died black for this mission, and the two additional sergeants were both Yemenite Israelis with dark features, fluent Arabic, and a healthy knowledge of Amharic. Eytan liked them all instantly. They were just like him, yet without the despair of too much age and experience, and their infrangible strength was infectious.

Karni beckoned Manchester to him and gestured for the healthy Brit to briefly take his aluminum pole while the commando jogged forward to speak to Eckstein and Baum. They were all churning up quite a racket with their tramping boots and the complaints of the children, so a breathless conversation was not going to make a difference. Besides, no one had any illusion that the rebels might have lost track of them; they had most probably regrouped and were hard on their heels.

"Eckstein." Karni addressed Eytan with typical IDF informality as he caught up to the major and loped along beside him. "We have less than four hours to set up a landing zone and markers on the other side."

"Thank you," Eckstein offered sarcastically as he huffed and puffed. "Until that bit of news I was completely unmotivated."

"Well, just wanted to remind you of the good parts." Karni grinned, sharp white teeth in a mahogany face. "We're headed for a soft spot in the border. Should be no problem to cross it."

"According to what genius?" Eckstein asked.

"A Mossadnik working in a refugee camp on the other side. And your commander really twisted the air force's arm to send in another C-130." He tore back the olive Velcro cover from his watch. "It's been in the air for over an hour now."

"Knowing Itzik," Benni commented, "he's probably got the plane picking up a load of used sneakers in Kenya on the way back."

Karni smiled again and jogged in silence for a moment. Then he jerked a thumb over his shoulder and lowered his voice.

"You know, Baum, that Czech back there. I understand he's not supposed to make the flight."

Eckstein and Baum glanced at each other, and Eytan realized that the *Mat'kal* mission was twofold. If he and Benni failed to "remove" Krumlov from the flight manifest, the commando officer had been ordered to finish him off himself. Eytan tripped over a dry stick of fallen acacia, and Benni snatched at his arm to prevent him from falling.

"So I suppose," said Benni to Karni, "that as of your jumpoff, no one had yet identified the *shtinker* back home." He used the Yiddish expression for traitor.

"Affirmative," Karni replied. "Which means . . ."

"Which means," Eckstein interjected soundly, "that Benni and I are in command of *Sorcerer* and we'll execute it as we see fit. You boys just do what you do best, run fast and shoot straight. At the *enemy*."

"*Ken, hamefaked.* Yes, commander." Karni cocked his head and fell back to his own men. When he was out of earshot, Benni grunted to Eckstein.

"There is going to be trouble."

"You mean, this *isn't* trouble?"

"Don't be dense," said Benni. "We'll *have* to kill Krumlov, just to keep him *off* the plane. He's a born-again Jew with a mission, and to be honest, I understand him."

"And what about your suspicions, Benni? If we let him on the plane, and he turns out to be dirty?"

"And what about your faith? If we truss him up and leave him behind, and he turns out to be clean?"

Eckstein had no immediate answer to this conundrum. Finally, he sighed through his hoarse gasps.

"Well, maybe we'll get lucky and they'll kill us all at the border."

"You always manage to look on the bright side."

Eckstein just grunted in reply. He wanted to conserve his last reserves of energy, for the sweat was pouring off him and he knew there was precious little liquid left in his body.

"Hullo, Colonel and Major." Manchester had suddenly appeared, taking Eckstein's flank and clipping along seemingly without effort. "Sorry to interrupt."

"Carry on, Manchester," said Eckstein in his best British upper-class.

"Right. Well, one of your young blokes back there has a set of NVGs."

Benni twisted his head around briefly, and indeed one of the *Mat'kalniks* was wearing a head brace with a pair of night vision goggles pulled down over his eyes.

"Yes?"

"Well, sir," said Manchester. "I don't understand your native jibberish, but I'd say he's spotted the rebels off to the south there, tagging along."

"Did you expect them to just run off, Manchester?" Eckstein asked. "Tails between their legs?"

"Not bloody likely, sir. But maybe we ought to hunker down here and fight it out. We've got your complement of superboys with us now."

"I think we'll just race them for it, Andrew," Benni said. "You're not having trouble running, are you?"

"Good god, no sir! I could run those wankers straight to Southampton!"

"Good man," said Eckstein, and as Manchester faded back he knew full well that the merc was preoccupied with Bernd's death and simply wanted revenge, and as much of it as possible.

The running slowed considerably as the troupe ascended a long dark razorback ridge, and both Eckstein and Baum were forced again to use their hands on their thighs and pump. They finally stopped on the ridge, gasping hard and bent over, and the follow-on line of adults and children slowly began to gather close, but the *Mat'kalniks* went around and made everyone squat so as not to offer silhouette targets on the ridgeline.

Benni straightened up partially and looked across a long dark valley that flowed from south to north. Above, the black sky was full of the whispy milk of crowded stars, and to the north the moon had risen behind a thin fog breathing off the mountains. Straight across the valley was another long razorback ridge, the mirror to the one they had crested.

"That's it." Karni had appeared again and was pointing off to the far mountains. "Maybe three kilometers, and it's not very high."

"When you're your age," said Eckstein, "nothing seems high."

Krumlov staggered up the crest, followed closely by Debay. But none of the Israelis would look at the Czech, and he knew why.

"Like Moses looking into the Promised Land, eh, Colonel?" Krumlov commented to Baum. "But I tell you now, *this* Jew will not be kept from his milk and honey."

Karni slowly turned his head to look at the Czech, then his wide eyes found those of Benni.

"Did I hear him right, Baum?"

"Yes."

Eckstein felt strong fingers on his elbow, and he found Dominique standing just below him on the ridge, her eyes glowing with challenge and her hair glistening at the brow with perspiration. She pulled him down to her and whispered.

"Jan told me that you do not want him to come to Israel. That you want him to stay in Ethiopia." Eckstein said nothing in response, and she went on. "Not that it should matter to you, Eytan. But I cannot go with you if he does not go. It would not be fair. I could not live with it." The last thing Eckstein needed at the moment was another ultimatum, and he simply sighed and nodded.

Karni had turned fully to Krumlov and, with the arrogance of his youth and stature as an Israeli spartan, challenged him openly.

"You say you're a Jew, Mr. Krumlov?"

"That is *Colonel* Krumlov to you, boy." The Czech straightened his weary shoulders. "And yes, I am a Jew, although dropping my trousers will prove nothing, because I came to it late."

"You came to it late," Karni repeated with cynicism.

"Yes. But I am a quick study."

"You don't say?"

Just like most intelligence and commando officers, Karni was certainly a skeptic when it came to the claims of probable impostors. His thin smile was hardly camouflaged as he turned away again and squinted across the valley.

But Krumlov stepped through the group and came to his full height on the ridgeline, and Karni made to pull him back but Eckstein in turn snatched at the commando's battle vest and held him still. Alone, the Czech watched the black sky as it began to take on the navy blue of a heralding dawn, and he stood there looking at the border of the Sudan and whispered, in perfect synagogue Hebrew.

"*Gahm kee ilech b'gai tzalmavet, lo irah rah. Kee Atah imadee . . .* Yea, though I walk through the valley of the shadow of death, I shall fear no evil. For Thou art with me . . ."

Rolf Feldheim drove his white United Nations command car along the crackling bed of a slim wadi, squinting in the glow of a red operations bulb at a detail map and inhaling deeply on the beginning of his third pack of the day. Mobote had summoned him to this godforsaken corner of the Gojam by radio, giving over the precise coordinates for a rendezvous, but it was like trying to find a black agate in a pool of motor oil.

The rebel leader had obviously lost faith in the mission, and with good reason, for his own incompetence had resulted in unnecessary casualties while failing to stop the Jews and their orphans and their prize Czech traitor. You simply could not teach blacks the subtleties of military tactics, diversions, ambushes, or encirclements. They went about everything like the bulls at Pamplona, straight down the alley, heads bent and flaring nostrils snorting. They obviously needed some direction from a European officer of high caliber, and he would give it to them, after sufficient beratement.

The wadi thinned further, then ended in a ramp of dried winter wash, and Feldheim coaxed the command car up the grade. He peered upward through the windshield and smirked when he saw the signal, a small green bulb flashing about 200 meters straight up a wide hill.

He gunned the engine and began to drive forcefully, already demonstrating his aura of command and control and his impatience with incompetence. There was a narrow path apparently used before by other vehicles and he followed it directly on, and it was only after some meters that he realized the path was flanked by a double line of Mobote's men, hunkered down with their weapons and waiting. At least they knew the basic procedures for night marches in the field. When your commander stopped, you crouched low and waited for orders.

At the top of the rise, just below the summit, Mobote stood with his fists on his garrison belt, the pearl handle of his .45 gleaming in the weak starlight. Feldheim stopped the command car, stepped out, and smoothed his uniform blouse. Then he slapped the map under one arm, stuck his cigarette in his mouth, and strode uphill.

"I see that you have no prisoners," Feldheim snapped as he stopped before the rebel leader. "So I assume that you summoned me for help." He looked Mobote up and down, noting smears of glistening blood on his camouflage jacket. But the African appeared unwounded, so the Austrian assumed it was the blood of someone else.

Mobote did not immediately answer, and a noncom approached him and spoke quickly in Oromigna and the rebel leader gestured at Feldheim's command car. Feldheim turned, and it was then that he saw the wounded men being helped to their feet, some slung over the shoulders of their comrades.

"I do not need your help, Major Feldheim," Mobote said as he shook his head. "But I do need your vehicle. We have buried our dead in the mountains, but the wounded must be taken to hospital."

Feldheim frowned deeply, and he glanced back at his vehicle again, where already the rebels were opening the rear cargo doors and gently laying their comrades inside. It would take weeks to get the blood and urine and stink out of his precious car.

"I am not an ambulance driver," Feldheim spat. "You should summon me to witness success, and nothing less."

"Then witness this," said Mobote as he turned and walked up the rise. "And maybe your tactical genius will be of some use."

Feldheim followed him up the hill, and when they crested it Mobote stood fully erect in plain sight and looked out over a long valley. Feldheim joined him, and although he did not favor this kind of exposure, he certainly could not do less than the African, and he stood as straight and tall as he could.

"Look there," said the rebel leader.

Feldheim squinted, following Mobote's pointed finger. The valley stretched from directly below their high perch and due north. It lay between the last mountain ridges of Ethiopa to the east, and the border humpbacks of the Sudan to the west. On the western side of the valley was a long slim road in the lee of the Sudanese hills.

"That is the border road," said Mobote. "The Israelis have already reached it, and they are about to cross."

"Where?" Feldheim squinted harder, but he was really not a combatant of any merit and his night fighting abilities were less than keen. He suddenly grunted as he felt something strike his chest, and he looked down to find Mobote's fist gripping a large pair of Steiner binoculars with infra-red filters.

The Austrian took them and raised them to his eyes. As his pupils adjusted, he indeed spotted a small cluster of men behind a brace of rocks on the eastern side of the road. He swung the binoculars to the left, and across the road on the western side he found a small wooden hut, long rows of concertina, and three Sudanese border guards toting AK-47s.

Feldheim snorted and lowered the binoculars.

"Why did you not stop them?"

"We tried, Major Feldheim," Mobote growled. "We nearly had them at Abu-Mendi, but they were joined by a band of commandos and they drove us off. I do not know where they came from."

"Where they *came* from? Are you mad? They were probably dropped in by parachute or helicopter!"

"It does not matter. They will cross the border now."

"Don't be absurd." Feldheim waved his cigarette in disgust, then realized he was making telltale red arcs in the sky and he dropped it and stamped it out. "They are led by Israelis and the Sudan is the most viciously anti-Israeli state in Africa. No one will let them cross over."

Mobote looked at him, nearly an expression of pity. "They are not going to ask for permission, Major." He gestured at the binoculars, and Feldheim raised them again and peered up the valley.

Sure enough, a series of small flashes burst from the rocky position on the eastern side of the border road, and when Feldheim swung his glasses west the three Sudanese border guards had already been felled into a heap. There was no report of gunfire. The Israelis had obviously used silencers.

A man sprinted across the road and crouched next to the three fallen guards. Then he swung and waved, and another man joined him from the eastern side.

"You see?" Mobote nodded sadly.

"Well?!" Feldhim spat, nearly hopping up and down. "Go after them! That border area is six kilometers thick and nothing lives there but leopards and goats! We can still bring them down. We can still hold the entire Israeli government in the palms of our hands!"

"We . . ." Mobote whispered, and the cruel scar on his cheek deepened in color, though no one could see it on his black visage under this black night. He turned and spat out some orders to his platoon leaders, and very quickly his men came to their feet, formed up, and began sprinting up to the crest of the hill. Mobote issued another order at close range to his junior officers, and then a long double line of rebels was charging down off the hill and headed for the valley, their weapons clanking and boots slamming the hardpack as they faded into the gloom.

There were many of them, and their passage continued for a long time as Mobote and Feldheim stood amid them like stiff trees in the midst of a stampede.

"I called for more men," Mobote said to no one in particular. "We have over one hundred again now. We will destroy these people, although I no longer care about taking any of them prisoner."

"Don't be a fool!" Feldheim spun on the African, and his eyes bugged and his cheeks went florid. "This could mean millions, don't you understand? Killing them will bring us nothing."

But Mobote clearly had made his command decision, and he was no longer going to be subject to the twisted intellect of some treacherous European sloth. At Feldheim's behest and following the Austrian's plan, he had lost good men whose families would not be comforted, the cause of the Oromos had been sullied, and worst of all, he had been humiliated. He looked past Feldheim and received a salute from two men who had remained behind and were now slipping into the cab of Feldheim's vehicle. He slowly began to remove his bloodstained battle jacket, and Feldheim frowned at him and then flicked his head around at the start of the command car engine, and then the Austrian turned back to Mobote and still he did not understand.

"What are you doing?" Feldheim demanded. "Do not do it this way, I tell you. Wait, let us sit down with a map and draw up a plan. We can still all get what we want from this venture!"

Yet even as Feldheim spoke, Mobote had drawn his pearl-handled .45 and was wrapping the weapon in his battle jacket. The barrel was buried deep inside a thick sleeve, and one hand was inside and with the other he gripped the cloth outside and cocked it.

"I thank you for your advice, Major . . ." said Mobote as he quickly placed the jacket against Feldheim's chest and pulled the trigger. A large white flash exploded between the jacket and the Austrian's heart, but there was little report and no echo of a gunshot split the night. Feldheim arched and flew back, his head struck a rock and lolled awkwardly to one side, and his corpse shuddered but once. "But I no longer need a partner."

Mobote reholstered his pistol, watched the command car turn and head back for the hospital in Dara, and then he slung his jacket over his shoulder and jogged off after his men . . .

20

Tel Aviv
May 10

THE COMMAND AND control center of the Israeli air force is an enormous steel and concrete cavern located fifty-seven meters below street level at IDF general headquarters in Tel Aviv. It is nuclear, conventional, and biological warhead-proof, and unaffectionately referred to as *Ha'Bor*—The Hole. The dimly lit network of operations centers, living quarters, and full-blown food services is much like a submarine, as many of its officers and technicians often spend countless days in the catacomb, emerging only for short leaves and squinting in the light of day like disrupted vampires. Fifty years of lightning warfare in the Middle East have proven that air power is the key to success in the region, and therefore The Hole has not been free of occupants for a single day since its construction. So, despite the air conditioners and ammonia washes and even the occasional stab at incense, the place stinks like a prison, which in many respects it is.

On this night, *Operation Sorcerer* was just one of many air force management concerns being handled in the subterranean lair. A flight of F-4 Phantoms was executing a bombing raid over Sidon in southern Lebanon, and a high-altitude reconnaissance mission was in progress over Baghdad. There were over forty-five IAF officers, noncoms, and clerks in The Hole. Coffee steam and cigarette smoke swirled beneath the fluorescent lighting, and in typical Israeli fashion, men and women shouted to each other without regard for rank or formality.

301 • • •

In one corner of the central C&C room three radar intercept officers and a communications sergeant had been assigned to the AMAN project, and they sat before large consoles with the green wash of radar screens flickering on their sallow faces. Itzik Ben-Zion paced behind the three young men and one woman, occasionally muttering to himself and unnerving the operators with his imposing presence.

An air force major named Ilan Kidon had been assigned as liaison to the AMAN general, because his wife was distantly related to the Ben-Zion family and he was adept at the peculiar sort of diplomacy necessary here. Kidon watched Itzik pace and felt some pity for his cousin by marriage, for in all the years of knowing him he had never seen Ben-Zion's uniform wrinkled so, nor the man reveal his worry and concern so openly. He reminded Kidon of a tiger shark flopping helplessly on the deck of a tuna boat.

"What's the location of the aircraft?" Itzik realized that he was pacing and fidgeting like a fussy old woman, and he stopped himself and thrust his hands in his pockets. For the first time in ten years he had almost bummed a cigarette from a corporal, but then he decided that the place was already so laced with smoke that he only had to inhale deeply to get his fill of nicotine.

"Ten kilometers farther south than three minutes ago," one of the radar officers muttered.

Itzik's face flushed and he stopped in his tracks, but Kidon intercepted the general's wrath.

"Don't be a *chutzpahn*, Yossi," the major snapped at his operator as he swatted him on the back of the head. "Just answer the general."

"Uhh, the C-130's approaching latitude thirteen degrees. Still over the water."

"Thank you," Itzik said to Kidon as he controlled his seething. "Do you have the F-15s in the air?"

"We can't launch them yet, Itzik." The air force major touched Ben-Zion's sleeve. "Remember?"

"Ken, ken." Itzik nodded. "Of course." And he continued his pacing.

The Hercules C-130 transport would have to cross over the African continent and fly a very low nap-of-the-earth pattern to remain below radar until it reached the landing zone. Once it set down in the Sudan and picked up its cargo, an air force fighter umbrella would roar in to cover its return. But if the fighters showed themselves *before* the Hercules slipped over the Eritrean shoreline and on toward the Sudan, one of the coastal nations might decide to scramble its own defensive squadrons.

"Anything from the navy?" Itzik asked.

Kidon turned to a young woman wearing a huge set of earphones and punching frequencies on a multiplex receiver. "Natasha?"

"Negative, Ilan," she said. An IDF missile boat had swung in close to Eritrea, staying put just off the international demarcation line. The small ship was equipped with highly sensitive sweep radar that could pick up scrambled fighters within a 500-kilometer range. "At last contact, just civilian stuff in the air."

Itzik grunted and continued pacing, rubbing his forehead and trying to sort out the flood of information that had set his heart beating and his conscience wrestling with his professional self as it had never done in his entire career. Upon Horse's discovery of the mole, the analyst had immediately called the general and jumped in a car with Yudit and Marcus, and they were now speeding en route to Tel Aviv. Badash had quickly identified Bluebeard as one Moshe Buzahglo, an engineering graduate of Be'er Sheva University and ten-year veteran of the Dimona reactor core. The Shabak agent had then split off from the AMAN officers in Jerusalem and picked up a load of his GSS field agents, commandeering an army helicopter at Atarot and taking off for Be'er Sheva. Until the GSS agents actually broke down the door of Buzahglo's home, Itzik would not have full confirmation of Horse's revelation and could do nothing to alter the fate of Jan Krumlov.

For the first time ever, he prayed that Eckstein and Baum still retained their infuriating tendency to disregard his orders. He hoped that the Czech was still alive, and that he would have the opportunity to greet the man and subject him to the most mild debriefing in the history of AMAN, and all of it done in the best five-star hotel the capital had to offer. He could not imagine himself actually apologizing, but he knew how to do that with actions rather than words. When he thought for a moment that Eckstein and Baum might not in fact survive *Sorcerer* at all, he felt a sharp pain in his chest and suddenly jerked fully upright. Kidon stared at him, and Itizk just grimaced and waved it off.

He turned to the sound of elevator doors opening and a female cry of exasperation that he instantly recognized.

"Get out of my way, idiot!" Yudit had been momentarily stopped by a pair of burly air force MPs, but she just shoved one in the chest as she spotted her commander and hurried toward him, with Horse in tow and Mack Marcus clunking along like Captain Ahab.

"Did you hear anything from them, Itzik?" she shouted as she nearly toppled a mess corporal carrying a tray of Turkish coffee demitasses.

"How could I hear?" Ben-Zion threw up his hands. "Am I a psychic?"

"The satcom?" Horse reminded his boss that the complex transceiver had been operating just two days before.

"They've probably lost it," Itzik said bitterly. "Or they're using it to make tea."

"Or it's all shot up," Marcus offered, then realized what he'd said. "Sorry."

"Anything else on this Buzahglo?" Itzik demanded.

"Badash called us from the chopper," said Horse, displaying a new-found self-confidence that instantly annoyed Ben-Zion. "But that was over an hour ago. He was about to set down in Be'er Sheva, but he had a commo link to the supervisor at Dimona." Horse fumbled for a slip of notepaper in his shirt pocket and peered at it through his thick glasses. "Buzahglo was secretly assigned to *Keshet* three years ago, and he even made two trips to Washington for the project. No one on his team knew about it. He was working in the anti-ballistic missile guidance section that uplinks to American satellites."

With this bit of indiscretion, Itzik instinctively swung his head in search of prying ears. Kidon was nearby and shrugged at him. "I didn't hear that."

For a moment, all heads turned to the shouts from a team of combat-control operators on the far side of the cavern. Apparently a pair of fighter-bombers had just scored a direct hit on a terrorist vessel just off the Lebanese coast, and the secondary detonations indicated a large shipment of arms and ammunition. The operators jumped from their chairs and slapped each other's backs as if their hometown soccer club had just won the playoffs, but their commanding colonel instantly berated them and they sat back down.

Horse stuffed the note back in his pocket and began to wring his hands and mutter. "I wish we could contact Eytan and Benni," he said. "Tell them about Krumlov, tell them he's . . ."

"If it isn't already too late," Yudit interjected, then shot Ben-Zion an accusatory look, as if he had decided to put the family dog to sleep.

"Itzik, maybe you should radio the Hercules crew," Mack Marcus suggested. "The *Mat'kalniks* have short range commo gear. They might be able to pickup a message."

"I can't *do* that, Marcus!" Itzik exploded, but as officers were always yelling down here, hardly anyone paid much attention. "And I'm *not* rescinding a general order until Badash confirms that this man is our traitor." The general's face was florid with frustration, but it was clear that his heart and mind were clawing at each other. He blew out a breath and swept a nervous glisten from his brow into his thick salt-and-pepper curls, and Yudit frowned, stepped up to him, and hooked a finger in his belt.

"Are you all right?" she asked with genuine concern.

"Yes, for God's sake." He swept her hand away, then lowered his voice. "No. I'm at least a hard two days' hike from all right."

There was another small commotion at the rear elevator, and the AMAN officers turned to watch Uri Badash snapping his Shabak ID in the face of an MP. Something in the counterintelligence officer's demeanor had changed. Yes, he was spent and exhausted and, like all of the them, running on empty. But his posture was slumped and his head slowly wagged from side to side as he came forward, his briefcase dangling from his hand. He walked up to the quartet of army intelligence officers, placed his briefcase on the floor, and extracted a cigarette from his pocket. He lit up even as he continued to shake his head.

"What the hell is it, Uri?" Itzik blustered. "You look like you've seen a ghost."

Badash snorted through his nose and a stream of smoke encircled his head.

"I wish I hadn't," he said, and seeing the confused looks stabbing at him, he sighed and quickly relayed the best first. "It was him. Moshe

Buzahglo was Bluebeard. We found a slick in his apartment in Be'er Sheva." He meant a secret hiding place commonly used by spies or saboteurs. Yudit reached out and gripped Horse's shoulder, as if she was watching a horror film and needed support. "There was a Minox and a small cache of microfilm," Badash continued. "Blueprints from *Keshet*, plus a one-time pad and contact numbers in Europe."

"Kidon!" Itzik called out, although he did not look for the air force major but kept his eyes locked on Badash's face. The major stepped close to the AMAN general, and Itzik's command came out staccato. "Have your people contact that plane immediately. When it lands, if Krumlov is still with our men he's to come aboard. I *repeat*, the Czech must board the aircraft, with full apologies and begging pardons from me personally. Is that clear?"

"*Ruth*," Kidon confirmed and he jumped to his commo sergeant.

"That's wonderful," Horse muttered, thinking of Eckstein and Baum and Krumlov. "I mean, it's not wonderful that we had such a traitor . . ." Then his brow furrowed and he stared at Badash.

"*You're* wonderul," Yudit said to Horse. "*You* did it"

Horse seemed not to hear her. "You used the past tense, Uri," he said to Badash. "You said Buzahglo *was* Bluebeard."

"That's right." Badash slowly nodded.

"Don't tell me he's escaped," Itzik snapped accusatorily.

"Worse than that." Badash smoked deeply for a moment. "The police showed up while we were tossing his flat. Buzahglo and his wife and baby were killed yesterday in a road accident on the Dead Sea highway."

Even among the mad bustle of the command and control center, the shock of Badash's news created a pallor of silence in the *Sorcerer* section. Yudit's mouth fell open, Horse pulled his glasses from his face as if that might improve his hearing, and Ben-Zion slowly raised a trembling palm to his forehead.

"You've *got* to be fucking kidding me," Mack Marcus exhaled in English.

"He was on leave," said Badash. "But only for four days. A nice little road trip to Eilat. He tried to pass a kibbutz tractor on a long curve, smashed into a gasoline truck." He paused for a moment and cursed under his breath. "Even the spies in this country drive like fucking fools."

"Oh my God," Yudit whispered. "He killed himself. And his family."

"No." Badash waved a finger. "It wasn't a suicide. The truck driver's shaken but okay, said Buzahglo tried to avoid him, skidded about a hundred meters. He obviously had no idea he was about to be blown." The Shabak officer moved to a chair and sank into it. "So not only was Krumlov on the level, he also guessed that Bluebeard's handlers wouldn't tell him even if they knew their mole was going to be unearthed. That way, they could have his intel right up to the minute he was taken down." Even the hardened counterintelligence man seemed stunned by the tragic irony of it all. "Krumlov knew how his own people worked, and he was just holding out so he could be here to bask in the glory. And it would have been well deserved."

They were all speechless, each of them thinking of the Game and its deadly gambits and how quickly God could just snap his fingers and turn their mole hunts and plots and counterplots into laughable dust. But just as quickly their thoughts turned to Eckstein and Baum, still out there in harm's way and striving for a prize that had just been immolated. Itzik, rooted to the floor and unable to move his arms, shouted over his shoulder.

"Kidon, for God's sake get me that Hercules pilot!"

But the air force major had already tried, and he rejoined the group and spoke in a pained and remorseful tone.

"I can't, Itzik," said the major. "They've already gone feet dry." The Hercules was over the African continent, racing for the rendezvous point, with all of its communications gear shut down. "They'll be in radio silence until they come out . . ."

21

* * *

THEY HAD TO carry the children up the last ridge before the Wadi of Dinder. It was only 200 meters high, but like the finish line at the end of a long footrace, when you see it you suddenly feel every tortured muscle in your legs and each breath seems as though the air you take is laced with poison. Half of the orphans were already limp with dehydration, and the other half were in shock and immobilized by fear. The adults, who were really no better off, accomplished this final feat in three full shifts, scrambling back down to the Sudanese border hut and piggybacking another load, until Eckstein finally picked up Adi and slung the boy's legs around his waist. Adi looped his arms around the Israeli's neck and held on tight while Eckstein pumped out his final reserves, hauling the both of them to the top of the ridge line.

"I am sorry, Etyan," Adi repeatedly apologized. "I am sorry." But Eckstein could only nod and grunt as he labored upward, and he just imagined that the little boy was Oren and he knew that he could have climbed Everest with him just so.

Karni, who had dragged the bodies of the three border guards behind the hut, remained below, wearing one of their field jackets and unconsciously fingering a bullet hole in the cloth as he briefly impersonated a Sudanese and watched the road for wayward vehicles. He checked the magazine on a silenced Beretta and slipped it into his pocket, deciding to keep the Sudanese jacket as a souvenir.

When the children and the rest of them had all disappeared over the rise above, he came up with a pocket scope and squinted across the road and along a wide wadi that snaked down from the Ethiopian mountains to the south. Then he nodded to himself and turned and sprinted up the mountain like a goat.

At the top of the ridge, all of the adults, including Manchester and Debay, had crumpled to the cool earth with exhaustion. They lay on their backs on a small slope on the western side, their equipment burdens immobilizing them like inverted turtles. Just below, the children were huddled in a pile beneath a broken acacia tree. A single *Mat'kal* canteen was passed around, just enough for the grownups to wet their lips, and then the rest of the canteens were given to the children and the water was done.

Eckstein rose shakily to his feet. Dawn was beginning to break over the Dinder, just slivers of pink above the distant purple mountains. Below was a wide bowl of hard-packed sand and prickly brush going gray in the early light, surrounded on all sides by small craggy ridges, like a miniature desert inside a moon crater. Near the far edge an incongruously lush oasis poked up from the barren earth, glistening palms and African bull grass waving in the morning breeze. There might be water there, but he knew that it was deceptively far away and there was no time to get to it. Closer to him, on the eastern side of the bowl and just at the foot of the ridge below, stood a man-made gate of ancient stones, sort of a half-moon wall with an opening in the center, as if this bowl had once been an amphitheater and there stood the ticket takers. But it was likely just an old shepherd's hut, or maybe a tomb.

"They're coming."

Eckstein turned to Karni's voice. The captain had just crested the rise and was breathing heavily but steadily. He looked at his watch. "There's a lot of them now. I guess we put the fear of God into them."

"Or just bloody pissed them off," Manchester commented.

"What's the air force ETA?" Baum asked. He was covered with a thin film of dust, and together with his sweat it had formed a strange cap of mud on his bald head. He was trying to stand up and having some trouble as he tried not to show how his thighs had turned to jelly.

"Thirty-seven minutes from now," said Karni.

"We can hold the fuckers off for half an hour," Manchester spat, and he got up from the ground and turned to squint back into Ethiopia.

"Maybe," said Eckstein. "But look." He pointed off to the northern end of the Sudanese wadi. "Wind's from the south. The Hercules will pop up over that ridge and drop into the crater. But we'll have to lay panels for him."

"Right," Benni agreed. "Otherwise he'll take one look at this cereal bowl and choose the better part of valor."

"Which is?" Eckstein cued his partner like a comic's straight man.

"Retreat," said Benni.

The air force Hercules pilots were absurdly brave and could land their hulking C-130s on a goat path, but if there were personnel on the ground they demanded orange touchdown panels at the very least. Such a signal indicated that the landing zone was smooth enough and free of obstructions, if not gunfire.

"But we can't lay signals yet," said Eckstein. "Right now, the rebels don't know we've called in a plane, but if one of them spots those fucking panels they'll bring up everything they have just to take him down."

Karni looked back down into Ethiopian territory again and clucked his tongue, as if a waiter had again brought him the wrong dish. He swung to two of his *Mat'kalniks*. "Yakir, Gadi," he called to them and pointed to two spots on the ridge. "*Mizvadot, po v'sham.* Suitcases, here and over there."

The two commandos unslung their heavy backpacks and removed a pair of dark green plastic boxes with molded carry handles. Remote detonators were Velcroed to the satchel charges, and they tore them off and quickly moved to set up the high explosives at Karni's behest.

Eckstein looked up at the sky. The stars were quickly fading, and although the sun had not yet shown itself, high wisps of morning clouds were already taking on the burnished copper tints of its rays. *This is insane*, he thought, to try to pull off something like this in broad daylight, where the enemy could see everything you did and your only salvation was a fat, hulking cargo plane as big as a barn.

Something banged off of a nearby rock and sent up a small plume of dust, and then the stutter of an automatic weapon reached up from the Ethiopian side. Karni immediately squatted down and everyone else followed suit.

"Somebody tell those *bâtards* you cannot shoot with accuracy uphill," Debay growled.

"*You* tell them," said Manchester. "We'll wait here."

Eckstein looked over at Krumlov, who was crouching nearby and staring at the Israeli major. Eytan had been avoiding making this final decision, but there was nothing for it now and he had to find a way to live with himself, if he was going to live at all. He felt Benni's eyes upon him, and when he glanced at his colonel Baum nodded his approval.

"Go, Jan." He kept his focus on the Czech as he pointed off into the Sudan across the crater. "Run for it. You can make the western hills in half an hour, just drop your pistols there and walk into one of the refugee camps."

"I will not," Krumlov said. Another staccato of weapons fire banged off the Ethiopian hills, and more dust spat up on the ridgeline.

"Get the fuck out, Jan!" Eckstein yelled now. "I'm giving you your fucking life, you fool! Now take what you have and go!"

"If you send him away I will go with him too, Eytan." Dominique had made her way up from the children and was on her hands and knees, wincing as the distant gunfire grew closer.

"Do what you have to, Dominique." Eckstein looked at her fully, hardening his heart and taking no responsibility for anything of what she felt, for him or for Jan or for Étienne. "You can be saved and taken to Israel or you can stay here in hell, and I can't do anything about that. Only you can."

She bit her lip and nodded as she realized that here was a man with much more on his mind.

"You can't just let him go, Eckstein," Karni called from his position a bit farther up the ridge.

"Shut up, Karni," Benni spat. "Eckstein's mission commander here. When you're in command I'll let you know."

Debay eyed the *Mat'kalnik* like a wary wolf, watching his fingers and his face.

"I am getting on that plane," Krumlov said to Eckstein, and he began to stand up, fumbling in his trouser pocket for something. "You'll have to kill me to stop me."

Eckstein started to respond, but Benni raised a hand and waved it and was about to say something when Krumlov suddenly pulled one of the Makarovs from his pocket. His hands were shaking, but he moved to cock the weapon, and Karni reacted instantly and yanked his own Beretta from his battle jacket.

Debay could have just opened fire on the *Mat'kalnik*, but something stopped him from his own ingrained instincts, and instead he leapt across five meters of earth and rammed his head into Krumlov's stomach just as Karni fired. Dominique screamed and the two men crashed to the ground as Benni stood up and roared at the *Mat'kalnik*.

"Are you out of your *mind*, boy?!"

Karni kept his smoking pistol trained on the forms of Debay and Krumlov, where they lay embraced in a cloud of dust.

"No. But are *you*, Colonel? The man draws a weapon and you expect me to just spit at him?"

Debay rolled off of Krumlov. The Czech was gritting his teeth and holding his thigh with both hands, and a stream of blood ran out from between his fingers and onto the ground.

"You're all a bunch of fucking *wankers*," Manchester spat, and he crawled up to the ridgeline, set himself in, and began to snipe back at the rebels on the other side. The rest was punctuated by his careful trigger squeezes and the concussive bangs of his Sterling.

Eckstein was on his feet, his fists balled, his knuckles white. He looked down at Krumlov, watching as Dominique quickly tied off his blood flow with a torn kaffiyeh and Debay gripped the Czech's hand as he writhed. The bullet had obviously struck a bone, and both Krumlov's nurse and bodyguard cursed the Israeli commando roundly in French. Eytan looked over at Karni, who now exhibited some remorse and had lowered his Beretta.

"Thank you very much, Karni," Eckstein hissed. The commando officer frowned at him. "Now you *have* to take him with you."

Benni stared at Eckstein, realizing that his comment had carried a strange syntax: Now *you* will have to take him with *you* . . . "Yes," said

Baum to the captain. "We cannot leave a wounded man in the field, no matter who he is or what orders you have."

Karni snorted. It was sacred IDF lore, the unbroken commandment, and certainly no one of *Mat'kal* would be the first to sully it.

"And *you* can carry him, Karni," Eckstein spat, adding insult to injury. "Right now. Get moving."

"*I* will carry the colonel," said Debay as he stood up, nearly beating his chest.

"You'll do exactly as I fucking say!" Eckstein shouted at the Belgian, and then he spun on Karni and his *Mat'kalniks* and everyone stared at him. "This isn't the fucking Parliament." He stalked over to Debay's fallen MAT-49 and tossed the submachine gun to the mercenary. "Get up on that ridgeline and help Manchester." Debay hesitated, looking down at Krumlov's ashen face and his lips nearly bloody with biting them. "Do it, goddamnit!" Eckstein shouted again and Debay turned and made for the ridge line.

Eckstein looked at Karni and jabbed a finger in Krumlov's direction. "Pick him up and take him down to those rocks." He swept his arm downhill toward the small gateway of ancient stones, and his voice was still loud and harsh and it grew louder as he had to shout over the sound of Debay's gun now joining Manchester's. "And take your men and get the children and Dominique down there, too. Then set out the panels." He looked at his watch. "You've got exactly twelve minutes."

Karni looked at Eckstein, then at Baum.

"Well, what the fuck are you waiting for!" Benni bellowed. "You heard the man."

Karni shrugged, walked to Eckstein, and handed him the pair of satchel charge detonators. Then he did something he had not done to another officer since he was a conscript at Sanure. He saluted.

"You've got balls, Eckstein," the commando said, and he meant it. "Big ones."

He bent to Krumlov and the Czech yelled as Karni heaved him to his feet, bent under his belly, and hauled him up over his shoulders. He started off down the hill and his three men followed along and gathered up the children. The orphans were able to stand now, and inasmuch as Karni could encourage them in their native tongue they found a bit of strength, and most of them managed to descend without being carried.

Adi broke from the little group and hesitated, turning and looking at Eckstein, who waved him down the hill and managed a brief smile of reassurance. Dominique took the little boy's hand and began to follow after the commandos, but then she suddenly stopped.

She left Adi and ran back to Eckstein, and he made to push her back but she only took his face in both her hands and her tears overflowed as she looked at him. An RPG banged from the Ethiopian side of the ridgeline, but the rocket was not made for ascending trajectories and it just thundered as it exploded somewhere on a rock, and Eckstein could not hear her as she whispered, *"Merci, mon brave."* And then she was gone.

Baum moved close to Eckstein and jabbed a finger at him.

"I don't know what you're planning . . ."

"Taksheev li. Listen to me, Benni." Eckstein reached out for Baum's wrist and gripped it as he spoke rapidly in Hebrew. "That plane has maybe three hundred meters to make a short-field landing. Am I right?"

Benni looked off at the crater, squinting and measuring with his eyes. "So what? That's what it's designed for."

"Listen to me." Eckstein reached for the cloth of Benni's soiled shirt now, gripping it and pulling and locking his partner's eyes to his own. "The pilot can't just rev up after that and make a straight takeoff. He'll have to taxi back and turn around and set up in a very small space. If we're all on the plane, who's going to hold those bastards off?"

Benni began to shake his head.

"Who, Benni? Someone has to stay here and suppress them while the plane turns around, otherwise it just won't work. You know that, you can see it."

"Not you."

"Yes, me."

"Manchester and Debay," Benni sputtered and pointed up at the ridge. "They'll do it."

"It's *our* mission, Benni. *Ours.* Right up to the end. You can't ask for volunteers. You want it written in the AMAN bible that we didn't have the balls to pull off our own mission, so we sacrificed a couple of brave Christians?"

"No." Baum began to wag his head hard.

"I'm right. You know I'm right and we don't have time."

"Okay," Benni finally relented. "But it's me. I'll stay."

"No, you won't."

"We'll flip a coin for it."

Eckstein almost smiled. "I'm afraid I'm flat broke. And I'm running this op and I'm not going to argue with you so don't even try to pull rank on me because you know damned well I couldn't give a shit anymore." He pointed downhill to the small gateway of fallen stones. "I'll set up right down there. Good cover."

Benni looked at the crumbled gateway, then back at Eckstein. "You can sprint for the plane just before takeoff," he said hopefully. "I'll hold it."

"Maybe," said Eckstein, but he knew there would not be time. "But if I can't make it, I'll just run my ass off to the far side of the crater. I'll do what I told Krumlov to do, walk into some refugee camp as Anthony Hearthstone, lost and befuddled photographer."

"No." Benni shook his head again, but Eckstein looked at his watch and now gripped his partner's shirt two-fisted.

"For God's sake, Benni, we've got seven minutes left for this! Now please, go down there and make sure those children get on the plane and to hell with everything else!"

"But, Oren . . ." Benni whispered.

And Eckstein felt the tears well in his own eyes and he tried very hard not to show that his heart was crumbling quickly. "He would be proud of me," he whispered. "He would do the same, if I've taught him anything at all."

Eckstein reached into his rear pants pocket, and he came up with his tattered copy of *A Farewell to Arms*. He handed the codebook to Benni, who just stared at it through glassy eyes. "Give it to him," said Eckstein. "It's not much, but it was a good book for both of us."

Benni's cheeks began to tremble, and he reached out and crushed Eytan's shoulders in his hands and Eytan gripped Benni's arms. And they said nothing else as Baum turned and began to run down the hill, and Eckstein wiped his eyes and hurried up to the ridgeline. He dropped to his stomach and crawled the last few meters, coming to rest between Debay and Manchester, who were laid up behind two large boulders and intermittently poking their gun barrels out and firing downhill. Return fire cracked overhead and plunked into the nearby earth, but Eckstein did not bother to try to get a look at the rebels climbing the far side of the ridge. He knew they were there.

"Give me your weapons," Eckstein shouted to the two men. "You can go."

Manchester rolled onto his right side and stared at Eckstein, while Debay just kept on shooting.

"Begging the major's pardon," Manchester yelled back. "But fuck off."

"You have exactly five minutes before that plane comes in," Eckstein shouted again. "Only one of us needs to stay."

"We are very comfortable here," Debay yelled as he changed magazines. "And your commandos were very generous with their ammunition."

"And with all due compliments, major," Manchester added as he resumed his sniping. "You're not bloody Lawrence of Ethiopia, so either join in or be gone, sir."

All right, so that was the way they wanted it. Eckstein showed them the pair of remote detonators and pointed back down the hill toward the crater. "Okay, then. I'm going to hold the second line. When they get close to you, come on down to me fast because I'm going to blow the charges."

Manchester stopped firing and looked over at Eckstein, extending a palm. "If you don't mind, Major, *we'll* blow the charges when we retreat."

"Not that we don't trust you, *mon ami*," Debay added.

Eckstein shook his head in wonder, but he tossed one detonator apiece to each man. "There won't be any transport," he warned one more time.

"We've got legs," yelled Debay.

"Cheers, now," Manchester added, and he plucked a grenade from his pocket and laid it down next to him.

Eckstein slid back down the slope on his belly, and then he turned and came to his feet and began to run downhill. He slung the Uzi from his shoulder and used both arms to keep his balance as he tried to make as much speed as he could without tumbling.

Before him the crater was splashed now with bright morning light, the distant oasis glistening wet with dew and sharp shafts of the sun stabbing from behind and the east. He could see the children huddled just beyond the low gate of stones at the foot of the ridge, with Benni and Dominique buzzing around them like mother birds, and Krumlov's form lying there stretched out on the ground. Out in the crater the *Mat'kalniks* had staked out either end of the landing zone in pairs, and as Eckstein watched, the two couples unfurled the plastic rolls of orange panels and stretched them across the imaginary strip, indicating the minimum touchdown point and maximum overshoot.

The gunfire from the other side of the ridge grew dimmer as Eckstein descended, and suddenly the roar of the big Hercules power plants split the air and the mottled camouflaged aircraft arched up from behind the northern crater ridge as if the pilot had only spotted the mountain at the last minute. The bulbous black nose of the C-130 dipped over and the engines screamed as the big plane dove for the ground, and then it leveled off sharply at only five meters altitude and a huge cloud of dust rushed up around it as it screamed in over the commandos and shook the earth and its flat belly seemed to thump the ground.

Even as the plane was struggling to stop, the *Mat'kalniks* had scooped up their panels and were running back for the children. The Hercules bucked forward and just barely halted at the end of the crater, and then it whined crazily and spun on its axis, heading back to set up for a quick takeoff again, its rear cargo hatch already yawning down.

Swarms of dust covered the entire crater, and the children were coughing and covering their eyes. Benni turned and looked back up to the ridgeline, but he could not see Eckstein or Manchester or Debay or anything else, and only the growing sound of gunfire reached out to him. Suddenly Karni appeared though the dust and he quickly scooped up Krumlov again as the Czech winced and groaned. The commando bounced Krumlov on his shoulders to settle the weight and he turned to Benni and yelled.

"*Bo, Baum!* Come on!"

The rest of the *Mat'kalniks* were already hustling the children from shelter toward the Hercules' takeoff point, but Benni could not move. He just stood there and stared up the hill until he felt a hard tug at his sleeve. It was Dominique, and he found her with tears streaming down her face, her mouth quivering and swollen.

"Come, Benni," she said. "Come. Eytan is giving us our lives. And dying now will only make you unable to do anything good ever again."

He nodded, and he began to back away with her, still staring up at the hill. But it suddenly struck his heart with a fear he had never known in battle or places where life was sure to be short and cruel. He had come to Israel alone, as a child from the camps after the war, his parents dead and not a single relative surviving. He had worked to forget, laughed and loved, labored and lived, and then his partnership with the German-born Eckstein had sewn up the final hole in the family he had re-created from whole cloth. And now, fifty years later, he realized that in many ways, he would be an orphan again.

Then Dominique pulled on him very hard, and they both began to run . . .

Eckstein burst into the low shelter of rocks. There was no one left there and he was glad, and he heard the plane very close now but he could not see it for the dust. There was a thin pool of blood where Krumlov had lain, and the *Mat'kalniks* had left him their Mini-MAG light machine gun and all their ammunition and grenades. He turned back toward the hill and quickly flopped down onto his belly and set up behind the MAG, opening the bipod and poking the barrel out between the rocks. He checked the belt feed, slammed the breech home again, and hauled back on the cocking handle.

He turned his head and looked behind him. The dust had settled a bit and he could see the green and tan fuselage of the Hercules moving from south to north along the hardpack, but it was so damned slow on the ground, and there to the north he could also make out the small crowd of humans crouched together, the *Mat'kalniks* bending over them protectively.

He turned back to his gun and looked up the hill. The firing on top was growing in intensity, the short whumps of grenades clear and ugly in the morning air. He thought he could hear shouts rising up from the Ethiopian side, but he decided that it was just his own fear screaming like a nightmare in his head. His mouth went dry as parchment and his heart began to pound against the ground and his palms went slick and slippery, and he smacked them down in the dust and then encircled the trigger grip again . . .

Manchester and Debay were done. They each had less than a magazine apiece and their grenades were long gone. The rebels were very close now, their forward elements less than fifty meters from the ridgeline, and they could hear Mobote shouting to his men and the thunder of rifle rounds and spinning steel jackets had grown into one endless storm of flying metal. Neither man could even hope to poke his head from cover, let alone return accurate fire. The rebels would be on them within the minute.

Debay turned his head to look back down into the crater, and Manchester watched him and he did the same. The big transport plane had almost taxied back to its takeoff point, and they could see the orphans and their shepherds huddled there and waiting. Within just a couple of minutes the contingent would be airborne, and there was no way now to make it to the plane even if they got up and sprinted like Olympians.

But if the rebels crested the ridge before the plane managed to take off, a tragedy could still befall the entire venture. With all that concentrated firepower from the ridgeline pouring down into the crater, and perhaps even an RPG rocket or a shoulder-fire missile, the vulnerable C-130 might well crash and burn. With all aboard. All for nothing.

The two mercenaries came to the same conclusion simultaneously. They looked at each other.

"Fuck it," Manchester shouted.

"Oui. D'accord," yelled Debay.

They each gripped their detonators in their left hands, their weapons in their right, and they stood up and yelled and opened fire . . .

* * *

The twin explosions shocked Eckstein from his groin to his feet. Two great blossoms of rock and dust burst up from the ridgeline, and as the debris tumbled down the hillside a follow-on shock shook his position like a small earthquake. He swatted the dust from his eyes and peered upward, searching, hoping, praying that the two mercs had somehow slipped down and into cover before they blew the charges. But then he heard a gathering storm of shouts from above and he knew that Manchester and Debay had died, as only men in their chosen profession should die.

He flicked his head back again, and now the Hercules was indeed finally reaching the turnaround point, its black propellers churning like demons and the pilots stamping on brakes and rudder pedals to swing the huge machine on its axis.

If he could just hold them off for another two minutes . . .

He tried to calm his racing heart, but his fear was not the problem. He had faced that before, many times, and always to prove himself the man he wanted to be, he had successfully ignored it and done foolish things. No, it was not the fear. It was the loss, deep and painful and coming in waves up through his body. It was like a bottomless pit and if he looked down into it he might just get up and flee, screaming.

So instead, he thought of the children. He imagined them hurt and broken and burning if the rebels succeeded in damaging or crashing the plane, and he found his will and his strength and he lay his cheek aside the cool steel of the MAG.

"There are things a man has to do, my son," he whispered aloud. And then he heard the surviving horde of rebels cresting the rise above. The explosions had certainly killed many of them, but the rest had recovered from the shock. They spotted the airplane and began to yell, and something in their rage and the momentum of the battle made them swarm down the hillside rather than opening up from right where they were. This was it. Just another minute or so and it would be over.

Something pounded the ground and Eckstein snapped his head around. It was Benni Baum's hefty girth, sending up a cloud of dust as he flopped on the ground next to Eytan, with Karni's Galil rifle cradled in his arms.

Eytan just looked at him.

A protest would be meaningless.

It was far too late for reproach.

And he could find no words.

"You think I'm going to spend the next twenty years of my life having nightmares about you?" Baum said.

Eytan just shook his head with wonder. Bullets began to ping off the rocks around them, but neither man flinched.

"Besides," said Benni. "Our families will find some comfort in knowing we were stupid together."

"They already knew that," Eckstein managed.

Baum reached into his pants pocket and slapped something down on the ground. It was Eckstein's copy of *A Farewell to Arms*, and it fell open to a place that Benni held with his finger, a passage that Eckstein had outlined in yellow.

Benni tapped the page. "What's that all about, Eytan?"

Eckstein looked at it.

If people bring so much courage to this world the world has to kill them to break them, so of course it kills them. The world breaks every one and afterward many are strong at the broken places. But those that it will not break it kills. It kills the very good and the very gentle and the very brave impartially. If you are none of these you can be sure it will kill you too but there will be no special hurry.

"It's just an observation." Eckstein tried to smile. "But I like it."

"You read too much." Baum shook his head. "When the hell do you find time to read?"

A grenade exploded somewhere close by and some shrapnel splinters clanged off the rocks like empty beer cans. Benni opened the bipod of his Galil and slammed the bolt handle back. Both men settled in, their right eyes squinting into their gunsights. Behind them, the Hercules suddenly revved to full power and jumped forward, picking up speed and rumbling like a thunderstorm as it hurdled down the sand of the wadi.

Its tones changed as it lifted off and arced up into the blue African sky, and both Eckstein and Baum smiled through trembling lips, even though Mobote and his rebels had just hit the bottom of the hill. With the rebel leader out front and waving his pearl-handled .45, they charged the Israelis from only 100 meters out, full frontal.

"*Ya Allah*, I wish I had a cigarette," Benni mourned as he opened fire.

"Well," said Eckstein as he joined in and his machine gun began to hammer, "you should quit anyway."